(leading to Very New Road and Even Newer Road)

BNFL dumping site

and cottage

nk e war d up →

a y

Mrs Cropley's marmalade and tuna casserole was buried here.

Bluebell Wood - where the Blair Witch Project was filmed.

D1203569

## THIS BOOK BELONGS TO

_____

## AND WAS PRESENTED TO YOU BY

_____

(who is a good friend, generous to a fault, and if they get into trouble
you won't hesitate to help them every way you can including financial).

## ON THE OCCASION OF

(*Delete as applicable*) Christmas/Birthday/Combined Christmas, Birthday,
and previous Christmas/sorry I ran over your cat/to cheer you up following
your acrimonious split from your partner, oh no, I've reminded you again,
please don't cry, that's what (he/she) wants/sorry I interrupted your wedding
with a very good reason you couldn't get married/well done on becoming
a vicar/rabbi/Lord of the Sith/thank you for springing me from Dartmoor

If the owner gets Brad Pitt/Britney Spears alone he/she would
like to cover him/her in _____

Denomination:

Lapsed _____

By the way, your good friend who gave you this book, does not want
anything in return. But imagine his/her face lighting up when you buy
him/her a lovely expensive _____

# THE VICAR OF DIBLEY

## THE COMPLETE COMPANION TO DIBLEY

Richard Curtis and Paul Mayhew-Archer

MICHAEL JOSEPH
LONDON

# MICHAEL JOSEPH

Published by the Penguin Group
Penguin Books Ltd, 27 Wrights Lane, London W8 5TZ, England
Penguin Putnam Inc., 375 Hudson Street, New York, New York 10014, USA
Penguin Books Australia Ltd, Ringwood, Victoria, Australia
Penguin Books Canada Ltd, 10 Alcorn Avenue, Toronto, Ontario, Canada M4V 3B2
Penguin Books India (P) Ltd, 11 Community Centre,
Panchsheel Park, New Delhi – 110 017, India
Penguin Books (NZ) Ltd, Cnr Rosedale and Airborne Roads,
Albany, Auckland, New Zealand
Penguin Books (South Africa) (Pty) Ltd, 5 Watkins Street,
Denver Ext 4, Johannesburg 2094, South Africa

Penguin Books Ltd, Registered Offices: Harmondsworth, Middlesex, England

This collection first published 2000
1

Copyright for original scripts as follows:
'Arrival', 'The Window and the Weather' and 'Animals' copyright © Richard Curtis
'Songs of Praise' copyright © Richard Curtis and Kit Hesketh-Harvey
All other scripts copyright © Richard Curtis and Paul Mayhew-Archer
Extra funny bits copyright © Kevin Cecil, Andy Riley and Paul Powell, 2000

All photographs of the cast and from the series copyright © BBC Worldwide;
White transit van © Stone Images; Recorder session © Stone Images; Publicans © Hulton Getty;
Sheep © Corbis; Food © Corbis; Parachutist © Corbis; Grumpy Old Woman © Corbis

Jacket illustration, endpaper map and line drawings for scripts copyright © Matilda Harrison, 2000
Illustrations for 'Dibley Fete', 'Ancient Chalk Figures', 'School Bible Competition',
'Alice Tinker/Horton's Puzzle Pages' and 'The Dibley Tower' copyright © Andy Riley, 2000
Illustrations for 'Dibley Road Sign' copyright © Margie Jordan, 2000

The acknowledgements on page 378 constitute an extension of this copyright page.

The programmes based on the scripts in this book were produced by
Tiger Aspect Productions and first shown on BBC Television.

The moral right of the author has been asserted
All rights reserved.
Without limiting the rights under copyright reserved above, no part of this
publication may be reproduced, stored in or introduced into a retrieval system,
or transmitted, in any form or by any means (electronic, mechanical, photocopying,
recording or otherwise), without the prior written permission of both the
copyright owner and the above publisher of this book

Scripts set in Blur Light, Joanna MT, Officina Sans Bold, Rotis Semi Sans Light, Woodtype Ornaments 2
Interior design by designsection, Frome, Somerset
Printed in Great Britain by Clays Ltd, St Ives plc

A CIP catalogue record for this book is available from the British Library

ISBN 0–718–14475–9

# Contents of Table

by Alice Tinker Horton

Let's see. Four legs, and one top. Oh, and maybe a few screws and glue and things to hold it together. That's about it.

Oh, hang on. That's not right, is it? Oooops! What it should be, of course, is a . . .

# Table of Contents

(Sorry!)

# Arrival

## Scene One: The Church of St Barnabus

*A beautiful old church in the centre of the picturesque village of Dibley. A service is taking place. A stern-looking man, David Horton, is giving a reading at the lectern.*

DAVID: The wrath of the king was mighty and knew no bound and so they did leave that country and did with heavy heart return unto Japeth and unto Gad. Here ends the lesson.

*He returns to his seat. An ancient-looking vicar, Reverend Pottle, is taking the service. Assisting him is Alice Tinker, the church verger.*

REVEREND POTTLE: Let us pray. Dear Lord, we ask thee to bless all the members of this thy congregation . . . (*Four people are sat in the pews*) And we especially ask you to remember the Queen who has been having trouble with her piles again. And Mrs Sinclair-Wilson and all her family. (*Alice leans forward and whispers in the Reverend's ear. He begins again.*) Mrs Sinclair-Wilson, who has been having trouble with her piles again, and the Queen and all her family.

DAVID: Amen.

REVEREND POTTLE: May you grant them happiness in this world and in the next, peace everlasting. Amen.

THE CONGREGATION: Amen.

*Reverend Pottle rests his head on his hand and closes his eyes. Alice nudges him and feels for his pulse. There is no heartbeat — he is dead. Alice does the sensible thing — she ignores this and carries on with the service.*

ALICE: Umm. We now sing hymn number 16, 'The Day Thou Gavest Lord is Ended'.

*They all start singing. The vicar sways and topples to the floor. Very dead indeed.*

## Scene Two: The Parish Hall

*Dibley's parish hall is an old building with wood-panelled walls, a curtained-off stage, and a large wooden table in the middle. Sat round it are David Horton, Frank Pickle, Jim Trott and Mrs Cropley, who is doing her knitting. David is Chairman of the Council and Frank Pickle is in charge of taking the minutes.*

DAVID: Are we all here?

FRANK: Yes, perfectly.

DAVID: Not can we all hear — are we all here?

*David's son Hugo enters and takes a seat. A lovely, bumbling chap, he is somewhat dominated by his father.*

FRANK: I'm sorry. Yes, all except Owen.

DAVID: Well, let's go on then, shall we? Owen's always late and we've got a lot of business. Right, I call this meeting of the Dibley Parish Council to order. David Horton in the chair, Frank Pickle taking minutes.

FRANK: Shall I minute that, sir?

DAVID: What?

FRANK: About my taking the minutes.

DAVID: Do you normally minute it?

FRANK: Well, I'd like to, yes.

DAVID: Then do it again.

FRANK: Oh, thank you.

DAVID: The agenda this week starts with the tragic news of the death of Reverend Pottle.

*All murmur their agreement.*

He had been a great servant of the village ever since his arrival here as a young-ish man in 1917.

JIM: Happy days.

DAVID: We all remember particularly fondly his famous Christmas sermon which I think we all know by heart. He shall be greatly missed.

HUGO: Hear, hear.

DAVID: Anyone want to add anything to that?

JIM: Ah, no, no, no, no, no, no, yes. Just one thing. If that's all right.

DAVID: Yes, fire away.

JIM: No, no, no, no, no, but I thought maybe we should mention the marrow.

DAVID: And what marrow's that?

JIM: Ah – he, he, he came second in the marrow-growing contest in 1956.

HUGO: Oh, bravo.

DAVID: Well, excellent – yes, we'll include that. Anything else?

JIM: No, no, no, no, no.

*David stares at him in irritation.*

DAVID: That's 'no' is it?

JIM: No, no, no, no, no, yes.

*Owen Newitt, a local farmer, arrives.*

DAVID: Right. Moving on.

OWEN: Sorry, I'm late.

DAVID: That's all right, Owen, we've only just begun.

OWEN: My bladder's been playing up again. I've spent so much time in the stables toilet I'm thinking of sending out change of address cards.

DAVID: Yes, thank you, Owen. Moving on, last week was the Village of the Year Competition and I have written to Buckingham Palace thanking them so much for Prince Edward's visit.

MRS CROPLEY: Hear, hear.

OWEN: Shame.

DAVID: I beg your pardon.

OWEN: I've nothing against Prince Edward, though I don't usually trust bald blokes. I'm just surprised though that we don't start with the Reverend's death.

DAVID: We dealt with that before you arrived, Owen.

OWEN: Oh.

DAVID: Now, moving on.

FRANK: Perhaps you'd like me to read the minutes back to you, Owen, so you can catch up.

DAVID: I don't think that will be necessary. We don't need to waste our whole evening because of Owen's dodgy waterworks.

FRANK: Shall I minute that?

DAVID: (firmly) No, thank you. Right . . .

FRANK: Shall I leave a gap then?

DAVID: Whatever you think, Frank.

FRANK: Well, it's not going to flow very well.

DAVID: (now very annoyed) Oh, for goodness sake, Frank – you are the Parish Clerk, not Alfred Lord Tennyson. Right – I'm sorry everyone for that rather annoying interlude, but if we can move on to the question of the successor to Reverend Pottle.

FRANK: Are you sure about that?

DAVID: What, Frank – what?

FRANK: Well, you just described Prince Edward's visit as a rather annoying interlude.

DAVID: I certainly did not.

FRANK: Well, I'm afraid you did – I cut that jolly interesting bit about Owen's bladder, so now it reads, 'So much for Prince Edward's visit. And if we can move on from that rather annoying interlude.'

DAVID: Oh God.

OWEN: Look, could we get on? I've got a worrying feeling in my colon.

MRS CROPLEY: Errm . . .

DAVID: Yes.

MRS CROPLEY: Nothing.

FRANK: Do you want that minuted, Mrs Cropley?

MRS CROPLEY: Oh, yes, I suppose so.

FRANK: Excellent. 'Then Mrs Cropley said nothing'.

DAVID: Now, moving on. I have, of course, asked the Bishop for someone a little younger than the Reverend Pottle.

MRS CROPLEY: Yes, please.

DAVID: But then I think it would be hard to find anyone older . . . without actually recruiting a member of the Rolling Stones.

*He laughs at his joke but no one else gets it.*

Right. If we can quickly move on through to the planning applications which I think you'll find on pink 7A. (*They all shuffle through their papers.*) The Herberts want a new barn. Rejected. The Franklins want a new kitchen. Rejected. And, my son Hugo here is putting up a conservatory for his South American flower collection which I think should be fine.

HUGO: Excellent news. Somewhere for the pool table at last.

DAVID: Right, any other business?

OWEN: Definitely not.

DAVID: Thank you all very much. We all meet again in a fortnight. Have you got all that Frank?

FRANK: Yes. '. . . without actually recruiting a member of the Rolling Stones.' What comes next?

*David looks at him in doomed exasperation.*

## Scene Three: David Horton's Sitting Room

*David and Hugo live in Dibley Manor – a huge detached house set in its own, very grand grounds. They are having a post Council Meeting drink. Hugo is seated whilst his father walks about the room.*

DAVID: Finally, we'll be able to get this village going again. Do you realize at last year's fête Potty Pottle awarded the prize for the best carrot to a cucumber?

HUGO: Yes, he was losing it a bit – though I did agree the Bishop of Oxford deserved first prize in the fancy dress competition.

DAVID: For being dressed as a Bishop.

HUGO: That's right. Brilliant.

DAVID: Well, those days are gone. Apparently this new chap is superb. Personally recommended by the Bishop of Wykeham.

HUGO: Isn't he that dodgy one, who says that Jesus didn't exist, and even if he did he definitely wasn't a Christian?

DAVID: It's about time we had someone with half a brain on the Parish Council.

*Hugo coughs.*

Oh yes, well, apart from your good self. At last we can give that frightful verger Alice the heave-ho.

*Hugo looks up at this mention of Alice. He rather likes her.*

HUGO: I don't think she'll be very happy about that.

DAVID: Tough luck. She's a famous imbecile. In last year's Christmas crib she had the Virgin Mary cradling a pig and the Baby Jesus being suckled by a black goat.

HUGO: But she's awfully keen.

DAVID: Yes – Eddie the Eagle was very keen. But the kind thing to do would still have been to shoot him between the eyes the first time he put on a pair of skis. No. I think the new chap will see sense. Sack Alice and sack Mrs Cropley – I've seen better flower arrangements on a compost heap. Whisky?

HUGO: Please.

DAVID: Excellent stuff. Keep it firmly locked away when the rabble come round. There's no point wasting good liquor on people who just adore Asda Sweet Amontillado.

HUGO: Actually that is lovely stuff, isn't it? Good old Asda.

## Scene Four: David Horton's Sitting Room

*It is a dark, stormy night a few weeks later. David is playing host and pouring sherry for the villagers gathered in his house. A fire is blazing and the room is very cosy.*

ALICE: Ooh, sherry – wow!

DAVID: Only the best here, Miss Tinker.

ALICE: Thanks very much.

MRS CROPLEY: (*offering round a tray of sandwiches*) Sandwich?

DAVID:  No thank you. Anchovy and peanut butter not quite my cup of tea. Frank, sherry?

FRANK:  Oh, thank you very much – lovely – my favourite.

DAVID:  Jim?

JIM:  No, no, no, no, no no – yes.

DAVID:  Don't drink it all at once – it's top stuff.

*He coughs to announce a formal word.*

As you all know we're all gathered here to greet our new vicar. I'm sorry it's such an awful night. I can't fix everything.

*They all force a laugh.*

HUGO:  Though, you did get our cat fixed, didn't you?

*The doorbell rings.*

DAVID:  I think our new vicar has arrived. Either that or the milkman's very late again!

### Scene Five: David Horton's Hallway

*It is pouring down with rain outside. A figure wearing a bright yellow raincoat is getting drenched on David's doorstep and is knocking frantically at the front door. It is Geraldine Granger. Dibley's new vicar.*

GERALDINE:  Hello. Hello. Can you hurry? It's tipping down out here. Raining very hard now. Please.

*David opens the door.*

Hello.

DAVID:  Hello.

GERALDINE:  David Honiton? Err . . . Hawtree?

DAVID:  Horton.

GERALDINE:  Horton. That's the chap. Could you just take these while I . . .

*She hands a couple of bags to David and turns to pick up the rest of her luggage.*

*Waving the taxi away, she squeezes past him into the hallway. David puts down Geraldine's bags and they shake hands.*

Hello. I'm Geraldine. I believe you're expecting me.

*She walks past him and takes off her coat to hang it up.*

DAVID: No, I'm expecting our new vicar. Unless, of course, you are the new vicar, and they've landed us with a woman (*he laughs at this — he really thinks that would be a joke*) as some sort of insane joke.

*Geraldine turns round to reveal that she is, in fact, wearing a dog collar and cross.*

GERALDINE: Oh dear.

*David is absolutely stunned by this revelation.*

DAVID: Oh my God.

GERALDINE: You were expecting a bloke: beard, Bible, bad breath . . .

DAVID: Yes, that sort of thing.

GERALDINE: And instead you've got a babe with a bob cut and a magnificent bosom.

DAVID: So I see.

GERALDINE: Well, don't worry. It'll be all right. You need a stiff drink. So do I. Come on, David.

*She takes him by the arm to guide him through to the living room. Hugo comes into the hall to see what's up.*

GERALDINE: Hello, I'm Geraldine. Call me Gerry.

HUGO: Delighted to meet you. I'm Hugo. Call me . . . Hugo.

GERALDINE: Right. (*She pokes Hugo's chest.*) Do you mind if I say that that is a devastatingly smart tie, Hugo.

HUGO: Is it?

GERALDINE: Yes. (*She points towards the living room.*) Shall we go in then?

## Scene Six: David Horton's Sitting Room

DAVID: Ladies and gentlemen . . . your new vicar.

GERALDINE: Hello – Geraldine.

*No one moves – they are all completely shocked that she is a woman. They can only stare at her.*

Boo!

*She laughs very loudly. Frank steps forward and extends his hand.*

FRANK: How do you do – I'm Frank Pickle. I take the minutes on the Council.

GERALDINE: Splendid. Very important job. Do forgive me if I instantly forget your name, won't you? I'm absolutely dreadful with names. Ask me to name the Virgin Mary's eldest son, and . . . nope – mind's gone blank.

*She laughs at this absurdity.*

FRANK: Jesus.

GERALDINE: That's it! Yes.

*Geraldine moves forward to Mrs Cropley.*

Hello, Geraldine. Gerry.

MRS CROPLEY: Letitia . . . er, Letty. Er, Cropley. I do the flowers in the church.

GERALDINE: Oh splendid. And what have we got in this week?

MRS CROPLEY: Well, we're in mourning for Reverend Pottle.

GERALDINE: Of course. Lovely. Carnations?

MRS CROPLEY: That's right. And I thought I'd put in a pineapple as well.

GERALDINE: Mmm. Unusual.

*She moves towards Jim.*

And you are?

JIM: No, no, no, no, Jim.

GERALDINE: Jim?

JIM: No, no, no, no . . .

GERALDINE: Not Jim.

JIM: No, no, no – yes Jim.

GERALDINE: Good, good. (*She walks over to Alice.*) And finally . . .

*They shake hands and Alice curtsies.*

ALICE: Delighted to meet you.

DAVID: This is Miss Tinker, she *was* the verger under the Reverend Pottle.

GERALDINE: Oh, splendid. Do you want to go on with the job?

ALICE: (*curtseying again*) Oh, yes please, Ma'am. I'd like that.

*David turns away in shock.*

GERALDINE: Good, good. Don't call me 'Ma'am'. Sounds like the Queen. Lovely lady – but very odd taste in hats. Don't you think – Miss Tinker?

ALICE: (*laughing*) Yes, yes I do! Oh, you can call me Alice.

GERALDINE: Right.

ALICE: Because it's my name.

GERALDINE: Right.

DAVID: Perhaps we should talk about all this in the morning.

*He offers her a sherry.*

GERALDINE: Thanks. (*She sips it.*) Urgh. Ooh. Do you mind – absolutely hate Amontillado. You wouldn't have any whisky would you?

DAVID: Ahm, certainly, ahm, yes.

*He sneaks to the cupboard to pour her a drink but Frank has overheard . . .*

FRANK: Actually, I wouldn't mind a whisky too, if there's one going.

MRS CROPLEY: Me too.

DAVID: *(weary)* Jim?

JIM: No, no, no, no, no . . .

DAVID: Please yourself . . .

JIM: Um, yes. I'll have one whisky.

*The doorbell rings and Hugo goes to answer it. Mrs Cropley offers her sandwiches to Geraldine.*

GERALDINE: Very unusual sandwiches. What's this with the ham?

MRS CROPLEY: Lemon curd.

GERALDINE: Good Lord. Mind if I just pop it down there? Just for a moment.

*She steps back and addresses the room.*

I'd like to say a big thank you to all of you for coming along on such a horrible night, when you could be in watching . . . *(She checks her watch.)* Top of the Pops. *(She looks at Alice.)* We're missing Top of the Pops.

*Alice dissolves into giggles. David hands Geraldine a whisky and she raises it to the room.*

Anyway, here's cheers.

*Owen enters. He's soaking wet.*

OWEN: Sorry I'm late. Been on the khasi since sundown.

DAVID: Ah, Owen. This is Geraldine – she's the new vicar.

GERALDINE: Hello.

*Owen ignores her completely.*

OWEN: No, she isn't.

GERALDINE: Why not?

OWEN: She's a woman.

GERALDINE: Ah. You noticed. *(She points to her breasts.)* These are such a giveaway, aren't they?

OWEN: Eh?

GERALDINE: Whisky, Owen?

OWEN: I think I might need one.

GERALDINE: Yep. Let's make it a double. Ooh, David, I think we might be needing another bottle. Did I spot a little Glenfiddich in there?

DAVID: I don't think so. No.

HUGO: No, no, no – there is. Or we could have that really expensive single malt you were keeping for very special occasions.

GERALDINE: Ooh. I think I feel a party coming on.

FRANK: Cheers!

## Scene Seven: David Horton's Sitting Room

*The next morning and David is on the phone.*

DAVID: Can I speak to the Bishop? He's where? Oh God. What's he doing there – they're all Muslims, aren't they? Really? Twenty-five million Christians. Oh well, fair enough. More than here. By about twenty-five million. Look, can I leave a message? David Horton rang – if he could ring me as soon as he returns.

*Hugo bounds in looking for something.*

This is outrageous – I won't have my village used like some laboratory animal to see if women vicars 'work'.

HUGO: Well, she seemed a decent sort of chap to me.

DAVID: That's the whole point – she's not a chap.

HUGO: No, not technically.

DAVID: Well, that is quite a technicality. I mean, what is happening? Are we to have topless bathing on the Rectory lawn come summer?

HUGO: The old vicar used to sunbathe topless, actually.

DAVID: He was a man; so it didn't matter.

HUGO: Well, actually it probably did – he had that sort of very fair skin that burns terribly . . . I read this article about Australia.

DAVID: Oh, get a grip, Hugo. If Jesus had wanted women to spread the Gospel, he would have appointed them. It's Matthew, Mark, Luke and John – not Sharon, Tracy, Tara and Debbie. No, it won't do. Hugo, I want you to call an extraordinary meeting of the Council. We will get this done before it's too late. They don't call me Sportin' Horton for nothing.

HUGO: I didn't know they called you Sportin' Horton. I thought they called you Dirty David, because of your enormous collection of Victorian pornogra –

DAVID: Oh for goodness sake, shut up!

## Scene Eight: Outside Mrs Cropley's House

*Jim, Owen and Mrs Cropley are looking over at the Vicarage. They see Geraldine and Alice leave the house together, making their way over to the church.*

OWEN: Well, it can't be right can it, really?

JIM: What's that?

OWEN: Having a woman vicar. I mean, Jesus didn't have any women disciples did he?

MRS CROPLEY: No, but things have to change, don't they?

JIM: That's right. I mean, look at traffic lights. Well, if they didn't change there'd be terrible congestion wouldn't there?

OWEN: On the other hand, there's gravity.

JIM: What about it?

OWEN: If gravity changed we'd all go floating up into space.

*Mrs Cropley cackles with laughter at this thought.*

And no one wants that.

JIM: So, there's good change and bad change?

MRS CROPLEY: That's right. I mean, there's the Changing of the Guard, isn't there?

JIM: Oh, wonderful.

OWEN: And then there's prawn-flavoured crisps.

JIM: Disaster.

## Scene Nine: The Vestry

GERALDINE: Well, here we are, Number 2 – base camp.

*Alice holds out the key and Geraldine takes it and unlocks the door. They enter the vestry.*

GERALDINE: Ah well, from here we launch our great mission. With, of course, proper rations . . .

*She takes handfuls of chocolate bars out of her cardigan and waves them gleefully at Alice.*

You're going to have to take me through a few things.

ALICE: Yeah.

GERALDINE: What kind of crowd are we pulling to the Sunday gigs here?

ALICE: Oh, er, about . . . four.

GERALDINE: A crowd of four?

ALICE: Yes. On a good day.

GERALDINE: Well, four's not bad is it? I mean, there were four Gospels, four Horsemen of the Apocalypse. Four *Rocky* movies. Until they made *Rocky* 5. Very bad move I thought.

ALICE: Well, it may go up to five if Mr Newitt's bowels settle down.

GERALDINE: Let me get this straight. We've got Mrs Cropley, Mr Pickle, Mr Horton . . .

ALICE: *(excitedly)* Oh! And sometimes Hugo comes . . . but not very often. *(She's got a huge crush on him.)*

GERALDINE: So who's the fourth one?

ALICE: Mr Newitt, I mentioned. With the bowels.

GERALDINE: No, no, no. He was the fifth one, wasn't he?

ALICE: Was he? Oh yes. Oh, well . . . *(She thinks hard and counts on her fingers. Then it hits her . . .)* Oh – me! Thickness! *(She points her fingers at her forehead, like a gun.)* Pow!

GERALDINE: Well, what about Christmas?

ALICE: Oh, Christmas! Well, that's special.

GERALDINE: *(feeling hopeful)* Good. How many?

ALICE: Three – Mrs Cropley always goes to visit her sister.

GERALDINE: I see. And what about you, Alice? What do you do when you're not in charge of crowd control here?

ALICE: I help the teacher in the nursery school. Art's my forte.

*She points out a shell collage of Jesus on the wall. It is not a masterpiece.*

GERALDINE: So it is.

ALICE: Reverend Pottle said that I was an undiscovered genius.

GERALDINE: Did he? Did he? Very remarkable man.

*Geraldine has a root around in the cupboard and finds a bottle of Ribena.*

Now, let's see. Oh, Ribena. Yum yum. For Sunday School?

ALICE: No – for Holy Communion.

GERALDINE: Unorthodox.

ALICE: *(leans in close and whispers)* Well, the Reverend had a tendency to get a little tipsy – so I used it instead of wine to avoid . . . *(She mimes the old man swinging about drunkenly.)*

GERALDINE: Quite right. I mean, I'm sure if this stuff had been around at the Last Supper Our Lord himself might have had a swig, you know, to keep a clear head for all those difficult questions Pilate was going to ask him.

ALICE: What is truth?

GERALDINE: Sorry?

ALICE: Oh. That was a question that Pilate asked – 'What is truth?'

GERALDINE: So he did. Good old Pilate. The sort of Magnus Magnusson of Palestine.

ALICE: Yeah.

*Geraldine sits up straight on a chair and takes the roles of both Magnus Magnusson and Jesus as contestant.*

GERALDINE: Name? 'Jesus'. Profession? 'Saviour of Mankind.' *(Alice giggles – she thinks this is just great.)* And for your specialist subject, Jesus, you've chosen Catering. Your first question – how many loaves and fishes does it take to feed five thousand people? 'Um. Pass.'

*Suddenly serious, Geraldine gets up.*

Oh God, Alice. Do you think we're going to be all right?

ALICE: Of course – I'm going to support you all the way.

GERALDINE: Well, then we can't fail, can we?

*Alice leans in close and grabs Geraldine's hands affectionately.*

ALICE: I know a lot about tropical fish as well.

GERALDINE: (*both smiling and frowning at this slightly weird statement*) Splendid, splendid. Then we shall be fishers of men.

ALICE: Yes. I don't know much about them, I'm afraid.

GERALDINE: Watch and learn, kid. (*She winks.*) Watch and learn.

## Scene Ten: The Parish Hall

*David has called a Parish Council meeting. All are present except Geraldine.*

DAVID: So I have drafted a letter which asks that she should immediately be removed from her new position. If you have any objections – if you want our village to become a national laughing stock, or if you actually believe what most right-thinking Anglicans still think is heresy – do speak up now.

*At that moment, Geraldine comes in.*

GERALDINE: Terribly sorry I'm late. Visiting my new parishioners. Honestly, I think they'd have been less surprised if the new vicar had been Mr Blobby. La-de-da. Anyway, challenges, challenges. Miss anything important?

DAVID: Ahm, well – there is one thing. We have drafted a letter to the Bishop.

GERALDINE: Oh, great – Bertie says all he ever gets are dull circulars, asking whether or not we should own up to the fact that most priests are as gay as Larry Hagman – do I mean Larry Hagman?

DAVID: Shall we get on?

GERALDINE: Grayson, that's it, Grayson. (*She does an impression.*) 'Shut that door', hilarious wasn't it?

DAVID: Ahm, Frank, as Secretary to the Council, I think perhaps you should read it.

FRANK: I'd rather not, thank you Mr Horton.

DAVID: Jim?

FRANK: Oh, all right – I'll read it. 'From the Dibley Parish Council.'

# Arrival

*Owen arrives.*

OWEN: Sorry I'm late – it's like the big ride at Alton Towers in my innards.

FRANK: I'm reading a letter from the Council to the Bishop.

OWEN: Right.

FRANK: 'My Lord. We are very sorry to take up your valuable time – but a very important subject has arisen.'

GERALDINE: Yes, sorry, it's just a suggestion, but, maybe you could mention his trip to Africa. Something like 'Welcome back from your triumphant conference.' Put it like that and he'll be putty in your hand.

FRANK: Thank you very much.

GERALDINE: Hugo – another stunning tie; girls just aren't safe are they?

FRANK: Yes. Ahem. 'Welcome back from your triumphant conference . . .'

GERALDINE: Excellent. Whatever it is he'll never turn you down now.

FRANK: 'We are very sorry to take up your valuable time.'

GERALDINE: Good, good.

FRANK: 'But, a very important subject has arisen. As you are aware, your new choice for vicar here has now arrived. And we must say that we are all deeply unhappy about her. We firmly believe that she will not fit in with our community at all.'

*Hugo is squirming with embarrassment and Geraldine can't believe what she is hearing. The atmosphere is tense.*

'We are profoundly angry that we should be used as an experiment ground for the more frivolous excesses of the modern church, and would ask you immediately, and urgently, to reconsider this disastrous appointment.' And it's signed by the Dibley Parish Council.

*A long pause follows.*

GERALDINE: Wow. You certainly know how to wind a girl. That's all of you is it?

DAVID: Yes, it is.

OWEN: Except me actually. As far as I'm concerned Potty Pottle was a regular old woman and if we have to have a lass, I'd much prefer it was a young one. Particularly, if I may say so, one with such an interesting taste in jumpers.

GERALDINE: Thank you. My grandmother knitted this. She's blind.

MRS CROPLEY: Did we actually vote on it?

JIM: No, no, no, no, no . . . I don't know.

DAVID: Of course we did.

FRANK: I'll just check that.

*David is very annoyed — this is why he hates minutes.*

No, in fact, we seem to have forgotten to vote.

MRS CROPLEY: Oh excellent. That is good news.

DAVID: Yes, but we had all agreed.

OWEN: I hadn't. Let's have the vote. I propose we give the Reverend a chance, at least see how she does on Sunday.

FRANK: Right. All those in favour of Owen's excellent proposition.

*They all vote yes.*

HUGO: Bravo!

FRANK: All those against.

*They all look at David.*

DAVID: Oh, this is ridiculous. All I can say is the proof of the pudding will be in the eating. I think you will find that our little community does not react well to the indignity of a vicar in high heels and rallies behind me in the desire to keep up the traditions that have made this village and the Church of England what they are today.

FRANK: I take it that's a 'no'.

DAVID: Yes.

GERALDINE: (to Hugo) God, your father's handsome when he's angry, isn't he?

## Scene Eleven: The Church

GERALDINE: In the name of the Father, the Son and the Holy Spirit. Amen.

CONGREGATION: Amen.

*The pews are full to bursting. Everyone from the village has turned out for Geraldine's first Sunday morning service.*

GERALDINE: I would like to start by singing 'Zippeedeedoodah' because it is such a thrill to see so many of you here, but I think we should stick with tradition and sing hymn number 199, 'Immortal Invisible God Only Wise' . . .

*And on to the most exciting part of the service, Geraldine's first Dibley sermon . . .*

I know a lot of you were surprised to find that your vicar's a woman. Not as surprised as me. All the way through my teens I was convinced that, naturally, I would become a supermodel and marry either Eric Clapton or David Soul, as you do. And then one day I read the Sermon on the Mount and it was so fantastic, that was it. I decided there and then to abandon the catwalk and give the dog collar a try. So, here I am. At your service, totally yours, any time, any day. Although if you come to see me first thing in the morning, wear dark glasses because before my face falls into place I look frighteningly like Bernard Manning. No, it's true – I do. It's scary. Now, let's sing hymn number 300, and I always think it's best if you shout on the 'bread of Heaven' bit.

*Sure enough, everyone sings VERY LOUDLY.*

CONGREGATION: 'Bread of Heaven!
Bread of Heaven!
Feed me now and evermore!
Feed me now and evermore!'

## Scene Twelve: The Vestry

*Alice is helping Geraldine take off her vestments. Her first service is over.*

GERALDINE: Marks out of ten Alice?

ALICE: Seventeen!

*There's a knock at the door.*

GERALDINE: Come in.

*It's Owen.*

Oh, Owen. What did you think?

OWEN: Missed most of it, I'm afraid. Otherwise engaged.

*Jim, Frank, Mrs Cropley and Hugo have all come in behind Owen.*

GERALDINE: Stomach still bad?

OWEN: To be frank, it's like the Battle of the Somme down there.

GERALDINE: Jim, did you enjoy it?

JIM: No, no, no, no . . .

GERALDINE: Oh, thanks.

JIM: You're welcome.

HUGO: You'll definitely be staying on now.

EVERYONE: (*in agreement*) Mmm, oh yes. You certainly will. Yes.

GERALDINE: Fingers crossed.

*Alice continues to help Geraldine disrobe.*

HUGO: Oh no, it's a dead cert. I haven't been more certain of anything since I opened the envelope telling me how many O levels I passed.

GERALDINE: And how many did you pass?

HUGO: None, I'm afraid.

GERALDINE: Oh, sorry.

FRANK: It's the most people we've had in the church since that Lady Godiva thing three years ago.

GERALDINE: Oh, what was that?

HUGO: We were celebrating the Summer Solstice, and we thought it would be fun to re-enact 'Lady Godiva'.

*Alice steps in and starts to unbutton Geraldine's final robe, in front of the others. Geraldine realizes what she's doing . . .*

GERALDINE: No, no, no. That's my dress.

*Alice jumps away. Very embarrassed.*

OWEN: A lot of people turned up, but unfortunately it was rather disappointing.

GERALDINE: Lady Godiva wearing a body stocking?

FRANK: No, she was absolutely stark naked.

GERALDINE: Wow!

MRS CROPLEY: Well, I hadn't had time to go to the hairdressers, so I wasn't looking my best.

GERALDINE: *(nudging Mrs Cropley)* I bet you were, you saucepot!

## Epilogue: The Vestry

*Late that night, Alice and Geraldine are sitting in the vestry having a cup of coffee.*

GERALDINE: So there's this nun, and she's having a bath – and a knock comes on the door.

ALICE: Oh dear.

GERALDINE: And she says, 'Who is it?' And the reply comes, 'It's the blind man – can I come in?' And she thinks for a moment, and says, 'Yes, come on in.' And the chap comes in and says, 'Nice tits – where do you want me to hang the blind?'

*There is a tiny pause. It sinks in and then suddenly Alice roars with shocked laughter. Everyone's happy.*

# Application for Lottery Funding

## SECTION 1

APPLICANT: Dibley Parish Council

NAME OF YOUR PROJECT: THE DIBLEY TOWER

BRIEF DESCRIPTION: The tallest building in the world

## SECTION 2

How much money do you want us to waste on this project? **£15,000,000**

Are you sure? Sure you don't want more? We've got billions kicking around. People keep buying these bloody lottery tickets like they're the secret to eternal life. Come on, you pansy. Put down a bigger number.

Okay. £70,000,000

That's more like it. Now, how many people do you think will visit your project in a 12-month period?

*(Note: take your personal estimate and multiply by nine to reach official estimate)* 18

Would you mind if Carol Smillie and/or Dale Winton interviewed you just before the lottery draw in a horribly patronizing way? Not in the slightest

## SECTION 3

*Congratulations! You may now have achieved lottery funding for your project. Don't wait for a reply, start building it and we'll send you the cheque.*

IMPORTANT Please enclose a drawing of what you think it will look like when it's finished

# The Dibley Tower

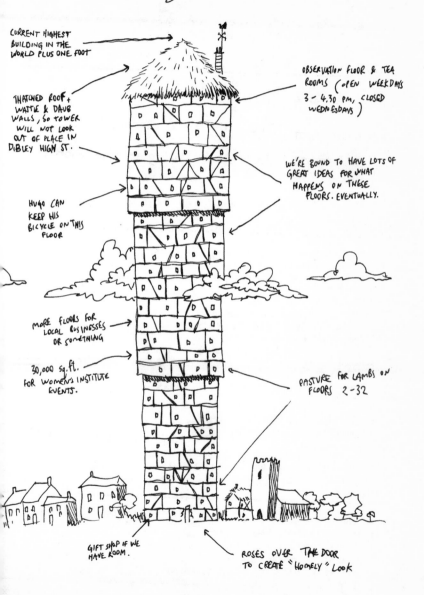

CURRENT HIGHEST BUILDING IN THE WORLD PLUS ONE FOOT

THATCHED ROOF + WATTLE & DAUB WALLS, SO TOWER WILL NOT LOOK OUT OF PLACE IN DIBLEY HIGH ST.

HUGO CAN KEEP HIS BICYCLE ON THIS FLOOR

MORE FLOORS FOR LOCAL BUSINESSES OR SOMETHING

30,000 sq.ft. FOR WOMEN'S INSTITUTE EVENTS.

OBSERVATION FLOOR & TEA ROOMS (OPEN WEEKDAYS 3 - 4.30 PM, CLOSED WEDNESDAYS)

WE'RE BOUND TO HAVE LOTS OF GREAT IDEAS FOR WHAT HAPPENS ON THESE FLOORS. EVENTUALLY.

PASTURE FOR LAMBS ON FLOORS 2 - 32

GIFT SHOP IF WE HAVE ROOM.

ROSES OVER THE DOOR TO CREATE "HOMELY" LOOK

# School Recorder Group Split Shock

*By Jacky Snow, Showbusiness Editor*

It seems as if the rumours are true. The Dibley School Recorder Group really has split up, citing musical differences as the main reason. Jessica Mathews, aged ten, said "It's been great playing *London's Burning* in the round, but I really feel like a new challenge. I want to take the recorder in exciting new directions, and that just wasn't happening in the Group." Jessica is already working on material for a solo project.

In a statement, descant player Emily Eden, aged eight, said "Our schedule was just too gruelling. We did the school hall, then the reference library, then the retirement home, all in a week. I'm just burnt out. I need two or three years off now, just to get my head together.

"When we began the recorder group three years ago, it was supposed to be a democracy. But it soon became apparent that Mrs Reid's word was law. When some of us became interested in avant garde atonal pieces with a darker industrial edge, Mrs Reid just didn't want to know."

Heartbroken Dibley School Recorder Group fans gathered at the school gates last night, crying openly, lighting candles and carving the word "WHY?" into the school sign. "I just can't believe it," sobbed one fan. "My life will never be the same again. But they'll leave a lasting legacy of great music, and wonderful memories. Their version of 'Frère Jacques' will never, ever be bettered."

At time of going to press Mrs Reid was unavailable for comment, claiming to be "marking books this evening".

# Your Letters

**We always appreciate your correspondence, because it means we don't have to write so many filler articles about farm open days, and we've got more time to write our CVs to send to the national papers.**

Dear Sir,
I heard the first cuckoo of spring the other day. Admittedly this is a lie, but I'm going to the pub tonight and the £10 you usually offer would come in very handy. I'll probably hear a cuckoo on the way, honest.
Yours,
Jim Trott

Dear Sir,
Does anyone know a good cure for pubic lice? It's for a friend.
Yours,
Owen Newitt

Dear Sir,
Don't y̶...

# Songs of Praise

## Scene One: The Parish Hall

*A Parish Council meeting is under way. Geraldine, Owen, Hugo, David, Frank, Mrs Cropley and Jim are seated round the table.*

OWEN: . . . as long as you wear plastic gloves up to your shoulder, so you can push your arm right up her.

DAVID: And I think that is that for today, except of course for Any Other Business. Any other business?

*They all shake their heads.*

Hugo.

HUGO: Yes?

DAVID: *(stressing his words) Any other business?*

HUGO: *(suddenly twigs)* Oh, yes, um. I would like to record the Council's gratitude for the completely anonymous gift of this wonderful new Bible.

*He produces a huge leatherbound Bible from underneath the table. Everyone murmurs in appreciation.*

DAVID: And I think you might add 'extraordinarily generous'.

GERALDINE: Mmm. And delete 'completely anonymous'.

DAVID: I'm sure everyone will agree that the King James text has infinitely more dignity than today's trendy rubbish. The glorious nobility of 'In the beginning was the word . . .'

MRS CROPLEY: Oh, lovely.

HUGO: Actually, *The Word* is quite trendy, if you watch it.

GERALDINE: Yes, it is.

DAVID: And while on the subject, am I alone on Sundays in preferring not to be asked to shake hands with the malodorous creature sitting in the next pew?

JIM: No, no, no, no – I quite like that bit.

DAVID: Let alone kiss them.

JIM: I *love* that bit.

OWEN: Look, could we move on? Some of us have got arms that are urgently needed up a certain sheep's backside.

GERALDINE: You flirt!

DAVID: (*looking at his watch*) Any other business?

GERALDINE: Yes, actually, there is one little thing.

DAVID: Farewell *Newsnight*.

GERALDINE: Well, I've had a letter from BBC Religious Programmes. A chap called Tristan Campbell. He says that he wants to film *Songs of Praise* here at St Barnabus.

DAVID: Heaven preserve us.

GERALDINE: Oh, not a *Songs of Praise* fan then, David?

DAVID: I am not. The BBC doesn't care about religion – they only cover it because they promised Douglas Hurd they'd look after Thora in her dotage. Chances are they'll have Mellors simultaneously shagging the living daylights out of Lady Chatterley on BBC2 to keep up their audience share.

MRS CROPLEY: I rather enjoyed *Lady Chatterley*. Some very useful tips.

DAVID: I beg your pardon.

MRS CROPLEY: Oh, gardening tips. Mellors was the gamekeeper – very good at hedge control!

DAVID: I see.

MRS CROPLEY: I thought the sex was jolly good fun as well.

FRANK: Do you want that in the minutes?

MRS CROPLEY: Better not – we don't want the Vice Squad raiding us, do we?

*Only Mrs Cropley laughs at her scandalous joke.*

DAVID: As I was saying, before I was so rudely interrupted by two tragic victims of experimentation with hormone replacement. I'd like to know of what possible interest our village church is to *Songs of Praise*?

GERALDINE: Well, it's a little bit embarrassing really. It says here it's to do with 'the fact that the present incumbent is a woman . . .'

DAVID: Might have known. *We're* the sex interest. 'Let's just flip over to BBC1 – apparently the vicar's got a nice pair of knockers . . .'

GERALDINE: *(teasing him)* I didn't know you'd seen my breasts, David.

MRS CROPLEY: He's certainly seen mine.

JIM: Everybody's seen yours.

GERALDINE: I *do* share some of your misgivings, David. I mean, personally, I'd rather leave television to Felicity Kendall and the other members of the Impossibly Tiny Bottom Club.

DAVID: Bravo. We are, for once, all agreed. *Songs of Praise* is cheapening and shallow and ridiculous. Isn't it?

HUGO: Oh yes, yes. Very cheapening.

MRS CROPLEY: Utterly shallow.

FRANK: Totally ridiculous.

DAVID: Excellent – well let's have a vote on this shall we? Anybody in favour of letting the morons from TV land into our church?

*They all put their hands up enthusiastically. Including Owen, who's just stretching up his arm to put on one of his shoulder-length plastic gloves.*

FRANK: I mean, it's got to be a hoot, hasn't it?

## Scene Two: Outside the Church

The church noticeboard has this poster on it:

## Scene Three: The Vestry

It is 6 o'clock on Thursday. Geraldine and Alice are ready to start the auditions.

GERALDINE:  Let the hordes in.

She readies herself behind the table and Alice opens the door. There stands one man on his own. He is a nerd. It is Cecil. Alice peers outside — no one else is there. She lets him in.

Hello. Are you all on your own?

CECIL:  Usually yes. I'm not married and I don't get out much.

GERALDINE:  I see. Well, welcome to our auditions for our choir. Can you sing?

CECIL:  No.

GERALDINE:  (writing a note) Can't sing.

CECIL:  I'd like to apply for the job of the choirmaster.

GERALDINE:  Can you conduct?

CECIL:  Oh yes.

He gives a quick demonstration, waving his hands around and nearly hitting Alice in the face.

GERALDINE:  Oh, wow. The job's yours. Welcome on board, er . . . ?

*They shake hands.*

CECIL:  Cecil. Can I enquire as to your current size?

*For a horrible moment she thinks he means her dress size.*

GERALDINE:  Sorry?

CECIL:  The choir?

GERALDINE:  Ahhh . . . Nil. Obviously we're going to have to rethink our advertising strategy.

CECIL:  (*shaking hands with Alice*) Cecil.

ALICE:  Alice.

CECIL:  I'm not married. I don't get out much.

## Scene Four: Outside the Church

*The poster for the auditions has been updated:*

## Scene Five: The Vestry

*It is six o'clock on Friday. The poster obviously has the right effect . . . a huge queue of people waits outside the vestry. Geraldine and Cecil are seated, ready to judge the applicants. Alice stands by to assist.*

GERALDINE:  Right, well, no time like the present.

CECIL: Except for the past. I used to love that.

GERALDINE: Yes, it was fun wasn't it? Alice, bring in the first contender . . . quickly.

*A very dour-looking man enters and begins to sing in a monotone.*

DOUR MAN: 'Lord of all Hopefulness, Lord of All Joy . . .'

*Geraldine realizes it is going to be a long and tedious evening . . . She glazes over. Next up, a very grand sixty-year-old dowager has a go.*

OLD WOMAN: 'Jesus wants me for a sunbeam, to shine for him each day.'

*Geraldine is bored, bored, bored. A young woman with long flowing hair sings the John Denver classic, 'Annie's Song', describing how her boyfriend fills up her senses.*

*Next up is a cardie-wearing nerd who sings exactly the same song: apparently his girlfriend fills up his senses, too.*

*An elderly man in dark glasses and biker jacket follows – his favourite song is also written by John Denver, and also features senses being filled up.*

*By this point, Geraldine is looking pained. A big, granite-faced beardy bloke comes in.*

BEARDY BLOKE: I'm very big in the gonads.

GERALDINE: Yes, I don't doubt that for a moment. Is that important for singing?

BEARDY BLOKE: The Great Otley and Netterton Amateur Dramatic Society. Character tenor.

CECIL: And what have you got for us?

*It's 'Annie's Song' again. Geraldine has had enough. She puts her hands to her head in despair and mimes a scream. A Gothic-looking housewife is next, who begins to bellow the great Robson and Green hit, 'Unchained Melody'.*

GERALDINE: (interrupting) Yes! Thank you.

*Owen comes in and Alice leads him to the centre of the room.*

Owen, what a surprise.

OWEN: Yes, well, I thought I'd have a go. Mum says I used to sing like an angel. I was just like – what's the name of that bloke? Lovely voice, youngster, in the charts, no testicles . . .

GERALDINE: Jimmy Osmond?

OWEN: No, Welsh bloke. Jones . . .

GERALDINE: I think you'll find, Owen, that Tom Jones had rather a lot of testicles actually. About five, I'd say.

OWEN: No – Aled Jones.

GERALDINE: Oh yes – definitely testicularly challenged that one.

CECIL: And what have you got for us, Owen?

OWEN: It's a little number I used to do called 'Jesu, Joy of Man's Desiring'.

CECIL: Oh lovely. That's one of my favourites. Very groovy. Fire away.

OWEN: All right then . . .

*He starts to sing . . . and he has an absolutely perfect singing voice. Geraldine and Cecil are stunned – they can't believe it.*

CECIL: Our very own Pavarotti.

GERALDINE: Yes. Thinner.

OWEN: And I've got more sheep.

## Scene Six: Geraldine's Hallway/Living Room

*Back at Geraldine's that evening. Alice is putting on her coat, about to leave.*

ALICE: I'm sorry Hugo didn't apply. He's very good at singing.

GERALDINE: You're fairly fond of Hugo, aren't you, Alice?

ALICE: Oh no, not at all. Not in the Romeo and Juliet/Dirty Den and Angie sort of way . . . Have you had lots of boyfriends?

GERALDINE: Well, depends what you mean by lots?

ALICE: Well, one really.

GERALDINE: Yeah, I've had lots, yeah. I've given up on it recently though – too much waxing for my liking. And you always get that funny feeling in your tum, don't you?

ALICE: Don't tell me. Every time I see Hugo, I just feel as though I've eaten a whole cow pat.

*Geraldine is about to show Alice out when there's a knock on the door.*

GERALDINE: Enter if you're sexy and love Jesus.

*She lifts her eyebrows and grins at Alice, who dissolves into giggles. Geraldine opens the door. It's David. Straight faced as usual.*

DAVID: Evening.

ALICE: I better be off then. (*She waves, leaves and then pops her head back round the door.*) Abyssinia!

GERALDINE: Ye-es . . . (*And she shuts the door.*)

DAVID: I just thought I'd tell you that I've put the new Bible on to the lectern. And dare I say, it looks slightly better than the paperback it replaces – you know, 'Funky News for Modern Man'.

GERALDINE: Why don't you come in, David. I'm waiting for that Tristan bloke from *Songs of Praise*.

DAVID: I wouldn't raise your hopes, Vicar. He'll be some sad old soak whose career peaked when he directed *Badger-Watch*.

GERALDINE: Yes. You always think people at the BBC are going to be glamorous – and then you remember Nicholas Witchell works there.

DAVID: Besides which, most of them are so homosexual they make John Inman look like Jean Claude Van Damme.

*There's a knock at the door.*

GERALDINE: Ooh. That'll be him now.

*She opens the door to a very gorgeous floppy-haired bloke.*

Oh.

TRISTAN: You must be Geraldine.

GERALDINE: Yes.

TRISTAN: Tristan.

GERALDINE: Yes, hi – come in. Do go on through there.

*He heads through to the living room and she falls back against the wall to have a quick bout of heavy breathing. Recovering her composure she follows him through.*

Tristan, this is David Horton, Chairman of the Parish Council. David, this is Tristan.

DAVID: How do you do?

GERALDINE: Have you ever worked with John Inman, Tristan? David's an enormous fan of his.

TRISTAN: 'Fraid not – camp comedy's not quite my cup of tea.

DAVID: No, mine neither. If you'll excuse me, I really must be going – there's some wrestling on I'm very keen to see. Goodnight.

*He leaves.*

GERALDINE: *(being cute and girly)* Coffee?

TRISTAN: Yes, thank you. It's very good of you to let us do this – I'm sure it's going to be wonderful.

GERALDINE: Mind Instant?

TRISTAN: No – that's great. I've only got a few minutes – but . . . great.

GERALDINE: *(gesturing for him to sit)* Do, do sit down, absolutely.

*She perches on the end of the sofa.*

TRISTAN: So. How's it going in the parish? Have you met a lot of opposition?

GERALDINE: Well, David's a bit hostile, but I can manage it.

TRISTAN: Yes – you often find it's the gay Anglo-Catholics who kick up the most fuss.

GERALDINE: Yes – although David's not actually . . . yes, yes, you're right.

TRISTAN: About the programme . . . Any ideas about hymns?

GERALDINE: Well, somebody did request 'Jesus Wants Me For A Sunbeam'.

TRISTAN: David?

GERALDINE: Yes, I think it was him, yes. *(She twists the lid off the coffee jar.)* Oh look – it's a new jar – I absolutely love that popping sound it makes, don't you?

*She pops the airtight covering with a spoon.*

Woo!

TRISTAN: *(not overexcited)* Yes. It is fun. Yes.

GERALDINE: *(blushing, now quite embarrassed)* Yes, it is, isn't it? Moving on then . . .

TRISTAN: Ahm. About the readings. We'd love one of the readers to be a woman.

GERALDINE: Not me?

TRISTAN: You've got to do the sermon.

GERALDINE: Of course, yes. Mustn't hog everything, must I?

*She does a tiny but very embarrassing pig impression and then quickly goes through to the kitchen to make the coffee.*

You'll be keeping the sermon in then, will you?

TRISTAN: Oh, yes. It's very much the heart of the programme. I'd really love people to get a glimpse of the woman underneath the cassock.

GERALDINE: I assume you're talking spiritually there?!

TRISTAN: Yes, I'm talking spiritually . . .

GERALDINE: *(back in the kitchen, to herself)* What else could he have meant? I want to get some close-ups of your pants.

*Embarrassed, she puts her head into her hands. Just then Tristan pops through into the kitchen.*

TRISTAN: Excuse me.

*Geraldine jumps.*

GERALDINE: Ah! Yes.

TRISTAN: I really better be going. I am very late.

GERALDINE: Absolutely. And the traffic this time of night is just . . .

TRISTAN: Non-existent.

GERALDINE: Non-existent. Yes.

TRISTAN: I'll send someone down to recce the church for the cameras, if that's okay?

GERALDINE: Yes. It's not just okay – it's okee-dokee.

TRISTAN: Goodnight, Geraldine.

*They shake hands.*

GERALDINE: Yes. You're lovely. No, sorry, you're welcome. Sorry, welcome to lovely to meet you. Welcome. Um, yeah.

*She shuts the door after him and leans back heavily against it.*

Oh God! I did a pig impression. I can't believe it.

## Scene Seven: Outside the Church

*A pretty young woman is looking at the gravestones. David approaches her, looking suave in dark sunglasses.*

DAVID: Can I be of any assistance?

RUTH: I don't know.

DAVID: I'm David. David Horton. Chairman of the Parish Council. Glorious little building isn't it? Very fine buttresses. (*He removes his sunglasses and casts an appraising glance over the woman's body.*) Lovely abs.

RUTH: I'm Ruth. I'm recceing for the lighting.

DAVID: Oh, I see. Part of the cameraman's team?

RUTH: I am the cameraman.

DAVID: Of course you are.

RUTH: I thought I might start with a shot of this old tombstone. Beautiful lettering. 'Here lieth Farah Fiffonf'.

DAVID: 'Sarah Sissons.' The f's are s's.

RUTH: Yes, I was joking.

DAVID: Of course you were. And underneath, look: 'Jane. Fister of the above'. Sister, one hopes.

RUTH: Come on, David. (*She walks towards the church.*) Let's check out your buttresses.

## Scene Eight: Geraldine's Living Room

*Geraldine is looking at herself in the mirror and talking out loud as if to Tristan.*

GERALDINE: Trist – not here! Oh, all right then. Just one little kiss.

*She kisses herself in the mirror, just as Alice enters.*

ALICE: Mind if I come in.

GERALDINE: Oh God!

*She leaps to the other side of the room.*

ALICE: Sorry. Just thought that I'd run through my lesson for *Songs of Praise* if that's all right?

GERALDINE: Yes – sit down. I was just, you know . . . licking the mirror . . . as you do . . . keeping it clean, you know. Anyway . . . (*She clears her throat.*)

ALICE: (*sighing*) I'm awfully nervous.

GERALDINE: Oh God. You're not the only one. Still, have a proper practice. Read on, Macduff.

ALICE: Okay. All right. (*She readies herself.*) 'Ye are the salt of the earth, and sainted. God shall seal your endeavours until ye sit on his right hand: therefore, fight the good fight, for his sake and he shall be your succour . . .' What's 'succour'?

*Meanwhile Geraldine is checking herself out in the mirror. Fiddling with her hair, pouting and admiring her breasts.*

GERALDINE: Sorry?

ALICE: You weren't even listening.

GERALDINE: Yes I was – I was just thinking about . . . Oh nothing. What were you saying about 'sucking' – erm – 'succour'.

ALICE: What does it mean?

*Geraldine joins Alice on the sofa.*

GERALDINE: Well, it means 'support, help, nourishment'. Like you, Alice, give me 'succour'. And I'll certainly need it tomorrow night. In front of all those people.

ALICE: And Tristan.

*Geraldine leaps up in a frenzy.*

GERALDINE: Who? Who?

ALICE: The producer.

GERALDINE: Oh hiiiim. Hiiim. God, I'd completely forgotten about him. I haven't thought about him once licking me up the legs.

ALICE: What?

GERALDINE: Well, I hope he doesn't expect me to make a special effort.

*Alice carries on reading the lesson to herself. And Geraldine makes gorgeous pouting faces in the mirror.*

It's not the job of a vicar to flirt, I'm afraid.

## Scene Nine: David Horton's Sitting Room

*David is standing in front of the fireplace. Hugo comes in from work.*

DAVID: Ah, Hugo. What would you think if ever I were to, say, find a girlfriend?

HUGO: Oh – I'd be terribly grateful. I just don't seem to be able to get one off my own bat.

DAVID: No – I meant, a girlfriend for myself.

HUGO: Oh right. Got you. Excellent. What, some sort of pleasant, plump, middle-aged, sort of . . .

DAVID: Not necessarily.

HUGO: No, of course. There are lots of older women who have really fought hard to keep their looks. I mean the necks are often a bit of a give-away, but . . .

DAVID: Yes, thank you, Hugo. I was in fact thinking of someone younger. All I wanted to say was that if I do bring someone round – I trust you'll behave with due discretion.

HUGO: Absolutely. Yes. Nudge, nudge. Wink wink, say no more. 'How are you, Davey, my older brother?' Nudge nudge. 'Sorry – must be going. Busy organizing a surprise thirtieth birthday for you – bro'!'

## Scene Ten: The Church

*The camera crew are busy setting up for the recording. Mrs Cropley is arranging a flower and lemon display as Ruth looks on.*

RUTH: They're very beautiful.

MRS CROPLEY: So are you my dear. (*Ruth smiles.*) In my youth I was what you call a corker. Can I give you a bit of advice?

RUTH: Of course.

MRS CROPLEY: Play the field. Snog everybody. Sleep with most. I didn't and I've been regretting it ever since. I do like young Frank but he's a bit of a slow-mover. Twenty-six years and not even upstairs outsideys.

*At the other end of the church Tristan is talking to Geraldine.*

TRISTAN: The cassock is splendid.

GERALDINE: Oh. Thanks.

TRISTAN: For the big occasion you can't beat a little black number can you?

GERALDINE: No.

*He leans forward and kisses her on the cheek. It surprises her.*

TRISTAN: And don't be nervous. It's just telly.

GERALDINE: That's right. Don't worry, I'll be fine. Cool as a cucumber me. (*Tristan walks off.*) And if Anne Diamond can do it . . .

*She can't believe he kissed her . . . as he walks away, she does a splendid impression of Munch's The Scream.*

## Scene Eleven: The Vestry

FRANK: I'm afraid we've run out of seats, Jim. We'll just have to stand.

JIM: But what about when we're supposed to sit down?

FRANK: We'll just mime it I suppose. (*He demonstrates mime-sitting.*) You know, down, down, down. Hold it and up.

*Hugo and Alice are also in the vestry. Hugo is in his best suit. Alice is in her verger's outfit. He approaches her.*

HUGO: Group hug?

ALICE: Oh, for energy?

HUGO: Of course.

*They walk towards each other until they bump. Alice leans her head into his chest and Hugo puts his arms around her. This is a momentous occasion.*

ALICE: Will life be different after this? Will we ever know privacy again?

HUGO:  Who knows? This time next week you could be a movie star.

ALICE:  Gosh, yes. I wonder which one?

## Scene Twelve: The Church

*The BBC outside broadcast unit is all set up and the service has begun. Geraldine is giving her sermon.*

GERALDINE:  Well, this is the first time I've been on television. I did once apply to go on *Mastermind* but they didn't like my special subject – apparently, there just aren't enough questions about the Wombles. (*There is a big laugh from the congregation.*) And also I was a bit young, being four and a half years old at the time. When I first decided to become a vicar, my life was a little bit like *Mastermind*. People asking me questions all the time – how? when? why? I know there are still people who can't understand why women are allowed to become vicars. People who are worried that soon there will be pantyhose drying on the vestry radiators and that 'hymns' will have to be called 'hers'. But, you know, they shouldn't worry because while they're worrying about these little things they're forgetting to worry about the big things. Issues like, well, how much you help those who need help, how much you love people and show your love to them . . .

TRISTAN:  And cut. Sorry, that was terrific but we're going to have to do it again. The flowers got in the way of the camera.

GERALDINE:  Oh, I see. (*She composes herself and begins again.*) In the name of the Father, the Son and Holy Ghost. Amen. Well, this is the first time that I've been on television. I did once apply to go on *Mastermind* but they didn't like my special subject – apparently there just aren't enough questions about the Wombles (*there is silence from the congregation*) . . . and, er, er . . .

TRISTAN:  Cut. Is something the matter?

GERALDINE:  Ahm. Yes, actually. Last time we did it there was a little laughter, wasn't there? A little titter. A mini laugh.

OWEN:  (*who has cleaned up well and is looking like an angel in his chorister's robes*) Problem is, we've already heard that joke once.

TRISTAN: Yes, I know. Everyone, can you pretend that this is the first time that you've heard this sermon. Try and laugh in the same places as you did first time round.

OWEN: How will we know which were the same places?

TRISTAN: Well, someone who remembers can hold up a hand and cue you.

OWEN: I'm damned if I can remember.

JIM: I think I can.

TRISTAN: Oh, well great. Everybody, watch this chap here, right?

*Geraldine is horrified that he's chosen Jim . . .*

And, take three and Geraldine cue . . .

GERALDINE: In the name of the Father, the Son and the Holy Ghost. Amen. Well, this is my first time on television. I did once apply to go on *Mastermind* but they didn't like my special subject – apparently there just aren't enough questions about the Wombles . . . (*she waits for the laugh . . . but it doesn't come*) and, er, also, they thought I was a bit too young.

*Jim lifts his arm at this point and the congregation roar with laughter.*

Er, no, no.

TRISTAN: Perhaps if you just raise your hand when you're expecting a laugh.

GERALDINE: Right.

TRISTAN: Cue.

GERALDINE: In the name of the Father . . . (*Everyone roars with laughter as she raises her hands to make the sign of the cross.*) No, no!!

## Scene Thirteen: The Vestry

*A small after-service party is being held. The wine is flowing and Tristan is talking to Geraldine . . .*

TRISTAN: Look, here's my number. Ring me when you've watched it.

GERALDINE: Oh, thanks very much. Perhaps if I'm beetling down the M40, you could show me round the Beeb. Introduce me to Uncle Bulgaria!

TRISTAN: Any time. I'm all yours.

*He smiles, waves and leaves.*

GERALDINE: *(to herself)* Attention, attention. Potential snogging situation developing!

*David approaches Ruth.*

DAVID: I was just wondering – I wouldn't mind having a bit of a chat with you about our next corporate video – 'The Potato in the 21st Century'. You couldn't give me your number or anything?

RUTH: Sure. If I had a pen . . .

*David already has a pen and card out. She takes them off him.*

## Scene Fourteen: Geraldine's Hallway/Living Room

*Alice arrives and takes her boots off in the hallway. She hears Geraldine talking in the living room.*

GERALDINE: Tristan. Hi, it's Geraldine. Oh you remember. *(She laughs.)* Yeah, well, what say you what we meet up after Evensong, Mr Producer, and reminisce?

*Alice walks in quietly. She watches for a second. Geraldine is talking to an empty room.*

ALICE: You've forgotten to pick up the phone.

GERALDINE: *(shouts in exasperation)* I know, I know. I know. Oh, come on, Geraldine, just do it!

ALICE: Do you want me to go?

GERALDINE: No, no, no. Sit down. Just sit down there. Right. Here we go.

*She picks the phone up – and hangs up.*

No, can't do it. Can't do it.

ALICE: Just a picking-cotton second here.

GERALDINE: What, what?

ALICE: You've gone and got a bit of a crush haven't you?

GERALDINE: No, I haven't! Well, maybe just a bit . . . Oh Alice. Blimey! Blimey! 'There's juice loose aboot this hoose!' I mean, it's all so right isn't it? He's a man – I'm a woman. He's a religious broadcaster – I'm a vicar. He's Scottish – and I love McVitie's biscuits. (*The phone rings.*) I've got a really spooky feeling here. Quite a lot of my future depends on this phone call. I mean it.

*Alice crosses her fingers. Geraldine picks the phone up and answers in a sexy voice.*

Hello.

DAVID: Geraldine?

GERALDINE: David.

DAVID: Yes. Slightly strange favour. Just wondered whether you had a number for that Tristan bloke. Wanted to speak to the lighting bod – Ruth, I think her name was – about some damage to the chapel – seem to have got her number down wrong.

GERALDINE: Hang on a moment, I'll look for it.

*She stamps on the spot, pretending to walk across the room when, actually, the number is right next to the phone . . .*

Hmm. I wonder where that number could be. I wonder, where I put it? Hmm, I'm such a butterbrain aren't I? Oh here it is, as luck would have it David. It's 0171 223 2129.

DAVID: No, sorry, I wanted Tristan's number.

GERALDINE: Yeah. That is Tristan's number.

DAVID: But that's the number I've been dialling . . . That's Ruth's number.

*The truth of the situation sinks in . . .*

GERALDINE: Tristan-and-Ruth's number. Yup.

*She replaces the receiver without another word.*

ALICE: So is the wedding off, then?

GERALDINE: Yes – looking a little less likely now. Yeah.

*She joins Alice on the sofa.*

Yes, yes. It's just the same old story, isn't it? He's taken. I'm Gitwoman. La de da. It's one of the disadvantages of the priesthood. If a bloke's looking for a hot chick, the vicarage is hardly his first port of call.

ALICE: I suppose not. Local disco . . . ?

GERALDINE: Yeah. Local disco – take your condom. Local vicarage – take a raspberry sponge. Oh well. Let's do the tea rotas, eh? There's more to life than just being happy.

ALICE: Could be worse. You could have behaved like the moron from Mars on *Songs of Praise* – like I did.

GERALDINE: Yes, I suppose so. God, that was a cock-up wasn't it? (*Alice is mortified.*) No, no, no, I didn't mean that, sorry. They'll edit it out – it'll be fine.

ALICE: Are you sure?

GERALDINE: Yes, absolutely. Trust me, I'm a vicar.

## Scene Fifteen: The Parish Hall

*A week later and everyone has gathered to watch* Songs of Praise *in the hall. Frank turns the TV on and they all sit down to start watching.*

FRANK: Settle down everyone. It's nearly on.

JIM: Hey, it's starting.

FRANK: Good luck.

*The opening images show Mrs Cropley playing the organ as everyone starts to sing 'Immortal, Invisible, God Only Wise'. The words to the hymn are shown over shots of the congregation, all singing keenly, and Geraldine, who is singing her heart out in the most attractive way she can, directly to the camera.*

DAVID: Well, if you can't sing in tune, I suppose you might as well make up for it in volume.

*The choir launch into a beautifully sung introduction to 'Love is All Around'. There are familiar faces from the auditions. Cecil is conducting with much enthusiasm.*

CHOIR: 'I feel it in my fingers . . .'

OWEN: 'I feel it in my toes . . .'

CHOIR: 'Love is all around me . . .'

ALL: 'And so the feeling grows . . .'

*Back in the hall . . .*

GERALDINE: Fab choice.

CECIL: Yes, I think it works.

*On screen, David is seen wiping his mouth trying to look attractive.*

GERALDINE: (*teasing*) You must, must give me the name of that mascara – it looks absolutely gorgeous.

*Back on the screen, Frank and Jim are seen squatting, pew-less.*

FRANK: You next, Vicar. This is your sermon.

EVERYONE: Bravo!

GERALDINE: (*on screen*) 'This is my first time on television. I did once apply to go on *Mastermind*, but they didn't like my special subject. Apparently, there just aren't enough questions about the Wombles.'

*There is a huge laugh from the congregation. Obviously edited into the sermon at the right moment.*

JIM: It's even funnier than I remember.

MRS CROPLEY: Oh, here comes Alice.

DAVID: Surely they've cut this?

ALICE: Oh no!! (*To Geraldine.*) You promised!

GERALDINE: Shush, shush, shush, everyone. It'll be fine, you'll see.

*She pats Alice's shoulders to reassure her, pulling an uncertain face at the same time. On screen . . .*

ALICE: 'The lesson is taken from the sixth chapter of the Song of Solomon . . . beginning at the second verse.'

*Alice stands behind the lectern and begins to read from the big old Bible.*

'Ye are the fault of the earth, and fainted. Um. (*She soldiers on – confused.*) Sainted. God shall feel your – seal your – endeavours until ye fit on his right hand.'

*Geraldine covers her face – she can't bear to watch.*

'Therefore fight the good fight, for his . . . fake, and he shall be thy . . . ff–fu . . .'

*The on-screen Geraldine jumps up and shouts at the same time as Alice says it.*

GERALDINE:  Succour! Succour. He shall be thy succour.

ALICE:  Thy succour.

*Back to the hall. And Geraldine leans in to comfort a distressed Alice.*

GERALDINE:  You see – nobody would have noticed, would they, David?

DAVID:  No. Of course not. Not if they were watching the other side.

## Epilogue: The Vestry

*It's night. Alice and Geraldine are having a cup of tea in the vestry.*

**GERALDINE:** So, two nuns are driving down the road in Transylvania.

**ALICE:** Ooh.

**GERALDINE:** And, all of a sudden, a great big, scary vampire jumps out right in front of the car.

**ALICE:** *(shuddering)* Oh no.

**GERALDINE:** Yeah. So one nun says to the other, 'Show him your cross.' So she winds down the window, leans out and says, 'Get out of the way, you toothy git!'

*She roars with laughter. Alice doesn't react at all.*

**ALICE:** I misunderstood that because I thought she meant 'show him your crucifix', whereas she actually meant 'show him you're really, really angry'.

**GERALDINE:** Ye-es. It is quite a confusing story, yes.

**ALICE:** I'm so stupid.

**GERALDINE:** No, you're not stupid at all.

**ALICE:** *(thinking further about the logic of the joke)* That is funny actually.

*She starts to giggle. Geraldine begins to realize that Alice will never, ever get her jokes.*

# Church of St. Barnabus, Dibley

*A glimpse into a voyage through the history of the heritage of the olde bygone past of yore.*

**by Frank Pickle**

**If you take this leaflet, please put 25p in the box by the door. We mean it. God is watching.**

Welcome to St. Barnabus'. The first mention of this church is in the Domesday Book:

"Nere to thys estate lyes the paryshe of Dybley, a small village wythe a nastie moderne-lookynge church. 30 acres of whete, 14 cattle, 2 mutton, 12 swine and a goate called Keith. The folke seeme slow of wit and greate of smelle. Easy to finde in the Highe Street is The Dybley B + B. Plentie of stable roome, tea and mead makyng facilities, and friendlie staffe. Dogges welcome."

From such humble beginnings began our little church; but as you walk through it, all of English history seems to unfold before you. As you enter, immediately above you is the **Bell Tower**. Two of

the bells are marked with Latin inscriptions: one reads 'Ego non tu latinum scio' meaning 'I know Latin and you don't', and 'Pagani dormire per hunc temptate!' meaning 'Try sleeping through this, heathens!'

Proceed through the **Nave**. On the wall to the North is the remains of a medieval wall painting depicting the Seven Deadly Sins. On the wall to the South is its modern companion piece, depicting the Seven Other Deadly Sins. These are, obviously:

Tetchiness, Gazumping, Hogging the Remote Control, Bonfires in Residential Areas, Not Leaving the Toilet Seat Down, Dithering and Overtaking on the Left.

At the end of the nave, you will pass the **Organ**. The organ was restored in 1976 with the addition of a Wah Wah pedal and a Bossanova rhythm switch. This year also saw changes to the outside of the church, which was completely covered in stone cladding. In a speech before the laying of the last block, the then vicar, Rev. Pottle, said: 'This

glorious cladding will add a lot of character. We'll really stand out from other churches. You could almost believe this black mortar is real! It's bound to increase the value of the property.' The stone cladding was removed in 1977.

In a glass case next to the organ is the original **Church Bible**. It was entirely written out by hand, and completed in 1477, exactly half an hour after the arrival of the first printed Bibles in Dibley. It is thought to be the only Bible in the country which ends with the words 'Oh, that's great, that's just terrific. Three years wasted. I'm going to jump off the bell tower. Goodbye.'

Above the **Choir** was the original location of the rood, a pre-Reformation painted carving of Jesus. When England became protestants and iconoclasts arrived in Dibley, the local inhabitants put a big bushy wig on top of the statue and said, 'No, that's not Jesus, that's a statue of Jesus's cousin Phil.' The Church of England believed this for another 173 years.

The **Pews** are from Ikea. They're not very old. Sorry.

However, do not despair, for the mighty climax of your voyage is near. As you reach the altar, look above and slightly to the left, and you will see Dibley's famous **Carving Of Something Or Other**. It might be an animal or something, and it's looking back at itself, if that lump is actually a head. It is thought to be the oldest carving depicting whatever it's supposed to be in Oxfordshire.

Leaving the church, you pass through the **Graveyard**. Nine generations of the Horton family lie here. Most of them were dead by the time of their burial.

Exiting the graveyard through the lych gate, you will see the **Bus Stop**. There has been a bus stop on this site since 1924. It is inscribed with the words 'Karen Little is a slapper, 12th October 1997'. A further inscription, not thought to be by the same hand, reads 'No I'm not, Melanie Spillane is a tart'.

Standing at the bus stop you will see **Me**. I stand here for a while most days, waiting for people to compliment me on my leaflet.

Please compliment me on my leaflet.

# Alice Tinker's

## PUZZLE PAGE

Fred wants to get to his house but it's in the middle of a maze. Can you help him? (Though actually, why should you? He bought a house in the middle of a maze in the first place. What did he expect, the great ninny with short legs.)

---

## RE-ARRANGE

These letters to spell the noise you make when you see a mouse!

| A | A | A | A | A | A! | A | A | A | A |

---

## Chess Problem
No. 86

This week's chess problem is: How do you play chess? Hugo and I can't figure it out at all. Though we do like the horsey pieces.

# The Window
# and the Weather

## Scene One: The Parish Hall

*An absolutely filthy night: dark, thundery and pouring with rain. Owen and Jim enter, a little early for the Council Meeting, the wind blowing them into the room. Owen shakes the rain off his cap.*

OWEN: Filthy weather!

JIM: No, no, no, I've known worse.

OWEN: Oh yes? When was that then?

JIM: The Great Storm, when the windmill got blown over.

OWEN: That wasn't the Great Storm – that was a moderately windy night – the *really* great storm was – The Great Storm.

JIM: When was that then?

OWEN: When Dave Batt got decapitated.

JIM: That wasn't the Great Storm!

OWEN: Well, it was pretty damn great!

JIM: No, no, no, the greatest storm was the one when old Harold got blown into the quarry.

OWEN: Oh that. The Great Wind.

JIM: What?

OWEN: The Great Storm has got to be rain – and in the Great Wind there was just wind.

*Enter Mrs Cropley and Frank, both shaking off the rain.*

MRS CROPLEY: Nasty night. It reminds me of the Great Storm.

OWEN AND JIM: Shut up.

*David enters, waving his umbrella.*

DAVID: Let's get this over and done with, shall we?

*He sits at the table.*

I've got apologies from Hugo and the vicar. First on the agenda, we've been asked to make a contribution to the South American Earthquake Appeal. I thought perhaps £10?

OWEN: Not much is it – hundreds of kiddies dying, we can only spare a tenner.

DAVID: What did you have in mind?

OWEN: I don't know . . . eleven quid?

DAVID: Done.

*Another crack of thunder.*

FRANK: Don't worry, sir – red sky at night, shepherd's delight.

DAVID: Yes. In my experience, it's more a case of 'red sky at night, thatched cottage on fire at the end of the village.'

*He pauses and takes his glasses off.*

I love this kind of weather. Do you remember the Great Snow?

OWEN: Oh yes – froze your balls off.

MRS CROPLEY: Poor old Gladys.

JIM: What about her?

MRS CROPLEY: Well, she died, didn't she? In the Great Snow. Froze to death one Friday.

JIM: No, no, no, no that was the Great Frost – it was the Bottle twins, Mabel and Edith, that froze to death in the Great Snow of '54.

OWEN: Rubbish! The Bottles died in the Great Freeze of '48.

DAVID: And I'm about to die in the Great Bore of '94.

*There is a huge roll of thunder. The Parish Hall is plunged into darkness.*

FRANK: How exciting! It's just like the Great Eclipse of '53.

DAVID: Shut up.

## Scene Two: Geraldine's Living Room

*Geraldine is wrapped up in a sleeping bag, with a mug of cocoa, reading* Hello! *magazine. Outside, Alice runs through the storm to the front door, and knocks frantically, disturbing her calm. Geraldine heaves herself off the sofa and hops to the front door in her sleeping bag. She opens the door to the terrified, dripping-wet Alice.*

GERALDINE: Hello.

ALICE: I just came to see if you were all right – not scared by the lightning and wind and everything.

GERALDINE: No, that's all right, Alice, I'm not.

*She moves to close the door.*

ALICE: No, neither am I.

*There is a huge clap of thunder. Alice screams.*

I am a bit, actually.

GERALDINE: Come on in.

*A little later and Geraldine pours Alice some cocoa. She has calmed down.*

ALICE: Do you remember in *The Sound of Music* when Julie Andrews was scared, she sang about her favourite things?

GERALDINE: Yes.

ALICE: Can we do that?

GERALDINE: Do you want the short answer, or the long answer?

ALICE: Both, please.

GERALDINE: The short answer is 'no'. And the long answer is 'nooooooo'.

*Alice is disappointed. Then there is another huge crack of thunder and lightning and she screams.*

Oh all right, we'll do it, we'll do it. Can you remember the words?

ALICE: Oh yes. I never forget the words of songs. I'm famous for it – never forgot the words of any song – never.

*She jumps up and stands in front of the fireplace.*

GERALDINE: OK – let's give it a go.

ALICE: Can you count me in please?

*Geraldine beats out the rhythm on the cocoa jug. Alice sways and sings.*

Raindrops on roses and whiskers on kittens, bright copper kettles and warm woollen mittens . . . um, um, um, um, um . . . ings.

*Geraldine starts beating faster to speed her up.*

These are a few of my favourite things . . .

*And then claps enthusiastically.*

GERALDINE: Yes – very nearly remembered all the words there! We're not scared any more are we?

ALICE: No, we're not.

*Thunder. Lightning. The lights go out. Alice screams very loudly. Then a horrid vision appears in front of them, with a torch in front of his face. It is Hugo.*

GERALDINE: (*holding a knife*) Oh for crying out loud, Hugo.

HUGO: Just checking everyone's fine.

*The lights come on.*

GERALDINE: We were just singing a Julie Andrews tune to stop us getting scared.

HUGO: Oh fab. I know a lovely song my mum used to sing me when it got stormy.

GERALDINE: Splendid. Fire away, O handsome troubadour.

HUGO: Well, I'm a bit rusty but here we go. 'When it's cold and stormy, And you're feeling a little sick, Cuddle up nice and warmy And play with your little dick.'

GERALDINE: Yes, that is very comforting, isn't it?

HUGO: Yes. Come to think of it, I'm not sure it was my mum who taught me that – think it might have been a bloke at school, actually.

*Another terrible crash. The lights go out again. A few seconds later, they come on again to reveal Alice sitting on top of Geraldine, smothering her.*

GERALDINE: Can you get off me, Alice.

ALICE: Sorry.

## Scene Three: The Churchyard

*A clear, sunny day, the morning after the storm. Geraldine walks through the debris-strewn churchyard, muttering to herself.*

GERALDINE: Good lord, what a mess.

*She stops to place a bunch of flowers back on a grave and carries on.*

I hate graves. I'm going to get burnt and put in a nice pot, and sit on my mum's mantelpiece.

*She reaches the church porch, and looks around her.*

Well, not too much damage, thank you, God. Dibley must be in favour at the moment.

*She walks into the church. A tree has smashed through the main stained-glass window.*

Or not . . .

## Scene Four: The Parish Hall

DAVID: I declare this crisis meeting open. We're looking at damage after the Great Storm.

FRANK: Are you sure you want to call it the Great Storm, because there was this tempest in '66 . . .

DAVID: All right – *all right* – we'll call it the Quite Great Storm.

JIM: How about 'big'?

DAVID: Oh for goodness sake! Over to you, Vicar.

GERALDINE: Yes. As you know, our window was smashed by a tree in the Storm With No Name. The first question is – do we replace it with the same image – OR do we go for something modern and exciting, like this Chagall window here.

*She shows them a beautiful illustration in a book.*

ALL: Oh yes.

MRS CROPLEY: I like the old one.

OWEN: Me too.

GERALDINE: Yes, of course, you're right. *(She closes the book.)* Load of arty-farty Froggie nonsense. So what we're looking for is a nice traditional rendition of Jesus and the Feeding of the Five Thousand, like the last one.

FRANK: Right.

JIM: No, no, no – I don't think it was Jesus, was it? He was too fat for Jesus.

GERALDINE: Not Jesus?

JIM: No, no, no – I think it was Moses.

GERALDINE: Moses and the Feeding of the Five Thousand does have a slightly odd ring to it.

OWEN: It wasn't Moses – Moses had a beard.

GERALDINE: So – not Jesus. Not Moses. Anyone got any idea who our mystery man was?

MRS CROPLEY: I always thought it was St Barnabus – seeing as how we are the church of St Barnabus.

HUGO: That is logical, Captain.

FRANK: There *was* a chap with a beard in the background though, holding a big lump of stone: that could have been Moses, carrying the Commandments for St Barnabus.

GERALDINE: I'm not sure Moses of Egypt and St Barnabus of Wolverhampton were the best of friends.

OWEN: Well, if it wasn't Moses – why was he holding the Ten Commandments?

JIM: Perhaps it wasn't the Ten Commandments. Perhaps it was just a big book.

GERALDINE: (*trying to sum up*) So, where are we? We've got St Barnabus and a mysterious chap holding a big book. Could it be that we have here the first depiction in stained glass of *This is Your Life?*

MRS CROPLEY: Perhaps the bloke with the book was a librarian.

DAVID: A librarian?

MRS CROPLEY: Yes. St Barnabus went into the library in Wolverhampton to borrow a holy book.

OWEN: If it was a library, why were there five thousand people in it?

JIM: I'm not sure they were people anyway.

GERALDINE: I'm sorry, Jim?

JIM: I always thought they were sheep. Jesus and the Feeding of the Five Thousand Sheep.

GERALDINE: But we've agreed it wasn't Jesus. It was St Barnabus . . . and the Librarian.

OWEN: Pretty bloody odd library, with five thousand sheep in it.

GERALDINE: All right. Hold it there – we're on the outskirts of Loony-Land, heading for City Centre. The best thing to do would be to find some old pictures of the window.

JIM: I might actually have one on me.

GERALDINE: Oh excellent. Problem solved!

JIM: Here we go.

*Geraldine looks at it, slightly perplexed.*

GERALDINE: Well, this is a picture of your dog, Jim.

JIM: No, no, no, no – that's right. But he was standing outside the church, so I thought you might be able to see the window in the reflection in his eye.

FRANK: Wait a second – I've had a thought. I could look through the old minute book and find the entry from when the window was actually built.

DAVID: Well, yes – I suppose it's worth a try. I think you'll in fact find that it depicted Jesus delivering the Sermon on the Mount.

HUGO: Absolutely – from a boat.

DAVID: I beg your pardon?

HUGO: Unless I'm much mistaken, Jesus was standing in a boat. Although I suppose it could have been a huge boat-shaped cigar.

GERALDINE: Ding ding! Everyone off. Loony-Land City Centre.

## Scene Five: The Parish Hall

*A week later.*

GERALDINE: Well, Frank's had a triumphant week! Tell us the whole story, Frank.

FRANK: To cut a long story short, I finally found the book of old minutes and there was a drawing by the original artist of our great north window and its beautiful portrayal of Noah's Ark.

JIM: Noah's Ark?

FRANK: That's right.

GERALDINE: So the man in the front was Noah, not St Barnabus.

FRANK: Right.

OWEN: And the five thousand were animals?

FRANK: Yes.

MRS CROPLEY: And the man in the background with the beard?

One Vicar, Female

One Verger, Human . . . just

The Happy Couple . . . not

The Three Stooges

Like Father, Unlike Son

We Few, We Happy Few, We Band of Idiots

Westlife

Sex God

No Sex God

Vicar and Creature with same-sized intellect as Verger

GERALDINE: A llama.

*Mrs Cropley finds this hilarious.*

MRS CROPLEY: Imagine Moses looking like a llama – no wonder everyone paid so much attention to him.

DAVID: Well, bravo Frank – unfortunately, I on the other hand have some rather bad news.

MRS CROPLEY: The last time I heard that, Vicar, it was the end of real teeth.

DAVID: I've spent the week investigating the prices of stained glass. The lowest quote we had was £11,000.

*Everyone mutters in outrage.*

OWEN: Bugger me – you could get someone killed for that.

DAVID: I'm afraid it puts us in an impossible situation. Sadly you must minute that Dibley can't afford a new window.

FRANK: 'Dibley can't afford . . .'

GERALDINE: Stop writing, Frank. 'Can't' isn't in the Christian vocabulary.

OWEN: Yes it is. You can't commit adultery, you can't steal . . .

JIM: . . . and you can't even covet your neighbour's ass, even if it's very alluring.

GERALDINE: No, no, no – what I mean is we can achieve anything if we want to. They said to Jesus, 'You can't walk on water – you'll get your dress wet', but he did!

HUGO: And they said to Rolf Harris, 'You can't do a "Stairway to Heaven"', but he darn well did.

JIM: Very successfully, in my opinion.

DAVID: Yes, that's all very well, but have you got any idea how to raise £11,000?

GERALDINE: Well . . . No, but I'll tell you this, what we're not going to do is stick a stupid thermometer outside the church for a hundred years, adding a nano-metre of red felt-tip pen each time someone gives us 2½p. I want our church to be a church – not an enormous church-shaped begging bowl.

DAVID: And I want Princess Anne to knock on the door and say 'I've dumped that ugly berk Tim Lawrence – I'm all yours big boy' but it's not going to happen is it?

*Eyebrows are raised all round. He's rather let this one out.*

Yes, well, enough of this – if you'll all excuse me. I actually have work to do. Thank you.

*He leaves, followed by Hugo. The others are highly amused.*

OWEN: Princess Anne eh? Well, who would have thought it!

MRS CROPLEY: She looked lovely on her wedding day.

OWEN: Everyone looks lovely on their wedding day. I bet even Margaret Beckett looked sexy as she walked down the aisle.

FRANK: I rather fancy Margaret Beckett.

GERALDINE: Shush! Boys! Has anyone actually got any idea how to raise this money?

OWEN: Well, lottery's the obvious answer, isn't it? Ask everyone for a fiver – I'll give them a lawnmower if they win.

GERALDINE: Perfect. Anyone else got any bright ideas?

MRS CROPLEY: I suppose I could finally yield to public demand and write my recipe book. 'One Hundred Exciting Things to do with Root Vegetables'.

## Scene Six: Geraldine's Living Room

*Geraldine answers the door. It is Alice. She holds up her piggy bank and marches inside.*

ALICE: Vicar! I've had a rather brilliant thought.

GERALDINE: Really?

ALICE: I've got this piggy bank. My dad used to put all his money in it, and he said when I grew up I could open it and buy a castle.

GERALDINE: Mmm. Did your dad have a reputation for telling the truth?

ALICE: Oh yeah. My mum knew all about his kids in the other villages.

*There is another knock on the door. Geraldine opens it.*

HUGO: Hello, Vicar.

GERALDINE: Hello, Hugo.

HUGO: I've just had this tremendous thought.

GERALDINE: My God! It's like being in Ancient Greece at the birth of philosophy here.

HUGO: We know Richard Branson, and maybe he could sponsor the window?

GERALDINE: Oh!

HUGO: I mean he looks like Jesus, what with the beard and the big smile and everything.

GERALDINE: Yes, yes.

HUGO: And he runs Virgin and Jesus's mum was a, well . . . you know.

ALICE: Hello, Hugo.

HUGO: Hello, Alice. Nice piggy bank.

## Scene Seven: Geraldine's Living Room

*Later, and Hugo, Alice and Geraldine are counting the money in Alice's piggy bank.*

ALICE: How much does it add up to?

GERALDINE: Well, excluding everything that actually isn't legal tender in the United Kingdom . . . a farthing.

ALICE: A farthing? Oh right. So quite a way to go then.

GERALDINE: Yes – but don't worry because Hugo's had his excellent idea.

HUGO: Red letter day!

GERALDINE: His father must know millions of millionaires like Richard Branson longing to find a short cut to heaven. (*She picks up the phone and dials.*) David. It's the Vicar here. Hi. Idea. Could you just give us the names of, say, five of your richest friends? I was thinking we could squeeze 'em for the money for the window. What do you think?

DAVID: It's a ridiculous and, may I say, very immature idea.

*He hangs up.*

GERALDINE: Thank you: what a kind and supportive man.

HUGO: What did he say?

GERALDINE: What a guy! He said he was a bit busy and could you give me the numbers.

HUGO: Oh right. Well, there's Lord Hanson.

GERALDINE: Very sexy.

## Scene Eight: Geraldine's Living Room

*Geraldine is on the phone trying to get donations.*

GERALDINE: Hello, it's Geraldine Granger – can I speak to Charles Kane please. Thank you. Ah – Mr Kane. My name is Geraldine Granger and I'm the vicar of St Barnabus Church. We were just wondering if you would like to donate some money for our new window. We're looking for eleven thousand pounds and . . . Sorry? I can stick it up my where, sorry? My jacksie. Excellent. Bless you.

*She hangs up, exasperated, and looks at her picture of Jesus.*

Look, I may have to fib a bit, but bear with me. It's for a very good cause.

*A little later and Geraldine is on the phone again.*

GERALDINE: Ahm . . . Could I speak to Mr Frobisher please? Ah, Daniel – it's Gerry Granger here . . . Um, Dibley Investments. You won't have heard of us – we're pretty new kids on the block – but I wonder if you'd be interested in a little investment portfolio we're putting together.

*Daniel Frobisher is in his glass office looking out over the city.*

DANIEL: Nothing to do with Dibley, Oxfordshire?

*Geraldine forgets her role.*

GERALDINE: Well, yes, actually! I'm the v . . . *(she remembers, and corrects herself)* . . . illage post mistress's daughter.

DANIEL: Friend of mine lives just outside. Hairless Horton. Bald by fourteen. Told me the other day they had a woman vicar.

GERALDINE: Yes, I heard that, too. My mother says she's fantastic. And pretty cute too. An all round bodacious babe in fact.

DANIEL: David says she's a bloody nightmare.

GERALDINE: Yup.

DANIEL: Probably fancies her. *(Geraldine grimaces.)* Interesting thought. Never know – she might be a virgin.

GERALDINE: *(with much emphasis)* I doubt it! I know a vicar, and she is famously the best kisser in Cheltenham.

DANIEL: Really?

GERALDINE: Yup. Her tongue is in the Home Counties Gymnastics Team. She can scramble eggs with it at twenty paces.

DANIEL: Ha. Now we're digressing, Miss Granger – tell me about your investment opportunity. I can't get that tongue out of my mind. Can you give me any sense of the range of your portfolio? Bonds, stocks, gilts, PEPs?

GERALDINE: Ahm . . . Yeah, we've got loads of those. How about I tell you over lunch Mr Frobisher?

*Daniel is intrigued.*

DANIEL: OK – I'll give you an hour. On Thursday. Lunch?

GERALDINE: Yes – I think I can find a window. Bye!

*She hangs up and looks at her picture of Jesus and her framed photograph of Mel Gibson.*

Boys, I think I have found a window.

## Scene Nine: A Lane in Dibley

*Owen and Hugo approach a villager weeding in his front garden.*

OWEN: Want to buy a lottery ticket, for the new church window?

Only a fiver, very worthy cause.

VILLAGER: What's the prize?

OWEN: A lawnmower.

VILLAGER: Got one.

OWEN: What do you fancy, then?

VILLAGER: A washing machine.

OWEN: Got one of those as well.

VILLAGER: Ooh, great! I'll take two tickets, then.

OWEN: God bless you, mate.

HUGO: Good luck!

*They walk off.*

But we haven't got a washing machine.

OWEN: No.

*He rips the villager's stubs out of the book of tickets.*

Well, then, he's not going to win, is he? Very worthy cause, though.

*He moves on to the next house. Hugo is impressed.*

## Scene Ten: Daniel Frobisher's Office, London

*Geraldine arrives outside the vast glass edifice. In Daniel's office, the telephone rings. He answers.*

DANIEL: Daniel here. Ah, Piers, listen, can I ring you back this afternoon? I've got a young lady visiting me. Don't be disgusting and childish. I'll ring you later.

*He puts the phone down. Geraldine is shown into his office — he has his back to her. She is wearing a smart black suit . . . and her dog collar.*

GERALDINE: Mr Frobisher?

DANIEL: Hello . . .

*He turns around.*

. . . Vicar.

GERALDINE: Fantastic office. It's a bugger to park round here though.

DANIEL: Yes, yes it is. Ahm . . . you don't often get members of the clergy heading up financial institutions.

GERALDINE: No . . . no, that's right. I fibbed about that. Bad. *Particularly* bad for a priest. I regret it.

*She bats her eyelashes at him.*

DANIEL: So, erm . . . what do you want. Sorry – what do I call you?

GERALDINE: Gerry's fine. Perhaps we could talk about it over lunch – if it's still on?

*Daniel nods pleasantly.*

It must be a very long time since you took a potential virgin out for a meal.

DANIEL: *(very embarrassed)* Oh Christ, I'm sorry about that.

GERALDINE: You said Christ! That's a thousand-pound fine, I'm afraid.

DANIEL: Jesus!

GERALDINE: Two thousand five hundred!

DANIEL: Oh, God, I'm not going to get through lunch at all.

GERALDINE: Three and rising! Still, at least you didn't say 'nob'.

DANIEL: I wasn't going to say 'nob'.

GERALDINE: Oh, you said 'nob'! Unbelievable! That's an extra five thousand.

*She grabs him by the arm and propels him towards the door.*

Come on. I want you to see our church.

## Scene Eleven: The Parish Hall

*A Council Meeting is in progress. Everyone looks bored to death.*

JIM: And then I said to them, I don't care what you say – this is my field. And they didn't take to it kindly, but finally, after a pretty fiery exchange of views, they moved on.

DAVID: Thank you, Jim for that report, and if you have any more trouble with those sheep, do tell us. So, finally, the window – how are we doing?

OWEN: Well, the village lottery has come up with a thousand quid.

*Everyone claps heartily.*

I've been delighted by the level of unquestioning generosity shown, especially in view of the fact that the prize is now only a tea strainer.

DAVID: Splendid. Any other news?

MRS CROPLEY: Well, I've started my recipe book, and the radish jam is a particular success.

DAVID: I bet. Anything else?

GERALDINE: (*coyly*) Well, I've got ten thousand pounds.

DAVID: I beg your pardon?

GERALDINE: Which means we can start work on our window instantly.

## Scene Twelve: The Parish Hall

*Alice watches as Geraldine addresses the village school.*

GERALDINE: Well, it's very kind of Miss Tinker to let me disturb your art class.

*Alice curtsies.*

And I love your papier mâché volcano.

ALICE: It's St Paul's Cathedral, actually.

GERALDINE: Right. Right. We're having a new window in the church. And it's going to be Noah's Ark – so I thought I'd ask you which animals you'd most like to be in it.

*A show of hands.*

GERALDINE: Oh good! Yes – you. George.

GEORGE: I'd like a velociraptor, Miss.

GERALDINE: A velociraptor – that's from *Jurassic Park*.

GEORGE: Yes, Miss.

GERALDINE: Yes, I'm not sure about that – but maybe. Any others?

*More hands shoot up. Geraldine points at someone else.*

Yes.

JANE: A tyrannosaurus rex, Miss.

GERALDINE: Right. Hands up for any animals not featured in *Jurassic Park*? Like a lion, for instance.

MARTHA: A football hooligan, Miss.

GERALDINE: Sorry?

MARTHA: My dad says football hooligans are all animals.

GERALDINE: Birds, any birds?

MARTHA: Samantha Fox, Miss – my dad says she's the sexiest bird in the whole world and he'd like to give her one, Miss.

COLIN So would my dad, Miss.

COLIN'S FRIEND: And mine.

GEORGE: My dad would like to give you one, Miss.

*Geraldine is shocked.*

GERALDINE: George! Shush!

*She pauses for a moment.*

Who is your dad?

## Scene Thirteen: Geraldine's Living Room

*Geraldine is in her pyjamas watching TV.*
*She's set up for a perfect evening: coffee, port,*
*chocolates and the Radio Times — all in reach.*
*Then there's a knock on the door. She pulls*
*a face.*

GERALDINE: It's open!

HUGO: Hello, Vicar.

GERALDINE: Hello, Hugo.

HUGO: I thought I'd see how the
window design's going. I had a couple
of animals I wanted to suggest.

GERALDINE: Certainly. I'm just about to watch the news — but do
sit down.

HUGO: Oh yes — frightfully important, the news. Must know
what's going on in the world. Who's Prime Minister and all that
stuff. Don't want Maggie Thatcher resigning and me never getting
wind of it.

GERALDINE: You're joking aren't you, Hugo?

HUGO: Yes, course I am. Maggie'll never resign — they'll have to
stab her in the back before she goes. Ah — here we go.

*The news begins. Grave stuff from South America.*

NEWSCASTER: There has, in the last four hours, been a second
earthquake in Colombia. Some of the pictures in this report may
cause distress.

REPORTER: It's hard to believe that things could be worse than last time, but this line of bodies, pulled out of a school in the suburbs tells its own tragic tale. Little Maria here has lost her sister.

*Geraldine starts to cry.*

GERALDINE: Oh dear. I'm sorry, Hugo – how embarrassing. I'm such a crybaby – I cry at anything and everything.

HUGO: Oh don't mind me – I'm the most frightful blubber too. At school they used to call me Blubber-box. That and Fartipants.

GERALDINE: This is just dreadful, isn't it?

HUGO: Just wish one could help more with this sort of thing. I sent money to Band Aid and all that. Bob Hope – excellent bloke.

*Geraldine carries on watching.*

Look, I'll leave you to it. Just wanted to put in a vote for a velociraptor. Damn fine specimens.

GERALDINE: Thank you, Hugo – a much valued contribution.

HUGO: Live long and prosper.

GERALDINE: Okay.

*Hugo leaves. She's left watching the TV.*

NEWSCASTER: If you have any donations for the Colombian Earthquake appeal, we'll be giving the address to write to at the end of the programme.

*Geraldine fetches a pencil and a piece of paper.*

## Scene Fourteen: The Churchyard

*Frank, Owen, Mrs Cropley and Jim are watching workmen going into the church to do the final preparations for the unveiling of the window.*

MRS CROPLEY: Someone told me it was going to be set in Jurassic Park.

JIM: I was told, on the underground grapevine, that the female figure is modelled on Samantha Fox.

MRS CROPLEY: Oooh, that'd be nice. Will she be topless?

OWEN: I suppose she may be. Anything to save money.

## Scene Fifteen: Inside the Church

*People are arriving for the ceremony. Daniel appears and is greeted by David.*

GERALDINE: *(looking at her watch)* Hmm . . . seven o'clock. Right, well here goes.

*She is standing in front of the window, which is covered with an awning.*

Ladies and Gentlemen, welcome. And we're very lucky to have with us today our wonderful benefactor, who gave us the remaining ten thousand pounds for our window. He very kindly said that any of the money we didn't spend, we could send to the earthquake appeal. Yes. So . . . the moment has arrived – Daniel, if you'd like to unveil it?

*Daniel steps forward.*

DANIEL: Certainly. But first I'd like to congratulate you on your new vicar. I'm a man from whom it's famously difficult to extract money . . .

DAVID: Hear, hear.

DANIEL: . . . My wallet has a burglar alarm on it. So. Now I am delighted to unveil the new window of the Church of St Barnabus, Dibley.

*He steps forward, and pulls back the awning, to reveal a plain glass window, through which a beautiful sunset glows. There is a murmur of amazement, and approval.*

JIM: You can see right through it.

ALICE: Lovely sunset.

OWEN: Well, bugger me.

MRS CROPLEY: It's turned into rather a nice evening, hasn't it?

DANIEL: It's beautiful.

*He moves over towards Geraldine.*

How much did it cost?

GERALDINE: About five hundred pounds.

HUGO: Nice work, Spock.

GERALDINE: Well, I felt that if I spent the whole eleven thousand pounds on the window, every time I looked at it all I'd see was those earthquake children.

DANIEL: What do you think of it, David?

*There is a pause. David is staring at the sunset.*

DAVID: Very beautiful. I've always thought it to be the finest view in the village. Good decision.

OWEN: Bloody marvellous. When it comes to it, you can't beat God's own creation, can you?

## Scene Sixteen: The Church

*The ceremony is over. Geraldine and Owen walk outside together.*

GERALDINE: Sorry we lost Noah.

OWEN: No! In my opinion Noah was a complete prick.

GERALDINE: Oh? Was he?

OWEN: Here's a bloke who's got the perfect opportunity to wipe out all the bloody useless animals in the world. Lice, moths, locusts, hamsters. What does he do? Takes the whole lot.

GERALDINE: Yup.

*He walks on. Mrs Cropley approaches.*

Mrs C – did you like the window?

MRS CROPLEY: Oh, yes. The sales of the turnip biscuits were a little disappointing. But you use the thirteen pence for whatever you see fit, my dear.

GERALDINE: Bless you.

*Mrs Cropley leaves. Daniel comes up behind her and whispers in her ear.*

DANIEL: Clever bastard.

GERALDINE: Oops! Pity – that's another thousand pounds I'm afraid. Good news, everybody! The Christmas outing's on again, thanks to Daniel!

*She takes his arm and they continue walking out of the church.*

## Epilogue: The Vestry

*Alice and Geraldine are having a cup of mint tea.*

**ALICE:** Right, I've got one for you today.

**GERALDINE:** Ooh. Fab!

**ALICE:** It's very funny.

*She clears her throat nervously.*

Knock, knock.

**GERALDINE:** Who's there?

**ALICE:** Ronnie.

**GERALDINE:** Ronnie who?

**ALICE:** Ronnie Barker.

*She screams with laughter. Geraldine is perplexed.*

It would be funny if Ronnie Barker came to your door, wouldn't it? He's hilarious!

**GERALDINE:** Yes. I'm not quite sure you understand how these jokes work.

**ALICE:** I've got a better one.

**GERALDINE:** Right.

**ALICE:** Knock, knock.

**GERALDINE:** Who's there?

**ALICE:** Billy.

**GERALDINE:** Billy Connolly?

**ALICE:** Yes! Oh well, you've heard that one. Well it's funny, isn't it?

**GERALDINE:** Not really, no.

**ALICE:** Well, don't worry. I've got hundreds more where they came from. Knock knock.

**GERALDINE:** (*closing her eyes*) Who the hell is it this time?

**ALICE:** Groucho.

**GERALDINE:** It's going to be a very long night, isn't it?

# LETITIA CROPLEY'S
# HOW TO COOK
## A BOOK FOR EVERYONE

the most unusual recipes ever

# A word from the author

These pages are kindly reproduced from the least best selling cookery book of the last century.

G.

Cooking is a joy, and it's easy. Some people try and mysticize it with fancy terms like 'boil' and 'scrape off the green bits', but really there's nothing to it. Cookery is simply the art of taking cold things and making them warm. So even if you don't have an oven, don't worry. My sausage casserole, heated gradually in the airing cupboard for a week, is always a great hit.

In this book, I'll be starting with the more traditional recipes like Chocolate Lettuce Pie and Pork in Bat. But being an open-minded lady, I've also been trying my hand at foreign muck. You're bound to relish my Chicken Sushi and Cajun Style Oak Bark Gumbo. I'll also answer some common questions like 'Just how dead does the lamb have to be before I cook it?'

Not all these recipes are mine; some were told to me by my mother, others by the voices I sometimes hear in my head. They're all tested, except for the ones I haven't got round to trying yet. Start on the easier ones first before you move on to more advanced dishes like 'Brace of Pheasant Cooked by the Power of Telekinesis'.

Happy Cooking!

*Letitia Cropley*

# The basics

*If your kitchen looks like this — the cook is ready to begin!*

Before you cook, you should get your kitchen in order. You should have everything out at once, because you never know which utensils you will need.

Getting all your utensils out is a wonderful opportunity to give your cupboards a thoroughly good clear. Recently, I threw out all the packets with sell-by dates prior to the Great War.

You must also learn a little about weights and measures.

## Weight conversions

100g – exactly a lump

200g – a big lump

300g – I hate metric

400g – I never use it

500g – Most of the packet, plus a lump and a smidge

1kg  – Just how big is this cake, fatty?

*Raw liver. How many puddings can we make from this?*

## A word about salmonella

I think it is best enjoyed as a garnish. More traditional folk may wish to serve it up as a starter.

# Animals

## Scene One: Geraldine's Kitchen

*It's late afternoon. Geraldine is busy preparing tea and scones as Alice chats.*

ALICE: You know that stuff they're selling now at the local shop?

GERALDINE: Which stuff?

ALICE: 'I Can't Believe It's Not Butter'.

GERALDINE: Oh yes.

ALICE: Well, you know – I can't believe it's not butter.

GERALDINE: No, well, I believe that is the idea, yeah.

ALICE: Then yesterday, I went to Crookenden and bought this other stuff, like a sort of home-brand, you know?

GERALDINE: Ye-es.

ALICE: And you know, I can't believe it's not 'I Can't Believe It's Not Butter'.

GERALDINE: Mmmm. I'm losing you now.

ALICE: Well, you know 'I Can't Believe It's Not Butter'?

GERALDINE: Yeah, yeah, yeah. You think it *is* butter.

ALICE: No, no – I mean, you know the stuff that I can't believe is not butter is called 'I Can't Believe It's Not Butter'.

GERALDINE: Probably, yeah.

ALICE: Well, I can't believe the stuff that is not 'I Can't Believe It's Not Butter' is not 'I Can't Believe It's Not Butter' and I can't *believe* that both 'I Can't Believe It's Not Butter' and the stuff I can't believe is not 'I Can't Believe It's Not Butter' are both, in fact, not butter. And I *believe* they both might be butter. In a cunning disguise. And in fact there's a lot more butter around than we all thought there was.

GERALDINE: Yes. I don't know what you're talking about – but I'm sure God does, and is intrigued by the whole thing. One thing I do know is that this is not butter – it's clotted cream. And do you know where it's going?

ALICE: Yes, in here. (*She points to her mouth, excitedly.*)

GERALDINE: No, it's going in my mouthpot, now.

*Geraldine pops it into her mouth. There is a knock at the door and she goes to answer it. Alice jumps up to take a scone. Geraldine spots her out of the corner of her eye.*

GERALDINE: Uh-uh-uh!

## Scene Two: Geraldine's Hallway

*Geraldine opens the door, with the scone wedged in her mouth. There stands a forty-year-old woman with a nervous smile.*

GERALDINE: Sorry – mouth just not big enough. Come on in.

*She beckons her inside.*

God got a lot of things right – for instance, men's bottoms are lovely – but he really should have made mouths scone-size. How can I help you?

MRS BARTLETT: It's our little Karl.

GERALDINE: Yes?

MRS BARTLETT: I'm afraid he's passed away.

GERALDINE: Oh dear. I am sorry.

MRS BARTLETT: (*crying*) It was rather sudden. We wondered whether you would have time to do the funeral tomorrow?

GERALDINE: Well, yes, certainly, of course. Can I ask how old Karl was?

MRS BARTLETT: He was just three.

GERALDINE: Oh dear. Would you like to come in?

*She gestures towards the living room but Mrs Bartlett is keen to leave. She turns towards the door.*

MRS BARTLETT: No, no. Thanks very much, Vicar. See you tomorrow.

GERALDINE: Of course. You take care.

*Mrs Bartlett leaves. Alice appears in the hallway.*

GERALDINE: How could I have said that about men's bottoms? And they're not lovely! Most of them are just horrible. My brother's bottom looks like Willie Whitelaw chewing toffee. Oh God. Alice, that poor woman. Imagine wanting to bury him tomorrow. Don't people cope with death in strange ways?

ALICE: They certainly do. When my father died my mum cracked open a bottle of champagne and went straight to Majorca. But that was probably because she hated him.

## Scene Three: Mrs Bartlett's Garden

*Geraldine, with Alice in attendance, is conducting a funeral service for Karl . . . a mouse. George, his small owner, is forlornly holding a matchbox, flanked by his parents. They are standing in front of a hole in the ground.*

GERALDINE: Dear Lord, you have seen fit to take Karl from us. We commend his soul to you, and pray that you welcome him into the Kingdom of Heaven. It is hard to understand exactly why Felix felt it necessary to eat Karl, especially since Felix had just devoured an entire tin of Whiskas.

*Geraldine looks at George. She whispers 'OK' to him. George steps forward with the matchbox.*

GEORGE: (*sadly*) In the name of the Father and of the Son and of the oily goose.

*He puts the matchbox in the hole.*

Amen.

## Scene Four: Geraldine's Living Room

*Alice is stuffing envelopes, Geraldine is cutting up a washing-up liquid bottle.*

GERALDINE: It's mad, isn't it, Alice? People genuinely love their animals more than they love each other.

ALICE: Animals are nicer than humans.

GERALDINE: Yup. Good point, Wonderland.

ALICE: I remember when my budgie Carrot first died, I was absolutely heartbroken. He was the only animal I'd not been allergic to.

GERALDINE: When he first died?

ALICE: That's right. Because he died and then two days later he came back to life again.

GERALDINE: Ye-es . . .

ALICE: Bit like Jesus, but with feathers. Then he died twice the next year, but both times he came back to life again.

GERALDINE: Are you sure he actually died?

ALICE: Oh yeah. He fell off the perch and everything. We buried him.

GERALDINE: Out of interest, how did he look when he came back to life?

ALICE: Well he always looked a bit different – but what would you expect? After all *he had died!*

*She laughs as if Geraldine's being thick.*

GERALDINE: Yes. You don't think perhaps your affectionate but technically insane mother just bought you a new budgie each time and called it 'Carrot' so you wouldn't be too sad?

*Alice thinks for a second. Then becomes really upset.*

ALICE: (*slowly*) Poor Carrot . . . actually did diedy?

GERALDINE: Er . . . yes.

ALICE: And little Carrot also diedy?

GERALDINE: Yes.

ALICE: (*her voice breaking*) And Carrot?

*Geraldine hugs her.*

GERALDINE: Yes. Come on now. We can pray for all of them. The whole bunch of Carrots. Alice, look . . .

*She puts a strip of detergent bottle on top of her dog collar: it says 'FAIRY' in big letters. Alice loves this and cheers up a bit.*

## Scene Five: The Parish Hall

*A Council Meeting is in session.*

DAVID: Right – I've had a letter from Florence Glover . . .

OWEN: Poor woman. That husband of hers is a monster – the most unpleasant man who ever lived in the village. What's the news, then?

DAVID: He's dead. Finally – the Pumpkin Show is on Saturday week. All entries should be in by Friday night.

OWEN: (*leaning across the table*) Well, I think I've got you this year, Jim. It's a big orange bastard and no mistake.

JIM: No, no, no – not a chance. They don't call you No-hope Newitt for nothing!

DAVID: All right, children. Now, if there isn't any AOB, *The Addams Family* is on television tonight and I'd like to take the opportunity to spend time in the company of normal folk.

GERALDINE: Actually, there is one thing.

DAVID: (*resigned*) I'll catch it on video.

GERALDINE: I thought you'd all like to know that I'm planning a special service. For the animals of the village.

MRS CROPLEY: Oh lovely. Sheba and Fishcake will be pleased.

DAVID: I beg your pardon?

GERALDINE: Well, I know you'll all think I've gone ga-ga – Miss PMT 1994 – but think about it. This is a country village, and people just adore their animals. So why not let St Barnabus be an ark for the morning. And Jim – you can be Noah.

JIM: No, no, no, no . . .

GERALDINE: No-ah, yes, that's right.

OWEN: Sounds barking mad to me.

DAVID: Yes, I think the vicar can do as she chooses with her own church. Perhaps we can return to this at the next meeting. We meet again in a fortnight. Oh, Vicar – I wonder if you could drop by after lunch tomorrow – for a little chat.

GERALDINE: Certainly.

DAVID: Splendid. I'd invite you to join us for lunch but Hugo's cooking and his food tastes like manure, doesn't it, Hugo?

HUGO: Sorry, Father?

DAVID: Your food, what does it taste like?

HUGO: (cheerily) Oh absolute poo, I'm afraid.

DAVID: See you after lunch.

## Scene Six: Outside David's House

Geraldine arrives and rings the front door bell.

GERALDINE: God it's cold out here. You should put your horse in the stable, David. Looks like it's got a great big stalactite hanging down between its legs.

She grins and brushes past him.

DAVID: Good afternoon, Vicar.

## Scene Seven: David's Hallway/Sitting Room

David helps Geraldine off with her coat.

GERALDINE: I must say, David – cheers – I really appreciate your support on this animal thing. When I first arrived, I had an awful feeling you and I were going to fight like Richard and Judy for the rest of our lives – but now something rather warm and cuddly and a bit Mr Kipling is happening, isn't it?

DAVID: Well, I'm delighted about that.

*They move into the sitting room.*

Port?

GERALDINE: Oh, yes – you know me. Bugger the gout – who needs two legs?

*He hands her a glass and she sits down.*

DAVID: Although actually there is one little thing I wanted to say about the animal service idea.

GERALDINE: Oh excellent. All ideas welcome.

DAVID: Are you absolutely and totally bollocking crazy?

GERALDINE: Beg your pardon?

DAVID: Are you seriously going to let animals into our church?

GERALDINE: Yes, I am. I think it's a great idea. People love animals.

DAVID: People also love food-mixers. But there are very few of us pressing the Archbishop of Canterbury for a special communion for the Moulinex Magic-Master.

GERALDINE: Are you hinting, albeit gently, that you're really not very keen on the idea?

DAVID: Have you actually thought this one through? Is there going to be any limit on size? Will hippopotamuses be welcome?

GERALDINE: You know perfectly well that there are no hippo-potamuses in the village. Well . . .

BOTH: . . . apart from Mrs Standford . . .

*David continues, unheeded.*

DAVID: Do nits get a blessing? Are fleas to be excluded? Should we bring along our free range eggs to have the unborn chickens blessed before we go home and scramble them?

GERALDINE: You know, for a big chap, David, you're being very childish.

DAVID: I'm being childish? I'm not the one who's going to bless the ickle wickle hamster! I mean, for heaven's sake! What if your congregation starts eating each other?

GERALDINE: Any animal caught swallowing another animal will be pretty sternly ticked off.

DAVID: And that is before we consider hygiene. One of the great joys I've found about having human beings in church is that they tend to be house trained.

GERALDINE: Yes, well, I don't deny there may be one or two puddly-type accidents, yes.

DAVID: If Mrs Fothergill's parakeet escapes, we will all be wearing protective headgear for the rest of our lives!

GERALDINE: (getting up crossly) I'm sorry. If you're going to start doing toilet gags, I'm afraid I just can't talk to you.

DAVID: So who will you talk to? The animals? Even Jesus, who had some pretty damn whacky ideas, didn't bless animals. Donkeys – he rode them. Fish – he ate them.

*Hugo enters in a fetching apron, wearing rubber gloves and wiping a plate.*

HUGO: Oh, hello, Vicar. Splendid idea about the animal service.

DAVID: (violently) Out!

HUGO: Absolutely, good idea – saucepans to scrub, plates to polish.

*He leaves smartly, then pops his head back round the door.*

Just one question, Vicar. Teddy bears – will they be welcome?

GERALDINE: Abso-bloody-lutely Hugo, yes.

HUGO: Splendid.

GERALDINE: I think I'd better be going too. I've got a doctor friend coming round. Perhaps you've heard of him? Dolittle. Lovely chap.

DAVID: Do me one favour though, will you, Vicar? Try not to publicize this fiasco outside the confines of our poor little village?

GERALDINE: Oh all right.

DAVID: And when you get home – do look up the word 'laughing-stock' in the dictionary.

GERALDINE: And while I'm at it, don't take it personally, but I'm also going to look up 'lips go unattractively thin when angry'.

*She waves her hand in front of his mouth, and leaves. David is unamused. He picks up the phone and dials.*

DAVID: Can I speak to the Bishop's office, please?

## Scene Eight: Outside the Parish Hall

*A man is leaning on his car, waiting outside the parish hall as children leave school. Alice comes out.*

REPORTER: So, you're really having animals in the church, are you?

ALICE: (flustered) Oh. Yes. Yes, we are.

REPORTER: Will gerbils be taking Holy Communion?

ALICE: Oh gosh, it's like being on *Blockbusters*. Um. I don't really know. You'd have to ask the vicar.

*Geraldine appears.*

Oh, Vicar! This gentleman wants to know about the service.

GERALDINE: Oh. Have we met?

REPORTER: No, I'm just an admirer, love. I've got a bulldog myself. Nags me every Sunday to take him to church. Particularly fond of the mass in Latin.

GERALDINE: I think you're taking the mickey.

REPORTER: Oh no. Everyone at the paper is really excited about it. Sheep singing hymns. It's a brilliant idea, isn't it. Can we have a picture, Vicar?

GERALDINE: What?

*A photographer appears and starts taking photos.*

Oh my God!

## Scene Nine: Geraldine's Living Room

*Next morning, very early. There is a knock at the door. Geraldine answers it and David enters, brandishing a newspaper.*

DAVID: Have you seen this?

GERALDINE: No – what? What? What is it?

*He flourishes the Sun in her face. There is a not particularly flattering picture of her on the front page.*

Oh my God – who is that? It's Jabba the Hutt, isn't it?

DAVID: 'In the name of the Father, the Son and the Holy Goat. Baa-men!' And listen, they've written a special 'Lord's Prayer' for you.

'Our Father who art in Doggy Heaven,
Hallowed be thy mane
Thy Kingdom come,
Thy Pedigree Chum,
On earth as it is in Battersea Dogs' Home.'

GERALDINE: Oh for heaven's sake.

DAVID: And you're actually quoted as saying that gerbils will be given Holy Communion.

GERALDINE: If that young journalist comes near me again, pretty soon after I'll be wearing an interesting pair of testicle-shaped earrings. What I actually said was . . .

*David interrupts her.*

DAVID: The point is that you shouldn't have said anything at all.

GERALDINE: Well, I know that! But they didn't have horns and tails, so we didn't realize they were from the tabloids.

*David sits next to her on the sofa.*

DAVID: The trouble is that you don't realize anything. You're a good woman with a good heart, but you should be running a cake stall, not a church. And I'm afraid, dear lady, the time has come, for the sake of this community, for me to begin proceedings to have you replaced.

GERALDINE: What?

DAVID: I will see myself out.

*He leaves. Geraldine lies back on the sofa, clapping her hand to her forehead. The back door slams and Alice enters, also wielding the paper.*

ALICE: Have you seen, Vicar?

GERALDINE: Yes. I have. I haven't been so depressed since David Bowie married a stick insect. Well, that's it, we'll just have to cancel. Alice – everybody is laughing at us.

ALICE: No – *some* people are laughing at us. But if I'd stopped doing what I was doing just because people were laughing at me, I'd have stood stock still all my life.

GERALDINE: The problem is, Big Chief David Wigwam-Head is *genuinely* on the warpath. I could soon be paddleless up a rather famous creek, the name of which rhymes with 'Britt'.

ALICE: Don't worry. I'll stick by you, and I can be a pretty scary opponent, as Gavin Hart discovered when he tried to look at my pants in the playground and I stabbed him in the head with a protractor.

## Scene Ten: The Parish Hall

*A lot of pumpkins are laid out on the table. Mrs Cropley is taking more out of boxes and arranging them. Frank is helping her, and Jim is loitering.*

FRANK: Are you going to go to the animal service, Jim?

JIM: No, no, no, no – I haven't made my mind up yet. I don't like missing *Little House on the Prairie*.

FRANK: What about you, Letitia?

MRS CROPLEY: Oh yes. The only question is whether to bring along the snails I've got for my new recipe.

FRANK:  What recipe's that?

MRS CROPLEY:  Bread and butter pudding surprise.

*Owen enters bearing a large bag.*

OWEN:  Oh dear, I've just trod in something brown – and it's certainly not chocolate cake.

FRANK:  Are you coming to the animal service, Owen?

OWEN:  Ah, I don't know – you see, I might not be fit for it, after all the drinking on Saturday night to celebrate my great pumpkin victory.

JIM:  Some hope. From what I hear, your pumpkins are no, no, no, no bigger than your balls.

OWEN:  Well, then, I'd better be buying myself some larger underpants, hadn't I?

*He opens the bag to reveal a pretty hefty pumpkin.*

JIM:  No, no, no, not bad I suppose. If you'll excuse me . . .

*Owen laughs derisively as Jim slopes out.*

MRS CROPLEY:  Have you heard this rumour, by the way? Mr Horton is trying to get the vicar the sack.

OWEN:  No, that can't be right.

*Jim opens the door, and wheels in a wheelbarrow, with a sheet covering something fairly big.*

Come on, Jim – second place isn't so bad. Germany came second in the war – and they've done all right.

JIM:  No, no, no – good. Then you'll enjoy being number two.

*He reveals an enormous pumpkin.*

OWEN:  Well, bugger me.

MRS CROPLEY:  You know, it's time the vicar did something about your bad language.

*She stops and looks at the pumpkin.*

It IS a big bugger though, isn't it?

## Scene Eleven: Geraldine's Living Room

*It is evening. Alice is hanging around, while Geraldine is ironing.*

ALICE: Ah – have you heard this rumour going round?

GERALDINE: If it's anything to do with butter, I'm really not interested.

*The phone rings. Alice answers it.*

ALICE: Hiya. Oh hello, how are you? . . . Oh I'm fine – been having a bit of trouble with a verruca but the big scab fell off today so it's better.

*Geraldine now is beside her, gesturing 'come on, come on'.*

No, she's here now – but may I just say I think you looked *gorgeous* in that frock you were wearing last time you were here. Right – here she is. Loads of love! Abyssinia!

*She hands the phone to Geraldine, with her hand over the mouthpiece.*

GERALDINE: Who is it?

ALICE: The Bishop.

*Geraldine is aghast.*

GERALDINE: Oh my God . . . Bertie, Bertie – hi, Gerry here. Sorry about that. Lobotomy – yeah, very slow progress. Sadly. How can I help? Oh, David Horton's been calling you, has he? He's a total nutter, isn't he? And one of your dearest friends. Yes. No, no, you're right. Yeah. He does represent the feelings of most of your community. Right, point taken, well, thanks for the . . . tip off. Big love to Luigi. Oh – Ivan. Sorry. Right. Lovely. Bye then.

ALICE: Did he tell you not to do the service then?

GERALDINE: Not as such, no. But he did say if it backfired, I'd have to take the consequences.

ALICE: Oh I'm sure it will be fine.

GERALDINE: You mean, like you were sure you'd win *The Krypton Factor*?

## Scene Twelve: Geraldine's Living Room

*It's Saturday night. Geraldine emerges from the kitchen in her pyjamas, talking to herself. She switches the lamp on.*

GERALDINE: It actually is the worst idea in the history of the world, isn't it?

*She takes a Crunchie out of her pyjama pocket.*

I shouldn't be eating this. Last time I felt this bad I ate 562 Crunchies in one night. That was fine until I washed them down with that tin of treacle, OD'd on sugar and woke up in a disgusting position on the sofa.

*She looks at the picture of Jesus on the wall.*

Oh God. I'm sorry I'm so gloomy. And I'm sorry I always say 'Oh God' when I am gloomy. Oh God. Look if it's a disaster tomorrow – if it's the ecclesiastical equivalent of La Toya Jackson's new nose – you'll give me a little hand, won't you? I like it here.

## Scene Thirteen: Geraldine's Living Room

*Dibley is waking up to a beautiful Sunday morning. Geraldine wakes up on the sofa in disarray, a tin of syrup next to her on the table.*

GERALDINE: Oh no.

*She is surrounded by about a hundred and fifty Crunchie wrappers. Her hair is a mess. She has overslept. She goes upstairs and runs back down a few minutes later, in her cassock – but with her bra over it. She realizes her mistake and runs back upstairs. She tries to brush her disastrous hair.*

*What she doesn't realize is that meanwhile, a hive of activity is happening outside as the village readies itself for the animal service. A girl checks something in a matchbox. A family loads a dog into a car. A horsebox is pulled along the motorway towards Dibley. Dogs are everywhere and horses ride over the fields towards the village.*

GERALDINE: I don't know what I was thinking of. I don't even like animals, particularly pets. There's always that one last poo that you can smell but you can't find until, come winter, you put your wellies on.

## Scene Fourteen: Geraldine's Living Room

*A little later and Geraldine is dressed, and ready. Alice is there.*

GERALDINE: Right, let's go. Face the total ignominy of a church empty apart from you, me and one very religious rat.

*Alice grins.*

What are you grinning about? You look like Sissy Spacek on ecstasy.

*Alice giggles but says nothing. They step outside. An amazing sight awaits Geraldine. Hundreds of people are walking to the church, with birds in cages, horses, sheep, cats and dogs in attendance. People smile and greet her — Geraldine is gob-smacked.*

## Scene Fifteen: David Horton's Living Room

*Meanwhile, Hugo and David are firmly seated on the sofa.*

HUGO: So, instead of going to the service, we'll sit here, and do nothing?

DAVID: Correct.

HUGO: Brilliant!

DAVID: Although I may drift along at the end to take some photos for the Bishop.

HUGO: Bravo. Superb plan.

*David takes another sip of coffee. Hugo looks wistfully out of the window.*

## Scene Sixteen: The Church

*Geraldine is meeting people on her way into church. She spots a sweet, floppy-haired dog. His owner is a scary looking skinhead.*

GERALDINE:  Oh, look at this one! Oh, let me see! (*She crouches down and pats the dog.*) Oh, look at you, little babyface! What's his name?

SKINHEAD:  Satan.

GERALDINE:  Satan? Right.
Good. Well, I hope he enjoys
the sermon. Rather brave of
him to come at all really.

*She stands up and strides off.*

## Scene Seventeen: David Horton's Living Room

*David and Hugo haven't moved from the sofa.*

HUGO:  Although . . .

DAVID:  Yes?

HUGO:  Actually . . . Actually . . .

DAVID:  Spit it out, boy.

HUGO:  Actually – I'm not sure it *is* such a ripping plan, in fact.

DAVID:  I beg your pardon?

HUGO:  Well, it seems to me that sitting here doing, if you'll pardon my French, *sod tout*, is, in fact, a pretty damn poor idea actually in comparison to taking old Bruno up to church to thank God for the animals upon which the economic and social life of our village is based, and thanks to whom the lonely and old people aren't lonely and don't feel old – even though most of them ought to have been buried before the war – and I'm talking about the Boer War here (*He's getting into his stride now.*) In fact, I suspect it's just being proud and waging a rather childish war against Mrs God and so it's not so much a good plan as the worst plan since Hitler's dad said to Hitler's mum, 'Let's go upstairs, Brunhilda, I'm feeling a little saucy tonight.'

DAVID:  You do what *you* think is right, then.

HUGO:  Right. Fair enough. Classic.

*He doesn't move — he's lost his nerve.*

## Scene Eighteen: The Church

*Geraldine is outside the church, with a multitude of animals and their owners.*

GERALDINE:  Ladies, gentlemen, and others — just before we go into the church, I'd like you to join me in a prayer.

*Everyone bows their heads — including some of the horses.*

Dear Lord, who rode into Jerusalem on the back of a faithful donkey, bless all these wonderful creatures here today. Give them shiny coats and full udders and tasty milk, and may one of them unexpectedly win the Grand National next year. At two hundred to one, when we've all had a little flutter. Amen.

## Scene Nineteen: David Horton's Living Room

*Hugo and David are both still sitting there. Then suddenly, very quickly, Hugo jumps up from the sofa.*

HUGO:  Come on, Bruno, let's go!!
Let's go, boy!!

*He and Bruno race out. Then, with his coat on, he bursts in and grabs the stuffed owl on the sideboard.*

Well, in for a penny, in for a pound, eh? Come on, Patricia — off to church you lazy old thing. Don't argue.

## Scene Twenty: The Church

*The church is full to bursting, with animals — and their owners — of all shapes and sizes. There is lots of squawking and growling. Geraldine makes her way down the aisle to the front, nearly stepping on a small creature on the way.*

GERALDINE:  Ooh, sorry, sorry!

*She squeezes past a goat, tethered at the front of the church.*

Now let's start with our first hymn, shall we? Which is, of course, the classic 'All Things Bright and Beautiful'.

*The congregation sings lustily. Cecil the choirmaster has a small mouse in his pocket that he gestures to during the phrase 'all creatures great and small'. An owl flaps its wings at the side of the church. A goat tries to eat Geraldine's surplice. Hugo appears halfway through and makes his way to the front. Alice waves at him, pleased. Meanwhile, David is leaving his house, armed with a camera. The hymn comes to an end.*

Please be seated.

*She gestures like Barbara Woodhouse.*

Sit. Sit. At this point, it's traditional to pray for the Royal Family. But today, dear Lord, we pray instead for the Royal Family's animals and pets. For the Queen's corgis, for Princess Anne's horses, and for anything that gets sat on by the Duchess of York.

*Then the choir sings 'Puppy Love' — the congregation is delighted. All this time, David is walking purposefully through Dibley. He arrives at the church, but can't get in — there are loads of people outside, with their animals. He looks around at the amazing sight in front of him. Inside, Geraldine continues with the service.*

. . . And the blessing of God Almighty, the Father, Son and Holy Spirit, be among you and remain with you always. Well, I think that's all we've got time for. I'd like to thank you all for coming. Especially you.

*She gestures at the goat, who bleats.*

I'd also like to thank most of you for behaving so well. For not biting each other. And for holding off from going to the loo for a whole hour. And thanks to your animals for the same.

## Scene Twenty-One: The Churchyard

*The service is over. Alice opens the doors of the church and the congregation streams out, carrying their pets. She and Geraldine say goodbye to everyone as they leave. A cow moos loudly. David is still watching from afar. A rather posh gentleman walks past him, on his way out.*

POSH GENTLEMAN:  It's wonderful, isn't it?

*David looks around him, quietly considering.*

DAVID:  It does make one wonder . . . yes.

*He is looking at Geraldine, as she says goodbye to everyone. She flaps her arms with exhaustion, hugs Alice, and they set off down the path together.*

## Epilogue: The Vestry

*Geraldine and Alice are having a cup of Bovril.*

**GERALDINE:** I don't know any more religious jokes – but I suppose I have got a couple of animal ones.

**ALICE:** Hurrah!

**GERALDINE:** Why did the lobster blush?

**ALICE:** Why?

**GERALDINE:** Because the sea weed.

**ALICE:** Because the sea-weed what?

**GERALDINE:** Because the . . . sea wee-ed.

**ALICE:** Did *what*?

**GERALDINE:** No, listen – the lobster was in the sea.

**ALICE:** Right.

**GERALDINE:** And the sea wee-ed . . .

*Long pause. Then suddenly Alice gets. it. She screams and puts her hands to her mouth.*

**ALICE:** Oh lordy, lordy – that's the rudest thing I've ever heard.

From: The Church of England
To: All C of E Vicars

# WHAT TO DO IF JESUS COMES BACK

### Jesus could return at any time. Be Vigilant!

He might not have a beard. He might not have robes. He might appear as a Frenchman asking for directions. Whenever you spy a stranger, THINK ONCE, THINK TWICE, THINK 'IS HE THE SON OF GOD?'

If you do see Jesus:

**FIRST:** **Offer him something to eat.** If you have no unleavened bread, wholemeal pitta will do.

**SECONDLY:** **Verify his Jesus-ness.** DO NOT do this by asking if He is the Son of God. DO remove the third floor slab from the vestry door. Underneath you will find a safe (combination 20442). Inside you will find "The Bumper Book Of 'Are You Jesus' Quizzes" and a consecrated biro. Ask Him to do a quiz.

### HOW DID HE DO?

Mostly As: Not Jesus.

Mostly Bs: A clever Jesus impersonator, but he's not fooling us.

Mostly Cs: **Hallelujah. He has come.** Ring the 24-Hour 'He Hath Come, Thank God, Let's Be Frank, Even We Were Starting To Have Our Niggling Doubts' Hotline immediately. We're back in business, baby!

# THE
# EASTER BUNNY

## Scene One: Geraldine's Living Room

*Geraldine is at her desk, writing. Alice comes through from the kitchen with a small watering can and goes to water the flowers on the coffee table.*

ALICE: These flowers are completely out of water.

GERALDINE: They're silk, Alice.

ALICE: Yeah, aren't they lovely.

*And she waters them thoroughly.*

Vicar – do you believe in magic?

GERALDINE: Hmm. Interesting question. If, on the one hand, you're asking me, 'Do I believe in magic as entertainment?' then my answer would be 'Yes' – Paul Daniels is the living and rapidly balding proof of that. If, on the other hand, you're asking me, 'Do I believe these magicians possess actual magical powers?' then my answer would be 'No' – although there is something pretty damn spooky about Paul Daniels' ability to make himself sexually attractive to the lovely and fragrant Debbie McGee. If, on the third hand, you're enquiring into the possibility of the magical manipulation of natural things by the Lord God, then my answer would be a resounding 'Yes'. Does that answer your question?

ALICE: I've got absolutely no idea. I was really only paving the way for asking if you believe in the Easter Bunny.

GERALDINE: Again – interesting question. Answer – of course not, you dozy donkey.

ALICE: *(disappointed)* Oh. Why not?

GERALDINE: Oh, all right, Alice. Brace yourself. This is going to be hard. But, as the BBC said to Esther Rantzen when they sacked her, 'That's Life'. Now, at ten, your mother sat you down and she told you that Kermit was just an old green sock. At twenty, she told you about Santa Claus . . .

ALICE: What about him?

GERALDINE: Moving on – this is the awful moment when I tell you that the Easter Bunny absolutely and totally does not exist at all.

ALICE: Well, maybe not where you come from – but here, we've got our very own proper Easter Bunny. I've seen it.

GERALDINE: No, you have not *seen* it.

ALICE: Yes, I have. Everyone in the village has.

GERALDINE: Alice, you're lying, and if you don't apologize I'm going to have to punish you, and this hairbrush features quite prominently in the punishment – and your pants don't.

ALICE: No, no, no. I'm serious. And be careful – anyone who questions the existence of the rabbit comes under the ancient curse.

GERALDINE: Whooh, I'm scared. What is the ancient curse?

ALICE: 'Whoever shall question the rabbit but once, their firstborn shall thenceforth be a dunce.'

GERALDINE: Right. And has anyone questioned it recently?

ALICE: Well, actually my mum did.

GERALDINE: (*making a 'spooky' noise*) Doo-doo doo-doo doo-doo doo-doo!

## Scene Two: The Parish Hall

*Mrs Cropley is in full flow before the whole Council. Geraldine is eating a chocolate bar, David has a particularly glazed expression on his face and Hugo tugs at a loose thread on his woolly jumper.*

MRS CROPLEY: I'm not asking for the moon. I think it's a brilliant plan, and if the Council would only just back us to get it started, I'm sure they wouldn't regret it.

HUGO: Bravo – excellent idea.

DAVID: And what exactly is the size of grant you need?

MRS CROPLEY: Seven million pounds.

DAVID: And what if Dibley is NOT successful in its bid for the 2004 Olympics?

HUGO: Ah, well, with the ski-slope, we can also host the Winter Olympics instead.

DAVID: Yes, well, thank you, Letitia, and supporters, we will of course give your proposal due consideration. (*He pauses.*) It's excrement.

MRS CROPLEY: Oh. How disappointing.

OWEN: Bloody Olympics! (*To Mrs Cropley.*) You're a tit short of an udder, you are.

JIM: No, no, no, no, no, yes, he's right. We should go for the Commonwealth Games first – build up to the Olympics.

GERALDINE: It's a mad old world, isn't it? I was talking to Alice the other day – this is hilarious. She said you've got a bona fide Easter Bunny in Dibley.

ALL: Yes, that's right. Yes.

DAVID: That's right. Finally, item six . . .

GERALDINE: Sorry, sorry, sorry! Have I just stumbled into *The X Files*? I mean, you're not all telling me you believe in the Easter Bunny, are you?

OWEN: That's right. The Dibley Bunny.

GERALDINE: (*looking at her chocolate*) Oh well, they've obviously started to put LSD in Crunchie bars. I didn't realize that.

DAVID: Oh for heaven's sake. We all know it's one of us – it's just a rather sweet tradition that's been handed down over the years, and no one knows who it is who actually dresses up in the costume.

OWEN: Right.

FRANK: Absolutely.

JIM: No, no, no, no, that's right.

*Hugo is utterly and totally mortified.*

HUGO: What? Oh no.

DAVID: Moving on. Any other requests for funding?

MRS CROPLEY: Yes – I think we should put in a bid for the Olympics.

DAVID: We've just done that, Mrs Cropley.

MRS CROPLEY: Oh, have we? Sorry – I've got a memory like an elephant that's lost its memory.

DAVID: Moving on. Vicar?

GERALDINE: Yes. Thank you, David. As you all know Lent starts tomorrow . . .

MRS CROPLEY: Ooh, that reminds me!

*She picks up two dishes from the table behind her.*

As it's Shrove Tuesday I've made you these pancakes from all my leftovers.

HUGO: Hot diggedy dog, Mrs C!

MRS CROPLEY: Now, these ones are lard and fishpaste, and these are the plain ones.

*They all dive for the plain ones and stuff them in their mouths.*

With just a hint of liver. Would you like one, Mr Chairman?

DAVID: I'd sooner eat my own scrotum, thank you, dear. Item six, Vicar.

GERALDINE: (choking) Yes, as I was saying, since it's Ash Wednesday tomorrow I thought, why don't we all try to give up something for Lent?

MRS CROPLEY: Like bondage, you mean?

GERALDINE: Possibly, yes, and then every time we fail we have to put a pound in this box.

*She produces a small box.*

Like you, for instance, Owen.
You could try to give up
swearing, couldn't you?

OWEN: I don't swear.

JIM: No, no, no, no, yes you do.

OWEN: I bloody do not.

ALL: Pound in the box. Pound in the box.

OWEN: What? 'Bloody' isn't swearing.

HUGO: I'm afraid it is.

OWEN: 'Bloody' bloody isn't. 'Bollocks' – now that is swearing – and 'arse' – but 'bloody' is just 'bloody' – it's a useful adjective, with biblical overtones.

*Owen gives up and puts five pounds in the box. He points at Mrs Cropley.*

She can give up cooking garbage then. I've eaten tastier slurry than this.

GERALDINE: And Jim. You could give up dithering. How about it, Jim?

JIM: No, no, no, no, no, yes, well, I'm not too sure.

*Owen slaps the box down in front of Jim. Jim puts a pound in for his dithering.*

OWEN: Ha bloody ha! Oh bugger! I mean sod it. I mean damn. Doh – arse arse arse!

*Jim passes the box back to Owen, who bungs another fiver into it.*

DAVID: Right. And might I venture that Frank can give up being such a pedantic old fart with the minutes.

FRANK: Ah. Good suggestion. Should I actually put 'fart' – or 'f', asterix, asterix, 't'?

*They all point to Frank, then pass him the box.*

GERALDINE: What about you David? Perhaps you could be a little more friendly to everyone?

HUGO: *(very buoyant)* Yes, Father. Everyone's fed up to the back teeth with you shouting at them all the time, like some great big bald shouty type person. (*He sees David's stern face.*) Except me, of course. I don't think . . .

FRANK: He's got a point, sir.

DAVID: Very well. Easy peasy. Although, I'd quite like to know where all this money is actually going to.

GERALDINE: Well, I thought we could start a neighbourhood video club, you know, on Friday nights in the hall. For people who don't have videos of their own.

JIM: I've got a video – but it doesn't work. I've plugged it in and switched it on – and nothing.

FRANK: I didn't know you even had a TV?

JIM: No, but I plugged the video into the radio instead.

DAVID: Right, fair enough. It's not a bad idea. And pray tell, what is St Geraldine giving up?

GERALDINE: Well, I thought I might give up bubble bath because I absolutely love the stuff – you know, all that wubbly bubbly bubbly – up your nosie, in your toesies, that sort of thing.

DAVID: Or, you could give up chocolate?

*Geraldine looks at the bar of chocolate she is nibbling.*

GERALDINE: No, I don't think so. Because, you see, I don't eat enough chocolate for that to really hurt me.

*David reaches over and opens the folder she has on the table in front of her. Inside is a HUGE bar of chocolate.*

DAVID: Chocolate.

GERALDINE: Oh, come on! You don't think I'm going to eat all this on my own, do you? This . . . this . . . is for all the tiny little orphan children of the parish.

*Hugo starts to fidget about with Geraldine's hymn book.*

Poor little mites. They're starved of love and tenderness . . .

*Hugo opens up the hymn book – and there's a recess cut into it which contains a chocolate bar.*

HUGO: Oh!

DAVID: Chocolate.

GERALDINE: Okay, chocolate, yeah, okay.

DAVID: Now we'll see who's got self control. Meeting's closed.
Let's go, Hugo.

*Hugo stands and turns. His jumper has unravelled up to his shoulder blades.*

## Scene Three: Geraldine's Living Room

*Geraldine goes over to the sofa and rummages under one of the cushions. She finds a chocolate bar hidden there. She looks at it lovingly.*

GERALDINE: I love you. You know that, don't you? You're lovely.
My little friend.

*She unwraps it and takes a deep sniff. But resists the temptation and puts it back under the cushion.*

No, stop – distraction – that's the answer.

*She switches on the television – only to see the Flake advert . . . This is just too much for her to take.*

GERALDINE: You bitch.

*She switches off the telly. The doorbell rings. She goes to answer it, muttering . . .*

Lord, give me a break. In fact, give me a Kit-Kat.

*She opens the door. It's Hugo.*

Hugo, lovely to see you. Come on in.

HUGO: Morning, Vicar.

*They go through to the living room. Hugo shyly acknowledges Alice, who has come through from the kitchen.*

HUGO: Oh. Hello, Alice.

ALICE: Hello, Hugo.

*They gaze at each other, too tongue-tied to speak. Geraldine watches them.*

ALICE: You all right?

HUGO: Yes, thanks. Er, hello.

ALICE: Hiya.

GERALDINE: It's gripping stuff isn't it? I've often wondered what it
would be like if you got Oscar Wilde and Dorothy Parker together in

the same room – and I think I'm getting a little flavour of it here. Why don't you just stop yakking on, Miss Tinker, and go out and make the tea.

ALICE: Right. Yeah.

GERALDINE: Now, Alice. (*Alice leaves.*) So, Hugo, what did you want to talk to me about?

HUGO: Oh, it's this Lent thingy. At the meeting you all had to give something up, and the thing is . . . nobody asked me. And I think perhaps it's because everyone thinks I'm such a bore that I couldn't possibly have anything interesting to give up. As if I didn't have a personality at all.

GERALDINE: You're not a bore at all, Hugo. You're a *riveting* human being. I'm sure you've got lots of vices you could give up. Like gambling, for instance. I bet you like a little flutter every now and again. (*Hugo's blank expression suggests otherwise.*) No. Smoking? (*She looks at him.*) I know, wearing a shirt without a tie.

*He pulls down his jumper to reveal a shirt and tie.*

GERALDINE: Ah.

HUGO: Does drinking coffee count as a vice?

GERALDINE: It does indeed. Coffee – the broth of Satan. It's a drug, Hugo, give it up now.

HUGO: No, no, I don't drink it, but I thought I could start, and then I'd have something to give up next year.

GERALDINE: Right, brilliant. Yeah, good.

HUGO: The only other thing is, I do think about 'It' quite a bit. You know, 'It'.

GERALDINE: No, not with you.

HUGO: You know. 'It.' With people like Mariella Frostrup and Sharon Stone. Norma Major. Naked.

GERALDINE: Aah. 'It.' Well, there you go then. Not that it's exactly an arrestable offence – although the Norma Major thing could land you in some kind of an institution. No, good, right, well, you stop thinking about 'It', and every time you do, put a pound in that box.

HUGO: Great. Old sinner me!

*Alice enters with a tray.*

GERALDINE: Yeah! Tea. Very good timing. Hugo and I were just finished, weren't we, Hugo?

*She turns to Hugo to see that he is staring at Alice. He fishes a pound out of his pocket and puts it in the box.*

ALICE: *(pouring the tea)* I know how you like it, Hugo. Hot and strong.

*Hugo gets another pound out and puts it in the box.*

Nice and wet.

*And another pound goes in the box.*

GERALDINE: On the other hand, I think it's best if Hugo goes now before he drifts into insolvency.

*She ushers him out. But Alice stands, not wanting him to go.*

ALICE: But I've got a lovely doughnut for you, Hugo.

HUGO: No thanks.

ALICE: Some chocolate fingers?

HUGO: Oh well, perhaps, I . . .

*He reaches for a chocolate finger, without looking directly at Alice.*

ALICE: They're such fun, aren't they? I love just sticking them in my mouth, and sucking and sucking till all the chocolate comes right off . . .

*She sticks a chocolate finger in her mouth and sucks on it, very quickly. Hugo can't stand this lustful torture. He has to leave.*

HUGO: *(to Geraldine)* I'm a bit strapped for cash – I'll pay you later.

## Scene Four: The Parish Hall

*All the regulars are at the Council Meeting, except Hugo and Owen. Geraldine has her Lent Box in front of her.*

DAVID: *(very relaxed and amiable)* Right. Well, I'll give them another minute or two.

*Hugo bounds in.*

HUGO: Sorry I'm late, mes enfants.

*He sits and drops several pounds into the Lent Box.*

HUGO: *(to Geraldine)* Anne Robinson was on the telly.

GERALDINE: Anne Robinson?

DAVID: Ah yes, how's your little collection going, Vicar? Had to put in many pounds yourself?

GERALDINE: None at all, David, thank you very much for asking. Hoping to collect a few tonight though. Jim, I expect you'll be contributing a few quid won't you?

JIM: Nope.

GERALDINE: Nope? As in 'nope, nope, nope, nope, yes'?

JIM: On the contrary. Nope as in 'nope'.

GERALDINE: *(amazed)* Right. Funky.

*Owen arrives.*

OWEN: Sorry I'm late. All my cows escaped.

GERALDINE: *(encouraging him to swear)* Bloody cows. They're a bloody, bloody nuisance aren't they?

OWEN: They can be a bit of a bore, yes.

DAVID: Right. We'll start. I declare open this meeting of the Parish Council, 3rd March, 1996. *(He notices that Frank is not writing.)* Frank – are you getting this down?

FRANK: Don't worry – I'll just knock off something at the end. No one reads the minutes anyway.

*Geraldine is very taken aback now.*

DAVID: Item one . . .

MRS CROPLEY: Ooh, Mr Chairman, if I could just butt in here.

DAVID: Of course, Letitia, you butt in to your heart's content, my little beauty.

*He beams at her and smiles smugly at Geraldine.*

MRS CROPLEY: Thank you. Now then, I just wondered if anyone would care to try my home-made orange juice.

*She produces glasses of orange juice on a tray.*

GERALDINE: *(clapping; she can see a fine coming on)* Aha ha ha! And what's in it, Mrs C?

MRS CROPLEY: Orange juice.

GERALDINE: Yes, but anything else? No yeast, no balsamic vinegar, no urine?

MRS CROPLEY: No.

*This is very disappointing.*

DAVID: Right, let's begin. Item one. The new video club. How's it coming on, Vicar?

GERALDINE: Yes, well, I've had some thoughts about the kind of film . . .

*She stops as she sees him unwrap a large chocolate bar.*

DAVID: Don't mind me. Didn't have any supper. (*He takes a big bite.*) Mmmm.

GERALDINE: (*completely distracted*) Yes. Yes, as I was saying . . .

DAVID: I'm sorry, forgetting my manners. Anybody else like a bar?

*He produces a huge bag full of chocolate bars and hands them out to all, except Geraldine. She can't take her eyes off the chocolate bar that Owen starts to eat.*

GERALDINE: Yeah, um. Right, as I was saying . . . Sorry, I'm feeling a bit faint actually. Owen, I think you had something to say, didn't you?

OWEN: Yes, well now, a few of us have been thinking about how we might kick off the video club . . .

GERALDINE: Oh that's it, that's it. Since we're a country parish, I thought we might start with an animal film – maybe *Black Beauty*, something like that.

FRANK: We chose an animal film, too.

MRS CROPLEY: Yeah.

JIM: The *Silence of the Lambs*.

OWEN: In a double-bill with *Reservoir Dogs*.

GERALDINE: Right, and maybe we could follow that with a romance?

FRANK: Our thinking again.

GERALDINE: Good. *Sleepless in Seattle?*

FRANK: *Last Tango in Paris.*

GERALDINE: Right. And I thought we could have something with a religious bent – you know, *Song of Bernadette*, or *Godspell*.

MRS CROPLEY: *The Exorcist*.

GERALDINE: David, I'm afraid I'm going to have to have that Mars Bar.

*She reaches over to grab it from him.*

DAVID: Ah, ah, ah – three long weeks to go, Vicar. Oh, and I've got a nice box of chocolates here to share round to celebrate my half-birthday.

*He produces a huge box of chocolates and everyone helps themselves.*

OWEN: Lovely one, Mr Horton. Thank you very much.

*Geraldine is not amused.*

## Scene Five: Geraldine's Living Room

*The next morning and Geraldine is looking at three chocolate bars laid out on the coffee table. Alice arrives.*

ALICE: Hello, Vicar.

GERALDINE: Hello, Alice. Can I just share a private thought with you?

ALICE: Oh, certainly, Vicar – as long as it isn't about tampons, 'cos I don't understand them at all.

GERALDINE: No, no, it isn't. I'd just like to share with you the fact that, well, I hate the people of this village.

ALICE: Oh dear.

GERALDINE: Yeah. Every single one of them. Self-righteous, small-minded, senile, chocolate-scoffing gits and that's true.

*The phone rings and Alice picks it up.*

ALICE: Hello, Geraldine's phone. Well, not actually her phone, because the phone can't speak – but Geraldine's phone meaning Geraldine is usually the person on the phone – even though actually this time it's Alice – so I might have said 'Alice's phone', but I didn't because it's not mine.

GERALDINE: Who is it?

ALICE: I don't know – they just hung up. People are weird, aren't they?

*The phone rings again.*

GERALDINE: I'll get it.

ALICE: *(waving Geraldine away)* No. Dibley Vicarage. Well, not actually the vicarage itself, 'cos it can't speak. It's just a building, but . . . Oh, hello!

*She listens and looks increasingly sympathetic.*

Oh right, right . . . I'll tell her. *(To Geraldine.)* It's Frank – he's at Mrs Cropley's – she's been taken ill. She's asking for you – what shall I tell him?

GERALDINE: Tell him I'm coming, you silly girl.

ALICE: She's coming . . . um, you silly girl.

*She puts the phone down.*

Oh dear – I hope she's all right. I love Mrs Cropley. She's been just like a mother to me – always wiping things off my face and telling me I look daft.

GERALDINE: *(rushing to get her coat)* No listen – she'll be fine. This is happy valley. People don't get sick here. Oh, and by the way *(she stops to look at Alice)*, I think that facial cleanliness is overrated. Spinach can be an attractive accessory. Not a lot of people get away with big lumps of it between the teeth, but you do!

## Scene Six: Mrs Cropley's Hallway

*Geraldine and Alice arrive. Jim, Owen, David, Hugo and Frank are there.*

GERALDINE: How is she, Jim?

JIM: No, no, no, no, no, no, no . . . not good.

GERALDINE: What happened?

FRANK: Well, it was a lovely morning, so I dropped round to see her – I'd chosen a sort of bright tie because . . .

GERALDINE: I'm afraid I'm going to have to press you for the shorter version, Frank.

FRANK: Right. I dropped around, in this tie, and I knocked on the door – not a loud knock, just a gentle tap, tap, tap . . .

GERALDINE: Even shorter than that Frank, I'm afraid.

FRANK: Right.

GERALDINE: Right.

FRANK: Very well. I came round, and now she's dying. And she wants to see you.

*Geraldine and Alice are very shocked by this.*

GERALDINE: She's dying?

DAVID: Well, it's not good. We've all been in and had a word with her – but the doctor says she's very weak.

OWEN: It's her heart, poor old girl.

GERALDINE: Oh Lord. Right, I suppose I better . . . I've never actually done anything like this before. Right.

*She turns to the bedroom door, and then back to the men.*

Look, it's not an April Fools, is it? And I'm going to go in there and she's going to be sitting up in bed with a custard pie?

*They all shake their heads.*

Damn.

❦

## Scene Seven: Mrs Cropley's Bedroom

FRANK: It's the vicar. She's come to see you.

*Mrs Cropley's eyes open and she smiles weakly at Geraldine.*

GERALDINE: Letitia, how are you?

MRS CROPLEY: Not so good, my dear. Breathing always seemed such an easy thing – but suddenly it's a bit of a bugger, to be honest. That Frank – he's a nice man, isn't he?

GERALDINE: Oh, he's a lovely man, yes.

MRS CROPLEY: Nice thighs.

GERALDINE: Is that so?

MRS CROPLEY: Oh yes. I haven't led a blameless life, Vicar.

GERALDINE: Oh, Letitia. Who has?

MRS CROPLEY: Anthea Turner.

GERALDINE: Yes, Anthea Turner and, of course, the lovely Jane Asher.

MRS CROPLEY: Mm. Prince William?

GERALDINE: Yeah. So, apart from Prince William, Anthea Turner and Jane Asher, who has led a blameless life, Letitia?

MRS CROPLEY: Hugh Grant.

GERALDINE: Well, hardly . . . You think so?

MRS CROPLEY: Oh yes. Fine in my book.

GERALDINE: Well, interesting book. I'm sure that God forgives your sins, Letitia.

MRS CROPLEY: I hope so, Vicar. (*She starts to have trouble breathing.*)

GERALDINE: Oh, do you want me to get the doctor?

MRS CROPLEY: No. Before you go – there are two things. You will be honest with me, won't you? I know I can trust you.

GERALDINE: You can trust me, yes.

MRS CROPLEY: My cooking.

GERALDINE: Ah . . . (*Less certain she can tell the truth now.*)

MRS CROPLEY: Was I a great experimenter, a pioneer whose rich command of unorthodox mixtures will be the stuff of legend in the new millennium – or was my food just ghastly? You can tell a dying woman the truth, Vicar.

GERALDINE: Very well. You are one of the greats. Mrs Beeton, Delia Smith, Letitia Cropley. That's the Trinity.

MRS CROPLEY: I thought so. And now – finally, let me bequeath to you my life's other great achievement. Say you'll do it. And promise me.

GERALDINE: Yes, of course I will – what is it?

MRS CROPLEY: It's something I've done for the past thirty years. And my father did it before me. (*She whispers something into Geraldine's ear. Geraldine looks aghast.*) You are my chosen one.

GERALDINE: Oh no.

MRS CROPLEY: You're a lovely girl, Vicar. Chunky, but lovely.

*And with that Mrs Cropley dies . . .*

GERALDINE: Oh . . .

*She leaves the bedroom, shuts the door behind her and shakes her head in sorrow at the others waiting outside. Alice bursts into tears and hugs Geraldine.*

### Scene Eight: Geraldine's Living Room

*After Mrs Cropley's funeral, and everyone is back at Geraldine's.*

HUGO: Splendid service, Vicar. Very moving.

GERALDINE: Thanks.

HUGO: I particularly liked your quote from Johnny Morris.

GERALDINE: I think you'll find that was Joni Mitchell, Hugo.

HUGO: That's right. Don't you always find that you don't really value someone until they're gone. And then it's too late.

*They all think about Mrs Cropley for a moment.*

ALICE: She was a wonderful woman.

FRANK: Ah, you didn't know her if you didn't know her when she was young.

GERALDINE: And what was she like, young?

JIM: No, no, no, no – rampant!

GERALDINE: Really?

JIM: Oh yes. She was a lovely looking girl. Red hair right down to her waist, eyes so bright they sparkled in the dark and a French kiss that would suck the tongue out of your mouth like an industrial vacuum cleaner.

GERALDINE: Is that right?

OWEN: Yes, I heard that too. My father used to talk about her, Luscious Letitia.

JIM: Cropley the Cracker.

FRANK: Titillating Tish.

OWEN: Always-lets-you-dock-your-boat-in-her-Jetty Letty.

DAVID: Come on, now, boys, show a little respect. It's been a very sad week. We won't be able to enjoy Easter with the usual relish.

GERALDINE: No – but we must remember the true Easter message – Jesus gives us hope of eternal life, in heaven. No one on earth lives for ever.

JIM: Except Bruce Forsyth.

GERALDINE: No, he just seems to have been alive for ever. He is, in fact, a surprisingly young man. No, I think the spirit of Letitia will live on in this village even though she herself has passed away.

DAVID: What – you mean there are some other nymphomaniacs lurking in the hedgerows?

GERALDINE: No, no, I mean . . . well, we'll see, won't we?

*She proposes a toast.*

To Letty.

ALL: To Letty.

OWEN: And all who sailed in her.

GERALDINE: Owen!

## Scene Nine: Geraldine's Living Room

*The next day and Geraldine is sitting on her couch, wearing fluffy bunny ears and counting out chocolate eggs on the table before her.*

GERALDINE: What am I doing? I should be writing my Easter Sermon, trying to work out ways to convince people of the miracle of the resurrection, instead I'm counting eggs and trying to work out how to make a Slinky into a bunny's bottom.

*Suddenly there's a knock at the door.*

Oh hell's bum! Coming!

*She remembers to remove the bunny ears, then opens the door brusquely. It is David.*

David. Lovely to see you. Just a little bit busy at the moment.

*She goes to shut the door, but he pushes past her.*

DAVID: Don't worry, this won't take a moment.

*She must stall him to stop him finding the Easter eggs.*

GERALDINE: David, David, David. Ahm, could you just take your shoes off, please?

DAVID: Why?

GERALDINE: Ah, it's a religious thing.

DAVID: But what about yours?

GERALDINE: Erm, mine have been blessed already. Just, put them there. Thanks.

*She leaves him to take his shoes off and rushes through to the living room, where she sweeps all the eggs off the table on to the sofa and covers them up with the throw.*

DAVID: Still holding off the chocolate?

GERALDINE: Yes, yes, haven't touched a morsel. Now, how can I help you then, David?

*She sits down on the sofa – a loud breaking sound – she realizes to her horror that she has crushed all the eggs. She moves gracefully on to the sofa arm.*

DAVID: Well, the thing is, I'm a little worried about Hugo.

GERALDINE: Yes?

DAVID: Well, yesterday, we were watching this rather good film on television – *An Officer and a Gentleman.*

GERALDINE: Oh lovely, Richard Gere. I'd swap places with that hamster any day.

DAVID: Which hamster?

GERALDINE: No, nothing. Nothing. Forget about the hamster.

DAVID: Anyway – this scene comes on where the two of them go off to a motel, well, they take their clothes off and they . . .

GERALDINE: Do 'It'.

DAVID: As you say, and I'm a little embarrassed in front of Hugo, so I look around – and he has his eyes closed!

GERALDINE: Ah.

DAVID: And I'm worried that Hugo might be, well, you know . . .

GERALDINE: No.

DAVID: Well, do I have to spell it out?

GERALDINE: I don't know what you're talking about, David.

DAVID: Oh, very well. J.O.H.N.

GERALDINE: John. You think Hugo might be John? John who?

DAVID: Let me finish. I.N.M.A.N.

GERALDINE: Inman. John Inman. You're afraid that Hugo might be John Inman? Oh, I see! You're afraid that Hugo might be homosexual.

DAVID: What do you think?

GERALDINE: Well, what I think is that it wouldn't matter a flying font if Hugo was homosexual – some of our finest Cabinet ministers are, as I'm sure you know, David – but no, the reason for this unusual behaviour is because Hugo's secret pact for Lent is to give up lustful thoughts.

DAVID: Really?

GERALDINE: Really. So poor old Hugo's just trying to save a few quid, bless him.

DAVID: Thank God for that. That's wonderful news. I have nothing against them of course – I'm as big a fan of Michael Barrymore as the next man.

GERALDINE: Of course you are, David.

DAVID: Bravo!

*He leaves and she unveils the crushed eggs.*

GERALDINE: Oh. That is the saddest sight I have ever seen. Oh, my poor broken darlings. But I promise your lives will not have been wasted in vain. Come Monday, I'll put you all in a lovely big gooey chocolate fondue. Come on darlings, come on darlings.

*As Geraldine is gently moving the crushed eggs on to the table, unbeknownst to her Alice has come in the room through the door left open by David.*

ALICE: Hello, Vicar. What are you doing with all those chocolates?

GERALDINE: Ahm, what, what, these chocolates? These . . . just trying to think up a convincing lie.

*Alice bundles up the chocolates to take them away.*

ALICE: Come on, hand them over, you little Miss Naughty.

GERALDINE: Alice, Alice, give me back those chocolates.

ALICE: Not till after Easter.

GERALDINE: Alice, I need those chocolates.

ALICE: No – you don't *need* them, Geraldine, you *want* them – and that's a very different thing.

GERALDINE: Unfortunately, Alice, I'm not legally allowed to kill you so I'm going to have to tell you something. Come and sit down now. Come on. Now, Alice, can you keep a secret?

ALICE: Of course I can. I've known the whole thing about David and his illegitimate daughter for ages and never said a word.

GERALDINE: Well it's not that . . . oh, thanks for that. It might be quite useful. No, this is about the Easter Bunny. Now, you still believe that the Easter Bunny buys all the eggs for the children and distributes them, don't you?

ALICE: That's right.

GERALDINE: Well, he doesn't. I bought these eggs for the children, to hide in the gardens on Easter morning.

ALICE: No. No, you don't mean it.

GERALDINE: Yes. Yes – you see, just before she died, Mrs Cropley . . .

*Alice is now all weepy. This news has upset her. Geraldine can't do it – she can't destroy the dream.*

Um, Mrs Cropley . . . got a phone call from the Easter Bunny, who said he was just too busy to buy them this year, you know, he's filling out all the forms for the Child Support Agency . . .

ALICE: What with being a rabbit and everything . . .

GERALDINE: Precisely – so he asked her to buy them and on her death bed, *she* asked me. She said I had to be sure to get them ready for tonight – otherwise the old Bunnyster would get all het up, and then I'd be dealing with a very hot cross bunny, wouldn't I?

ALICE: Oh fine. Well, here, let me help then. (*She kneels on the floor with the eggs.*) I feel a bit sad about doing this. It does rather take the magic out of it, preparing the chocolates for the Bunny – but I suppose that's what becoming an adult is all about, eh?

GERALDINE: Yes. That's right.

## Scene Ten: Geraldine's Living Room

*It's two o'clock in the morning. Geraldine is awake and moving around upstairs.*

GERALDINE: Well, as the old saying goes: 'Cometh the hour, cometh the woman in a silly rabbit costume'.

*Geraldine comes down the stairs and turns the light on. She is in full, wondrous, rabbit costume, complete with two huge ears sticking up — one of them suddenly flops over in front of her face, as she looks at herself in the mirror.*

Oh, bugger.

*She straightens the ear back up again.*

If I'd have known becoming a priest would entail dressing up in a rabbit costume, I'd have had a complete rethink and taken up prostitution — as, indeed, my headmistress originally suggested. Mind you, I would probably have ended up in a rabbit costume then, as well.

*She turns the light out and heads to the front door.*

## Scene Eleven: The Village

*Geraldine puts one furry foot outside, then the other. She scampers down the garden path and into the village. She tries to open the first garden gate she comes to. It's jammed. She looks up the path — in the doorway there is a terracotta pot full of earth and one little plant. Geraldine takes aim and throws an egg. It lands in the pot. Then she does an overarm lob. Again she hits the target. She clenches her fist in triumph — she could quite enjoy this. The third she throws without looking — it sails through the air and into the pot. She crosses the road — in front of an approaching milk float — and stands transfixed in the glare of the headlights. Then she looks for somewhere to hide and stands utterly still behind a hopelessly narrow lamp-post. The milk float sails past.*

MILKMAN: Morning, Vicar.

*A farmer is in his field on the very edge of the village. He holds a gun, along which he takes aim at a rabbit. It scampers off and the farmer tries to catch up with it, still looking along the gun. He loses sight of it, but immediately sees another — this one much bigger. Five foot tall in fact, and holding her hand up in front of her.*

GERALDINE: No!

*Geraldine is moving quite confidently now — even experimenting with hopping. She places a few eggs outside a cottage then turns into the lane — and bumps straight into another huge Easter Bunny.*

GERALDINE: Aaaaaaghh!

OTHER BUNNY: Aaaaaaghh!

*They both stare at each other for a moment. Then the other bunny takes off its head.*

GERALDINE: David!

*It is indeed David. He tries to maintain some dignity.*

DAVID: Vicar!

GERALDINE: Sssshhh!

DAVID: What are you doing?

GERALDINE: I'm the Easter Bunny.

DAVID: You can't be. I'm . . . (*he lowers his voice*) the Easter Bunny. I promised Letitia Cropley I'd do it.

GERALDINE: Well, so did I.

DAVID: Mad bat must have forgotten she'd already asked me. How demeaning — and after all the time I've spent on these bloody ears.

*He puts his rabbit head back on and they start off down the lane together.*

GERALDINE: I must say, you look surprisingly cute in that.

DAVID: Shut up.

GERALDINE: That's a sexy little tail you've got there!

*She gives it a squeeze.*

DAVID: Get off. I suggest we keep very quiet about this. You do one end of the village and I'll do the other. This will remain our secret.

GERALDINE: Fair enough. You're sure you don't want to come back to my burrow afterwards for a little bit of bunny funny business?!

DAVID: Quite sure.

*They turn a corner and are rather surprised to find a dozen more full-sized Easter Bunnies in the middle of the road. They all freeze. Owen is one of the rabbits.*

OWEN: Oh hell. Any more and we'll be able to stage a production of bloody *Watership Down*.

*A little later and the rabbits all make their way home. Geraldine walks along with four other rabbits – David, Hugo, Frank and Owen.*

GERALDINE: Dear old Mrs C. I bet she's up there right now, having a good giggle at us.

DAVID: She better be. If I find she's down here, I'll kill her.

GERALDINE: Hugo – lovely ears.

HUGO: Thanks. I didn't know you could see them under this costume.

OWEN: Your ears aren't much cop, Vicar. What did you use?

GERALDINE: A couple of coat hangers.

FRANK: Not pipe cleaners?

DAVID: I found you can't beat chicken wire and papier mâché. Worked a treat.

OWEN: I just took mine off a real rabbit.

❦

## Scene Twelve: Geraldine's Kitchen/Living Room

*Everyone is round at Geraldine's enjoying a post Easter service drink. Hugo and Geraldine are in the kitchen fetching nibbles to offer round.*

HUGO: Lovely service, Vicar.

GERALDINE: Thank you.

HUGO: Nice hairstyle, too – is it a shaggy?

GERALDINE: No, it's a couldn't-find-my-hairbrushy.

HUGO: Groovy.

*David comes through from the living room.*

DAVID: So tell me, Vicar – what's the final total on the video fund?

GERALDINE: Well, we raised the princely sum of twenty-six pounds.

DAVID: Oh dear me.

GERALDINE: No, let me finish. That was Thursday. On Friday it shot up to seventy-four pounds because ITV showed the uncut version of *Basic Instinct*. Thanks very much, Hugo.

*In the living room, Frank taps his glass.*

FRANK: I wonder if I can make a little announcement? I know we're all missing Letitia terribly so I've decided, as a tribute, to carry on her great work in the culinary field.

DAVID: Oh no.

FRANK: As a start, therefore, I've made what we always used to call 'our cake' from her original recipe and I'd be thrilled if you'd all like to try a slice.

*He offers it to Jim and Owen, who back away, but they realize they must take a slice.*

JIM: Won't say 'no, no, no, no, no'.

OWEN: Thank you.

FRANK: There we are, everybody.

*The others all take a slice and consider the taste like experts.*

HUGO: What is that?

ALICE: There's definitely coconut.

HUGO: Er, there's something else in there.

*There's a pause, then realization hits.*

GERALDINE AND DAVID: Anchovy.

*Jim, disgusted, puts his slice back on the plate.*

FRANK: What do you think of it, Owen?

OWEN: Lent's definitely over now, isn't it, Vicar?

GERALDINE: It most certainly is . . .

199
203
346
294

'Ahm . . . where was I?'

Delia Smith's Guru

The President of the Teletubbies' Fan Club

One Family, One Brain Cell

One Very Intelligent Bunny

My Congregation and Other Animals

'Baa . . . men!'

Stupid Cupid

The World's Greatest Ballerina, and Darcey Bussell

The World's Greatest Broadcaster, and Terry Wogan

Owen Newitt-berg

Robson & Jerome

Mr and Mrs Horton (née Tinker)

*She opens up her cardigan to reveal lots of chocolate bars attached to the inside of it. She beams at David, happy to be back in the world of chocolate.*

OWEN: To be perfectly frank, Frank, it tastes absolutely fu . . .

GERALDINE: *(butting in quickly)* Funnily enough, I've got an announcement to make as well, Owen. Due to the fantastic success of our Lent fundraising, we can actually open our video club this Friday night. And I thought the first night should be totally in honour of Letitia. So we're going to show *My Fair Lady*.

*There is lots of agreement from everyone.*

Obviously, in a double bill with *The Adventures of Emmanuelle*.

*Lots more agreement from the lads.*

DAVID: To Letitia.

GERALDINE: *(raising her glass)* Letitia – the finest Easter Bunny Dibley ever knew.

ALICE: Eh? What?

GERALDINE: No, she wasn't, she wasn't . . .

## Epilogue: The Vestry

*Geraldine and Alice are enjoying a cup of cocoa together.*

**GERALDINE:** Right, this is a goody. Knock, knock.

**ALICE:** Ooh, I love these. Who's there?

**GERALDINE:** OJ.

**ALICE:** OJ who?

**GERALDINE:** Okay, you can be on the jury.

*Geraldine laughs uproariously, as does Alice. Then...*

**ALICE:** *(puzzled)* No, I don't get it.

**GERALDINE:** OJ is OJ Simpson ... American footballer ... very famous.

**ALICE:** Ah. So he plays in the First Division?

**GERALDINE:** No. American footballer as in 'plays American football', not 'footballer who's American'.

**ALICE:** So he's not American?

**GERALDINE:** No, he *is* American.

**ALICE:** He *is* American?

**GERALDINE:** Yes, and he was on trial and they had to find twelve people who'd never heard of him.

**ALICE:** I've never heard of him.

**GERALDINE:** No. So, they should have come here really. Anyway, pathetic joke, don't worry about it.

**ALICE:** No, no, no. It's a good joke. You just need to explain who he is before you tell it.

**GERALDINE:** Right. That's the problem about telling jokes about famous people – they just aren't famous enough, are they. Next, I should tell a joke about a very very famous person – John Major. Someone like that.

**ALICE:** John ..?

**GERALDINE:** Or maybe not.

# Frank Pickle's Village Year

Here in Dibley we do our very best to keep the old local traditions
going. And although sacrificing virgins between the standing stones
died out way back in the 1970s, there's still plenty to enjoy. Here
are some of our annual favourites.

## January

| | |
|---|---|
| 1st | Dibley Village Shop Sensational January Sale starts. Prices slashed on all marrowfat peas |
| 2nd | Taking Unwanted Presents Back to Marks and Spencer Day |

## February

| | |
|---|---|
| 4th | Blessing of the Answerphones |
| 12th – 18th | Drizzle Week |
| 19th | Sodden Sunday |
| 20th | Sodding Monday |

## March

| | |
|---|---|
| 2nd | The Bus comes |
| 22nd | Procession of the Merrie Men: all Dibley folk go to the next village to smash up their pub and steal their women |

## April

| | |
|---|---|
| 2nd | So-so Wednesday |
| 3rd | Mediocre Thursday |
| 4th | Good Friday |

## May

| | |
|---|---|
| 1st | May Day: Prettiest girl in the village is crowned Queen of the May |
| 5th | Second, third and fourth prettiest girls in the village stop crying about May Day and shouting 'Why wasn't it me, I'm so ugly, I'm a freak' |

## June

| | |
|---|---|
| 9th | Blessing of the Gas Barbecues |
| 21st | Dibley Open Garden Day. A splendid day on which everyone visits all the other gardens in the village, and goes home safe in the knowledge that theirs is the best |

## July

| | |
|---|---|
| 4th | Annual Dibley Festival of Dutch Gabba |
| 15th | Take Your Dog To Work Day – unless you are a sheep farmer, in which case it's 'Leave Your Dog At Home Day' |

## August

| | |
|---|---|
| 1st | Clooney Kissing – a recent tradition, particularly popular with the local clergy |
| 12th | Shooting season starts. Rabbits, Grouse and Ramblers |
| 29th | Village Brothel reopens. Three for the price of two before 7.30 |

## September

| | |
|---|---|
| 9th | A quick drink to celebrate the bringing in of Harvest |

## October

| | |
|---|---|
| 5th | The quick drink to celebrate the bringing in of Harvest ends |
| 6th | The harvest is actually brought in |
| 23rd | Blessing of the Remote Controls |

## November

| | |
|---|---|
| 15th | The Dibley Football Match – by tradition, a pig's bladder is used as the ball, one goalpost is on the village green, and the other goalpost is in Kirkwall on the mainland of Orkney. Despite the 500 mile long pitch which includes a sea crossing, someone did manage to score in 1909 |

## December

| | |
|---|---|
| 13th | Lighting of the Nativity Chickens |
| 14th | Hiding from the RSPCA Inspectors |
| 20th | Overambitious Posting of Christmas Cards to Australia |
| 25th | Queuing starts for the Dibley Village Shop's Sensational January Sale – prices slashed on all marrowfat peas |

## MISSING

### *Holy Grail of Christ's Blood*

Formerly property of St Joseph of Arimathea. Last seen in the Camelot region circa 450 AD. Contact Holy Knights of St John Templar, Dorking.

Call 08677 786 and ask for Bernard.

### £10 Reward

## Save £££

By not going out & not spending any money.

Simply by staying inside your house all day with no electricity, gas and water you can save yourself up to £50 per day!

For more details call

**07777 321 321**.

But use someone else's phone.

## Colossal Turkey farm

Do you need a turkey the size of a dinosaur?

**Phone 4521**

### ROTA ASSISTANTS WANTED

TO OVERSEE ORGANISATION OF FLOWERS ROTA, CLEANING ROTA, PRAYER ROTA, BIBLE ROTA, SIDESMAN ROTA, COMMUNION ROTA, REFRESHMENTS ROTA, ORGAN ROTA, OVER-HEAD PROJECTOR ROTA AND ROTA MOTOR ROTA.

PLEASE ADD YOUR NAME TO THE ROTA ASSISTANTS ROTA AT THE REAR OF THE CHURCH AND THEN WAIT FOR THE ROTA ASSISTANT'S ROTA ROTA ASSISTANT TO CONTACT YOU. OR SEE RITA THE ROTA WRITER.

BOARD

PARISH ✝

WANTED!
White plastic cups which split right down the side when you fill them up, leaving you badly burnt.
Urgently needed for post-service refreshments
contact Alice, verger, St Barnabus, Dibley

**Bell Ringers Wanted For Church Summer Concert**

Musical pieces include: 'Ding Dong Ding Dong Ding', 'Ding Dong Ding Ding Dong', 'Ding Dong Ding Dong Dong Dong Ding' and 'Theme From The Great Escape (Ding Dong Mix)'.

## Massage Service

Performed in the privacy of your own home by a fully qualified masseuse. Just massage. Really. Nothing funny. Just a straightforward, no-nonsense, clean, simple, perfectly respectable massage.

**Also available: sex for money**

**Phone Sandi, 22901**

Ever wanted a scrap of paper with a phone number on it?

Please take one!

0911 154 381
07777 851052

Lost cow. Tethered outside pub 4.30pm, missing by 11.30pm last Friday. Of great sentimental value. Need by Sunday as am planning to eat.

# The
# Christmas Lunch Incident

## Scene One: Geraldine's Living Room

*Geraldine and Alice are decorating the Christmas tree.*

ALICE: Vicar, what are you looking forward to more than anything else at Christmas this year?

GERALDINE: Well, my highlights are going to be *Jurassic Park* and the Queen's speech. Written this year by Ruby Wax, I believe. And what about you?

ALICE: I'm totally excited about your first Christmas sermon. It's going to be an experience I'll never forget.

GERALDINE: Alice, my first Christmas sermon was last Christmas.

ALICE: Oh yeah, I forgot. Not that it's your fault. You probably just chose a boring subject.

GERALDINE: What, the birth of Jesus Christ? Otherwise known as the greatest story ever told.

ALICE: Well, yeah, the first time you hear it, but after that it's a bit predictable, isn't it? I mean, man and woman get to inn, inn full, woman has baby in manger, angels sing on high, blah, blah, blah . . .

GERALDINE: You have forgotten to mention that the baby is, in fact, the Son of God.

ALICE: Oh yeah, I know, I mean that's a nice twist.

GERALDINE: A nice twist?

ALICE: Yeah, but there aren't exactly a lot of laughs. I mean the Christmas *Only Fools and Horses*, oh that's much funnier. That Rodney, what a plonker!

GERALDINE: I think we'd better change the subject, because frankly if we stick with this one I'll be forced to put this somewhere dark that will make it impossible for you to walk.

*Geraldine brandishes a sharply pointed Christmas decoration in front of Alice. Then her watch starts beeping.*

Chocolate time. Now then, Alice, tell me, exactly how many chocolate Advent calendars is the maximum a greedy person should have?

ALICE: I don't know – I would have thought thirty.

*Geraldine walks over to her desk. Both it and the wall are covered with chocolate Advent calendars.*

GERALDINE: Good, good, I've got it about right, then. And there's just enough time before David's big party to open two more windows on my Oasis one. Do you want Liam or Noel?

ALICE: Liam.

GERALDINE: All right then.

*She holds the Liam chocolate out to Alice, but pops it in her own mouth just as Alice reaches for it.*

Mmm, Patsy Kensit's right, you know. Liam is tasty.

## Scene Two: David's Sitting Room

*An elegantly decorated tree stands in the window, the coffee table is covered with nibbles and the drinks are flowing. Hugo and Geraldine are chatting. Jim and Frank are also chatting, with David who is sporting a new beard.*

HUGO: Got anything planned for Christmas?

GERALDINE: Well, one or two things, yes. I am the vicar, remember.

HUGO: Oh yes. Yes, of course. Can be quite a sad time though, Christmas, can't it? I always feel sorry for people who are alone on Christmas Day. Solitary sad acts watching *Jurassic Park* and opening Advent calendars.

*Exactly what Geraldine does . . .*

GERALDINE: Yes, yes that is tragic, isn't it? What's the idea with your father and the er . . .

*She gestures to her chin.*

HUGO: Oh, he says it makes him more attractive to women.

GERALDINE: Right. So he's gone completely mad now, then?

*David taps his glass to get everyone's attention.*

DAVID: Welcome, everybody, and thank you all for coming. May I take this opportunity of wishing you all a Merry Christmas.

*A group of carol singers are heard outside.*

I hope we all find this a time of joy and peace and goodwill to all men. Hugo, tell that lot to go and drown themselves, will you?

HUGO: All right. Or I could ask them to come in and cheer our hearts with their childish joy.

DAVID: I think not.

GERALDINE: Shame.

DAVID: Oh, all right, we'll take a vote. Who wants to hear little Miss Loony and her tuneless tots kill some carols?

*All raise their hands, except David.*

HUGO: Three cheers for Crimbo. (*And out he goes.*)

FRANK: Vicar, Vicar – Jim and I are getting together on Christmas Day.

GERALDINE: Oh?

FRANK: Not that we're an item you understand, not in that sense. But, er, we're joining forces for the day.

JIM: Just the day, not the night.

FRANK: And we wondered if you'd consider being our guest.

GERALDINE: Oh!

JIM: The thing is, my wife's away on a Competent Grandparenting course and we used to have lunch, Christmas lunch, at Letitia's but since she, well, you know, sort of . . .

GERALDINE: Died.

JIM: Yes – it's just us. And, er, we wouldn't half mind a bit of totty to take her place!

GERALDINE: I see, so, a sort of rock and roll lunch with the guys.

JIM: No, no, no, yes that's right. Yes, sex and drugs and rock and Swiss roll.

FRANK: We promise you a delicious repast and a potentially thrilling game of charades.

GERALDINE: Well, I can't deny I am totally available for Christmas lunch, so I'd be delighted to accept.

FRANK: A result!

*Frank high-fives Jim in excitement.*

GERALDINE: Except for the charades. Which I enjoy as much as colonic irrigation.

FRANK: I've not played that.

*Hugo has let the carollers in – they are an angelic-looking bunch of children from the village, with Alice leading them. Their version of 'Ding Dong Merrily on High' continues interminably on the 'Gloria' bit, till Geraldine has to butt in.*

GERALDINE: Well, that's lovely. Now then before you finish, a little test for you. We all know that Christmas is a very very special time, but who can tell me who started it all?

*All hands in the room are raised.*

Yes, James.

JAMES: Noel Edmonds.

GERALDINE: No.

JIM: *(lowering his hand)* That's me out.

GERALDINE: Any other guesses?

BETHANY: Baby Jesus.

GERALDINE: That's right, Bethany, and what's so special about Jesus?

PATRICK: His name's a swear word.

GERALDINE: Yes, but I was thinking rather more of the fact that he's the Son of God. And where was he born?

TREVOR: In Dunstable.

GERALDINE: In Dunstable?

CHILDREN: Yeah, that's right.

GERALDINE: Who told you that?

*They all look to Alice.*

ALICE: Well, I always thought it was a bit odd but that's what my mum told me. Jesus was born in Dunstable.

GERALDINE: In a *stable*.

DAVID: Is there any chance of getting on with it?

*Owen arrives. He doesn't notice the carol singers in the room.*

OWEN: I'm sorry I'm late. I was just leaving when that daft girl and her horrible gang of talentless dwarfs came in. I haven't heard a racket like it since I caught that cow in the shredder.

*Geraldine gestures towards the children and Alice. Owen turns to see them.*

Hello Alice. Hello dear little children, nice to see you again.

GERALDINE: On you go, Alice.

ALICE: Right. Our final song is an old favourite in a new version the children taught me. I'm a great believer that you must listen to the culture of the young.

DAVID: Get on with it.

ALICE: Okay. On the count of four. Four.

ALICE AND CHILDREN: 'While shepherds watched their flocks by night all seated on a bank.'

GERALDINE: Oh God.

ALICE AND CHILDREN: 'An angel who was bored came down and taught them how to . . .'

GERALDINE: (*shouting and clapping to drown them out*) Merry Christmas, everybody!

*Alice sees the children out and Hugo follows her into the hallway.*

HUGO: Fabulous. Deeply moving. So nice to know the shepherds really had some fun at Christmas, isn't it?

*Hugo notices that they are standing directly beneath some mistletoe. He bends down to kiss Alice — she lifts her lips to his . . . but they can't do it. It's too embarrassing.*

# The Christmas Lunch Incident

ALICE: Bye then.

HUGO: Bye.

*Back in the sitting room . . .*

GERALDINE: I can't deny it, I have heard more pleasant sounds coming from very recently castrated cattle.

DAVID: Look, Vicar, I know we have our differences. I believe in hanging and birching and you're not normal. But the thing is, I've decided to make some changes in my life and my image, as you can see from this.

GERALDINE: Yes, I noticed that. It's very, very . . . beard-like, isn't it?

DAVID: Well, thank you. The truth is, at last I'm putting right some of the things that forced my poor wife to leave me all those years ago. So I finally learned how to cook.

GERALDINE: Oh!

DAVID: With the help of Delia Smith.

GERALDINE: Saint Delia.

DAVID: Yes. Which means I'm doing a real Christmas lunch this year and I'd be thrilled if you'd like to come along and taste it.

GERALDINE: Oh, David, what a sweet offer. Unfortunately I can't.

DAVID: No, no, you're right. Forget I mentioned it, a leopard can't change his spots. To you I shall always be a sad and bitter old bachelor.

GERALDINE: No, no – I don't think that at all, David.

DAVID: Oh, so you will come then?

GERALDINE: Er, er. Yes, yes. I'd love to come and taste your stuffing.

DAVID: Splendid.

GERALDINE: Will you excuse me just a moment, I've got to . . . Yes. Frank, Jim, look, er . . .

JIM: It's going to be the most exciting Christmas of our lives.

FRANK: What a catch, eh?

*They are so excited about Geraldine coming to lunch with them that she just can't cancel on them.*

GERALDINE: It's going to be great, isn't it? It's going to be really great. Will you excuse me just a moment? I've just got to, er, David . . .

DAVID: I am *so* excited that you'll come.

GERALDINE: Good.

DAVID: The stuffing. Do you think I'd be mad to try Delia's exotic cranberry one?

GERALDINE: No, no, that'll be lovely.

DAVID: Splendid. Now tell me, Vicar, on a more serious note, how's the Christmas sermon going?

GERALDINE: Oh it's fine, I haven't thought about it much.

DAVID: Oh dear.

GERALDINE: What? Problem?

DAVID: Well, I know I wouldn't think about anything else for months.

GERALDINE: Wouldn't you?

DAVID: No.

GERALDINE: Why?

DAVID: It's the key-note speech at the party conference, isn't it?

GERALDINE: Is it?

DAVID: Deliver a stinker, again, and you'll lose them for the whole year.

GERALDINE: Will I?

DAVID: They're back to Satan until next December.

GERALDINE: *(now very shocked by this thought)* Are they?

DAVID: Indeed.

GERALDINE: Right. Right.

### Scene Three: Geraldine's Living Room

GERALDINE: Alice, ready to hear this?

ALICE: I'm all ears.

GERALDINE: Right.

ALICE: Well, not all ears. I'm face and tummy and legs and lots of other bits – including some rather private bits I only let a doctor see. Only he wasn't a doctor and he got arrested soon afterwards. But my ears are all ears and they're listening to yoooou, Geraldine Granger, vicar extraordinary.

GERALDINE: Right. Picture the scene. Christmas morning, full house. Girl Vicar with special new hairdo.

ALICE: I'm so excited I could just burst like a great big blister when you stab it with a pin.

GERALDINE: Well, please don't. A hush descends and I start. 'I take as my text today St John Chapter One, Verse One. "In the beginning was the Word and the Word was with God", and Alice please put that magazine down.'

ALICE: Oh, sorry. It was great though, great beginning. Fantastic.

GERALDINE: *(sitting at her desk)* Oh well, good. Glad you enjoyed it. I'll have to rethink the whole thing now.

ALICE: Vicar.

GERALDINE: Verger.

*Alice hands Geraldine a flat present.*

Oh Alice, how sweet. Oh, I wonder what it is? Is it a ball?

ALICE: No.

GERALDINE: I wonder if it's a book? Can I open it now?

ALICE: Yeah, yeah.

GERALDINE: Oh thanks, I love books.

ALICE: Something a bit intellectual, just to get your teeth into – you know, just drift away on a carpet of storytelling and imagination.

GERALDINE: Right. 'Zigazig Ha. The Authorized Biography of the Spice Girls.' Fantastic!

ALICE: Yeah, it's a brilliant story.

GERALDINE: Oh, I can believe that, and look at this. 'Chapter One, The Beginning – we decide which one of us is going to have red hair.'

Fabulous. Look at this. 'Chapter Eight, Big Trouble – we all fancy the same bloke in Boyzone. Oh no, what do we do?' Thank you so much, Alice.

ALICE: Oh, I'm glad you like it. I was torn between that and the book about Des Lynam's mum.

GERALDINE: Well, you made the correct choice. I've got to get on with my sermon now though.

ALICE: Oh fine. Well I'll see you at the service and lunch will be about one o'clock.

GERALDINE: Right . . . What? Lunch?

ALICE: Yeah. I mean usually it's just me, my sister and my mum but this year I said, 'Can I bring the vicar along?' and Mum said, 'Oh, the vicar won't come. She'll have far more important people to have lunch with.'

GERALDINE: It's funny you should say that . . .

ALICE: And I started to cry and I said, 'No she won't. Because I'm her best friend in the universe,' and Mum said, 'All right, ask her to come then', and I said, 'I don't need to ask her.'

GERALDINE: (mortified) Yeah, funny you should say that.

ALICE: And anyway if she didn't come I'd kill myself.

GERALDINE: Right. Right, well I'm looking forward to it.

*She shows Alice to the door.*

ALICE: And, um, by the way, about my sister. She's lovely but she's not quite as, well, you know, on the ball as I am. So don't, you know, let's get into the heavy deep philosophical stuff that you and I go in for, if you get my meaning.

GERALDINE: Yeah, you mean steer clear of the Jesuitical heresy, that sort of thing.

*Alice looks completely blank at this.*

ALICE: Well, I'd better go and get my last-minute shopping.

GERALDINE: All right. Bye. Don't go mad. (She shuts the door.) Oops, too late, you did.

*Immediately, there's a knock at the door. She opens it . . .*

GERALDINE: Owen.

OWEN: Hello, Vicar. I've got something to ask you.

GERALDINE: Please say it's not about Christmas lunch.

OWEN: No.

GERALDINE: Oh, thank God.

*She reaches up and gives him a kiss on the lips.*

OWEN: (*taken aback*) No, I just wondered whether it would be all right if I missed the service tomorrow. Only my favourite sheep is sick. I won't bore you with the details but she swallowed this fish hook and I tried to yank it out but it seems to have caught on one of her ventricles, so I've now tugged it up in her throat.

GERALDINE: No, no, you deal with that Owen. But actually, since you're not coming to the service, you wouldn't do me a favour would you?

OWEN: That depends.

GERALDINE: Well, it's just that I've just this second thought of an exciting new beginning for my sermon. I'd love to know what you think.

OWEN: Right, okay, I'll give it a listen.

GERALDINE: Oh great, come on in. (*They head in.*)

OWEN: To be honest, anything to put off scraping the cow dung off the stable walls.

GERALDINE: Right, right. Do sit down. I've decided to steer clear of the traditional Christmas sermon, so I'm going to start, 'I take my text today not from the Bible, but from a rather beautiful poem by Christina Rossetti, called "The Hidden Heart". "I look this morn upon my face, and whence . . ." '

*This is too much for Owen.*

OWEN: Actually those stable walls are pretty mucky. I'd best be going. Bye.

*He leaves and Geraldine is left to contemplate her situation.*

GERALDINE: Bye. I quite understand, yeah, yeah. Right. Now some frightening facts. It's the biggest gig of the year. It's a one-woman show, there's twelve hours to go. I have NO ideas at all.

## Scene Four: Geraldine's Living Room

*Christmas Day morning dawns bright and crisp. The church bells are pealing . . . and Geraldine is still waiting for inspiration at her desk. Balls of screwed-up paper are all around her.*

GERALDINE: Oh no. This is a major essay crisis now. (*She appeals to her picture of Jesus.*) Listen Birthday Boy, if you don't help me now I'm afraid I'm going to have to tell them you actually are Noel Edmonds. It's up to you. Please. Help me.

## Scene Five: The Vestry

*The service is over and Geraldine hangs up her robes. She's wearing a bright red festive waistcoat with a picture of Jesus on the back and the slogan 'It's My Birthday'. David and Hugo come through to see her.*

DAVID: Oh well done, Vicar, first-class sermon.

GERALDINE: Oh, thanks, David.

DAVID: Interesting text, fascinating parallel between the two stories. Just like Mary, the Spice Girls were also virgins thrust into the public eye at a young age. Very illuminating.

HUGO: Yes, and like them, Jesus wants us to tell him what we want.

GERALDINE: What we really, really want.

HUGO: That's right. Brilliant stuff, Vic.

DAVID: Come along, Hugo.

HUGO: I fancy the blonde one.

DAVID: See you at one, Vicar.

GERALDINE: Right.

*They leave, and Frank and Jim come through.*

FRANK: Jolly good sermon, Vicar. Don't you agree, Jim?

JIM: No, no, yes, yes. I like the way you moved from the superficial and facile messages of popular music to the subtle and complex revelations of the Nativity.

GERALDINE: Right.

FRANK: Lunch at one?

GERALDINE: Could we have it just a little bit earlier?

FRANK: Like when?

GERALDINE: Like in about five minutes.

FRANK: Right. She's keen Jim, she's very keen. Better get that turkey in the microwave.

*They leave, followed by Alice.*

ALICE: See you at lunch.

GERALDINE: Oh Alice. Please remember I haven't got a very big appetite.

ALICE: You! Pull the other one. 'Thirds please, Alice' more like.

*Geraldine leaves the vestry and makes her way to Frank's house. A couple greet her outside.*

MAN/WOMAN: Merry Christmas.

GERALDINE: Merry Christmas. *(Then, to herself.)* Right, let's have a little practice. 'Just a tiny portion for me, thank you. No thanks, I won't have any pudding.' Oh, that one's going to be tricky.

## Scene Six: Frank's Dining Room

*It's small and tidy with lots of pictures of trains.*

GERALDINE: Just a couple of slices of turkey and a few veg for me, thanks.

FRANK: Absolutely.

*He places Geraldine's plate in front of her. It is huge, and full of food.*

GERALDINE: And how many types of vegetable is that?

FRANK: Sixteen.

JIM:  Meat and sixteen veg. That's always been the way in Dibley.

FRANK:  Tuck in, Vicar, there's more where that came from.

GERALDINE:  Lucky, lucky me, eh?

*A few minutes later she has cleared her plate.*

Well, that was scrumptious. Thank you very much indeed.

*Frank takes away her plate and Jim deposits a whole Christmas pudding in front of her.*

JIM:  Pudding.

GERALDINE:  Well, perhaps I'll just have a small portion. (*Then Jim brings in two more Christmas puddings.*) Right, just one each. A whole one each.

*A little later and Geraldine has just about finished off her pudding.*

FRANK:  Found the money yet, Vicar?

GERALDINE:  Not yet, no.

FRANK:  Well, you ought to find some, I put five pounds in every pudding.

GERALDINE:  Oh . . . Actually.

*She fishes something out of her mouth — it's a five-pound note.*

FRANK:  Well done.

*Jim reads out his cracker joke.*

JIM:  What do you do when you see a spaceman?

GERALDINE:  Oh I don't know, know, know, know, know, Jim. What do you do when you see a spaceman?

JIM:  Park in it, man.

# †HE CHRISTMAS LUNCH INCIDENT

*There is much hilarity and laughter.*

FRANK: Now, that is most amusing. How do they think up these new jokes every year. Do you get it, Vicar?

GERALDINE: Not as often as I'd like.

FRANK: Oh saucy.

JIM: I heard a really funny joke last week, hilarious.

GERALDINE: Did you?

JIM: *(laughing)* It's very funny.

GERALDINE: In your own time then.

JIM: Knock, knock.

GERALDINE: Who's there?

JIM: *(can't stop laughing now)* No, no, no, no, no, no, no wait, wait, no, no, no, Doctor.

GERALDINE: Doctor Who?

JIM: Yes.

## Scene Seven: The Village

*Geraldine is on her way to David's house. She looks at her watch and realizes she is late.*

GERALDINE: Oh Lord!

*She starts to run, goes a few paces and runs out of breath.*

Unrealistic.

## Scene Eight: David's Sitting/Dining Room

*The table is set for the three of them. A covered plate at each place setting.*

GERALDINE: For what we are about to receive may the Lord make us truly grateful.

ALL: Amen.

*David lifts the lids on the plates to reveal pasta underneath.*

GERALDINE: Well, that's original, not going for the traditional turkey then?

DAVID: Well, not as a starter, no.

GERALDINE: So this family-sized portion of pasta is, in fact, the starter, is it?

*Hugo, beaming at her, nods.*

Excellent. Tuck in.

*She manages to finish the pasta.*

Well, you'll have to forgive me, I won't be having that much turkey.

DAVID: Oh you won't be having any turkey.

GERALDINE: Oh?

*Hugo places another dish in front of her.*

DAVID: Till after the fish course.

GERALDINE: Excellent. A whole fish.

*Geraldine eats the whole lot and has to undo her waistcoat.*

DAVID: Now the turkey.

He brings in an enormous golden-brown done-to-perfection turkey. Geraldine looks positively ill. But she eats . . .

HUGO: (*reading his cracker joke*) Here's a good one. What do you do when you see a spaceman?

GERALDINE: I don't know. What do you do when you see a spaceman?

HUGO: Park in it. Humour's getting very surreal these days. I blame Nicholas Witchell.

DAVID: More sprouts, Vicar?

GERALDINE: Er no, no they're lovely, but I really couldn't eat another one.

DAVID: (punches the air and laughs) Yes!

GERALDINE: What, what, what?

DAVID: No. No, no, no it's nothing. Hugo and I have a silly Christmas wager each year. I bet that I can eat more sprouts than the guests and he bets that I can't. Never won in twenty years have you, Hugo?

HUGO: No, Father. As usual you win. Like every tennis game, every game of backgammon, every game of cards we've ever played since I was born. I suppose you're just a better person than I am.

DAVID: Right. Thought he was on to a winner with you though, Geraldine – no such luck.

HUGO: No, I'm a loser.

DAVID: That's my boy.

GERALDINE: Just wait one cotton-picking-minute here. I think perhaps I could manage a couple more after all.

*Hugo looks up, surprised at this turn of events. He is to chair the competition – David and Geraldine sit at opposite ends of the table, Hugo in the middle. He dishes out the sprouts.*

HUGO: (in a Scottish accent like the man from 'Gladiators') Contestant David. You will go on my first whistle. Vixen, you will go on my second whistle.

*Hugo blows the whistle and David begins to eat. He chews and chews and finally cannot manage any more.*

DAVID: I'm through, finish those and you win.

*Hugo blows the whistle and Geraldine begins. She chews and chews . . . and finally – in an act of superhuman squeezing-in, she manages to fit all the sprouts into her mouth. She's won.*

HUGO: (in an American accent) At last I know the taste of victory and it sure is mighty fine. Put it there, partner.

*He shakes Geraldine's hand. She stands up, but her bottom is stuck in the chair. Hugo helps her out of it.*

GERALDINE: Well, while I'm up I think I'd better call it a day. Couldn't eat another thing.

DAVID: *Au contraire*, Vicar. Bring in the winner's reward.

*Hugo brings in an enormous Christmas pudding.*

HUGO: We made it especially big, because we know how you like your puddings, Vicar.

GERALDINE: Mmm . . .

## Scene Nine: A Lane in the Village

*Geraldine is crawling along on her hands and knees, too full up to walk.*

GERALDINE: If I ever actually meet Delia Smith in person I'm afraid I'm going to have to strangle her with my bare hands. And stuff cranberries into every available orifice.

## Scene Ten: Alice's House

*Alice is dressed in a pink fairy outfit, with bauble earrings. She lets Geraldine in.*

ALICE: Are you all right? You don't look very well.

GERALDINE: No, no I'm, I'm fine. It's just I'm, you know, a little bit sort of . . .

*She sits down and the chair collapses beneath her.*

Oh, I'm sorry about that.

ALICE: It doesn't matter. Don't you worry, you know you're probably just faint from lack of food.

GERALDINE: Right.

ALICE: Sit down and we'll have you full up in no time at all.

GERALDINE: Good.

*Alice calls for her mum to come through. A fierce but slightly vacant-looking woman.*

ALICE: Geraldine, this is my mum.

GERALDINE: Oh, Mrs Tinker. How lovely to meet you, I've heard so much about you.

MRS TINKER: Have you?

GERALDINE: Yes, I have.

MRS TINKER: Have you?

GERALDINE: I certainly have.

MRS TINKER: Oh, you have, have you?

*Alice's sister appears in the doorway. An odd-looking girl with frizzy hair, wearing a bunny jumper and old-fashioned skirt.*

GERALDINE: Yes. And this must be Alice's sister.

ALICE: Yes, this is Mary.

GERALDINE: Oh, hello Mary.

MARY: Hello. You're much taller than I imagined you'd be.

GERALDINE: Am I?

MARY: Yes. Because I always imagined you sitting down.

GERALDINE: Right.

MARY: Alice never stops talking about you. I know absolutely every little thing about you.

GERALDINE: Really, Alice?

MARY: She says you're the best vet in the world.

GERALDINE: I'm the vicar.

MARY: Are you?

ALICE: 'Course she is, you silly billy. Come on, Vicar, sit down, otherwise we'll never eat.

GERALDINE: Well, that suits me, I'm not really very hungry.

*Alice and Mary crack up laughing at this.*

ALICE: I told you she was a card, didn't I?

MARY: You told me she was a vet.

ALICE: No I didn't. (*To Geraldine.*) Guess what Mum's cooked up for us today?

GERALDINE: Oh, would it be turkey and sixteen veg?

MARY: Don't be silly. Not for Easter.

ALICE: It's Christmas.

MARY: Is it?

ALICE: Of course it is, you nit.

MARY: So why am I wearing a cardie with a large bunny on it then?

ALICE: I've been meaning to ask you that all morning.

*Mrs Tinker brings in the turkey.*

GERALDINE: Ah. I've heard wonderful things about your cooking, Mrs Tinker.

MRS TINKER: Have you?

GERALDINE: Yes, I have?

MRS TINKER: Have you?

GERALDINE: Yes, I have.

MRS TINKER: Oh, you have, have you?

*Fed up with this carry-on, Geraldine diverts attention to the food.*

GERALDINE: À table! À table! Now, for what we may be about to receive may the Lord make us truly thankful.

ALL: Amen.

GERALDINE: Now then, just before we start eating, I'd like to tell you a little story.

ALICE/MARY: Oh, hooray.

GERALDINE:  It's about the lovely kind woman who's a vicar.

ALICE:  Oh, just like you.

GERALDINE:  Yes, and because she was trying to be kind to her parishioners she agreed to have three different sets of Christmas lunch.

ALICE:  Oh, that's hilarious.

GERALDINE:  Isn't it, yes. I mean the first lunch, well, she was okay, by the second lunch she was trying to manage to get it down. But by the time she got to the third family, you know, she was *absolutely stuffed*.

MRS TINKER:  Was she?

GERALDINE:  Yes, she was.

MRS TINKER:  Was she?

GERALDINE:  Yes, she was.

MRS TINKER:  Oh she was, was she?

GERALDINE:  *(annoyed now)* Yes she was, she couldn't eat another bite.

ALICE:  I bet the thought of one more slice of turkey made her absolutely sick.

MARY:  I bet it made her absolutely sick.

MRS TINKER:  Did it?

ALICE:  I bet it did.

MRS TINKER:  It did, did it?

GERALDINE:  Yes, it certainly did. But since the third family was where her absolute best best friend lived . . .

ALICE:  Oh, like I'm your best friend?

GERALDINE:  Yes, she decided to tell her best friend all about the three meals problem.

ALICE:  Oh, good idea.

GERALDINE:  Yes, because she knew her best friend would take pity on her and say, 'Hey, you don't have to eat all that food if you don't want to. Just have a cup of tea instead.' You know, to help her out.

ALICE:  Oh, that's where it's not like me at all.

MRS TINKER:  No.

MARY: No.

GERALDINE: No?

ALICE: No, because if she was my best friend and we'd cooked a meal for her like we've cooked this one for you and it turned out that she'd eaten already, I'd just cry and cry and my sister would cry – look she's crying already just hearing the story. And I'd probably be scarred psychologically for the rest of my life by this dreadful tale of betrayal and deceit.

GERALDINE: Right. Well, we'd better tuck in then, eh? Now this starter is . . . ?

MRS TINKER: Stuffing.

GERALDINE: Balls of stuffing . . .

*A little later and Geraldine is about to leave . . .*

Well, goodbye everybody and thank you so much. Very interesting chat, Mrs T.

MRS TINKER: Was it?

GERALDINE: And thanks for the lovely present, Mary.

*It's an Easter egg.*

MARY: You're welcome, doctor. Maybe we can do charades next Easter.

*Alice grabs Geraldine's hand affectionately.*

GERALDINE: Yes. Over my dead body. Right, I've got to go now, I've got a taxi waiting. Thank you, I've got to go now, Alice. (*Alice won't let go of her hand.*) Alice, let go, Alice.

*Geraldine leaves.*

MRS TINKER: Who was that then?

*A taxi is, indeed, waiting outside. Geraldine climbs in and it drives away – to the vicarage the other side of the road.*

## Scene Eleven: Geraldine's Hallway

*At last, Geraldine is home. She opens the door and falls over, flat on her face. Owen arrives at the door. Geraldine is still on the floor.*

GERALDINE: I think I'll skip supper tonight.

OWEN: Hello, Vicar. May I have a word?

GERALDINE: *(not moving)* Yeah, you carry on.

OWEN: The other night, you said, 'Was I going to ask you to Christmas lunch', and I said 'no', and then you snogged me.

GERALDINE: Did I?

OWEN: Yes. Now I've realized that was your subtle female way of angling for an invite.

GERALDINE: I don't think it was.

OWEN: And I missed it, because I'm not a subtle female. So now I'm asking. Would you come to lunch?

*Geraldine pulls herself up off the floor.*

GERALDINE: Oh, Owen, I would love to but . . .

OWEN: It's just that you're alone and I'm alone and it's not that I want the company or anything, though it might be nice to hear a human voice on Christmas Day, since I've spent every Christmas alone since my uncle died, in the year they introduced decimal currency. Not that you have to come, of course, because I know I'm a misery, though I have got a lot of love in my heart as any of my cows will tell you, if they could talk, which they can't, which is a shame in one way and a bloody relief in another. Because what would they say? 'Oh, what have you been up to today?' 'Oh, standing in a field, what about you?' 'Standing in a field. What about you?' 'Yes, standing in a field . . .'

GERALDINE: Yes, I think I got that bit.

OWEN: So what do you say? Join me at Christmas lunch for the first time since 1971 or reject me, just like I've been rejected every day by everyone ever since I was born, what do you say?

*Very long pause.*

GERALDINE: I say 'yum, yum, in my tum'.

## Scene Twelve: Owen's House

OWEN: Here, let me.

*He takes Geraldine's coat, rolls it up and then throws it on the floor.*

GERALDINE: Thanks.

OWEN: I hope you're not too hungry.

GERALDINE: Oh, do you know, that's the sweetest thing you've ever said to me.

OWEN: Only I know how families are famous for big spreads, but I'm not a cook so I've not done one.

GERALDINE: Oh, wonderful.

*He shows her through into the dining room, where the table is covered with platters of food.*

OWEN: Ha ha, only joking.

GERALDINE: Ha, ha, ha. Right, there's quite a lot of food here for just the two of us.

OWEN: No, I'm not eating. Stomach upset, but don't you worry, I shall get just as much pleasure from watching you tuck in. (*He pulls out a chair for her.*) Particularly my pièce de résistance, the traditional Christmas fare.

*He lifts the lid off a platter to reveal a wobbling mass of white stuff. Geraldine looks like she may faint.*

GERALDINE: Is that tripe?

## Scene Thirteen: The Village

*Owen is driving Geraldine back home in the tractor. He's up in the cab, she's lying in the scoop with the hay, singing.*

GERALDINE: '. . . nobody likes me!
I'm going out to eat worms
Big long slimy ones
Big tall juicy ones
Fuzzy, buzzy, uzzy, wuzzy worms . . .'

## Scene Fourteen: Geraldine's Living Room

*Geraldine is lying back on the sofa.*

GERALDINE: If anyone ever asks me to have Christmas lunch again, I'm going to say, 'Thank you very much, but frankly I'd rather have sex with Jimmy Hill.' Why don't they *leave me alone?* I suppose they have left me alone now. Yeah, they have. Should have asked a friend over. Definitely should have asked a friend.

*The doorbell rings and she puts her slippers on before going to answer it.*

Coming! I should be there in about twenty minutes. I swear if these are Jehovah's Witnesses I'm joining. Anything to get out of this village. I try to be nice to people, they turn me into the EC turkey mountain.

*She opens the door to Tristan, the ever-so-lovely television producer from 'Songs of Praise'.*

TRISTAN: Hello.

*She slams the door shut in total shock. It's really him! She re-opens the door.*

Tristan Campbell. You probably don't remember me. I was the producer when we did *Songs of Praise*.

GERALDINE: *(over-excitedly)* No, of course I remember you. Do come in. Go through.

*She ushers him into the living room.*

TRISTAN: I'm terribly sorry to disturb you. This is crazy, but Christmas makes one do crazy things.

GERALDINE: Yes, it certainly does. I mean look at the three wise men. Trekking thousands of miles just to bring a baby a couple of bottles of perfume.

*She laughs loudly at this, slightly embarrassed.*

TRISTAN: Quite. Well, it's just that – oh heck, I know I've only met you the once but I've never been able to get you out of mind. And, well, I think you're perfect, so I just wondered if you'd marry me?

GERALDINE: Pardon?

TRISTAN: I wonder if you'd marry me?

GERALDINE: Yes, I thought that's what you said. But then I thought, AAAAAAHHHH! You mean you actually want me to decide now?

*She cannot believe this is happening.*

TRISTAN: No, well, of course not. But it's just if you could find it in your heart to say yes, then you'll make me the happiest man alive and I'll love you for ever.

GERALDINE: Oh well. Well then, yes. I mean – yes.

TRISTAN: Fantastic. Back in a sec.

*He leaves.*

GERALDINE: He loves me. Completely and utterly in love with me. Loved me from the moment he saw me. Forsaking all others. Utterly obsessed with me. I'm afraid you're going to have to butt out, Mel. (*She takes down her picture of Mel Gibson.*) Three's a crowd, babe.

*She goes over to the mirror and puts on a party headband with bouncing antennae.*

I'm going to put this on. He loves it when I'm cute.

*A bit of lipstick and then the doorbell goes again. She runs to get it.*

TRISTAN: Hi.

GERALDINE: (*looking cute and gorgeous*) Hi!

*Tristan has a girl with him – he introduces her to Geraldine.*

TRISTAN: And this is Aoife. I didn't bring her in just now in case you said no, but, well, she'd love to meet you.

GERALDINE: Hello, Eva.

AOIFE: Aoife.

GERALDINE: Either.

AOIFE: Aoife.

GERALDINE: Yes, Eee whatever. And you are?

AOIFE: I'm Tristan's fiancée.

GERALDINE: I don't think so – ha ha ha! Of course you are. Do come in. Just go on through, the fire's on.

*She cannot believe she made such a big mistake. The antennae hairband comes off in humiliation. She gathers herself together and goes through to the living room.*

Drink?

TRISTAN: Thank you.

AOIFE: Oh, yes please.

TRISTAN: Aoife's been dying to meet you.

GERALDINE: *Has* she? *Has* she?

*She hands them both a glass of wine. Her heart is sort of broken.*

TRISTAN: I always said if I ever got married then the only person I'd want to marry me was Geraldine Granger.

GERALDINE: Superb. Superb. Well here's to love and marriage, which go together like a horse and carriage, according to Cole Porter. He should know, he was gay. (*She laughs.*) Here's to Tristan and his young Heifer.

AOIFE: Aoife.

GERALDINE: Yes, it's a strange name isn't it? How do you spell that?

AOIFE: A.O.I.F.E.

GERALDINE: Oh, you didn't bother to leave any vowels for anyone else then? You greedy hussy!

TRISTAN: Actually, actually there's no U in it. I once, the soppy thing that I am, I left a message for Aoife: 'Aoife, missing "U", always'.

GERALDINE: That's lovely, isn't it? Oh you Irish, you love your wacky spelling, don't you?

TRISTAN: You can say that again, her brother's called Barrfhionn.

GERALDINE: Oh, what, spelt K.R.T.N.Q.Z.?

AOIFE: That's the guy.

TRISTAN: (*looking at Aoife tenderly*) But I love her with all my heart, that's all I can say, despite the name thing.

GERALDINE: Good. Good.

AOIFE: And I love him with all my heart. And I would be thrilled if you could marry us. I'd love a woman to do it. I'd so love you to do it.

*Geraldine is won over.*

GERALDINE: And I'd be honoured to do it, Aoife. You're lovely.

AOIFE: Oh, look, we're really sorry to interrupt your Christmas, it just seemed like the perfect time to fix a wedding and, after all, it's what Christmas is all about, isn't it? Love.

GERALDINE: It is, it is. That and overeating till you spew. Well, cheers.

*With that she takes a swig from the bottle of wine.*

## Scene Fifteen: Geraldine's Living Room

*Later that night and Geraldine is lying on the sofa in her pyjamas. The doorbell rings and she rolls off the sofa on to the floor, then drags herself up.*

GERALDINE: I must get some callipers for my knees. These have surrendered completely.

*It's Alice, in her pink anorak, wearing a pink sparkly tiara.*

ALICE: Hello, Vicar, I thought you might be lonely.

GERALDINE: Yes, I am a bit, come on in. Did you have a good day?

ALICE: Oh yeah. Best Christmas we've ever had. We were just sitting round and I said, 'I have never had such a good Christmas.' And Mum said, 'Haven't you?' And I said, 'No, I haven't.' And she said, 'You haven't, haven't you?' and I said, 'No, I haven't.'

GERALDINE: Yes, yes, I think I've got the hang of that bit.

ALICE: And then I thought, actually everything is better in the village since the vicar arrived.

GERALDINE: Oh, Alice, thank you.

ALICE: And I thought I wonder if the Vic knows it, so, I thought she probably doesn't know it . . .

*The doorbell rings.*

GERALDINE: Oh no, who can that be? Not another Scottish sadist and his Irish tart come round to torture me.

*Alice follows her to the door, still talking.*

ALICE: Well, as I was saying, I thought she probably doesn't know, so I went round and . . .

*Geraldine opens the door to Jim, Hugo, Frank, Owen and David.*

. . . got everyone.

ALL: Happy Christmas!

GERALDINE: Well, I don't know what to say!

JIM: I do.

GERALDINE: What's that, Jim?

JIM: Charades.

GERALDINE: All right, come on in. But anyone who does that disgusting mime for *Gone With the Wind* is straight back out again.

HUGO: Don't worry about the catering, Vicar. We've all got together and produced a rather splendid selection of . . . turkey sandwiches.

GERALDINE: Not for me, I don't think.

FRANK: Do have one, Vicar, we've put so much effort into it.

HUGO: Some of them have got cranberry jelly. Some of them have got piccalilli — we've been at it all afternoon.

GERALDINE: All right, then. I don't think I should really.

*She takes a big bite of a sandwich and immediately regrets it.*

No, just as I thought. Big mistake, excuse me.

## Scene Sixteen: Geraldine's Living Room

*A little later and charades is in full swing. It's Alice's turn — she is holding two jars in front of her. The men are all trying to guess the charade.*

DAVID: It's definitely a film?

ALICE: Yes.

FRANK: And it is one word?

ALICE: Yes. Give up?

ALL: Yes.

ALICE: It's Jars.

JIM: Jars?

ALICE: I've not seen it but apparently it's about these big jars that attack people.

OWEN: *Jaws*, you stupid girl. It's *Jaws*.

*Hugo gets up to say something.*

HUGO: All right, settle down, settle down. Now, now I'm not a great speech maker, I get so nervous I usually start gibbering absolute talkish. But I – I just wanted to say, this village didn't amount to doodle squat before the vicar arrived and now it's a fantastic place to live.

ALL: Hear hear.

OWEN: She's the first person ever to make me feel genuinely desirable.

HUGO: Exactly, Owen. So I'd like you all to raise your glasses to our own dear Vicar. To the Vicar.

*They all turn round and raise their glasses towards the hallway.*

ALL: The Vicar.

HUGO: And we hope she soon recovers from what seems to have been a truly sensational bout of indigestion.

GERALDINE: *(from the toilet)* Yes. Thanks a lot. I should be out just after New Year.

## Epilogue: The Vestry

*Geraldine and Alice are having a cup of Earl Grey together.*

**GERALDINE:** Right. Knock, knock.

**ALICE:** Who's there?

**GERALDINE:** The interrupting sheep.

**ALICE:** The interrupting sheep...

**GERALDINE:** Baa! (*roars with laughter*) Do you get it?

**ALICE:** No, sorry, because I hadn't finished my bit. Do it again.

**GERALDINE:** No, it's the joke. The interrupting sheep. Always interrupts people, see.

**ALICE:** And that's funny?

**GERALDINE:** Yes, it's hilarious.

**ALICE:** Oh well, in that case I know hundreds of hilarious jokes like that.

**GERALDINE:** Do you?

**ALICE:** Yeah I do. Er, knock, knock.

**GERALDINE:** Who's there?

**ALICE:** The interrupting cow.

**GERALDINE:** The interrupting cow...

**ALICE:** Moo. (*She laughs.*) Knock knock.

**GERALDINE:** (*bit bored now*) Who's there?

**ALICE:** The interrupting rabbit.

*This will be interesting...*

**GERALDINE:** The interrupting rabbit who?

**ALICE:** What noise does a rabbit make? I know they sort of twitch their noses and ...

*She makes her hands into 'ears' and makes a 'rabbity' noise.*

**GERALDINE:** I wonder if I can get the church to agree to the idea of verger culling?

CATHOLICISM
SINCE 30AD

Cardinal Jose Minguez
Miracles Unit
St. Peter's Church
The Vatican
Rome

8/9/2000

Alice Horton
Dibley Church
Dibley
HP21 5TJ
England

Dear Mrs. Horton,

Thanks for your enquiry. However – bad news I'm afraid – we don't think that on this occasion we can bestow sainthood on Rev. Geraldine Granger. There are a number of reasons; firstly, she's not a Catholic. Secondly, she's still alive, and that's usually a bit of a stopper as far as canonization goes.

But the big problem is this – although we think it's just great that Geraldine can stop a baby crying by pulling a funny face, it isn't technically a miracle. If she manages to do something else by pulling a funny face, like parting the clouds or bringing tears of blood to a statue of Our Lady, do let us know and we'll get two priests down there quicker than you can say 'Domini Spiritu Sancti Septulum In Christi Amen'.

In the meantime, best wishes. We've enclosed a complimentary car sticker. It always makes us chuckle here at the Vat.

Yours Eternally,

P.S. In reply to your other queries; no I don't know why the Vatican never enters the Eurovision Song Contest. Perhaps we should. I will investigate. And yes – I have heard the one about the Pope in his bath looking down on the unemployed – hilarious every time!

MY OTHER CAR IS
A POPEMOBILE

# Children's Questions About God

**Children often ask penetrating and succinct questions about God. As a vicar, I think it's important to answer these questions in a way that keeps them quiet for a bit. Here's how I reply to the tricky ones.**

*Child: Why does God have a beard?*
**Me: Because he's too busy looking after all of us to shave.**

*If a Pokémon dies does it go to heaven?*
**Ummm...**

*Can I send e-mails to Jesus?*
**No. Jesus is very holy so he's not rich enough to buy a proper computer. He has to make do with an old Amstrad PCW which, unfortunately, can't load Outlook Express.**

*Is Jesus on the light or the dark side of The Force?*
**You're getting confused there. You see there's Star Wars, and there's reality, and they really are two different – oh, all right then. He's on the light side of The Force. And Darth Maul is his enemy.**

*If God is everywhere, is he in my wee-wee?*
**No he isn't. Your wee-wee consists entirely of Sunny Delight, the most godless drink on this earth.**

*Why doesn't God show himself? It would be easier to believe in him if I could see him sitting up in the clouds.*
**He doesn't want to make it too easy for people to believe in him; you have to find God within yourself.**

*But he showed himself to Abraham. Why not me?*
**I'm sure there was a good reason why Abraham had to see him. I just can't think of it right now.**

*He also showed himself to Moses.*
**Is that right?**

*Yes, it is. Why?*
**Stop asking questions. It's none of your business.**

*But you said you wanted to answer all our questions. You're such a hypocrite.*
**Go and watch telly.**

*But what if –*
**Go and watch telly.**

*All right.*

### God: You didn't handle that very well, did you?

**Oh, that's right, God. Absolutely typical. Turn up when the kid's gone away, why don't you...**

# ENGAGEMENT

## Scene One: The Parish Hall

*A Council Meeting in full flow . . .*

DAVID: Right . . . any other business?

GERALDINE: Yes, I was just wondering, did everybody enjoy the village play?

OWEN: Don't make me laugh. I've seen amputations with more all-round entertainment value. Hamlet's supposed to be a dashing student.

FRANK: I'm not as sprightly as I used to be.

OWEN: Sprightly? You spent the second half in a wheelchair.

FRANK: I pulled a thigh muscle.

GERALDINE: I thought you manoeuvred yourself beautifully, Frank. A momentary blip when you reversed into the grave, but then who'd have thought it would only take you fifteen minutes to climb out?

HUGO: Best bit of the evening. Hilarious stuff.

GERALDINE: I'm only sorry more people didn't come to see it.

JIM: Yes, the night I went I was the only one there.

HUGO: That must have been disappointing for the cast.

JIM: No, they weren't there either. I went on the wrong night.

FRANK: Did you enjoy it, sir?

DAVID: Mmm. About as much as having my nipples pierced.

FRANK: Did you like my big speech, 'To be or not to be.'

DAVID: Very good. I was rooting for you not to be as soon as possible.

GERALDINE: Well, I think Frank deserves our congratulations. So, well done, Frank! Bravo, bravo, encore, encore!

*She claps, but no one else joins in, so she stops, embarrassed.*

DAVID: So is that everything?

GERALDINE: I'm still looking for items for the Parish Newsletter, or rather the Parish 'There's Sod All News' Letter, to be more precise. At the moment, the only thing we've got is a piece from David about his missing watch, which actually is quite a mystery.

*Jim produces a watch from his pocket.*

JIM: Err . . . is that it?

DAVID: (*taking the watch*) Oh yes, thanks.

*Geraldine screws up the piece of paper she has been reading from in disgust.*

GERALDINE: Oh, well. Right. There's only three days to go before I have to go to print. And now my headline is 'Hen lays quite large egg'. So please could everyone contribute just one piece?

OWEN: I could do a review of Frank's play if you like.

GERALDINE: Oh, that would be lovely, yes.

OWEN: As long as I can use the word 'dickhead' in the headline.

GERALDINE: Maybe you're not the man for the job.

## Scene Two: Geraldine's Living Room

*Geraldine is sitting at her typewriter, reading an item for the newsletter.*

GERALDINE: 'New members urgently sought for the Dibley Bondage Club. If interested, please ring Frank Pickle.' At last, a juicy item!

*She starts to type excitedly, then looks again at the item.*

Oh, Dibley Bridge Club. Oh . . . pity.

*She carries on typing, disappointed. Alice comes in.*

ALICE: Hi, you.

GERALDINE: Hello, Alice, come in and shut up. I'm having a serious crisis with the newsletter.

ALICE: Will you be telling us when Jesus is coming?

GERALDINE: Sorry?

ALICE: Well, in last month's newsletter you wrote about how Jesus is coming. But you didn't mention any dates. So Mum wants to know when to get the house tidy.

GERALDINE: No it won't be like that, Alice, he'll just sort of turn up.

ALICE: Oh, that's a bit rude! I might be on the toilet or something.

GERALDINE: No, it won't feel rude, it'll feel just lovely.

ALICE: Oh, that's all right then.

GERALDINE: You haven't got anything for Gossip's Corner, have you?

ALICE: Oh yes, well I have actually!

*Geraldine swivels round in her chair to face Alice.*

GERALDINE: Do you? Go on then.

ALICE: I heard the other day, and don't tell anyone . . .

GERALDINE: (*crosses her heart*) Of course not! Yes?

*She licks her pencil and holds her notepad, poised to write.*

ALICE: That Mr Garrett was seen in the street kissing someone that wasn't his wife.

*Geraldine gasps in horror.*

GERALDINE: Who was it?

ALICE: His mother.

GERALDINE: So, sod all gossip if we're honest.

*She flings the notepad down in disgust at this lack of scandal.*

ALICE: The recipe page is always my favourite. I mean, surely you've got something there?

GERALDINE: (*holding up a piece of paper*) Well, funny you should say that, actually – this is our most exciting item so far. An anonymous person's donated their recipe for chocolate pudding. It's a little bit idiosyncratic.

ALICE: Anonymous . . . What, you say they didn't give their name?

GERALDINE: No, no.

ALICE: So, it could be someone in this room, or . . .

GERALDINE:  Well, no. Not unless it's you, or me. (*She pauses.*) It's you, isn't it?

*Alice smiles, pleased with herself. Geraldine is very disappointed*

GERALDINE:  I should have guessed when it said 'With chocolate pudding, you can never have enough haddock.'

ALICE:  Oh dear. Well I'll let you get on.

GERALDINE:  No, I doubt that very much.

ALICE:  Actually . . .

GERALDINE:  There we go.

ALICE:  There is just one tiny thing.

GERALDINE:  (*resigned*) Is there?

ALICE:  Do you think that I'm unattractive, and will never be kissed by any man, and die without ever knowing the joy of true love?

*Geraldine stops typing at this outburst and shows Alice some sympathy.*

GERALDINE:  Oh no. Don't tell me that Hugo hasn't even kissed you yet?

*Alice starts crying.*

ALICE:  I just don't think that he loves me.

GERALDINE:  Oh that's nonsense. It's just you've got to give these things time, that's all. How long have you known him?

ALICE:  Um . . . twenty-six years.

GERALDINE:  Right. Well, the fact is, he *does love you*, so maybe you've just got to tell him exactly how you feel.

ALICE:  Oh, I feel like I, like I want to marry him and have fifteen children in a fortnight!

GERALDINE:  Right. Well, maybe not *exactly* how you feel then.

ALICE:  It's just so hard. I mean, how did you tell your boyfriends that you loved them?

GERALDINE:  Well, I usually stuck their hands down my blouse. But I don't think that's going to work for you and Hugo. No, you need a cupid that's not stupid and that cupid is me. Right, plan of action. You, virgin, go home and come back here after lunch looking really nice, okay?

ALICE: Why?

GERALDINE: No, no questions. One little hint though, no garlic for lunch. And perhaps you could remove those little bits of biscuit in the corner of your mouth. Go on, shoo!

*Geraldine picks up the phone and starts dialling. Alice turns to her, all excited now, and rubs her arm in gratitude.*

ALICE: This is great! I haven't been so excited since I got the card saying I'd won that beauty contest, do you remember?

GERALDINE: We were playing Monopoly at the time, weren't we?

ALICE: That's right. I was so proud.

GERALDINE: Ye-es. Off you go then, sad little lunatic. (*Alice leaves and Geraldine starts speaking on the phone.*) Hugo, it's Geraldine here. I'm inviting you over to my house about two o'clock this afternoon. And for God's sake, try to look sexually attractive, would you? All right. Bye-bye. Sorted.

## Scene Three: Geraldine's Hallway/Living Room

*The doorbell rings. Geraldine opens the door and there is Hugo, wearing a pair of extremely bright patterned trousers.*

GERALDINE: Hugo. Come on in, lovely to see you. Oh, lovely trousers! Oh, *bon pantalons!*

HUGO: Yes, you said sexy. I've brought you something for the newsletter.

GERALDINE: Oh great.

HUGO: It's an advert.

GERALDINE: (*reads*) 'Sock for sale. Bottle green. Would suit person with similar sock.' Well that's very exciting isn't it? You go on in and sit down.

*Hugo goes into the sitting room. Geraldine follows, screwing up the sock advert and throwing it away.*

Now Hugo, you're probably wondering why I've asked you to come here today.

HUGO: Well, actually, no. I think I've worked it out.

GERALDINE: Oh really?

HUGO: Yeah. You know the film *The League of Gentlemen*, where they gather together the seven master criminals of the world? Each of them skilled in their own particular trade. Master of disguise, master lock breaker, explosives expert, etcetera. All assembled in order to pull off the greatest robbery of all time.

GERALDINE: Mmm. *Vaguely* remember it, yes.

HUGO: Well, I assume it's that. Am I right?

GERALDINE: Er no. Right, moving on. I'm going to come to the point straight away. Hugo, do you love Alice?

HUGO: *(completely flustered by this directness)* Oh, um, well. I never really . . .

GERALDINE: *(firmly)* The answer is 'yes', Hugo.

HUGO: *(quietly)* That's right. I absolutely adore her.

GERALDINE: And you're going to lose that girl if you don't kiss her soon. And that would be a tragedy, wouldn't it?

HUGO: Yes, because I love her like Romeo loved Juliet.

GERALDINE: Good.

HUGO: Like Richard loves Judy.

GERALDINE: That's *less* good. Will you promise me that the next time you see Alice you'll give her a great big kiss?

HUGO: Okay, I promise.

GERALDINE: Good.

*The doorbell rings.*

Oh! Ooh! I wonder who that could be?

*She goes to the door and comes back with Alice, wearing a very girly dress.*

Oh! Look who we have here!

# Engagement

ALICE:  Hello, Hugo.

HUGO:  Hello, Alice.

GERALDINE:  I'll just go and make some tea then, shall I? Hugo, I believe there's something you have to do?

*She goes into the kitchen and leaves Hugo and Alice together in the living room. She is very pleased with herself.*

Oh this is easy. I should take this up for a living. All you have to do is create the right social situation and love will flower like a flower, flowering in the right social situation. Two lovely young people, their tender lips meeting for the first time. In a whirlwind of passion that is, in fact, true love.

*Going back through to the living room, she finds Hugo and Alice still standing there awkwardly. She shouts.*

Oh for heaven's sakes just kiss, you morons! I'm so sorry. Did I say that out loud? What I actually meant to say was, 'Please don't worry, it's perfectly simple and you're going to enjoy it.' All you have to do is close your eyes and go forward.

*Alice and Hugo close their eyes and stumble towards each other. Not quite on target.*

Then open your eyes again, look where you're going, that's right, and go forward. (*Geraldine guides them towards each other.*) Docking procedure almost complete. And then . . .

HUGO:  Can't we just shake hands?

ALICE:  Yeah, yeah, I love shaking hands. It's an excellent way of communicating affection without getting wet.

GERALDINE:  (*desperate now*) Just do it!

HUGO:  Right, right. Good luck, Alice.

ALICE:  Good luck, Hugo.

*Their lips meet and they kiss. And don't stop ...*

GERALDINE: Yes! Houston, we have kiss-off. Oh lovely, oh well done, you two, that's excellent. Actually you can stop now, Hugo, if you want. Hey, why should you stop? Nothing like a nice long kiss is there? Other than an even longer kiss obviously. Alice, you can sort of stop. No, look, okay, here's what's going to happen. Er, you carry on kissing, okay? I'm just going to get on with my work. Don't mind me at all. I'll just sit here, no, look, I'm going to pop out. Be back in a while.

## Scene Four: Outside the Vicarage

GERALDINE: Oh, Owen, you wouldn't give me a hand with this shopping would you?

OWEN: What's in it for me?

GERALDINE: Um, eternal salvation.

OWEN: Anything more, you know, un-nebulous.

GERALDINE: Chocolate Hob-Nob?

OWEN: Let's do it!

## Scene Five: Geraldine's Living Room

*They enter the hallway, bearing shopping.*

GERALDINE: Oh, thanks, Owen. Just bung those in the kitchen for me if you would.

OWEN: Right-oh.

*Owen chucks the bags casually into the kitchen. There is a loud breaking sound.*

GERALDINE: Yes, thanks. Now. What did you want to see me about?

OWEN: I want to put an advert in the newsletter.

GERALDINE: Oh hurray!

OWEN: I've got a four hundred piece jigsaw for sale.

GERALDINE: Oh, good for you. We really need stuff.

OWEN: It was five hundred and fifty pieces but one of the dogs got to it.

GERALDINE: Right. And how much are thinking of charging for it?

OWEN: I thought about a hundred quid. They're £4.99 new but mine's unique now, so I think it's a bit of a collector's item.

GERALDINE: Yes indeed, and the next collection is on Thursday morning in a big truck! (*She laughs sardonically at her own joke. Owen is unamused.*) I'll just type this up then.

*Owen catches sight of Alice and Hugo, actually still there, still kissing.*

OWEN: What's this then?

GERALDINE: Oh, that's Hugo and Alice. They've been at it for four and a half hours now. Provided quite a talking point in my confirmation class, I can tell you. So what have we got? One jigsaw for sale, partially eaten. What's the puzzle of?

OWEN: Er, it's a woman with no clothes on. But it's very tasteful.

GERALDINE: What, a painting of some sort: Reubens, Renoir?

OWEN: No, it's a Page Three Girl, but the labrador's eaten her knockers.

*Alice and Hugo suddenly break apart.*

GERALDINE: Right. Oh, they're back! Welcome home! How was it then?

*Alice's lips have gone numb from all this kissing action. When she speaks it is with difficulty.*

ALICE: Fantastic.

GERALDINE: In English, Hugo?

HUGO: (*also unintelligible, but enthusiastic*) It was really . . .

GERALDINE: Right, they're speaking in tongues. Cup of tea?

ALICE: Oh no thank you, Vicar. I used to love having tea with you, but now I've realized in comparison to some things it's a total and utter yawn-making bore of bores. Come on, big boy.

*She drags Hugo off.*

HUGO: Bye.

GERALDINE: Oh, well, the joy of those first kisses, eh, Owen?

OWEN: Well, I wouldn't know, I've never had a proper kiss.

GERALDINE: Oh, haven't you?

OWEN: Except for Daisy and she was a cow, so that doesn't really count does it?

GERALDINE: What, you *kissed* one of your cows?

OWEN: No, the gamekeeper's daughter. Right cow she was. She said if I gave her all my pocket money she'd let me feel inside her bra.

GERALDINE: What, and then she didn't let you?

OWEN: No she did, problem was she wasn't wearing it at the time.

GERALDINE: Oh dear.

OWEN: Some folks' lives – they're full of love and softness. Other folks they never get to know the sweet tenderness of human contact. 'The sun is out, the sky is blue, there's not a cloud to spoil the view, but it's raining, it's raining in my heart.'

GERALDINE: Oh, go on then you great big loser, give us a quick kiss.

OWEN: Really?

GERALDINE: Yes, but no burping though.

OWEN: Okay. Here goes.

*They lean in and kiss each other. It lasts longer than it should. Geraldine bangs Owen on the back and he releases her. He is very very satisfied.*

Aah! Sizzle my sausage! Can I have another?

*He advances towards her again.*

GERALDINE: No! No! No! Oh God, what's this?

*She picks something out of her mouth.*

OWEN: Oh great! I got that bit of pork stuck in my tooth last week. I thought I'd never get it out. Thanks for that! I'll see myself out.

GERALDINE: Oh no, he's got one of my fillings.

## Scene Six: A Lane in Dibley

*Alice and Geraldine are walking together.*

ALICE: I reckon he'll come on a Saturday. 'Cos there's less traffic then. What do you think?

GERALDINE: Look, Alice, I don't know exactly when Jesus will come, okay?

ALICE: He'll probably get a bus from High Wycombe I would imagine.

GERALDINE: Morning, Hugo.

*She carries on walking and then realizes that Alice is no longer next to her. She is snogging Hugo.*

Alice.

## Scene Seven: The Church Porch

FRANK: Tell me, Vicar, is Alice all right?

GERALDINE: Oh, she's absolutely fine. Please feel free to just step right over them.

*Alice and Hugo are lying on the ground kissing, in front of the church porch. Now they've discovered it, they just can't stop.*

## Scene Eight: David Horton's Sitting Room

*David is sitting alone, watching the television.*

TV REPORTER: A report from Birmingham University suggests that over fifty per cent of single people in Britain now talk to themselves as a way of combatting loneliness.

DAVID: *(talking to himself)* Ridiculous. How can they know that?

TV REPORTER: And over thirty per cent talk to their televisions.

DAVID: *(to the television)* Of course they don't!

*Hugo enters. David turns off the television.*

Ah, Hugo!

HUGO: *(looking shifty, and hovering in the doorway)* Evening, Father.

DAVID: What have you been up to?

HUGO: Oh . . . er, nothing. You wouldn't be interested.

DAVID: No, you're probably right. You've never done anything interesting up till now.

HUGO: Actually, I have been up to something. There's something I have to tell you, Father.

DAVID: Mmm?

HUGO: I've fallen in love, with the most beautiful and wonderful woman in the world.

DAVID: Jill Dando?

HUGO: No, Father. Even more beautiful than the wonderful Jill Dando.

DAVID: Well done you. Anything to get you away from that ridiculous Alice creature. She was ghastly, wasn't she? Less a human being than a genetically modified stick insect with the brain removed. So, what's this new bird called?

HUGO: (crushed) I don't know.

DAVID: Don't even know her name? Well! You rogue! Good on you, son.

HUGO: Actually, actually I do know her name, Father.

DAVID: Well splendid. Spit it out then.

HUGO: Her name is, well, the, the thing is, her name is Alice.

DAVID: You're joking?

HUGO: No, my girlfriend's name is Alice.

DAVID: What an incredible coincidence. Pestered for a decade by a cabbage-patch doll named Alice Brain Bypass and when you finally do find yourself a girlfriend she's also called Alice. What's her surname?

HUGO: Actually, Father, can we start the conversation again? Just, just ask me a simple question and I'll give you a simple answer. Just ask me who my girlfriend is.

DAVID: Very well, Hugo. Who is your girlfriend?

HUGO: Er, well . . .

DAVID: My daughter-in-law. The mother of my grandchildren. The mistress of this great house. The co-inheritor of every penny I've ever earned in my long and unhappy life. The woman who will cherish me in my old age, and tend to me in my waning years. The female vessel into which all my hopes and dreams are to be poured.

HUGO: Right . . .

## Scene Nine: Geraldine's Living Room

*Hugo has gone round to relay all this to Geraldine.*

GERALDINE: So what did he say?

HUGO: Well, I can't tell you what he *actually* said because, because you're the vicar. Well, let's say a certain word is represented by another word that, that sounds a little like that word, like um, 'duck' for instance. He asked me what the duck I was playing at. He said he didn't give a flying duck if I ducking loved Alice ducking Tinker and if I ducking kissed her again, he'd make sure that I was well and truly ducked.

GERALDINE: Oh – duck me.

HUGO: I don't know what to do. I love Alice with all my heart, but I also love my dad.

GERALDINE: Of course.

*The doorbell rings.*

HUGO: (*solemnly*) If – if that's Alice I'd better not see her. I have a big decision to make and her radiant beauty and subtle seductive charms may cloud my mind as I grope towards an answer that is both right and true.

*Alice enters and growls at Hugo.*

HUGO: Oh dollocks.

ALICE: Come here, Mr Moist.

*He ignores her.*

HUGO: Well, I'd better be going. Bye everyone.

ALICE: Oh my God, I knew this was going to happen. He doesn't love me any more! He's sucked out all my juice and discarded me like an empty carton of Ribena.

GERALDINE:  No, poppet, it's not like that at all. The truth is that he's . . . he's sprained his tongue and the doctor says he's got to give it complete rest for a few days. You see?

ALICE:  Oh, that's all right then.

GERALDINE:  Yes! So you keep away from him, Miss Lusty Lips.

ALICE:  I'll try. Oh let's have some tea.

GERALDINE:  Yes, and I can get on with this newsletter. Things aren't getting any better. At the moment the headline is 'Dibley Voted Village of the Year'.

ALICE:  Well, that's pretty exciting!

GERALDINE:  No, let me finish. 'In a Dream I Had Last Thursday'.

*The doorbell rings. Alice goes to the kitchen. Geraldine opens the door to Owen.*

Owen, how are you?

OWEN:  I think this is your filling.

GERALDINE:  Oh, thank you.

OWEN:  I would have brought it sooner but I've only just passed it.

GERALDINE:  (*absolutely horrified*) I, err . . . I won't be putting it back in right now then. Is that all?

OWEN:  No! It's that kiss! Ever since that kiss I've been feeling all churned up!

GERALDINE:  Yeah my tummy's been feeling a bit dodgy too.

OWEN:  And I decided I need a woman. Only I don't want to pay for it. And I reckon the only way to get a woman is to marry one. So I was wondering, how about it?

*Geraldine laughs hysterically for several seconds. Then stops abruptly.*

GERALDINE:  Oh, sorry Owen. Sorry, for one insane moment there I thought you were proposing to me.

*She chuckles again. Owen, meanwhile, drops to his knee.*

OWEN: I am.

GERALDINE: (*suddenly serious*) Right, yes, I see.

OWEN: I know I'm not much of a catch, but then you're not getting any younger yourself.

GERALDINE: Thank you.

OWEN: And although I'm not rich I have got a bit of money, not to mention what I might get for that jigsaw. Also, I've been told that old stamps that have got something wrong with them are very rare, so I thought I might sell this one. You see that flaw?

GERALDINE: Er, yes, you've drawn a moustache on the Queen's face.

OWEN: I'm not stupid. And I wouldn't expect you to do a lot around the farm. Except, of course, when the cows get the squits. In which case they produce it quicker than I can clear it, and it's all hands to the mops.

GERALDINE: That's a lovely image.

OWEN: And I'm pretty confident I could satisfy you in the bedroom because, quite frankly, I'm so desperate for it that I could keep going for months on end.

GERALDINE: Yep. This is romantic stuff.

OWEN: I don't expect you to give me an answer now. I know you women like to think about things when it comes to romance. You're different from us men, you've got smaller brains.

GERALDINE: Well, now I feel *very special*.

OWEN: So I'll come back later and you can say 'yes' then and make me the happiest man in the world. Well, apart from Kris Akabusi, that is – he's always happy. You've only got to say 'hello' and he's laughing. But I'll be pretty damn happy I can tell you. So, see you later then, Mrs Newitt, my little love bucket.

*Alice comes back into the living room . . .*

ALICE: What did Owen want?

GERALDINE: (*in a complete state of shock*) He's asked me to be his wife.

ALICE: That is brilliant! I'm so happy for you! And you're the vicar! You can do your own wedding service! 'Geraldine, do you take this man to be your lawful wedded husband?' 'I do.' 'Owen . . .'

GERALDINE: Shut up! Shut up, Alice! I don't want to marry Owen.

ALICE: Why? What's wrong with him?

GERALDINE: How long have you got? His breath smells like nerve gas. That gel he puts on his hair, that is *actually lard*! If I was looking for charm and good conversation I'd sooner marry a courgette! Other than that I'm sure he's gorgeous. It's just, I don't love him.

ALICE: Oh poor you, you're going to marry somebody you don't love. That's terrible, Geraldine, don't do it, please don't do it!

GERALDINE: No, no, no, no, no. I'm not going to do it. That's the point, you see. Next time I see him I'm just going to have to be very honest and just say that I can't marry him.

*The doorbell rings.*

ALICE: *(jumping up dramatically)* Oh, God, that's him! That's him!

GERALDINE: Right, answer the door, Alice. It's just a question of being mature and grown up and adult and mature.

*It is not Owen . . . it is Frank and Jim.*

ALICE: Oh hello. Come on in! The vicar's in the living room.

GERALDINE: So, Frank, Jim, how can I help you?

JIM: We want to put a notice in the Parish Newsletter.

GERALDINE: Oh, thank goodness!

JIM: See if you can spot my little joke.

GERALDINE: Right. 'Want to have a go at bell ringing? Then come along to St Barnabus and let us show you the ropes.'

JIM: 'Show you the ropes.' Get it? It's very funny because it's 'show you the ropes', as in the actual ropes that ring the bells . . .

GERALDINE: I know, I know.

JIM: And it is also, 'show you the ropes' as in 'teach you the ropes of bell ringing'. Show you the ropes.

GERALDINE: Yes, I promise you I do understand.

ALICE: I – I don't get it.

JIM: Ah, well, you see . . .

GERALDINE: *(shouting)* No, no, no! *(She calms herself down.)* Actually, there is something you two could help me with, if you'd like to just sit down. Now, you're going to think this is completely crazy and totally ghastly, but Owen 'I've had my hand up more cows' botties than James Herriot' Newitt has asked *moi*, sophisticated, *glamorous* vicar of this parish to be his wife!

*She laughs, as if such an idea is clearly ridiculous.*

FRANK: Well done, Vicar. Off the shelf at last!

GERALDINE: No, no, you don't understand! I'm going to turn him down.

FRANK: Did you hear that?

GERALDINE: And you chaps know him much better than me, and I don't want to hurt his feelings. I need some reassurance that he won't be too upset. Yes or no?

JIM: No, no, no, no, no, no, no. No, no, no.

GERALDINE: Good.

JIM: You see he's known so much sorrow and tragedy, a bit more won't hurt him.

GERALDINE: Sorrow and tragedy?

FRANK: Yes, you know his brother drowned himself?

GERALDINE: Oh no, I didn't know that.

JIM: Yes, it was all over some nonsense with a girl. She wouldn't marry him, so he chucked himself in the river.

FRANK: But Owen's quite different. Owen takes after his father. And he was a much more cheerful chap.

JIM: Until he shot himself. But of course he had good reason to shoot himself because his wife had just left him. Yes, and he'd already lost both his parents because, you see, when his mother tried to leave, his father shot her.

GERALDINE: Yes, well. Thanks very much guys.

FRANK: Oh not at all, Vicar. Come along, Jim.

GERALDINE: I think I'll just top myself now and save Owen the bother.

*Jim has one more go at his joke before he leaves.*

JIM: 'Show you the ropes!'

GERALDINE: Oh, Alice, what am I going to do?

ALICE: Well, I have got one thought. When my mum's got like a really difficult problem to deal with, like, um, oh I don't know, like choosing her lottery numbers, she always has a little drink before hand – you know – just to calm her nerves.

GERALDINE: Er, no, I don't think so.

ALICE: Oh.

GERALDINE: Think I can deal with this problem without having to drink myself into a stupid Tinker stupor. Actually, being a priest does sort of equip you for dealing with this kind of complex human dilemma.

ALICE: Oh good. Well, I'd better be off home because it's Rollover Week and mum's probably unconscious by now. Bye.

*She leaves. Geraldine deliberates for a good thirty seconds over whether or not to have a whisky. It gets the better of her and she has a huge swig.*

GERALDINE: Oh yes, now I'm thinking clearly. Um, 'Owen, I would love to marry you but I'm already married. To Gordon Brown, the Chancellor of the Exchequer.' No, he'll never buy that. (*She takes a second swig.*) 'Owen, I would love to marry you, but I'm not the woman for you. In fact I'm not a woman at all. I'm one of the lobster people from planet Neptune.'

*The doorbell rings. It is time to give him an answer.*

Owen.

*He is dressed in his best clothes, his hair slicked down like a schoolboy. This is clearly a momentous occasion for him.*

OWEN: I've come for your answer.

GERALDINE: Owen, I would love to marry you . . .

*Owen grabs her. He is overjoyed and celebrates by giving her a huge snog.*

OWEN: Oh, thank you! I'll go and get the condom.

GERALDINE: No, Owen, I haven't finished. Owen, I haven't got to the 'but' bit. Owen, I would love to marry you BUT – I can't.

OWEN: Oh why?

GERALDINE: Because I don't love you. You're a good man Owen and

I'm sure there's a very suitable woman out there somewhere for you. Somewhere, a nice insatiable woman with no sense of smell. But that woman isn't me. Promise me you're not too upset, eh?

OWEN: Well, I don't know exactly how upset I am.

GERALDINE: But not so upset that you'd go and commit suicide or anything like that?

OWEN: Well, I haven't decided. But before I do, you've got to answer me one question.

GERALDINE: Oh, anything.

OWEN: Right. Have you been drinking?

GERALDINE: Ahm . . . Have had one little dropsicule, yes.

OWEN: Because if there's one thing I can't stand it's a woman who drinks. So the answer to your question is 'no'. I'm not in the slightest bit upset at all. In fact, I'm very grateful to you for saving me from marriage to a disgusting old lush who smells of gin from dusk till dawn. Madam, I bid you farewell, you revolting old soak.

*He leaves.*

GERALDINE: That is one helluva charming dude.

## Scene Ten: David Horton's Sitting Room

*Geraldine has gone round to see David.*

DAVID: Whisky?

GERALDINE: No thanks, I don't actually.

DAVID: How's the newsletter coming on? Today's the final day, isn't it?

GERALDINE: Er, yes. It's not our *best* issue.

DAVID: What's the lead story?

GERALDINE: Well, at the moment I'm torn between 'Almost Time to Plant Radishes' and 'Lost Cat Not Lost'.

DAVID: Well, be that as it may, the reason I asked you round today was because I need your help with a project I'm working on. Can you tell me: is Kylie Minogue married?

GERALDINE: Er, no. I think the beauteous midget is still unattached. Why, thinking she's the right woman for you, eh David?

*She cackles with laughter. He's not amused.*

DAVID: No, not me. Hugo. You see, I've drawn up a list of all the women he fancies. One of them is bound to want him. According to Debrett's he's the 108th most eligible bachelor in this country. Look, there he is, under Dale Winton.

GERALDINE: Oh, an interesting place to be. Let's have a look at that list. Posh Spice, Kate Moss, Anne Widdecombe . . . Hugo fancies Anne Widdecombe?

DAVID: Well, he liked the way she took on Michael Howard.

GERALDINE: You've even got *me* on this list!

DAVID: You think I'm being a bit silly about all this, don't you? I just can't *bear* the thought of that Alice thing in my family.

GERALDINE: David, I *completely* understand. Alice does indeed have all the intellectual capacity and charisma of a cactus. Alice is Cactus Woman. But the trouble is – and it pains me to tell you this, David – you are the father of Cactus Man. And these simple succulents were made for each other. Actually, as cacti go, I think they're rather wonderful together.

DAVID: Well, then it will have to happen over my dead body. Look, this is my new will, leaving Hugo nothing. (*At that point, Hugo enters.*) Ah, Hugo! Just in time. I was just showing the vicar my new will.

HUGO: Oh, come on, Papa, you're not that angry. It's just some great big bluff.

DAVID: I can assure you that it isn't.

HUGO: It's like that time you tried to convince me you were Father Christmas. I saw through that and I can see through this, too.

DAVID: Then you see wrong! If you continue to consort with that Tinker twerp you will no longer be welcome in this house. You will no longer be my son and as this will attests, you will have nothing.

HUGO: (*standing up for himself for the FIRST TIME EVER*) On the contrary, sir, I will have everything in the world that I desire.

### Scene Eleven: The Parish Hall

*The next day. Hugo and Alice are there, alone.*

HUGO: Hi.

ALICE: Hi!

HUGO: I'm sorry I couldn't see you yesterday. I had to sort something out with my father.

ALICE: Oh. Plumbing?

HUGO: No, no I was talking to him about you actually. And now that's sorted the time has come to er . . .

*He offers Alice a chair and then drops to his knees.*

ALICE: Oh, have you dropped something, where is it?

HUGO: No, no I have to be on my knees, that's all.

ALICE: Oh, shall I come too? It looks fun down there.

HUGO: No, you have to be sitting. Alice, in the words of Sigourney Weaver in the film *Aliens*, I just want to say . . .

*Alice knows this film. The words come tumbling out . . .*

ALICE: 'Get away from her, you bitch.'

HUGO: No, no. Earlier, to the little girl.

ALICE: Oh. 'You stay in the ventilation shaft and I'll check the corridor.'

HUGO: Just let me finish.

ALICE: Yes, sorry.

HUGO: Alice, in the words of Sigourney Weaver in the film *Aliens*, I just want to say, 'I will never leave you. That's a promise.' I love you, Alice Tinker, and I have to know, will you do me the greatest honour in the world and consent to be my wife?

ALICE: No.

HUGO: But I thought that you . . .

ALICE: No, I mean, let me finish. No . . . question I've ever been asked has been easier to answer. Apart perhaps from when my mum asked me which of the Teletubbies I most liked. Because the answer was Tinky Winky, absolutely just like that, but even including that, to no question I've ever been asked has my answer been more certainly, and more positively . . .

HUGO: 'Yes.'

ALICE: That's right!

HUGO: Crackerjack!

*Geraldine arrives at that moment.*

GERALDINE: Well, what have we here?!

HUGO: She said 'yes'!

GERALDINE: Oh that's a relief, otherwise you'd have completely ruined my scoop.

*Geraldine shows Alice the front page of the newsletter.*

ALICE: Oh! 'Verger towed Hugo Horton.' Where to?

GERALDINE: No, no. 'Verger to wed Hugo Horton.' To wed Hugo Horton, see?

ALICE: Is that true, Hugo? Are you going to marry the verger?

*She starts to cry.*

GERALDINE: But you *are* the verger, Alice.

*It dawns on her.*

ALICE: Oh yes! Oh right. Oh yeah, nice.

GERALDINE: (*to Hugo*) Good luck.

## Epilogue: The Vestry

*Geraldine and Alice are having a soothing cup of camomile tea.*

**GERALDINE:** What do you get if you eat too many Christmas decorations?

**ALICE:** I don't know. What do you get if you eat too many Christmas decorations?

**GERALDINE:** *Tinselitis.*

**ALICE:** Oh dear, I'd better be careful.

**GERALDINE:** What about?

**ALICE:** Well, eating Christmas decorations. I'd no idea it was bad for you.

**GERALDINE:** What?

**ALICE:** You get tinselitis.

**GERALDINE:** Yes. Which is a made-up disease!

**ALICE:** Oh. That's all very well for you to say that, say it's all in the mind, but for people who have tinselitis it's painfully real.

**GERALDINE:** Now stop right there, Alice.

**ALICE:** Of course they shouldn't eat the Christmas decorations in the first place, but once they have wolfed down a couple of Santas, society shouldn't go on punishing them.

**GERALDINE:** Are you interested in being alive on New Year's Day?

**ALICE:** No, I can't bear to think about it actually. Always happens at Christmas, everyone else is happy . . .

**GERALDINE:** Oh God.

# COUNTRY
# DIARY
## OF A DIBLEY LADY

~ MAY 1906 ~

"May is come and birds sing their tune
May starts after April but stops before June"
                                    Byron.*

May 1st: A joyous
spring morning. found a
glade of delightful Hollyhocks,
and picked a few to adorn
the evening table. Such
delicacy, such scent!

Wild Hyacinth
(Lychnis
   Diurna)

May 2nd: Did more
paintings of flowers.
Ho hum.

Some sort
of flowers,
I don't
know they're
all the
same.

May 3rd: More flower stuff.
Do sometimes wish life could
be more exciting. Began
to think — if I had a young
man to spoon, would I need
to spend so much time hanging
round sketching daffodils?!
To control such wicked thoughts,
went to the churchyard to
sketch our delightful
St Barnabus.. found some
most unusual purple mushrooms.
Will take them home to
bake myself and my mother
a delicious tart.

* Darren Byron, of 3 PigLane

Dibley Church

May 4th. A most unusual day. Went back to the churchyard to paint once more, taking only the mushroom tart for victuals. After a short while, an eagle with the head of a dog started talking to me. Then my head expanded to the size of the world and I found I could taste sunbeams.

    Somewhere round tea I think I shagged the young vicar. In the evening, returned home, where I found mother very dead.

Dibley Ch
after I ate
the mushr

May 5th. The roses are looking splendid today....

### The Very Badly Drawn Horse of Dinton

Believed to have been created by the same tribe who made 'The Man No It Really Is a Man, Look That's His Nob' of Devizes and 'The Odd-Looking Cow with Six Legs and a Nob' of Haddenham.

### The Great Britney Spears of Bishopstone

No one knows how it got there or why, just like the real Britney Spears.

### The Noughts and Crosses Game of Terrick

This 200-foot high, incomplete parlour game is believed to have been started circa 600 B.C., and was gradually added to over 1000 years. It is thought that it was the turn of noughts when the Vikings invaded.

# Figures of the Area

### The Extremely Small Man of Dunsmore

Made by a very unambitious local tribe, this figure measures six centimetres from head to foot. He is frequently obscured by a dropped crisp packet.

### The Green Hill of Wantage

No soil has been removed from this hill, so no white figure is visible at all. The observer is drawn into the work, and imagines the countless potential shapes which exist in the hidden chalk. The observer is forced to question their preconceptions about what constitutes art.

The Green Hill of Wantage is proof that artists could be contrary and annoying even 3000 years ago.

117 Rue De Siecle
Paris

Dear Jim

I am thanking you for your letter and for telling me so m
about your exciting life in Dibbley. I am so pleased to h
a pen pal in Britain and I hope we can be the most best frie
I was very happy to get your colour photograph. You're right, y
do look just like Tom Cruise. And what a coincidence you were
ning next to his wife Nicole Kidman when the picture was take

I was interested to read about your life. Being a fighter
pilot must be fun. I am sad to hear of your split from Naomi Ca
It must be very hard telling her to leave uour penthouse suite o
Woodberry Close.

Dibley sounds like a très mode place to live and much mo
fun than boring Paris. I have never played skittles before bu
sounds like the best game in the world. And I cannot wait to see
car boot sale. It sounds, how do you say, so sexy.

It was nice of you to invite me to stay. Are you sure you
have room for my four girlfriends? Of course we would be more than
happy to help uou with your scientific research. Unfortunatel
I am not sure we will be able to do all those things you suggeste
because I cannot find the words in my dictionary

Please write back soon. Your dear French friend,

Isabelle

xxxx xxxx xxxx x

P.S. I have asked all my girlfriends to send you their unwash
underwear so you can examine it for tiny listening devices. I
must be so exciting working for the British Secret Service. xx

**ALICE:** . . . and there in the loneliness of their bedrooms, with little bits of bauble and angel sticking out of their mouths . . .

**GERALDINE:** Mercy, mercy, mercy.

**ALICE:** The forgotten millions. The victims of tinselitis. Or TI as we call it.

*Alice has worked herself up – she starts crying for the victims.*

**GERALDINE:** I'm beginning to think that Herod had the right idea. Kill 'em when they're young. It's the kindest thing to do.

# Miss Dibley

THE FINALISTS FOR THIS YEAR'S MISS DIBLEY COMPETITION ARE AS FOLLOWS:

### *Alice Horton (28)*

**HOBBIES:**
Sellotape, bouncy castles, collecting novelty pencil sharpeners, sharpening pencils with novelty pencil sharpeners.

**AMBITIONS:**
To win the Nobel Peace Prize, go flying in the Starship Enterprise, get a blue Pokémon pencil sharpener.

**I WOULD LIKE TO BE MISS DIBLEY BECAUSE:**
I would get to travel, and model some of the sexiest anoraks in the world.

### *Suzanne Milligan (5¹/₂)*

**HOBBIES:**
Running, playing, swimming, skipping.

**AMBITIONS:**
Go to Disneyland, get a blue Pokémon pencil sharpener.

**I WOULD LIKE TO BE MISS DIBLEY BECAUSE:**
My Mum has spent £300 on my dress and make-up.

### *Edith Evans (83)*

**HOBBIES:**
Same as last year

**AMBITIONS:**
Same as last year

**I WOULD LIKE TO BE MISS DIBLEY BECAUSE:**
I have been entering this contest for 63 years and I'm bound to win if I keep trying.

### *Jim Trott (61)*

**HOBBIES:**
Car boot sales, the pub, Thai women.

**AMBITIONS:**
To meet a Thai woman at the pub car boot sale.

**I WOULD LIKE TO BE MISS DIBLEY BECAUSE:**
I want to be exploited for my good looks, and no no no no no no yes, I want to marry a racing driver.

Parish Council Minutes : 16/02/98

Present : Rev. Granger, David Horton, Hugo Horton, Jim Trott, Owen Newitt,
Frank Pickle

7.06   Mr D. Horton states "We should start soon, we're half an hour
late, we really should get going."

7.08   Biscuits and Mr H. Horton arrive.

7.09   Rev. Granger takes a Bourbon.

7.10   Mr Trott takes a pink wafer.

7.11   Rev. Granger's hand hovers over Jammy Dodgers.
Rev. Granger takes shortcake instead. Hugo goes for Dodgers.

7.12   Mr D. Horton states "You really don't have to write down that sort
of stuff. Just write down the important things. Which I hope we shall
be getting to quite soon."

7.13   Mr D. Horton states "You also didn't have to write down what I just
said about not writing down the stuff about the biscuits."

7.14   Mr D. Horton states "And you didn't have to write THAT down either.
Oh God, we're stuck in a never-ending loop. I'll die here, I know I will.
Unless I do something I'm going to perish in this very spot."

7.15   I am now taking these minutes with my left hand, as Mr D. Horton
has damaged my right hand with the edge of the biscuit tin while
shouting "stop it, stop it, I shall go mad."

7.16   Rev. Granger uses this diversion to conceal the last Jammy Dodger up
her sleeve. Mr H. Horton states "I saw that Vicar - now come on - be
fair - one piece of shortcake is worth at least two pink wafers,
and the Jammy Dodger's got my name on it. Come on, come on -
coochi-coo - come to Daddy."

7.17   I am now writing this with my teeth as Mr
D. Horton has broken both my hands with
the full weight of the entire biscuit tin. Rev.
Granger uses the diversion to eat the Jammy Dodger.

7.18   Item 1 on the agenda : Violence in
the village — an unsettling upsurge.
Mr D. Horton very concerned.

# DIBLEY LIVE

## Scene One: The Parish Hall

*A Council Meeting is in progress.*

DAVID: Moving on. I've received an entry form for the 'Best Kept Village' competition. Any thoughts?

OWEN: Yes. Tear it up.

DAVID: I beg your pardon?

OWEN: Months of effort, and what will we win? Some pointless poncy piece of paper saying 'Dibley: Best Kept Village'.

JIM: No, no, no, no! It's not just a piece of paper, it's a title! A trophy! It's a cheque for two hundred and forty thousand pounds, presented by the Duchess of Kent!

GERALDINE: No, that's Wimbledon, Jim.

JIM: Yes, that is Wimbledon.

GERALDINE: Actually, I agree with Owen on this, David. I think our feelings towards last year's competition are *very* similar to Prince Andrew's feelings towards Fergie. You know, something we wish we'd never entered.

DAVID: Oh come on! We did all right.

GERALDINE: We came fifty-fourth out of fifty-four!

DAVID: Is that right?

GERALDINE: Remember Denfield?

DAVID: Well, how could one forget those poor people?

HUGO: Yes, who'd have believed a lorry load of BSE-infected toxic waste would have crashed into a nuclear fuel tanker, causing a crater two hundred feet wide and the evacuation of the entire village.

GERALDINE: And they came fifty-third.

DAVID: Point taken, let's forget it. Item five. Frank, you wanted to say something?

FRANK: Yes, I do. (*There is a long pause.*) No, I don't.

DAVID: Gripping stuff. Vicar?

GERALDINE: Yes. Next month, St Barnabus will be six hundred and fifty years old. Exactly the same age as Esther Rantzen. And to celebrate I've got a licence for one week to set up our very own local radio station.

HUGO: Oh, I say, bravo, Mrs God.

GERALDINE: Yeah, I thought it was a chance, you know, to drag people away from the television for a week.

JIM: Sex, sex, sex. That's all you get on television these days.

GERALDINE: Is it?

JIM: It is on mine. I watch the Playboy channel.

DAVID: I think I'm losing the will to live.

GERALDINE: Well, I'll give you all a week to think up programming ideas, okay? But I warn you, I'm streets ahead. Listen to this. (*She starts to rap.*) 'Nothing could be hotter, nothing could be slicker. Lock up your son and dotter, cos here comes the vicar.'

*Everyone looks very unimpressed at this outburst. Geraldine is chastened.*

It's a work in progress obviously.

## Scene Two: Geraldine's Living Room

*Geraldine is at her desk writing. Alice is visiting.*

ALICE: Very exciting news about Radio Dibley.

GERALDINE: Yes, it is, isn't it?

ALICE: I'm thinking of being a shock jock. 'Hello everyone this is bloody well Radio Dibley.'

GERALDINE: Can you just give me a minute, Alice? I've got to finish off this crucial sentence here.

ALICE: Oh, I love your sermons.

GERALDINE: Thanks.

ALICE: They're so clever and holy. Let's have a peek.

*She looks over Geraldine's shoulder.*

GERALDINE: (*trying to stop her from seeing*) No, no! No, no, no . . .

*Alice snatches the paper from Geraldine's hand.*

ALICE: (*reading*) 'I love chocolate because . . .'

GERALDINE: Well, look, the only reason I'm doing that is because, apparently, the runner up gets a year's free supply which she would share with her parishioners. Obviously. I've got to finish this sentence in under ten words.

ALICE: Oh, that's easy. Yeah! I've got it!

GERALDINE: Have you?

ALICE: Yeah, yeah. 'I love chocolate because it's very, very, very nice.'

GERALDINE: Yeah, I was working on something a little bit *less* predictable than that.

ALICE: Less predictable. Okay I've got it. 'It's very, very, very nice . . . with sausages.'

*She smiles, very pleased with herself.*

GERALDINE: That's perfect, isn't it?

ALICE: Yeah, that's it. That's the one.

GERALDINE: Yes. Do you mind if I write it in later? Okay. So tell me. How are things going with Hugo, you juicy young bride-to-be, you?

ALICE: They're lovely. But a big gloomy about his dad, though. He thinks I've got the intellectual capacity of a prawn sandwich.

GERALDINE: When did he say that?

ALICE: Oh, just after he said that my only value in life was as an organ donor.

GERALDINE: Right.

ALICE: If only I could find a way to show him that, you know, beneath this quite simple exterior lies the razor-sharp intellect of an Andrew Einstein.

GERALDINE: Albert.

ALICE: Albert Einstein.

## Scene Three: The Parish Hall

*A week later, the Council Meeting is in progress.*

DAVID: Item three, Vicar.

GERALDINE: Yes, I thought everyone would like to see a copy of our radio schedule. Sorry about the ideas I didn't have room for. For instance, Frank, Desert Island Desks.

FRANK: Well, it would be just like Desert Island *Discs*, only I would choose the eight desks I've most enjoyed sitting at.

DAVID: So Frank won't be broadcasting at all. Splendid.

FRANK: Oh yes I will. I'm doing a talk show. An hour of Frank talking. That's me, you understand, not someone called Frank Talking, because, of course, that would be an hour of Frank Talking, talking.

GERALDINE: Yeah. Don't speak too soon, Frank. And the next night is 'The Moral Maze with Jim Trott'. What's your subject, Jim?

JIM: 'Is sex with poodles always wrong?'

GERALDINE: I see. And you've found someone to speak on both sides of that argument?

OWEN: *(confidently)* He certainly has.

HUGO: *(looking at the schedule)* Oh, oh, oh, this sounds good. 'David Horton in conversation'.

GERALDINE: Well, I thought it would give the week some gravitas, David.

HUGO: Councillor David Horton MBE talks about his distinguished life and work . . . in conversation with Alice Tinker.

DAVID: *What?*

GERALDINE: Well, she was desperate to be involved.

DAVID: Then nail her feet to the floor and use her as a mike stand. No offence to anyone present, but that girl really is the most pointless thing ever put on the planet. With the *possible* exception of the Pope's testicle department.

*Geraldine pats Hugo's arm sympathetically.*

GERALDINE: Aaah. Well, moving on, I thought we might finish the week with a bang and have the village quiz.

*Everyone groans.*

Oh, I know, I know. David has won it for the last few years . . .

DAVID: Last *twenty-seven* years.

GERALDINE: Yes, the last twenty-seven years, but I'm sure we can find him a worthy opponent.

JIM: Yes. I've learnt every single answer from last year's contest, so this year I can get them right!

GERALDINE: And what about if the questions are different, Jim?

JIM: Oh, sod it.

GERALDINE: Still, I'm sure some genius will emerge. And to add more excitement, I've decided to award a prize for best broadcaster of the week.

*This news is greeted with genuine excitement.*

HUGO: Oh, what's the prize?

GERALDINE: I think a book token is always . . . *(everyone groans in disappointment)* completely boring and unwelcome, isn't it, so it certainly won't be that. It'll be something *seriously sensational.*

*She looks very mysterious and winks.*

### Scene Four: Geraldine's Living Room

*Geraldine walks down the stairs carrying an old cardboard box. Alice is there with her.*

GERALDINE: It's perfectly simple. All I've got to do is find a prize that everybody in this village would die for in this box of total rubbish.

*She takes out a horrible troll doll with long fluffy hair. Alice snatches it off her, very pleased, and strokes it.*

ALICE: Sweet.

GERALDINE: Oh! Oh, this takes me back.

*She lifts out an old Black Sabbath LP.*

ALICE: Are they gospel singers?

GERALDINE: No. See your thinking, but no. A boy called Peter gave me this. Look: 'From Peter Rabbit to his Flopsy Bunny.'

ALICE: Oh! 'Thank you for letting me fill your burrow.'

GERALDINE: (*embarrassed*) Yeah.

ALICE: How sweet!

GERALDINE: Alice, I've got to have a little talk with you about your interview with Mr Horton.

ALICE: Oh yeah. I've been working really hard on some very probing questions.

*She produces a notebook and opens it.*

GERALDINE: Right. (*She reads.*) 'Councillor David Horton of Dibley, sir. If you could meet any character from fiction which Womble would it be?' That's fabulous, isn't it?

*The phone rings.*

Will you answer that, Alice? I've got to find something before the meeting.

ALICE: Hiya, this isn't the vicar speaking, so I can't help you at all. Oh, I see, yeah, yeah. I'll tell her, hold on. (*She turns to Geraldine.*) It's the people from that chocolate competition. You didn't win the chocolate.

GERALDINE: Oh, that's just my luck. I *knew* mentioning orgasms was a mistake.

ALICE: You won their first prize! A holiday to Disneyland Paris!

GERALDINE: Don't be stupid, Alice. (*She snatches the phone.*) Hello, Geraldine Granger here. (*She listens.*) I won their first prize! A holiday to Disneyland Paris!

ALICE: You haven't!

GERALDINE: I have! (*Into the phone.*) Thank you very much. (*She makes a thumbs-up sign to the picture of Jesus above her desk.*) Cheers mate.

## Scene Five: The Parish Hall

*A week later, another Council Meeting is in progress.*

DAVID: Right. Prize for the best broadcaster. Any luck, Vicar, or can we assume this idea's another defunct duck?

GERALDINE: Mmm probably, yeah. I mean all I've managed to get is two tickets for a luxury weekend in Disneyland Paris with five hundred pounds spending money. Thank you, thank you!

*There is complete amazement from all, except David.*

DAVID: (*grudgingly*) So we have a prize. Not bad. Hallelujah! Moving on. Item seven.

OWEN: (*getting up*) Oh, sod item seven, I'm going to practise my microphone technique.

JIM: (*also getting up*) Me too.

## Scene Six: Geraldine's Living Room

*It is kick-off time for Radio Dibley and everyone is present. A desk has been set up with all the necessary equipment.*

GERALDINE: Right, we've got one minute to go. Let me just check everybody knows what they're doing. Owen you're . . .

*Owen is wearing shades and trying to look cool.*

OWEN: The sound man, man.

GERALDINE: Right, and Alice, you're . . .?

ALICE: Alice.

GERALDINE: Doing what?

ALICE: I'm just kneeling here.

GERALDINE: Yes, you're manning the phones, aren't you Alice? And you two are?

FRANK AND JIM: (*in unison*) We're your posse.

GERALDINE: Yes. And what does it mean when that red light's on?

JIM: You're a prostitute.

GERALDINE: (*desperately*) We're on *air*!

*Owen panics and scrambles for the switches.*

OWEN: What? Bloody hell!

GERALDINE: What are you doing?

OWEN: You said we were on air.

GERALDINE: Not *now*!

OWEN: Sorry.

*Geraldine looks at the clock.*

GERALDINE: Three, two, one . . . Now!

*The red light comes on. Geraldine points at Owen for the jingles, but he doesn't notice her. She waves at him in desperation, silently trying to attract his attention.*

JIM: (*conversationally*) This is the first time I've noticed it. The vicar's got a very nice arse.

FRANK: Ssssh!

*Geraldine is trying to stay calm.*

GERALDINE: Hello, and welcome to Radio Dibley. I'm Geraldine Granger and I'm inviting you . . .

*Jim creeps up behind her.*

JIM: I'm sorry about that, Vicar.

GERALDINE: *(trying to push him away)* All right, Jim.

JIM: I didn't mean to mention your arse on the radio.

GERALDINE: No, thank you, have a seat. *(in her smoothest broadcasting voice)* Let's kick off with the phone-in. Where you'll have your chance to tell me . . .

*Owen comes and stands next to her.*

OWEN: When do you want the jingle, Vicar?

GERALDINE: No, you've missed it already.

OWEN: Bugger.

GERALDINE: *(back to her broadcast voice)* It'll be your chance to ring in with your memories of Dibley.

OWEN: Bugger, bugger, bugger, bugger.

*Geraldine, in desperation, stands up, grabs Owen and rams her fist into his mouth to shut him up.*

GERALDINE: *(still in broadcasting voice)* So please ring in on 5216. Share with us your magical memories. *(She releases Owen and sits back down.)* Memories of some of the big events that have happened in Dibley. Doesn't even have to be interesting frankly. Um, perhaps, oh, I don't know – the first time you saw a dog. Or any recent tummy aches . . . *(Alice tries to chip in.)* No, not you. We're eager to share them with you, so please . . . *(The red light goes on.)* Yes, yes, yes, thank you, God, I think we have a caller on line one. Hello caller.

DAVID: Vicar, is that you?

GERALDINE: *(eagerly)* It is indeed. Is that David Horton, local Councillor, Chairman of the Parish?

DAVID: You know bloody well who it is. I'm ringing up about this interview tomorrow.

GERALDINE: David, I feel I should warn you we are actually on . . .

DAVID: I'm cancelling. I'm sorry, I don't want that Alice moron asking me damn fool questions.

GERALDINE: David . . .

DAVID: And it's no good telling me that you'll get someone else, because frankly they're all zombies. Frank, Owen, Jim. I've got sheep who'd do a more probing interview. It'd be ruinous to a man. Have to cancel, talk to you later.

GERALDINE: *(gently)* David, just before you go. Just between you and me, how are your haemorrhoids?

DAVID: Well, they're terrible if you must know.

GERALDINE: Aah. Really painful? Very embarrassing? A little bit like a bunch of grapes hanging out your bottom?

DAVID: Yes. Well, it is actually, my lavatory hasn't known what's hit it in the last few weeks.

GERALDINE: Oh, oh well. Thank you David 'Haemorrhoid' Horton for sharing that with us LIVE on the Dibley Radio Phone-In. Anything else you'd like to add?

*There is a long pause.*

DAVID: *(in a silly voice)* And this is Rory Bremner now, using my real voice. Bet I had you all fooled eh? Ha, ha, ha!

OWEN: Zombies! He's got a nerve.

JIM: No, no, no, no, that's right. I'm not going to watch his show any more.

FRANK: Nor me.

OWEN: Bloody Bremner!

## Scene Seven: Geraldine's Living Room

*It's Hugo's turn to DJ. He is wearing a terrifying snakeskin jacket and shades.*

HUGO: This is Hugo 'Hotdog' Horton, playing your requests from my collection.

*He lifts his shades.*

And next up, Mrs Lawrence, of Sunnyview Farm, says: 'Please play something to cheer up my husband. He's not been well, but it looks as though his new pills are now taking effect.'

*He puts his shades back on.*

Well, Mrs Lawrence, that's wonderful to hear. And here's a favourite of mine from last year. It's The Verve, and their hit, 'The Drugs Don't Work', coming up after this.

*He gestures to Geraldine, who plays his jingle: 'It's Hugo Horton, with music that's important.' They smile at each other, and Geraldine goes into the kitchen, where Alice is looking very downcast.*

GERALDINE: Hey, what's the matter?

ALICE: Well, I just can't believe my future father-in-law described me as a moron to the whole village.

GERALDINE: Oh that! Oh, don't worry about that. To lots of people 'moron' is actually a very friendly word. Like 'How are you doing, me old moron?' You know, it can be very affectionate. You know like, 'I love you, you little moron.'

*She hugs Alice as she says this.*

ALICE: Well, be that as it may – I'm determined to prove him wrong. And I've hatched a plan.

GERALDINE: (to herself) I won't raise my hopes too high.

ALICE: I'm going to take him on at the village quiz.

*Geraldine laughs uproariously at this.*

GERALDINE: Oh, you are funny. That's what I love about you, that naughty, scampy, impish sense of humour. You're serious, aren't you?

ALICE: Oh, you agree with David! You think I'm a moron too!

GERALDINE: No! No, no, no, no, no, no, no.

ALICE: No?

GERALDINE: No, I think it's a very good idea.

*Alice grabs Geraldine's hands, very excited now.*

ALICE: Ask me a question? Any question you like.

GERALDINE: Right, what's the capital of France?

ALICE: F.

GERALDINE: Sorry?

ALICE: Well, at the beginning of France there's a capital letter, and it's F.

GERALDINE: I smell victory.

*Back in the living room . . .*

HUGO: Almost time for me to go now, but first here's a request from Mr Brown of The Chestnuts who says he's lost his wife! Bit careless of you, Mr Brown. (*He realizes that the wife has, in fact, died.*) Oh I see. Sorry. Anyway he says he'd like to hear Joan Sutherland singing 'Ave Maria' as it always moves him to tears. But, um, but I haven't got that. So here's a saucy little number that always gets my eyes watering. It's by Louise, and she's 'Naked'!

*Geraldine comes through from the kitchen with a cup of tea for him.*

GERALDINE: Hugo, look you've got to have a word with your father. He's being really, really horrid to Alice.

HUGO: Oh, I know. What can I do? He's got a real bee in his bonnet. (*At this disastrous moment Alice enters from the kitchen.*) Every time I mention her he says, 'You know as well I do, Alice is as thick as two short planks glued together with stupid glue and there's less activity in her brain than inside Cliff Richard's underpants.'

*Alice runs out, crying. Hugo and Geraldine realize she has overheard.*

GERALDINE: Oh no. Big, big, big, big disaster. Huge!

HUGO: I'd better follow her. Can you take over?

*Geraldine points threateningly at her picture of Jesus on the wall.*

GERALDINE: I could go off you.

*The doorbell rings and she goes to answer it.*

Still, as the song says, 'things can only get better'.

FRANK: Hello, it's the Frank Pickle Hour.

GERALDINE: Spoke too soon.

## Scene Eight: David Horton's Sitting Room

HUGO: Father, can I have a word? I'm in a bit of a rotten state and I need to talk.

DAVID: Well, of course you can, Hugo. If you can't talk to your father who can you talk to? Only make it quick, because I've got a lot to do.

HUGO: (*hesitantly*) Um.

DAVID: I'll have to hurry you.

HUGO: Well, it's about Alice, sir. I've had enough.

*David is pleased to hear this.*

DAVID: Haven't we all? She's monstrous!

HUGO: No, I mean I've had enough of you getting at her. I know she's not what you call academic . . .

DAVID: Academic? Last week she asked me why they needed a foreign secretary in the cabinet when there are so many English girls who can do shorthand.

HUGO: Yes, well, you know, she's very good on the things she knows about. Like the church . . . and, and, Jesus.

DAVID: Oh yes. She's *very* knowledgeable about Jesus. Last week she told me she had all his records.

HUGO: Really?

DAVID: Well, she says he was one of the Carpenters.

HUGO: Yes, well there is more to life than just being clever. There's being good and true and loving.

DAVID: I don't deny it. And I have fully accepted that you will marry her. But don't expect me ever to concede that she is anything but a genetic throwback who belongs in a pond with all of her fellow tadpoles. Now if you will excuse me . . .

*David walks out and Hugo picks up his teddy which is on the sofa.*

HUGO: Come on, let's listen to the radio, that always cheers us up.

*He turns on the radio and hears Geraldine's voice.*

GERALDINE: And coming up soon, the Frank Pickle Hour.

HUGO: Spoke too soon.

## Scene Nine: Geraldine's Living Room

*Frank is settling down in front of the microphone.*

GERALDINE: Right, you're on in fifty seconds, Frank, and I need to hear a little bit for level. So tell us what you had for breakfast.

FRANK: Toast.

GERALDINE: Yeah, I need a little bit more than that. So just make something up, you know, let your imagination run wild.

FRANK: Wild. Great. Two pieces of toast.

GERALDINE: Right, perfect. You're on. (*Under her breath*) God bless us all.

FRANK: (*speaking very slowly and clearly*) Hello. I'm Frank Pickle and I'll be here for the next hour. Or maybe a little longer in fact, because I have to put my coat on afterwards and say goodbye to the vicar, which should take a few minutes. Anyway, I'll be with you for quite some time. So, I'll start by telling you something I think you'll find very interesting. (*Geraldine is lying on the sofa, yawning.*) I first discovered I was gay when I was eighteen and I fell in love with a young farmhand called Justin. (*Geraldine sits up, absolutely amazed.*) He was beautiful. I've been trying to tell you, dear friends, for twenty years but it's tricky. That's the lovely thing about radio. Speaking into this microphone here, alone, tonight, I can say things I could never say to you face to face . . .

## Scene Ten: The Parish Hall

*Geraldine and Frank are waiting for the others to arrive.*

GERALDINE: I'm sure they'll understand, Frank. I mean, Owen's always going on about that new Julian Clary series.

FRANK: He said he should be strung up by his privates and shot.

GERALDINE: Well, yes, but only in a kind and affectionate way. Now be brave. Evening, Owen.

*Owen enters, followed by Hugo, David and Jim.*

OWEN: Evening, Vicar. Hello, Frank. Hell of a good show last night.

JIM: Brilliant.

DAVID: Most enlightening, Frank.

FRANK: Oh, thank you. You are such dear friends. Excuse me a moment, I need a minute to gather myself.

*He is overcome by their understanding, and hurries out.*

GERALDINE: Well, you've made an old man very happy. Very proud of you guys, I really am.

OWEN: I thought we'd better say something.

HUGO: Didn't want him worrying all evening.

GERALDINE: No. One thing, little detail. Did anyone actually hear his show?

DAVID: Good God, no.

JIM: No.

OWEN: Must be joking.

HUGO: No way, José.

GERALDINE: Thought not.

DAVID: Let's get on. Frank?

*Frank reappears, wearing a choice pink jacket. He sits down proudly. David is perplexed.*

Well, yes. Any matters before we get down to business?

OWEN: Yes, I'd like to congratulate the vicar on this week. Radio Dibley's brought the whole village together, and I think it's down to her.

GERALDINE: Oh, thank you, Owen!

JIM: Hear, hear. I couldn't wish the prize of a trip to Disneyland to be awarded by a more wise and wonderful lady.

GERALDINE: Ah. Penny dropping now.

OWEN: Yes. Not only a very wise and beautiful lady, but also a very sexy lady, and I'd like her to accept this small token of my appreciation.

*He produces a box of chocolates.*

JIM: And I'd like her to accept this much bigger token of my appreciation.

*He hands over a bigger box of chocolates.*

DAVID: Gentlemen, gentlemen!

FRANK: And I'd like her to accept this, though it does seem a bit pointless now.

*He takes out a small chocolate bar.*

GERALDINE: Yes. I hope you don't think that gifts like this are going to sway me.

OWEN: No? Well, how about this very large box of fresh cream Belgian truffles?

*He produces a huge box of chocolates. Geraldine is tempted. She takes them and looks at them greedily.*

GERALDINE: Well, I – I, er, I can't deny, Owen, that your report on bovine fleas was broadcasting of the very highest . . . what am I talking about? It was oral tripe!

*She bangs the box of chocolates back on the table.*

No, I'm sorry everybody, I'm just going to have to be completely honest about this.

OWEN: Well, I'll have these back then.

*He takes both boxes of chocolates.*

GERALDINE: Jim –

*She holds out his box to him. Jim shakes his head.*

JIM: Oh, no, no, no.

GERALDINE: Oh! Thanks!

JIM: They were past their sell-by-date anyway.

GERALDINE: (*reading the label*) 'October fifty-three'?

DAVID: I applaud your principles, Vicar.

GERALDINE: Well, I'm just glad you weren't tempted to join in, David.

DAVID: Oh, no! Some of us have integrity.

HUGO: So we'll be taking these home again then, Father?

*He holds up a vast, huge box of elaborately wrapped chocolates and a bottle of port. David desperately tries to wrench them out of sight. Geraldine glares at him.*

*Later . . . David and Geraldine are the last to leave.*

DAVID: Well, Vicar, see you at tomorrow's quiz?

GERALDINE: Yes. Now David, as you know, Alice Tinker is your challenger. You will be gentle, won't you?

DAVID: Oh, I'd absolutely love to be, but you're forgetting the Horton motto, which I'm afraid I must abide by.

GERALDINE: Which is?

DAVID: '*Veni, vidi, spurios brutos detruncavi*'.

GERALDINE: Which means?

DAVID: 'I came, I saw, I tore the thick bastards limb from limb'.

GERALDINE: Right, I see. It's war.

## Scene Eleven: The Parish Hall

*The hall is set for the quiz and the audience is seated. Alice and David are ready to go head-to-head. Geraldine is chairing the quiz.*

DAVID: How's Alice in Dunderland? Ready to take me on?

GERALDINE: Absolutely. Fear not my little moron.

*She kisses Alice for luck.*

OWEN: *(on sound control duties again)* Three, two, one. You're on.

GERALDINE: Hello and welcome to our final special programme, 'Brain of Dibley'.

*Owen plays a jingle: 'Tune into Dibley Radio, For fun with the holy lady-o!'*

Our contestants tonight are the reigning champion, Councillor David Horton MBE, MA, FRCS, and the challenger Miss Alice Tinker GCSE, PMT, TTFN.

*The audience applauds.*

And tonight's quiz has a local flavour, so let's kick off and fingers on buttons. *(Alice puts her fingers on the buttons of her cardigan.)* That's the button on the table, Alice. Question one for ten points, who lives in Dibley Manor House?

DAVID: *(buzzes)* I do.

GERALDINE: Oh, sorry, David, haven't quite finished the question there. Five point penalty I'm afraid. Hugo, if you will. *(Hugo is keeping score. David now has minus five points.)* So that's over to Alice now. Who lives in Dibley Manor House with David Horton?

ALICE: *(buzzes)* Hugo Horton.

GERALDINE: Correct! And question two. Which famous singer once opened the Dibley Fête?

DAVID: *(buzzes)* Kylie Minogue.

GERALDINE: Oh sorry, David, it's a two-part question, another five point penalty there for you. So Alice. Which famous singer opened the Dibley Fête and which Dibley resident is her biggest fan?

ALICE: *(buzzes)* It's Kylie Minogue and Hugo Horton.

GERALDINE: Yes. Well, this is surprising. Thought you'd be doing better than this, David. I do hope your haemorrhoids aren't affecting your performance, Councillor. And now, questions about the Tinker family.

DAVID: Oh my God.

GERALDINE: For ten points which Tinker was commonly known as Donkybonker?

*Alice buzzes and raises her arm in the air – this she knows. David doesn't stand a chance.*

*A little later . . .*

And so to our final scores tonight. Councillor David Horton has clawed his way back up to nil, that's nil. While Miss Alice Tinker has two hundred and forty-five points.

*The audience applauds.*

So the incontrovertible winner of this year's Brain of Dibley is Miss Alice Tinker! And I think it would be just lovely if the runner-up, just to show there's no hard feelings, were to present the cup to the winner.

DAVID: Um, yes, all right. (*He hands the cup to Alice, ungraciously.*) There we go.

ALICE: Thank you very much.

GERALDINE: With a word of congratulation.

DAVID: Er, yes, all right. Congratulations on your victory.

ALICE: Thanks.

GERALDINE: And now you can kiss her. Properly please, remember this is radio and our listeners will want to hear it.

*David grudgingly kisses Alice, who wraps her arm around his waist.*

ALICE: Oh Daddy.

GERALDINE: Bravo. And the winner of the broadcasting prize is, of course, our resident cool dude Mr Hugo 'Hotdog' Horton.

*Hugo bunny hops to the stage and sweeps Alice into his arms.*

And on that happy note it's farewell from Radio Dibley. Hit it, Newitt.

*Owen plays the farewell jingle: 'Oh damn, oh no, Radio Dibley's got to go!'*

## Epilogue: The Vestry

*Geraldine and Alice are having a cup of decaffeinated coffee.*

**GERALDINE:** So there's this man vicar and he's playing golf with his friend John.

**ALICE:** John.

**GERALDINE:** John, yes, and John misses a three-foot putt . . .

**ALICE:** Oh dear.

**GERALDINE:** Yeah. And he says, 'Damn it! Missed the bugger.' And the vicar tuts and he says, 'John, you say that once more, and God will open up the heavens and send a thunderbolt down to strike you dead.' Well, the next thing that happens, John misses a two-foot putt, and he says, 'Damn it! Missed the bugger.'

**ALICE:** Oh-oh!

**GERALDINE:** Yes, so the heavens open and a great big thunderbolt comes down and strikes the vicar dead. And God says, 'Damn it! Missed the bugger.'

*As ever, she roars with laughter at her own joke. Alice stays stony-faced.*

**ALICE:** No, no that can't be right, can it? Because God wouldn't miss. 'Cos he's God. I mean, even though he was standing *really* close, he'd still hit the right one, and he certainly wouldn't swear.

**GERALDINE:** It's a very tiny brain you're housing in there, isn't it?

# Census Results: Dibley, Oxon
## Home Office Ref: J210H 5TQ2

**Beliefs and Faiths**

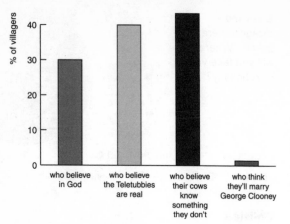

% of villagers

- who believe in God
- who believe the Teletubbies are real
- who believe their cows know something they don't
- who think they'll marry George Clooney

**Personal Finances**

Villagers were asked: "Where do you keep your savings?"

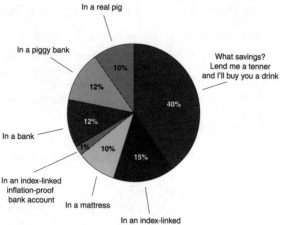

In a real pig

In a piggy bank — 12%

What savings? Lend me a tenner and I'll buy you a drink — 40%

10%

12%

In a bank — 1%

In an index-linked inflation-proof bank account

In a mattress — 10%

In an index-linked inflation-proof mattress — 15%

**Housing**

Villagers were asked: "How many people live in your household?"

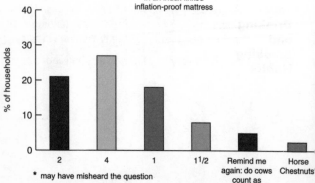

% of households

- 2
- 4
- 1
- 1½
- Remind me again: do cows count as people?
- Horse Chestnuts

\* may have misheard the question

## Leisure

Villagers were asked: "Where will you take your next holiday?"

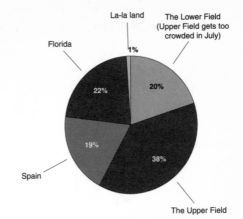

La-la land
The Lower Field (Upper Field gets too crowded in July)
Florida
1%
20%
22%
19%
38%
Spain
The Upper Field

## Politics

Villagers were asked: "If there was a general election tomorrow, how annoyed would you be that no one had told you until today?"

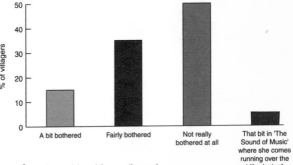

% of villagers

A bit bothered | Fairly bothered | Not really bothered at all | That bit in 'The Sound of Music' where she comes running over the hills singing*

\* may have misheard the question again

## Drinking and Smoking Habits

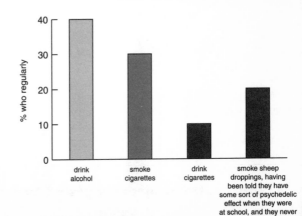

% who regularly

drink alcohol | smoke cigarettes | drink cigarettes | smoke sheep droppings, having been told they have some sort of psychedelic effect when they were at school, and they never stopped believing it

**Traffic control project suggested by David Horton MBE**

*(Artist's impression by Mr J. Trott)*

# CELEBRITY VICAR

## Scene One: The Parish Hall

DAVID: Right, we've got a lot of stuff to get through tonight, so if I could ask you all not to waste time with the traditional distractions, repetitions and general annoyances that are the usual content of these Parish Council meetings?

OWEN: Good idea.

GERALDINE: You're the boss.

DAVID: Excellent. Ready Frank?

FRANK: Absolutely.

*David is pleasantly surprised by their co-operation.*

DAVID: Bravo. Point one. The Gala Night: I thought St Valentine's Day, with all the profits going to the upkeep of the village hall. Happy with that, Jim?

JIM: Yes.

DAVID: Marvellous.

HUGO: Father . . .

DAVID: Later, Hugo.

HUGO: I didn't say anything.

DAVID: What do you mean?

HUGO: Father, Father.

DAVID: Oh no, it's a dream isn't it?

GERALDINE: Yes, David, I'm afraid it is.

*Geraldine is dressed as an angel. David wakes up — Hugo has been shaking him gently.*

HUGO: Father, Father. Time for the Council Meeting.

DAVID: Oh God.

HUGO: Highlight of the week!

DAVID: You're the saddest person in the kingdom and that's including Rolf Harris.

## Scene Two: The Parish Hall

DAVID: Right, well, we've got a lot of stuff to get through tonight.

*Geraldine arrives.*

GERALDINE: Oh, sorry I'm late. Did I miss anything?

DAVID: No, we were only just starting. As I was saying . . .

GERALDINE: Is there a lot of stuff to get through tonight?

DAVID: Yes, there is.

GERALDINE: Well, can we try to do it without all the traditional distractions and repetitions and general annoyances that are the usual content of these Parish Council meetings?

DAVID: Well, quite.

OWEN: Good point, Vicar. The way I see it, a slightly firmer hand on the rudder might get us through these things a little quicker.

FRANK: Do you want to take a vote on that?

DAVID: On what?

FRANK: On the proposition by the Vicar, seconded by Mr Newitt, that there should be a slightly firmer hand on the rudder.

DAVID: Well, of course we don't want to take a vote on it.

FRANK: Right. All those in favour of not voting? (*David raises his hand.*) That's one. All those in favour of a vote? (*Everyone else raises their hands.*)

'Carried overwhelmingly.'

DAVID: For God's sake, this is exactly the kind of interruption we're trying to avoid.

JIM: Oh. I thought you meant the kind of thing like where, you know, you're talking about Owen's cattle and I think you're talking about Owen's kettle. And I say I'll lend him mine but it's fused at the moment.

DAVID: Yes. Well that kind of thing can be pretty annoying too. Moving on.

HUGO: Your kettle really not working, Jim?

JIM: No, it's absolutely knackered.

OWEN: I can lend you mine at a very reasonable price.

DAVID: (banging his gavel and shouting) Stop it right there!

ALL: Oooooo!

DAVID: Point one. The date of the Gala Night. I thought Valentine's Day, February the fourteenth.

GERALDINE: Yeah. That sounds fine to me.

DAVID: Thank God for that.

GERALDINE: So long as you don't mind it being on the same day as the Cattle Show.

JIM: Oh, are we having a kettle show?

DAVID: Very well, February the fifteenth.

OWEN: Old folks' Valentine Dinner.

DAVID: Sixteenth?

GERALDINE: Old folks' Valentine Dinner.

DAVID: I thought that was the fifteenth?

GERALDINE: Yes, but so many of the old dears forget the first one, we always have another one the next day.

DAVID: Very well then, the seventeenth?

GERALDINE: Old folks' Valentine Dinner.

DAVID: There's a third one?

GERALDINE: No, just teasing. Gotcha!

Everyone except David falls about laughing.

DAVID: Very well, the seventeenth it is.

GERALDINE: Yep. So long as you don't mind us missing Hugo's wedding.

*She smiles at Hugo. Everyone else looks excited.*

DAVID: I do hate you all very deeply.

*A little later . . .*

Right, so that's settled. The Valentine Gala night is on November the twenty-third. Anything else?

JIM: No, no, no, no . . . no.

DAVID: Very well, item two.

JIM: Oh there was this one other thing. I don't think I can make November the twenty-third.

DAVID: Lord help me.

GERALDINE: Sorry, I've just checked my diary and actually your original suggestion of Valentine's Day is in fact fine because the Cattle Show's the week before. Silly me, sorry.

DAVID: Moving on. We can at least agree that the money will go to upkeep of the hall.

ALL: No!

GERALDINE: No! Can't it go to something people can feel passionate about?

ALL: Yes.

DAVID: Like what, for instance?

OWEN: Ulrika Jonsson. Jim and I are very passionate about her.

JIM: She can climb on my travelator any old time.

GERALDINE: No Jim, I was thinking more of a village nursery. I just think it's very important to get the toddlers interested in reading and writing when they're very young.

DAVID: Oh, what nonsense. I had a charming farmhand here for years who couldn't read a single word. Never did him any harm.

HUGO: Apart from that time he couldn't read the sign saying 'Caution: Faulty Chainsaw'. He cut off his nose and one of his hands and Dad had to go to Court . . .

DAVID: (hurriedly) The nursery it is.

## Scene Three: Geraldine's Living Room

*Alice is round at Geraldine's. The phone rings and she rushes over to answer it, beating Geraldine.*

ALICE: Hello?

GERALDINE: Alice.

ALICE: One second please, caller. Yeah?

GERALDINE: Could you please let me answer my own phone?

ALICE: Oh sorry. Sorry.

*She slams the phone down – cutting the caller off.*

GERALDINE: I didn't mean hang up.

ALICE: Oh sorry. (*She picks up the phone again.*) Oh sorry. Oh no, they've gone.

GERALDINE: Well, of course they've gone, because you hung up!

*The phone rings again.*

Leave it! (*She answers the phone in a very polite voice.*) Hello, Geraldine Granger here! Right. It's for you.

*She grumpily hands the phone over to Alice.*

ALICE: Hello? Oh yes, yes, right yes, I'll be straight home, okay, bye. Oh, it's just my mum reminding me Sister Wendy's on. Oh, she's lovely, don't you think?

GERALDINE: Yes, she reminds me of Ken Dodd. I do sometimes wonder what the hell she thinks she's doing on TV, pointing at all the nobs on statues and saying 'Oh, good lord, that's nice isn't it?' People don't seem to feel they exist any more unless they're on television or in the papers.

*The phone rings again and, once more, Alice runs to answer it.*

ALICE: Hello, Vicarage. Right . . . right . . . right . . . yeah. I'll ask her. It's *The Times* of London. They heard you on Radio Dibley and wonder if they could do a feature on you?

GERALDINE: No! No, the answer is no. I am a vicar. I am not a celebrity.

ALICE: They'd pay you five hundred quid.

GERALDINE: Yes! Yes! An unequivocal yes.

## Scene Four: The Parish Hall

DAVID: Item six, the Gala Night. Ideas for content?

JIM: No, no, yes, yes. I saw this film the other night – The Full Monty. You get some music, I'll take all my clothes off.

DAVID: And that would be entertaining, would it?

JIM: They'll certainly get their money's worth. I'm taking off my truss and everything.

FRANK: (turning to David) Good idea. I'm intending to do my impressions, sir.

*He narrows his eyes and pretends to be smoking a cigarette.*

'How do, how are you diddling?'

DAVID: And who's that?

FRANK: My grandfather.

DAVID: Right. Owen, any ideas?

OWEN: Well, I might be able to talk the duck into a return performance.

HUGO: I did have one idea but it's only very much in the formative stages. But I suppose I might like, you know, give it a dry run as far as I've got.

GERALDINE: Yeah! Fire away, Hugo.

HUGO: Okay, well, I come on stage in some sort of costume. I haven't quite decided what.

GERALDINE: Mmm. And . . .?

HUGO: Well, no, that's as far as I've got. It's very much in the early stages of development.

GERALDINE: Yes, well, very good, Hugo, yes.

HUGO: Thanks. I can't deny I'm pretty excited.

DAVID: Any other business?

FRANK: There certainly is. I'd like to congratulate the vicar on her feature in *The Times*.

GERALDINE: Oh, well, thank you, Frank.

OWEN: Yes, I like *The Times*. It's not too rough on the buttocks.

GERALDINE: Actually, I have to say it was very good fun, and they did give me five hundred quid towards the nursery. But don't worry, my media career stops here. My place is in the pulpit – not in the papers.

## Scene Five: Geraldine's Living Room

*The phone rings. Geraldine comes through from the kitchen to answer it, wiping her hands. Alice leaps in from nowhere and beats her to it.*

ALICE: Hello, Dibley Vicarage, can I help you? . . . Oh, I'll ask her, but I'm afraid she's going to say no. Her media career is over.

GERALDINE: Who is it?

ALICE: Hang on. It's the people from Terry Wogan's 'Pause For Thought'. They read your article and want you to come on, but . . .

GERALDINE: Oh um . . . er . . . I, no, no. Wait, wait, wait! Um. No, wait, wait, wait! Go on then. (*She grabs the phone.*) Hello, Geraldine Granger here.

*She is trying desperately to act cool.*

Thanks. Yeah, thanks. When would you want me? Tomorrow morning? Good Lord, somebody dropped out? Dropped *dead*? Oh dear. Right, right, well that in itself gives one 'Pause for Thought', doesn't it, you see. Yes, okay, well, thanks very much, yes. And big licky love to Tezza. Thank you.

*She puts the phone down and launches into a football chant.*

'Pause For Thought', 'Pause For Thought', 'Pause For Thought', 'Pause For Thought', 'Pause For Thought', 'Pause For Thought'!

ALICE: I thought you weren't going to do any more of those things.

GERALDINE: Really, what gave you that idea?

*Hugo comes in.*

HUGO: Hello.

ALICE:  Hi, Hugey.

GERALDINE:  Hello, Hugo. Guess who's going on Terry Wogan's show tomorrow?

HUGO:  Terry Wogan.

GERALDINE:  No, *apart* from Terry Wogan.

HUGO:  Don't know.

GERALDINE:  All right, I'll give you one clue. Only your favourite vicar.

HUGO:  Archbishop Tutu's going to be on Wogan?

GERALDINE:  No! Me, me, me! I'm doing 'Pause For Thought' on Terry Wogan's show!

ALICE:  Oh, by the way, just in case you haven't got a thought . . .

GERALDINE:  No, I have.

ALICE:  I've got quite a good one.

GERALDINE:  Right.

ALICE:  I was thinking, wouldn't it be lovely if some kittens were actually born with pink fur? And you didn't have to paint them pink yourself.

GERALDINE:  Yes. Thanks for that.

ALICE:  That's all right.

GERALDINE:  Just imagine it. Tomorrow morning about this time, me and Tezza face to face.

*She tries to do a Irish accent . . .*

'Well bejabbers, and top of the morning to you, Geraldine.'

HUGO:  Is Terry Welsh, then?

GERALDINE:  Beam me up, Scotty.

## Scene Six: Dibley, Early the Next Morning

*Various households are listening to Terry Wogan's radio show.*

TERRY:  Well, that's 'Love Letters' – the pleasing baritone of Alison Moyet. Now it's time for 'Pause For Thought', just a moment or two out of your busy day. Today it's a she vicar! Geraldine Granger.

GERALDINE: Hello, Terry.

*David and Hugo are at home listening.*

TERRY: Hello, Geraldine. So what's your keen brain been working on?

GERALDINE: Well, I've been thinking about a cause very close to my heart actually and that's nursery schools. I mean surely everyone should be able to read and write. Except Edwina Currie of course. I mean if she writes another novel we should lop her arms off immediately!

*Hugo laughs at this but David is unimpressed.*

DAVID: Slippery slope, I tell you. Slippery slope.

## Scene Seven: The Lobby of Broadcasting House

*Geraldine and Alice come out of the lift and walk across the lobby. Geraldine bumps into someone by accident.*

GERALDINE: Oh sorry.

*It's Darcey Bussell. Her complete and utter favourite dancer.*

DARCEY: That's all right, no harm done.

GERALDINE: Wait a minute. Wait a cotton-picking tutu-wearing minute here. It's Darcey Bussell, isn't it?

DARCEY: That's right.

GERALDINE: This is very very exciting! (*To Alice.*) It's Darcey Bussell! You know, plié, plié, bend, plié. Well, you really are just my most favourite dancer in the entire world.

DARCEY: (*politely*) Oh, thank you.

GERALDINE: I actually very nearly became a ballerina myself. You can probably tell by my décolletage, can't you? It's just my ballet teacher said that unfortunately my ankles are a little bit too bendy. Oh there are thousands of us in the church who started off as dancers. Terry Waite for example. Yeah, yeah. Spent the first twenty years of his life in pink tights. This is Alice, by the way. Ignore her. So, *Darcey Bussell*, what are you doing here? I've been doing 'Pause For Thought'.

DARCEY: Oh yeah, I just heard it in the car, it was brilliant.

GERALDINE: Thank you!

DARCEY: If there's ever anything I can do for the nursery, please count me in.

GERALDINE: You're sickening, aren't you, Darcey? I mean, not only the best dancer in the universe but such a lovely personality as well. You don't mind me calling you Darcey, do you?

DARCEY: No, no, not at all.

GERALDINE: And you can call me D'Geraldine if you like! Ha ha!

*A woman approaches.*

WOMAN: Excuse me, could I have your autograph?

*She is actually asking Geraldine.*

GERALDINE: What?

WOMAN: I heard you on Terry, and I thought you were absolutely brilliant.

GERALDINE: Um, well, um. I suppose I'll have to get used to this sort of thing! Price of fame, eh?

YOUNG WOMAN: (*to her friend*) I won't be a sec, Carol. I'm just getting Alison Moyet's autograph!

*Darcey waves goodbye and politely moves away.*

GERALDINE: Right.

ALICE: (*to the autograph hunter*) Actually, she's not . . .

GERALDINE: Shut it. (*She signs the piece of paper.*) 'Alison Moyet.'

WOMAN: You wouldn't just sing a song for me, would you?

GERALDINE: Not today, I've completely lost my voice, you see.

## Scene Eight: The Parish Hall

*All are seated round the table.*

DAVID: Item two. Jim.

JIM: Yes, I'd like to congratulate the vicar on her performance on 'Pause For Thought'.

OWEN: And 'Any Questions?'

FRANK: And 'Countdown'.

HUGO: And 'Noel's House Party'.

GERALDINE: *(feigning modesty)* Oh stop, stop, stop! Well, actually, Noel wants to turn 'Find The Vicar's Knickers' into a regular slot. Amazing!

DAVID: Let's move on to the Gala. Any progress there, or is the climax of our show still Owen and his amazing farting duck? Hugo, has your idea developed at all, since you first workshopped it here last week?

HUGO: Well, yes. I've had a bit of a breakthrough.

DAVID: Take us from the top.

HUGO: I'm wearing – just what I'm wearing now. I come out on stage . . .

*And he fades away – that's it – as far as he's got.*

DAVID: So the quantum leap is that you've decided on your costume?

HUGO: That's right. Keep it pure.

GERALDINE: And the content?

HUGO: Still working on it.

GERALDINE: Right, right.

HUGO: Something profound, something possibly very deep.

DAVID: And why not? And what news on tickets, Frank?

FRANK: Well, I won't mince my words, but tickets aren't going too well.

GERALDINE: Oh, not sold out?

FRANK: Not sold any. But don't panic, it could be worse.

GERALDINE: What's worse than not selling any tickets at all?

OWEN: Well, selling one ticket. But selling it to a serial killer.

JIM: No, no, no, no, that's right – who comes on the stage and slits all our throats and then leaves us all in a great pool of blood.

DAVID: *(wearily)* Does anyone actually have this serial killer's address?

GERALDINE: Don't worry, everybody. Rev. to the rescue as usual. As it happens I'm doing rather an important spread for one of the Sunday papers tomorrow. So I'll mensh our little show and we'll get loads of peeps in after that.

HUGO: Bravo Holy hero!

DAVID: I thought you said no more media?

GERALDINE: Yes, I did and this is positively my last. Apart from the photo shoot for *Vogue* and *Loaded* and *What Car?*

DAVID: I hope you know what you're doing.

GERALDINE: Yes, thank you, David, I think I do.

## Scene Nine: Geraldine's Living Room

*Lots of increasingly salacious photo shoots later, Geraldine is sitting on her sofa wearing a glamorous suit and dark glasses. Hugo and Alice come in.*

ALICE: How did the interview go?

GERALDINE: Well, I think I grooved. What am I talking about, 'I think'? I was a total triumph! The journalist is coming here to speak to people about 'Saint Geraldine of Dibley'. Yes that is the headline! I tell you, kids, if I don't watch out I'm going to turn into the most famous religious personality in the country.

ALICE: What, more famous than Jesus?

GERALDINE: Well, not as famous as Jesus, obviously. He's had longer to work on his act. But as for Sister Wendy – well, out of the pool, toothgirl.

ALICE: Ah. The thing I love about you is the way you're famous but you haven't changed at all.

## Scene Ten: Geraldine's Living Room

*The next morning and Alice enters, carrying a newspaper.*

ALICE: Morning, Vicar. I got the paper.

GERALDINE: Oh, exciting! My moment of glory. What's it like, what's it like?

ALICE: Well, it's not exactly what I expected.

*Geraldine opens the paper and her expression freezes in surprise.*

GERALDINE: Oh my . . .

## Scene Eleven: The Parish Hall

GERALDINE: . . . God knows how this happened. What's the story, Frank?

FRANK: Well, he came round asking for crazy anecdotes about you and I told him about the service for animals and you dressing up as an Easter bunny.

GERALDINE: Right.

FRANK: And he waited while I double-checked the dates and tried to get absolutely all the details right. And then he wrote this.

*Frank holds up the paper. There is a big picture of him next to the headline 'Is This the Most Boring Man in Britain?'*

GERALDINE: I'm so sorry, I don't know what to say. Oh, and Hugo.

HUGO: I don't think they meant to be rude.

*He is holding up another paper. This time featuring a big picture of Hugo with the headline 'Rich as Croesus, Thick as Shit'.*

DAVID: Though you can't deny it's a possibility.

OWEN: I'm damn sure they meant to be rude about me.

And yes, there is a picture of him too, with the headline 'Britain's B.O. King'.

JIM:  And me.

Jim's headline says 'No, No, No, No Brain'.

DAVID:  (*speaking to Geraldine*) I told you it would all end in tears. You've put yourself above your own community. You've forgotten why you came here. Frankly we feel used and we feel betrayed. Have you anything to say? (*Geraldine shakes her head, chastened.*) Well let's move on, shall we? It's a sad day.

## Scene Twelve: The Parish Hall

*After the meeting Geraldine is alone at the table. Alice comes in and pats her head gently.*

GERALDINE:  Oh, Alice, I've been such a fool. How am I ever going to sort this mess out?

ALICE:  Well, I do have one idea that I think just might work.

GERALDINE:  Really?

ALICE:  Mmm.

GERALDINE:  Let's hear it then.

ALICE:  Well, there was this man on TV and his girlfriend was quite ill – in fact she was dead. And what he did was, which was quite clever really, he flew up into outer space and he flew round the world so quickly that he made time go backwards so the girl actually got better again and I thought maybe you could do the same thing. And make everyone like you again.

GERALDINE:  This man, he wasn't called Superman, was he?

ALICE:  Yeah.

GERALDINE:  I don't think that idea's going to work, Alice.

ALICE: Oh, well, it's on to Plan B then.

GERALDINE: Which is?

ALICE: Quite clever.

GERALDINE: Mmmm.

ALICE: You kill yourself.

GERALDINE: Right.

ALICE: And then everyone will say, 'Oh that's a pity, I quite liked her actually'.

GERALDINE: Anything else a little less final?

ALICE: Oh, well, there's always Plan C, of course, which actually is, in fact, my personal favourite and it all takes place on the night of the Gala.

## Scene Thirteen: The Parish Hall

*It is the night of the Gala and all attention is focused on the stage. Jim is up first doing a striptease. Then Owen with the famous farting duck under his arm.*

OWEN: Wait for it, wait for it.

*The duck farts and Owen takes a bow. Frank comes on stage.*

FRANK: And now an impression of my second cousin Wilfred. 'Hello, Frank, I've got to have my tonsils out.'

*It is a very bad impression of a total nonentity.*

OWEN: (to David) I've got my shotgun in the van.

DAVID: Load both barrels.

FRANK: And now an impression of my second cousin Wilfred after he had his tonsils out. 'Hello Frank.'

*Owen has had enough.*

OWEN: Get a move on, you strange and insane idiot.

FRANK: Right. Ladies and gentlemen I am proud to introduce – raising money for the nursery – our star guest. In a unique performance entitled 'The Mirror', the star of the Royal Ballet, Miss Darcey Bussell.

*A large 'mirror' is positioned on stage. Darcey Bussell begins her performance. She dances beautifully across the stage – as she passes in front of the 'mirror' Geraldine appears in a matching costume as if she is Darcey's mirror image. Back and forth they dance – it is a dream come true for Geraldine. Maybe she doesn't dance quite as well as Darcey – but at least she lasts till the end. There is explosive applause. The evening is a triumph.*

# CELEBRITY VICAR

## Scene Fourteen: The Village Green

*After the success of the Gala, Geraldine and Alice take a moment to reflect. They sit together on the village green's bench.*

GERALDINE: Why would anyone be stupid enough to want fame and fortune, when you can have the stars at night and a proper friend by your side?

ALICE: I always make a wish when I look at the stars.

GERALDINE: Do you? What do you wish for?

ALICE: Well, Saturday repeats of *Teletubbies*.

GERALDINE: Oh, good call. Anything else?

ALICE: Well, Sunday repeats of *Teletubbies*.

GERALDINE: Mm. Apart from *Teletubbies*. Anything else?

ALICE: Oh, well, you know . . . I always make a wish about Hugo, and me, and happiness. Well, he's the most wonderful man in the world, isn't he?

GERALDINE: He was rather remarkable tonight.

ALICE: He was, wasn't he?

*They think back to Hugo's performance at the Gala. Geraldine, still in her ballet gear, announces the last item.*

GERALDINE: And finally, ladies and gentlemen, with an item he has simply named 'Item', is Mr Hugo Horton.

*Hugo steps on to the stage. He clears his throat.*

HUGO: It's a week today till I get married and today is St Valentine's Day, so I just want to say a few words by the Everly Brothers for lovers everywhere, and particularly to the woman I love.

*He looks at Alice.*

'I bless the day I found you,
I want my arms around you,
Now and for ever, let it be me.
So never leave me lonely,
Say that you love me only,
And that you'll always
Let it be me.'

*Back under the stars . . .*

ALICE: (*remembering what Hugo said*) Oh, nice.

## Epilogue: The Vestry

*Geraldine and Alice are having a cup of warming five-spice tea.*

**GERALDINE:** So. What do you call a budgie that's been run over by a lawnmower?

**ALICE:** I don't know. What do you call a budgie that's been run over by a lawnmower?

**GERALDINE:** *(laughing)* Shredded tweet!

**ALICE:** So the budgie's dead then?

**GERALDINE:** Yes, I should think so, it's shredded tweet.

*She cackles again. Alice is really upset.*

**ALICE:** Poor little thing, it didn't even see the lawnmower coming. How could it know that death was just round the corner?

**GERALDINE:** Alice, I'm not going to tell you these jokes any more if you're going to keep on responding like this. It's not a *real* budgie, okay, it's not a *real* lawnmower, it's just a joke.

**ALICE:** So the budgie's not dead?

**GERALDINE:** No! It never got born.

**ALICE:** Never got born?

**GERALDINE:** No.

**ALICE:** Oh, poor little thing. So much beauty, so much potential and never got born. Never saw the light of the sun nor felt the gentle rustle of the breeze through its feathers. Never went 'Twiggle, twiggle, twiggle! Give me my cuttlefish!'

*This is too much for Geraldine.*

**GERALDINE:** Get out now. Go on, get out!!

# Farmer finds Saxon Treasure

A farmer in the Dibley area struck it lucky last week, when he found a trove of Saxon treasure on his land. Owen Newitt, 52, said "I was just digging away in the Long Paddock and suddenly my shovel hit something. I dug a bit more, and there it was; the treasure of a Saxon king. His armour, his sword, everything." Mr Newitt is eager to play down rumours that the treasure bears an uncanny resemblance to the insides of a Morris Minor. "It's true that the sword does look a bit like an axle, and I suppose the breastplate is a bit like a gearbox. And the shield does say 'Morris' on it as well, but I reckon that was the name of the king. King Morris. King Morris of Leyland actually."

The rusting Morris Minor body which serves as a hen coop/occasional cowshed in Mr Newitt's yard is utterly unrelated to the find, he claims. He is also keen to brush aside allegations of profiteering. "It's only archaeology I care about, it's not the money. That's not why I'm going public with this find. Not at all. Though obviously, anything I do get for the used parts, sorry, ancient Saxon Treasures, I'll split fifty-fifty with any buxom young blonde who wants to marry me for my vast wealth."

# GREAT DAYS OUT
# NEAR DIBLEY

## MATTRESS KINGDOM

The Only Leisure Park Actually Based on Someone Mishearing Something

The people who put up the money thought they were paying £40 million for a Theme Park based on the Keanu Reeves film, The Matrix. Instead, they got:

* Some Mattresses
* Some More Mattresses
&
* The 3-D IMAX film –
'How to Spring a Mattress'

**Off the B21 near Wantage**

## MISPLACED APOSTROPHE WORLD

* Pick your own strawberry's

* Water Slide's

* Fun for boy's and girl's

"Its brilliant!" Charle's Hughe's of Leed's

## The 1996 House

Come and see a full re-creation of a mid-nineties family home. Immerse yourself in a gentler time when a pint was less than £2 and only businessmen and drug dealers had mobile phones

**Near Didcot – off the A249**

## Visit the
## Museum of Broken Milking Equipment

£10

Children & Pensioners £12

The Old Barn,
Owen Newitt's Farm,
Dibley

# Love and Marriage

## Scene One: The Parish Hall

*A Council Meeting is under way.*

DAVID: Item six. The naming of the new road. Any suggestions?

FRANK: Yes. I think we should call it 'New Road'.

DAVID: Brilliant. Not to be confused with the similarly named 'New Road' at the other end of the village?

FRANK: Yes, but that's quite an old road now, sir. So I thought we could rename that one 'Quite Old Road'.

DAVID: Not forgetting, of course . . .

FRANK: That we already have a 'Quite Old Road' – a-ha-ha! I'm ahead of you, sir!

DAVID: I feared you might be.

FRANK: So I thought we could rename old 'Quite Old Road' 'Really Quite Old Road Now', and, so as to leave a gap for any new roads, I thought that we could free up the name 'Old Road' by renaming 'Old Road' where I live 'Very Old Road'.

DAVID: Or we could just go for 'Pratt's Lane'. Hugo, do you have a suggestion?

*He stares significantly at Hugo, who looks completely blank, and then remembers.*

HUGO: Oh, yes, yes. I think we should name it after the Chairman of the Council. David Horton Road.

*David pretends to be surprised and flattered.*

DAVID: Good Lord, what a thought! Ah . . . shall we take a vote?

*Just at that moment Geraldine comes in.*

GERALDINE: Sorry I'm late. Where are we?

HUGO: Voting on a name for the new road.

GERALDINE: Oh good! So long as we don't name it after any of us. I hate all that puffy puffy self-publicity stuff, don't you? So what's the suggestion?

HUGO: David Horton Road.

GERALDINE: Oh, please! In the name of all that is holy, no!

DAVID: Actually, I agree with the vicar on this one. Very poor idea, Hugo. Personally, I'd rather we named it in memory of someone who is no longer with us. Someone like, say, my predecessor as Chairman of the Parish Council?

*Everyone murmurs their approval at this very selfless proposal from David.*

OWEN: Very good idea.

DAVID: Excellent.

GERALDINE: Your predecessor being, let me just get this right, your father's cousin? Whose name was?

DAVID: David Horton, that's right. All those in favour of naming it David Horton Road after my predecessor?

*Everyone, except Geraldine, raises their hands.*

Carried. Now, Vicar you have a couple of things?

GERALDINE: Yes. Well the main thing is that by the next time we meet, Hugo here will have married the lovely Alice Tinker.

HUGO: That's right. Dibley's answer to Michelle Pfeiffer – only much, much prettier.

GERALDINE: Well, quite! And I thought this was the ideal opportunity to offer him a few words of encouragement. So, anyone?

OWEN: Oh, well, certainly, yes. I've not known what it is to be married, Hugo, though I still live in hope of planting my seed in a certain acreage of womanhood.

*He makes a point of looking directly at Geraldine.*

But I reckon if you treat Alice like I treat my prize cow you won't go far wrong, apart from making her eat grass and getting her mounted by a bull. If you do that you'll get arrested like my father was.

HUGO: Well – well, that's very helpful. Thank you, Owen.

GERALDINE: Yes. Any words of wisdom from you, Jim?

JIM: Well, I've been married forty-three years and the secret of a successful marriage, Hugo, is sex and plenty of it.

HUGO: Well, hooray!

JIM: With as many different women as possible.

GERALDINE: Oh no!

JIM: Especially Orientals, because they can go for hours without . . .

GERALDINE: (*swiftly interrupting him*) Well, thank you, Jim. I think that's enough of that. What about you, Frank?

FRANK: Well, I've never had sex with an Oriental.

GERALDINE: No, no, no! I meant, have you got any words of advice for Hugo?

FRANK: I could do no better than read from this week's horoscope. (*He looks at the paper.*) 'Libra. Romance is in the air, and happiness shall be yours eternally.'

HUGO: That's absolutely splendid.

GERALDINE: Yes, except you're Capricorn, aren't you, Hugo?

FRANK: (*again, reading from the paper*) Capricorn. 'Forget romance. You are heading for total catastrophe.'

## Scene Two: Geraldine's Living Room

*Geraldine is on the phone to the Bishop.*

GERALDINE: Good Lord. Well, this is totally out of the blue, Your Grace. I don't know. I'm totally aware of the importance of inner-city work and I've always wanted to do genuinely missionary stuff. You know how fond I am of all things missionary. It's just that – oh dear – it really would be very hard indeed to leave Dibley.

*Alice lets herself in.*

ALICE: Ding dong, Avon calling. Or rather ding dong, Verger calling, I suppose.

GERALDINE: On the other hand, leave it with me. Okay, bye. And love to Rocky.

*She puts the phone down.*

So what can I do for you, quivering bride-to-be?

ALICE: Well, as you know my mum's making my wedding dress, and I just want to run it by you before she actually starts knitting.

*She opens a scrapbook to show Geraldine.*

GERALDINE: Knitting?

ALICE: As you can see, we're going for the traditional white.

GERALDINE: Good idea.

ALICE: With red and blue stripes just to give it that British look.

GERALDINE: Right. Hence the policeman's helmet also? Right. And the flopsy bunnies? Do you think they'll work?

ALICE: Oh yeah, definitely. Well, they balance out Tarka the Otter. It would look very odd with just an otter.

GERALDINE: Well, that I don't deny.

ALICE: And then for my train she thought . . .

GERALDINE: Thomas the Tank Engine?

ALICE: Right, along with Percy and Gordon.

GERALDINE: That's quite a lot to pull up the aisle don't you think? Three steam engines?

ALICE: No, they'll be very light. She's making them out of lino. What do you think?

GERALDINE: Can I be brutally honest?

ALICE: You can be as brutally honest as you want.

GERALDINE: Good.

ALICE: As long as you don't say anything nasty or critical in any way.

GERALDINE: Right, well, working within those particular parameters then . . . I love this dress!

ALICE: Oh brillo pads!

*The doorbell rings and Geraldine gets up to answer it.*

GERALDINE: Excuse me.

ALICE: *(to herself)* Mrs Alice Horton.

GERALDINE: David, Hugo, come on in.

ALICE: Hello, husband-to-be!

HUGO: Hello, wife-to-be!

ALICE: Hello, father-in-law to be!

DAVID: *(sourly)* Hello, Miss Tinker.

GERALDINE: *(indicating that Alice should leave the room)* Tea, Alice?

ALICE: Okay. Bye bye, daddyo!

*She pinches David's chin affectionately. He flinches.*

DAVID: It's like the planet of the Clangers in here. I'll come straight to the point. I've invited a lot of family and friends, so I want to make sure this wedding's not a total bloody embarrassment.

GERALDINE: Oh, fear not. Hugo and I have kept a very careful eye on things, haven't we, Hugo?

HUGO: Well, that's right.

GERALDINE: All the catering for the reception's sorted out.

HUGO: Good old Burger King.

GERALDINE: Yes, you can't have too many gherkins at a wedding, I always say. And we've been tweaking your speech haven't we, Hugo?

HUGO: That's right. I knew I'd cracked it when I put in your joke about the Australian who gets stung by a snake on his todger.

*He laughs at this. David remains stony-faced.*

I'll just go and help Alice with the tea.

GERALDINE: *(to David)* Would you like to come in and sit down?

*David sees the wedding-dress scrapbook open on the sofa.*

DAVID: Oh, my God! *Please* tell me she's not wearing this.

GERALDINE: No, that's a piece of paper with a drawing on it. She'll be wearing the finished dress sculpted from only the finest quality wool and linoleum.

*David looks through the scrapbook in utter disbelief.*

DAVID: Is that an otter?

GERALDINE: Yup. It's to balance out the bunnies.

DAVID: And what's that?

GERALDINE: That is Bobby Moore receiving the World Cup in 1966.

DAVID: I tell you now, if she wears this dress I am not coming. This is just what I feared. Vicar, I will see you at drinks on Tuesday, by when I expect to hear that changes have been made.

*He stalks to the door, and looks into the kitchen, where Alice and Hugo are entwined.*

Hugo!

HUGO: Bye, Alice.

*Alice wanders dreamily into the living room.*

ALICE: Oh, when he kisses me I go all goose pimply like a great big pimply goose! It's all going to be so perfect.

GERALDINE: Yes. Although I have been having second thoughts about you wearing this dress.

ALICE: Really? You think I should go nude?

GERALDINE: No.

ALICE: It's a thought.

GERALDINE: No, no, no. I just think it should be simpler, that's all.

ALICE: Oh, what you mean like lots of hearts or something?

GERALDINE: Yeah, it could be, yeah!

ALICE: With a different Doctor Who in each one?

GERALDINE: (firmly) No.

## Scene Three: David Horton's Hallway/Sitting Room

*It's the Tuesday night drinks do. Alice arrives and Hugo is there to greet her in the hallway.*

HUGO: Hi, welcome to the party, come in. Let me take your coat. Oh, nice blouse.

ALICE: Oh, thank you. My mum knocked it up from some curtains. Look.

*She pulls a cord under her arm and the sleeves slide up.*

HUGO: Fun!

*Geraldine comes in.*

Hello, Vicar.

GERALDINE: Hello, Hugo.

HUGO: I got so lucky. So many girls don't have any dress sense at all.

*He moves behind Alice and tugs at both her sleeves, delighted. Geraldine studies her face in the mirror.*

GERALDINE: Oh God, I've forgotten to put my make-up on. Oh hell. Who cares? It's the woman inside who counts isn't it, Ally-Pally?

ALICE: Every time, Vic Stic.

*They make a 'V' sign at each other.*

GERALDINE/ALICE: Girl power!

*Geraldine goes through into the sitting room.*

DAVID: Geraldine, I'd like you to meet someone. This is my little brother Simon.

SIMON: Hello.

*Geraldine is gob-smacked. First thought: this man is absolutely gorgeous. Second thought: I am wearing absolutely no make-up.*

GERALDINE: Would you excuse me just one tiny second?

*She leaves the house. She sprints through the village. She enters her house. She exits her house. She sprints back through the village. She re-enters David's house and starts up the conversation exactly where it left off.*

GERALDINE: Hi, I'm Geraldine.

SIMON: Yes, I know. I've heard you on the radio. Very amusing.

GERALDINE: Was I? *Was* I?

SIMON: Very funny story about the choir boy and the cucumber.

GERALDINE: Well, thanks. So you're the prodigal brother? In what way 'prodigal'?

SIMON: Too much drink, too much sex. Too little responsibility.

*Geraldine growls in her most flirtatious way.*

GERALDINE: Well, that's my kind of prodigal. So here we are – total strangers, trying to find out more about each other. So, just plucking a question totally at random . . . are you married?

SIMON: No, my wife died six years ago.

GERALDINE: Good . . . God how awful.

SIMON: Yeah, well it's a long time now.

GERALDINE: Right. So is there another special lady in your life at the moment?

SIMON: No, not at the moment.

GERALDINE: Bet you'd like one!

SIMON: Yes, I'd love one. Point me in the direction of a buxom blonde and I'd be out of that door like a bullet out of a great big gun.

GERALDINE: Blonde. Right, blonde. Well, I suppose blondes are valuable people, too, aren't they?

SIMON: I'm looking forward to the wedding rehearsal tomorrow.

GERALDINE: Oh, you're not going to that are you?

SIMON: Wild dinosaurs wouldn't keep me away. I'm very eager to see you in action, Vicar.

GERALDINE: Oh please, just call me Geraldine. Hey – just call me Gerry. Actually, forget the ruddy vowels, just call me 'Grrr'.

SIMON: 'Grrr' it is.

*The chemistry is fizzing here.*

## Scene Four: Geraldine's Kitchen

*Geraldine walks into the kitchen with a towel slung over her shoulder, carrying a plastic bottle. She is reading its label.*

GERALDINE: 'No animals were harmed in the testing of this product.'

*It's a bottle of peroxide called 'Gentlemen Prefer Blondes'.*

Although some rats have become horribly conceited. So let's see. 'To use: Proceed with care, and apply gradually and with great caution.' Right.

*She empties half of the bottle haphazardly into the kitchen sink.*

Right. Well, goodbye to no-action-in-the-pants department . . . hello, Simon Horton!

*She bends her head over the sink.*

## Scene Five: Geraldine's Hallway/Living Room

*Geraldine answers the front door to Jim, with a towel on her head.*

GERALDINE: Hi, Jim, come on in. What can I do for you this merry day?

JIM: There's something I'd like to try out on you!

GERALDINE:  Oi, oi!

JIM:  It's my best man's speech.

*When he's not looking, Geraldine groans, but then pretends to be delighted.*

GERALDINE:  Nothing I'd like better. Okay, right, well. 'Ladies and gentlemen pray silence for the best man.'

JIM:  I would like to begin with a quotation from that great song of Abba's. 'Know, know, know, know, knowing me, know, know, know knowing you.'

*Geraldine realizes this could take a while.*

GERALDINE:  I'm just going to get some water to drink all right? I'll be in the kitchen – I'll still be listening.

JIM:  Right. 'Know, know, know, knowing me, know, know, know, know, knowing you. Aha. There is nothing we can do. We'll just have to face it this time we are through.'

*Geraldine comes back through.*

Now I hear you saying 'Why has he chosen "Know, know, know, knowing me"?'

GERALDINE:  I'm just going to get a biscuit as well.

*She jumps up from the sofa again.*

JIM:  'Know, know, know, knowing you' – surely that song is about divorce?

GERALDINE:  *(reappearing)* Right.

JIM:  But that is my point. You see, know, know, know, knowing Hugo and know, know, knowing Alice I am sure, unlike Abba they will never divorce.

GERALDINE:  *(clapping)* Well, that's fantastic, Jim. It's gripping stuff. The only dodgy bit for me is the 'Knowing Me, Knowing You' stuff, but the rest of it is perfection.

JIM:  No, no, no, no, no, you're too kind.

*Geraldine gestures him towards the door.*

GERALDINE:  Right. So, if you'd just like to . . .

JIM:  I would now like to conclude . . .

GERALDINE:  Right, there's more. OK.

JIM: . . . with a quotation from my favourite musical, 'No, no, no, no, no, no . . .'

GERALDINE: Ooh, look at the time. Best be going, I think.

JIM: 'No, no, no, no, no, no . . .'

*Geraldine is escorting him firmly to the door.*

GERALDINE: Very good speech.

*Jim is pleased, but he still wants to tell Geraldine the name of the musical.*

JIM: Oh, no, no, 'No, no, no, no, no . . .'

GERALDINE: Oh, well, safe journey home then.

*On the doorstep, Jim finally comes out with it.*

JIM: 'No, No, Nanette.'

## Scene Six: The Church

*The wedding rehearsal. Everyone is waiting for Geraldine.*

FRANK: She definitely said ten. I can't imagine what's held her up.

*Geraldine arrives. Her hair is wild peroxide blonde. She feels great.*

GERALDINE: Morning.

ALL: (totally stunned) Morning, Vicar.

*She casually walks over to David.*

GERALDINE: Simon not here?

*David can't stop staring at her hair.*

DAVID: No, something else came up.

GERALDINE: Right, right. Some dinosaurs perhaps.

DAVID: Pardon?

GERALDINE: Nothing. Right, let's get started, shall we? Jim, have you got the ring?

JIM: No, I haven't.

GERALDINE: No, I know you haven't got it now, but you will have it on the day.

JIM:  That's right.

GERALDINE:  Right. So, have you got the ring?

JIM:  No, I'll have it on the day.

GERALDINE:  Right. Moving on then.

*Owen is hanging from the ceiling of the church holding a camera lens, trying to capture the right angle.*

Owen, it's a wedding video, it's not *Schindler's List*. And, Frank, this is when I'll ask, 'Who giveth the hand of this woman in marriage?'

FRANK:  Yes, well, look, I've been worried about that.

GERALDINE:  Ah.

FRANK:  You see, I've been thinking. People may think that I'm the actual father of the bride.

GERALDINE:  And that's a problem, is it?

FRANK:  Yes. I thought we might put this in the order of service.

*He hands a note to Geraldine, who reads it out.*

GERALDINE:  'Frank Pickle would like to point out that he is an old friend of the family and is definitely not Alice's father, as he has never had sexual relations with Mrs Tinker in any way.'

FRANK:  Yes, well I thought it might help.

## Scene Seven: The Vestry

*Alice is helping Geraldine on with her surplice, getting ready for Evensong.*

HUGO:  Thanks for all that, Vicar. The wedding's going to be just fabuloso.

GERALDINE:  Yup. And the er . . . wedding night, Hugo?

HUGO:  Oh absolutely. We're both packing hot-water bottles and I've got a brand-new pair of Rupert Bear pyjamas.

GERALDINE:  Right, right.

HUGO:  And, of course, a copy of *Basic Instinct*.

GERALDINE:  Oops! Suddenly too much information there.

*She glances down at her surplice. There is a huge red wine stain on it.*

Oh, Alice, this one's filthy! I'm sorry, Hugo. You'll have to excuse me. I've got to get ready for Evensong.

*She wrestles the surplice over her head, where it gets stuck. Alice goes to find a clean one.*

HUGO: Right, well, I'll leave you to it.

*As he is leaving, Simon appears.*

Hello, Uncle Simon.

SIMON: Hi, Bogbrush. *(to Geraldine)* I'm sorry I missed the rehearsal. It's that bloody motorway.

*Geraldine is still stuck in her surplice.*

GERALDINE: No, don't worry really.

SIMON: Can I help you with that?

GERALDINE: No, I do it every day. Actually, if you could just help me at the back here. Thanks.

*Simon pulls the surplice off.*

SIMON: Well, hello Blondie!

GERALDINE: *(going all girlie)* What – this? This is just a whim, a whimsical whim. That's me for you, born whimmy.

SIMON: Look, I was planning to go out for a spot of dinner this evening. Get away from big brother. I was wondering if you would consider joining me?

*Geraldine begins to hyperventilate, but then manages to regain her cool.*

GERALDINE: Yeah. Wouldn't mind.

*Alice comes back into the room.*

ALICE: Don't forget my hen party tonight, Geraldine. I'll be round at eight.

GERALDINE: Ah. God obviously hates me.

SIMON: Oh well, never mind, another day.

GERALDINE: Another day. How about tomorrow?

SIMON: I have to get back to Liverpool straight after the reception I'm afraid.

GERALDINE: Liverpool?

SIMON: Yes. I'm your friend in the North. I'll see you at the wedding.

*And he leaves. Geraldine gazes after him, and sighs.*

ALICE: Nice arse. He can give me one any time.

GERALDINE: I beg your pardon, Alice?

ALICE: Oh, I'm just practising. I've been reading this book about hen parties and apparently we have to watch this man take all his clothes off and then the bride has to say 'Nice arse. He can give me one any time.'

GERALDINE: Does she indeed? Who's coming to this party then?

ALICE: Oh, you know. All my girlfriends.

GERALDINE: Ballpark figure so I can get the booze in? Ten?

ALICE: No.

GERALDINE: Twenty? Forty?

*Alice points downwards.*

Oh, down. Twenty?

*She points down again.*

Ten?

*And again.*

Less than ten.

*Alice nods. The penny drops.*

Ah.

## Scene Eight: Geraldine's Living Room.

*The party is in full swing. Guests: Geraldine and Alice. Alice has devil's horns on her head; Geraldine has a hairband made out of two of Michelangelo's 'Davids'. Alice has a matching red bra and suspender belt over her dress. Geraldine is sporting a luscious T-shirt with a green bra with tassels on the front and 'Alice's Best Friend' written on the back. She pours Alice a drink and hands it to her.*

ALICE: *(giggling excitedly)* Now I'm anybody's! This is the best party I've ever been to in my whole life.

GERALDINE:  Is it? Yeah, me too. It's wild isn't it?

ALICE:  Everybody's been so nice haven't they? I can't imagine a better best man than Jim.

GERALDINE:  No, I think his speech is going to be a real highlight.

ALICE:  And Mr Newitt's been ever so thorough with the wedding video. He's even letting us pay for him to come on the honeymoon, just so he can take a few pictures!

GERALDINE:  He's all heart, isn't he?

ALICE:  I know. Oh, dear Frank agreeing to give me away. It would have been nice to have had Mr Horton, being my actual biological father, but you know for obvious reasons that's not possible and Frank's lovely . . .

GERALDINE:  Sorry, *sorry*. Just slipped into a strange parallel universe where absolutely nothing made sense there for a moment. You said Mr Horton was your father?

ALICE:  That's right. Oh, he didn't bring me up or anything. But Mum said that one night they had a stand together. And that makes him my biological father.

*Geraldine is completely horrified.*

GERALDINE: Gateway to hell wide open now.

ALICE: I suppose that's one of the reasons that Hugo and me get on so well, being related.

## Scene Nine: Geraldine's Living Room

*It is the morning of the wedding. Geraldine is alone, weighing up her options.*

GERALDINE: Nobody would know. Nobody would know . . . Until the day the first child was born, with eight legs and webbed feet and fur.

*She hums a horror tune. The doorbell rings. It's Owen with his video camera — he's filming.*

OWEN: And there she is, our first glimpse of the vicar on this very special wedding day.

GERALDINE: Owen, what are you doing?

OWEN: You all right, Vicar?

GERALDINE: I'm just feeling a bit off colour. I think I've got a cold coming.

OWEN: Would you like me to rub some Vick on your chest?

GERALDINE: No, that won't be necessary, thank you, Owen.

OWEN: Shame.

GERALDINE: Owen, I'm going to have to cancel the wedding.

OWEN: Because of a sniffle?

GERALDINE: No, because I've just found out last night that Alice's biological father is David Horton.

OWEN: Yes, that's right. What's the problem?

GERALDINE: Sorry? Sorry? Has the British legal and ethical system entirely by-passed Dibley? David Horton, you do know who I mean by David Horton?

OWEN: Yes, the cousin of our David Horton's father. His predecessor on the Council. Dirty Dave Horton, the Stud of Stadhampton.

GERALDINE: Oh right, right! Obviously! Oh, Owen, I love you.

The Christmas Fairy

People the same age as:
Winston Churchill and Lloyd George

S Club 7

Alice Amazing and Vicar Velociraptor

The Three Wise Men . . .

ZZ Top

Virgin Verger and Family

Alice and Mad Babysitters

Geraldine and Mad Bishop

Bishop and Mad Parents

Proud Relatives and Very Mad Baby

Miss Dibley 1994–2000

*She kisses him warmly on the cheek.*

OWEN: Shall we go to bed then?

GERALDINE: No. (*The church bells start to peal.*) Oh, I'd better hurry.

*She rushes upstairs to get ready.*

## Scene Ten: The Church

*The church is packed to bursting with friends, families and flowers.*

*Hugo is at the front of the church with Jim, looking nervous. Owen is filming the whole thing as if he is Spielberg. David and Simon look ravishing in their morning suits. All wait expectantly for Alice to arrive.*

*Finally she sweeps into the church on Frank's arm, under a decorative arch of flowers. A tiara to outdo all tiaras is on her head, whilst her dress, a huge froth of pink and white, says it all . . . a huge pink heart is on the front, with 'I Love Hugo' inside it. She is radiantly happy and dances down the aisle with Frank, who is wearing a sign on his back that reads 'Not Alice's Father'.*

*And that is not all. Behind them are Alice's bridesmaids . . . in hyper-realistic Teletubby outfits. Alice takes her place beside Hugo, who thinks himself the luckiest man in the world. Geraldine, in all her peroxide glory, starts the service.*

GERALDINE: We come together to witness the marriage of Alice and Hugo. But before we start the service we're going to sing one of Alice's favourite hymns. I say hymn . . .

*The organ starts, to the tune of 'Two Become One' by the Spice Girls. Everyone sings loudly. Alice holds up two fingers to Geraldine's one as they sing – she adores this song.*

*Then it's time for the serious stuff.*

GERALDINE: If any person here knows of any just cause or impediment why these two should not be joined together in holy matrimony, let them speak now or forever hold their peace.

*And suddenly, from the back of the church . . .*

WOMAN: Yes! I do.

*She walks up the aisle.*

The groom is already married. He married me three years ago and don't let him deny it. I've got the marriage certificate to prove it.

*She waves the certificate in the air. Hugo turns round and looks at her. She stares at him.*

Oh sorry, wrong church.

*She walks out. Hugo picks Alice up off the floor, where she has collapsed in shock. The service continues.*

GERALDINE: Have you got the ring?

JIM: Yes.

*He searches through his pockets.*

No.

*Instead they have to settle for a pair of vaguely ring-like 'Hula Hoops'.*

GERALDINE: With this ring I thee wed.

HUGO: With this ring I thee wed.

GERALDINE: With my body I thee worship.

*Hugo laughs nervously. We move on to Alice's vows.*

Repeat after me. I Alice Springs Tinker.

ALICE: Take thee Hugo Horton.

GERALDINE: *(confused)* Take thee Hugo Horton.

ALICE: To be my lawful wedded husband.

GERALDINE: To be my lawful wedded husband. *(She tries to get ahead again.)* To have and to hold.

ALICE: To have and to hold.

GERALDINE: From this day forward.

ALICE: For richer for poorer.

GERALDINE: For better for worse. Till death us do part. Amen.

ALICE: Amen. In sickness and in health.

GERALDINE: Yes . . . and that too.

*On to Geraldine's wedding sermon.*

I know true love when I see it. And I saw it in this pair from the moment I arrived in Dibley. I also know true insanity. I think I've had a little glimpse of that too.

*Alice presses a button and instantly her tiara turns into a halo of flashing lights. She grins proudly at Geraldine.*

*A little later and it's the end of the service . . .*

And so, by the power vested in me, I now pronounce you man and wife. You may kiss the bride.

*Jim steps forward and grabs Alice.*

No, no, Jim. You. *(She glares at Hugo.)* You kiss the bride.

## Scene Eleven: Outside the Church

*Alice and Hugo make their way through the crowd of guests to the awaiting horse and carriage. Simon and Geraldine stand back to watch the happy couple depart.*

SIMON: Splendid service, Vicar.

ALICE: I'm going to throw my bouquet, are you ready?

SIMON: I wonder who the next bride will be?

GERALDINE: Oh, please. Don't tell me you believe in all that superstitious nonsense?

*Alice throws the bouquet and suddenly Geraldine ploughs through the crowd, knocking over guests left and right, like a demented, vicious American Footballer. She leaps high into the air to catch the flowers. Victorious, she turns and smiles sweetly at Simon.*

Gosh! Looks like it's me.

## Scene Twelve: David Horton's Sitting Room

*The wedding reception is in full swing. Geraldine hands Frank and Jim a drink.*

GERALDINE: Here you are.

FRANK: Oh, thank you. Cheers.

GERALDINE: So, did you enjoy the service then, Jim?

JIM: Oh, you bet I did. That Alice snogs like a nymphomaniac on Death Row.

GERALDINE: Yes. And did you settle on a present?

FRANK: Well, I noticed there was a dishwasher on the wedding list.

GERALDINE:  Ah, lovely!

JIM:  So we clubbed together.

OWEN:  And bought them a bottle of Rinse-Aid for it.

GERALDINE:  Right. What are you guys like, eh? Spend, spend, spend.

OWEN:  Perhaps we could have got away with a sachet?

*Geraldine looks longingly at Simon, then she taps a decanter with a teaspoon to attract everyone's attention.*

GERALDINE:  While Alice and Hugo are getting ready, I'd like to make a small announcement.

FRANK:  Oh, good old Vicar. Speech for every occasion, eh?

GERALDINE:  I'd just like to say that today was a very special wedding for me, because I am, in fact, going to be leaving Dibley, and so it was, in fact, my last marriage here. (*There is total shock from everyone.*) I'm going to miss you all to bits obviously. It's just that I feel spiritually the real problems are in the inner cities, so I'm going to a new parish in Liverpool. (*She looks significantly at Simon.*) I happen to know a couple of tall people there, so I think the whole experience will be very satisfying. Thank you.

FRANK:  Vicar, for the first time in my life I'm speechless. Well, not the first time. As a baby I was speechless, obviously and in 1972 I lost my voice for a day, so in a sense I was speechless then . . .

*Geraldine silences him by smothering him with a hug.*

GERALDINE:  Oh, dear Frank.

OWEN:  I want you to know you're the best vicar we've ever had.

GERALDINE:  Thank you, Owen.

OWEN:  All the others were ugly bastards.

GERALDINE:  You're a very tender human being, Owen.

JIM:  You've been just wonderful. And after you we definitely want another woman vicar . . .

GERALDINE:  Hooray! Turned you into a feminist, Jim!

JIM:  . . . with a lovely arse like yours.

GERALDINE:  Spoke too soon.

*Simon approaches her.*

SIMON: So you're becoming a Liver Bird?

*Geraldine attempts a Liverpudlian accent.*

GERALDINE: Certainly am. It's going to be great!

SIMON: What a cruel sod fate is. David's just asked me to come here and run the estate for him. I shall be moving to Dibley.

GERALDINE: (mortified) Really? Dibley?

SIMON: Oh, it's such a pity. We could have really got to know each other. Grrr . . .

*Geraldine bangs the decanter loudly.*

GERALDINE: Sorry, just another teeny little change of plan.

*She hears Alice and Hugo approaching, and changes her mind.*

Oh, sod it, I'll tell you about that later. Okay, ladies and gentlemen, big hand please, for the bride and groom who are, I believe, in their going away gear.

*Alice and Hugo walk into the sitting room – each wearing wet suits, snorkels and flippers.*

HUGO: We're off to Barbados.

*A few minutes later Frank, Jim and Owen head off to the car to see the happy couple off.*

FRANK: Quite amusing actually, I put a little firework in the exhaust pipe.

JIM: No, no, no, no, so did I.

OWEN: Oh dear, me too.

*The car starts, followed by the sound of a massive explosion. Back in the sitting room, Simon and Geraldine are watching through the window.*

SIMON: I must say – I think marriage looks rather good fun, don't you, Vicar?

GERALDINE: Well, don't quote me on it, but – er – yes, I do.

*Watch this space.*

# LOVE AND MARRIAGE

## Epilogue: The Vestry

*In Alice's absence, David, still in his morning suit, is having a late-night cup of tea with Geraldine.*

**GERALDINE:** So, the man from McDonald's goes to the Pope and he says, 'Holy Father, I have a proposition for you. I will give the church a million quid if every time you say the Lord's Prayer you say "Give us this day our daily hamburger." '

*David is listening intently.*

Well, the Holy Father thinks about this and he says, 'My son, I cannot change the holy text.' So the man says, 'Okay, fifty million quid.' So the Pope thinks and he says, 'Well, I'll put it to the Cardinals.' So he goes to his Cardinals and he says, 'Cardinals, I've got some good news and some bad news. The good news is that I can get the church fifty million smackeroonies. The bad news is we're going to have to lose the contract with Wonderloaf.'

*David laughs heartily as Geraldine starts to explain the joke to him.*

You see, they already had a deal going over the . . .

**DAVID:** The daily bread. I know, I get it!

**GERALDINE:** You get it?

**DAVID:** Brilliant!

*They laugh together – at last, someone to share her jokes!*

**GERALDINE:** Oh you get it! What a relief.

*David stops laughing and looks at her intently.*

**DAVID:** Stay.

✝

See Dibley from the air!

Join the Catapult Society

*Pick your own*
*WHEAT*
*Phone 2188*

## CALLING ALL THESPIANS!

Dibley Amateur Dramatics Society seeks performers for summer production of 'The Matrix'. No acting experience necessary. Basic martial arts and ability to freeze frame in mid-air and slow down time an advantage.

Villagers may be interested to know that the Xmas production of 'Star Wars Episode One: The Phantom Menace' raised thirty pounds and led to only one fatality, and he was just a nipper.

YOU'VE TRIED THE
REST NOW TRY
THE BEST

**JIM TROTT**
**AFTER-DINNER**
**SPEAKER**

WILL SPEAK FOR AS
MUCH AS TWELVE
HOURS OR AS
LITTLE AS SIX.

Single woman seeks George Clooney type to share fun, chocolate and vicarage. Must have GSOH, American accent, athletic build, furrowed brow and look exactly like George Clooney. Preferably should actually be called George and related to the Clooney family. Will accept Sean Bean if in good condition. Contact Box 12.

## Join the
# Dibley Morris Society!

### It's fun.
### It's been going for three years.

**All we need is one more member, and then we'll have two members, and then we can actually do some dancing.**

**Village Green – 11am – Every Saturday – bring a hankie**

# Cakerobics

*Come to our classes in the village hall.*

Gentle exercise through lifting cakes and then eating them. As fitness improves we will progress to heavier and heavier cakes.

## MILKERCISE
MILK COWS TO DISCO MUSIC.
ONLY £4 A SESSION
AND ALL THE MILK
YOU CAN DRINK.

## Newcomers Club

**Do you have a second home in Dibley which you just come to at the weekend?**

Then why not join us, and have a good grumble about the locals who never seem to be very friendly when you complain about the noise of their farm machinery half a mile away.

# Alice Tinker Horton's
# PUZZLE PAGE 2

## QUICK CROSSWORD

1. ACROSS: A name you call yourself.
2. DOWN: The thing you see with, but spelt wrong.

Electrician Phil has got his wires in a tizz. Can you help him find which appliance goes with which plug? Get the answer right, you win – get it wrong and poor Phil fries to death, unfortunately.

One of Mr Newitt's cows has been genetically modified. Can you spot which one?

ANSWER: The cow in the top right hand corner, which has an IQ of 312 and Grade 6 piano.

# Autumn

### Scene One: Geraldine's Living Room

*Alice and Hugo, just back from their honeymoon, are round at Geraldine's, showing her their photos.*

ALICE: So, this is the first day of the honeymoon.

GERALDINE: Oooh.

ALICE: And here's . . . Who is it?

HUGO: That's me at the airport.

ALICE: Yes. Oh and this is a nice woman we met on the flight. She was a bit tired when we got to Turkey, so Hugo was *ever* so sweet and carried her case through Customs.

GERALDINE: Right, well, I think I can anticipate the next photo.

ALICE: That's the Customs opening the case.

GERALDINE: Well, how much cocaine is that, Hugo?

HUGO: I'm told the street value was eighty-four million pounds.

GERALDINE: Impressive.

ALICE: Still they let him go the minute they realized he was innocent.

GERALDINE: Which was?

ALICE: Er, fourteen months later.

HUGO: Actually, I'd better go. I've got an appointment with my post traumatic stress counsellor. Awfully nice chap. Have to pretend to be a bit doolally. I don't want him thinking he's wasting his time.

*Hugo crawls out of the room.*

GERALDINE: So, how's married life, little Miss Coke Donkey? Everything all right in the bedroom?

ALICE: Nice! We had a bit of trouble early on, you know we couldn't quite work out what went in where.

GERALDINE: Well, that's always tricky.

ALICE: But, you know, once we got a wardrobe we were fine. I just hope Hugo doesn't go off me now.

GERALDINE: Why's he going to go off you, you strange little idiot?

ALICE: Well, I might lose my potent sexual allure. I'm already putting on weight. I've put on four pounds in the last month. That's a pound a week.

GERALDINE: Is that right?

ALICE: Yeah. I mean if I go on at this rate, by the time I'm fifty I'll weigh eighty-two stone, which is more than a walrus. And I don't want to look like a walrus.

GERALDINE: You haven't been sick at all have you, Alice?

ALICE: Yeah, every single morning.

GERALDINE: Well, in that case, young lady, I think I've got some very important news for you.

ALICE: I qualified for the Vomit Olympics?

GERALDINE: No, the truth is, my dearest darlingest little verger, I think you might be pregnant.

ALICE: But . . . no, no, no, that can't be right.

GERALDINE: You mean you haven't actually . . .

ALICE: No, no. We've certainly played the odd round of hide the purple parsnip. No. I've done the test and it said I wasn't pregnant. The hamster didn't turn blue or anything.

GERALDINE: I'm not entirely sure I'm familiar with this particular pregnancy test.

ALICE: Oh yeah, it's the way we've always done it in Dibley. You get a hamster and you wee on it and if turns blue you're pregnant.

GERALDINE: Right.

ALICE: It's true, yeah.

*The phone rings and Alice gets up to answer it.*

Hiya, Vicarage. Alice Horton née Tinker speaking. That's 'née' as in born, obviously, not the neigh a horse makes. That would be (*and she neighs like a horse*) neeiigh! (*Geraldine looks pained.*) Who's calling? Oh hello, Uncle Simon. (*Hearing this, Geraldine jumps up off the sofa and grabs for the phone.*) Oh, sorry we haven't . . . there's so much news, the honeymoon was . . .

*Geraldine manages to prise the phone away from Alice.*

GERALDINE: Simon. Hi, haven't heard from you for ages. Ever think of dropping by? On Saturday? This Saturday? Well, obviously, I'll have to check my diary . . . just see if I've got any time at all.

*Alice hands her the diary but Geraldine just chucks it over her head – no need to bother checking.*

Yes, it does seem that I have got a hole available – window – window available. So, any idea what we might get up to? You want to do what to me? Sorry? Wouldn't that melt? (*Alice just has to hear this but Geraldine holds her away, against the wall.*) You mean it would be nicer if it did melt? Okay well, can't wait then, see you Saturday. Bye.

*Moaning with delight, Geraldine goes and lies face down on the sofa. Alice copies her and lies on top of Geraldine.*

ALICE: You know something, I think Uncle Simon might be quite keen on you.

*She bumps herself up and down on Geraldine.*

GERALDINE:  Off, off, off, off off!

*Alice slides down on to the floor.*

ALICE:  If you want any tips on how to attract a man, from someone who's got one . . .

GERALDINE:  Yeah?

ALICE:  I have got one or two sure-fire seduction techniques.

GERALDINE:  Oh, such as?

ALICE:  You can't beat a nice pink anorak. Hugo's always loved me in mine. When I'm naked he makes me wear it . . .

GERALDINE:  No, stop, stop – too much detail, sorry. (*She jumps up.*) Horrible mental picture there.

ALICE:  Then once you're married you can go to bed together too, which is absolutely scrummy.

GERALDINE:  So I'm told.

ALICE:  Though it isn't scrummy if you're not married, of course, because then you go to Hell and all your bits drop off.

GERALDINE:  Well, not necessarily.

ALICE:  Well, you know all that. You know all about eternal damnation and pneumatic drills in your brain tissue if you so much as look upon a man with lust. Especially as a vicar. God would probably have to strangle you with his bare hands.

GERALDINE:  Well, yeah, well spotted. Good point . . .

## Scene Two: The Parish Hall

*A Council Meeting is in session.*

DAVID:  Right, we've got quite a lot to get through, so let's not waste any time, eh? Item one, apologies for absence.

JIM:  No, no, no, no, yes I've got one.

DAVID:  Who from?

JIM:  Me.

DAVID:  But you're here.

JIM:  Yes, I am here now, but I'm not here at the next meeting.

DAVID:  You really don't need to apologize until the next meeting.

JIM:  Oh. But I'm not here at the next meeting.

DAVID:  Yes, I know. You send your apologies before the next meeting.

JIM:  That's what I am doing.

GERALDINE:  Actually, if that's the way we're doing it now, I'd better send my apologies for the meeting after that, because I won't be at that one.

HUGO:  Me too, I'll be missing the one next April. There's a Captain Scarlet convention in Bristol.

DAVID:  Stop right there. This could go on for ever. I could apologize for missing a meeting in 2010, for God's sake. Moving on.

FRANK:  Which meeting?

DAVID:  What?

FRANK:  Which meeting in 2010 are you apologizing for?

DAVID:  I'm not apologizing.

FRANK:  Well, you should.

OWEN:  There's no point in holding the bloody meeting if the chairman's missing.

DAVID:  I'm not missing it, you raving lunatics.

OWEN:  I am not a lunatic. I have the psychiatric reports to prove it. A slender majority of the panel decided in my favour.

DAVID:  All right, you're not a lunatic but you are a famous idiot.

OWEN:  Now wait a minute, Baldylocks.

GERALDINE:  Hey, hey, hey, guys calm down. You're acting like a couple of schoolkids.

OWEN:  Well, he started it.

DAVID:  I did not. He started it, Beardy Weirdy.

GERALDINE:  Now seriously, come on. You seem to be forgetting that we're partners here. If you ever needed me I'm there for you, aren't I?

My house is your house and I like to believe that if I ever needed you, you'd be there for me wouldn't you?

OWEN: Ready and erect at your service.

GERALDINE: So, no more bickering, okay? From now on Dibley Council stands for friends. Friends who are working together for the village with support and love.

HUGO: Hear, hear.

FRANK: You know, Owen, for five years I actually was in love with you. And even today, when I see you on the farm in your wet weather gear . . .

GERALDINE: Moving on, Mr Chairman. Double quick now.

## Scene Three: David Horton's Sitting Room

DAVID: By the way, my brother's popping down this weekend. Simon.

GERALDINE: (*ultra casual*) Is he? Oh.

DAVID: He's coming round for Sunday lunch, if you'd care to join us. Good old-fashioned pork on the menu.

GERALDINE: Well, I think I may be having that on Saturday.

DAVID: So, what are you up to on Saturday night? Now Hugo's left me, I'm all on my own, thought you might like to come round. Watch Lulu, play a bit of Scrabble.

GERALDINE: No – I'll be busy working on my Simon, er, *sermon*.

DAVID: Pity. What's your text?

GERALDINE: Sermon on the Mount I hope.

*Hugo and Alice arrive.*

ALICE: Hello, Vicar. Hello, daddy-o.

HUGO: Sorry for barging in, but we've got the most fantastic news.

DAVID: Are you getting divorced?

ALICE: No, silly. (*She scolds him like a child.*) Naughty Papa, spank bot.

HUGO: No, the long and the short of it is, in short, we're expecting a baby.

GERALDINE: Oh, that's brilliant! (*She hugs Hugo, then Alice.*)
Oh fantastic!

ALICE: I know.

*David sits down, stony-faced.*

GERALDINE: Brilliant, absolutely brilliant isn't it, David?

*They all turn to him, he shows absolutely no emotion.*

Oh look, he's so happy he can't speak. But I know that look
for sure. That's his old familiar, 'this is the best news I've ever
had' look.

ALICE: Is it?

GERALDINE: Oh yes, he's smiling inside. (*She goes up behind David
and pulls his face into a smile.*) Look, see!

*Geraldine pushes Alice into the hallway.*

Fantastic news, Alice!

ALICE: I know, isn't it?

GERALDINE: Yes.

ALICE: I'm going to be a mummy.

GERALDINE: I know.

ALICE: (*assuming stern 'mummy' voice*) Naughty La La, stop that or I'll
put you down the toilet and flush.

GERALDINE: Er, yes, worrying. (*Now, on to what she really wants to discuss.*)
Um, Alice just something that's been on my mind. You know, I've
been thinking, I don't think it is such a mortal sin these days for an
unmarried vicar to have sex. You know, so long as she doesn't rub
her parishioners' noses in it.

ALICE: Rub her parishioners' noses in what?

GERALDINE: In the sex.

ALICE: I'm starting to feel a bit sick.

GERALDINE: Yes, yes, forget that.

## Scene Four: Geraldine's Living Room

*It's Saturday night. Geraldine is looking absolutely gorgeous in a sexy red dress. The bell rings.*

GERALDINE:  Coming.

*She quickly places a couple of candles out around the room.*

That's romantic. So is that. (*to her picture of Jesus*) I just don't think it's going to be your sort of evening.

*She turns the picture round to face the wall, then goes to open the door, expecting it to be Simon.*

*Geraldine opens the door, expecting it to be Simon . . .*

GERALDINE:  Ta da! Owen.

OWEN:  (*surprised at Geraldine's sexy dress*) Bloody hell!

*They walk through to the living room.*

It's what you said at the last meeting. About us all being polite and civilized.

GERALDINE: *(impatiently)* Yep, yep, yep.

OWEN: Well, it's just that I'm a rough country type so I thought I'd write down all my favourite words and you can tell me the ones I can still use in polite society.

GERALDINE: Right. Okay, here we go. *(She reads down the list he has made.)* No, no, nope. 'Cucumber'?

OWEN: Yes.

GERALDINE: Nothing wrong with 'cucumber', Owen.

OWEN: Yes, well, there may be if you're telling someone you're going to stick it up his backside.

GERALDINE: Okay, that also goes for 'grappling iron' and 'full-size ceramic doll of Sir Cliff Richard', does it?

OWEN: Right.

GERALDINE: Moving on. No. No. No! And the last one . . . *(She slaps his cheek.)* If that's all I'm very busy, Owen, so perhaps I'll see you in church on Sunday.

*She opens the door to show Owen out and standing there is the very sexy Simon.*

SIMON: Hello.

GERALDINE: Simon! Um, what a surprise, I didn't expect to see you today.

SIMON: Oh, yes, I was just passing, purely by chance after my unpremeditated return from . . . Prague.

OWEN: Yes, well, you'll have to come back later – she's busy. Don't you worry, I'll see him out . . .

GERALDINE: Well I . . .

OWEN: Come on, big guy. Nice to know when you're not wanted. Goodnight, Vicar.

*Owen pulls Simon away with him – Geraldine can't believe it.*

GERALDINE: Night then.

*She walks back inside, only for the doorbell to ring immediately.*

Thank you, God! Thank you, God!

*It is Alice and Hugo.*

ALICE: Hello. Is Simon here yet?

GERALDINE: No.

ALICE: Thank goodness. I brought you a lovely pressie.

GERALDINE: Oh, you shouldn't have, Alice. (*Alice produces a pink anorak, just like hers.*) No I mean it – you really shouldn't have.

ALICE: Go on, put it on. Hugo can't resist me in mine, can you, Hugo?

HUGO: No.

ALICE: Come on. Let's have a look. (*She puts the anorak on Geraldine.*) Oh, oh yes. Most moist-making!

HUGO: Grr . . . ruff ruff!

*The doorbell rings again.*

ALICE: Aha, I wonder who that can be?

GERALDINE: Oh, don't get excited. Knowing my luck today it'll be Anne Widdecombe.

*Alice answers the door.*

ALICE: Uncle Simon, come on in.

SIMON: The gorgeous Mrs Horton.

*Geraldine tries to hide but there is nowhere to go.*

HUGO: Hello, Uncle Simon.

SIMON: Hello, Nitwit.

ALICE: Here she is.

GERALDINE: (*very embarrassed*) Hi.

SIMON: Ruff ruff!

*Hugo puts his thumbs up. It worked!*

ALICE: Well, Hugo, time we left these two love birds alone, I think.

GERALDINE: (*surprised at her tact*) Thank you, Alice.

ALICE: We'll have a nice cup of tea in the kitchen until Simon's ready to leave.

HUGO: Then we can give you a lift home.

SIMON: Lift, where?

HUGO: Well, to Father's, that's where you're staying, isn't it?

SIMON: Um . . .

GERALDINE: Um, no, er, your Uncle Simon's booked into a hotel tonight.

HUGO: We'll give you a lift there then. Which one?

SIMON: Actually, I think it's a little bit out of your way.

HUGO: We don't mind that.

GERALDINE: It's in Wales.

HUGO: Wales?

GERALDINE: Yeah, Wales, yeah, yeah.

HUGO: But I thought you were going to Father's for Sunday lunch?

SIMON: Yes, yes, that's right. Er, so I can go to my hotel in Wales . . .

GERALDINE: Wales.

SIMON: . . . and tomorrow I come back again. It's a very good hotel.

HUGO: Ah, right.

GERALDINE: So, there's absolutely no need for you two to stick about. You'd better go.

HUGO: Right.

GERALDINE: Okay then.

*She ushers them out.*

ALICE: Righty-ho. *(last minute advice . . . )* Loads of chapstick, no tongues.

*So, Geraldine has, at last, got Simon to herself.*

GERALDINE: So.

SIMON: So.

*He gestures to the anorak which she immediately takes off and stamps on.*

GERALDINE: Hate it! Hate it! So, thanks for dropping by. *(She is suddenly nervous.)* Do you know any jokes, because I do, here's one. Where does Saddam Hussein keep his CDs? In a rack!

*With that, Simon pulls her towards him and they kiss. Quite a kiss. They part.*

GERALDINE:  No, sorry, that just didn't work at all I'm afraid. We're going to have to try it again! (*And she kisses him again.*) I've got some champagne in the fridge.

SIMON:  I'm told champagne's even better at altitude.

GERALDINE:  Is it?

SIMON:  Even one flight of stairs can make all the difference.

*He kisses her again, then takes his coat off and runs upstairs. Geraldine is reeling, slightly dizzy with the effects of Simon.*

GERALDINE:  Okay. I'll just get it then.

*She goes to the fridge and is about to go upstairs when the doorbell rings.*

Oh no, no. Ignore it, ignore it.

*She can't . . .*

I hate being a vicar, I hate it, I hate it. I hate it, I hate it. (*Sweetly.*) Hello.

*She has opened the door. It is Frank and Jim.*

FRANK:  Sorry to trouble you, Vicar.

GERALDINE:  (*yawning*) Yes, I was actually just going to bed.

JIM:  No, no, no – it's just that you said that Dibley was all about neighbourliness and if we ever had a serious problem we should come and see you.

GERALDINE:  Yes.

FRANK:  We need to see you now. Desperately.

*Their urgency makes her relent – they obviously need to talk to her.*

GERALDINE:  Of course, guys, of course. Come on in.

FRANK:  Oh, thank you, Vicar.

GERALDINE:  Go on through. Make yourselves comfortable. Right then, guys, tell me, what's the problem?

*Pulling up a stool, she readies herself to hear their problem.*

JIM:  It's seven down.

GERALDINE:  Seven down?

FRANK: We've been struggling with it all day. It's been hell, I can tell you.

JIM: It's eight letters. The first letter P and the third letter O.

GERALDINE: 'Plodipop'.

JIM: No wonder we didn't get it. I've never heard of it.

GERALDINE: Well, you have to have a pretty eclectic vocab to do the . . . (*she checks*) *Sun* quick crossword. Right then, chaps. No more problems then?

JIM: Well, I've just found out that my wife is having sex with her cousin Brenda – but that will keep until the morning.

GERALDINE: Yes, I think so, off you go then.

*The doorbell rings again and Geraldine roars in irritation.*

Argh! Sorry, Frank, it's just been a rather plodipoppy sort of a day.

*David comes in, carrying Scrabble.*

DAVID: If Muhammad won't come to the mountain, the mountain must come to Muhammad.

GERALDINE: David! Let joy be unconfined. But I am not playing Scrabble. No.

*But, oh yes. The four of them end up playing but Geraldine is desperate for them to leave. Jim spells out PLODIPOP.*

DAVID: Plodipop?

FRANK: Yes. Your turn, Vicar.

GERALDINE: Um, do you think that perhaps, you know, it's time for bed, you know, it's getting on a bit isn't it?

DAVID: You can't stop in the middle of a game, Geraldine.

GERALDINE: Right.

*Suddenly behind them Simon appears dressed only in Geraldine's very short dressing gown.*

SIMON: Geraldine, is there any chance of you coming to bed soon?

*She cannot believe it. Embarrassment is an understatement.*

I'm so sorry to interrupt. It's just that I've been waiting for this gorgeous creature for hours. She won't tell you herself, of course, she's your vicar – she always puts your happiness above her own. But I can't help thinking on this one occasion she might quite like you to go.

*David cannot look at either of them.*

DAVID: Yes, of course. Jim come on.

JIM: (turning back confidentially) Need any condoms?

GERALDINE: No, thank you, Jim.

JIM: I always carry half a dozen in case I get lucky.

*At the door . . .*

DAVID: I hope you know what you're doing, Geraldine.

GERALDINE: I'm sure it will come back to me.

FRANK: Good luck, Vicar. There you go, just in case.

*He hands her a packet of Polos.*

GERALDINE: Thank you, Frank.

FRANK: I think he'll make you very happy.

GERALDINE: Thank you.

JIM: And if he doesn't, I'll have a go.

GERALDINE: Thank you, Jim.

SIMON: I'm sorry, I thought they'd never leave.

GERALDINE: Oh, come on!

*She grabs the champagne, grabs Simon's hand and heads upstairs. The doorbell rings again, so she pushes Simon back downstairs and goes to answer it. It's Jim, offering her two cigarettes which he has lit for her.*

JIM: For afterwards.

*She takes them, shuts the door and, at last, heads upstairs.*

## Scene Five: Outside Geraldine's House/Around Dibley

*The lights go out, electricity sparks from her room and then fireworks go off above the house. It was worth the wait.*

To the tune of Boyzone's masterpiece, 'No Matter What', their relationship blossoms. Geraldine and Simon enjoy romantic country walks and picnics. She delicately consumes an entire chocolate bar in one huge bite, and then elegantly jumps neck-high into  a puddle. But despite these little hiccups, it's definitely love.

## Scene Six: David Horton's Sitting Room

*David, Hugo and Owen are having a cup of tea and discussing Geraldine's relationship with Simon.*

HUGO: So, you mean he stays the whole night?

DAVID: That's what I'm saying. In her bed.

HUGO: Golly. So where does she sleep?

DAVID: With him.

HUGO: Good lord.

OWEN: It seems all right to me.

DAVID: What, for a vicar to go around having sex willy-nilly in front of her parishioners?

OWEN: I shouldn't think it's a case of willy-nilly. Willies got to be willing. You can't do it with a willy that's nilly.

DAVID: Be serious, Owen.

OWEN: I am serious. On principle I'm a great believer in sex before marriage. Otherwise I wouldn't have had any sex at all.

DAVID: Well, unfortunately my memory is that Jesus was against it. Which I think is a problem when we're talking about our vicar.

OWEN: Yes, but things were very different in his day. Women weren't emancipated and they hadn't yet launched Minx magazine. I mean, Hugo, I bet you and Alice were at it like rabbits before you were married?

HUGO: Oh, right, yes.

OWEN: What did I tell you?

DAVID: *(sceptical)* Hugo?

HUGO: Yes, well, we certainly ate a lot of carrots together.

DAVID: Well, I'm still worried. There's something not right at all. And I mean Simon's just not . . .

OWEN: Rubbish. As long as she's private about it, I think we should let her and Simon and their lovemaking be.

DAVID: Okay, okay.

OWEN: Although I wouldn't mind seeing a few Polaroids.

## Scene Seven: Geraldine's Living Room

*Geraldine and Simon are snuggled on the sofa.*

GERALDINE: So, time for bed?

SIMON: Um, let's have a coffee first.

GERALDINE: Okay, good idea. Fancy some ice-cream?

SIMON: Yes, please.

GERALDINE: What flavour?

SIMON: What have you got?

GERALDINE: You don't want to ask that question . . .

SIMON: Why?

GERALDINE: Because I just got myself a brand-new freezer. (*In the kitchen she shows him the huge freezer, filled top to bottom with all kinds of ice-cream.*) Yum, yum, yum. What do you fancy?

SIMON: I'll just have that little one.

GERALDINE: Oh, well, please yourself. You get a nice little dinky plastic spoon with that one.

SIMON: Thanks.

*He goes back through to the living room. She turns back to the freezer.*

GERALDINE: So happy you're here!

*And then she heads back into the living room merrily.*

SIMON: I'm sorry, Gerry, but this just isn't working.

GERALDINE: Oh, I'll get you a proper spoon.

SIMON: No, er, I don't mean the spoon. I meant us. You and me.

GERALDINE: Ah. Ah. That's . . . unexpected.

SIMON: The thing is, it's been fantastic, but I think we've been taking things a little too fast. I feel we ought to apply the brakes for a second, if you get my meaning.

GERALDINE: Yes, I mean you're speaking English, aren't you, and I understand English, so I don't think meaning is the problem.

SIMON: The thing is, there is, was, no is . . . another girl in Liverpool.

GERALDINE: Another girl?

SIMON: Yes. We've been going through a lot of troubles. I thought it was definitely all off but I've spoken to her a couple of times in the last week or so and I don't know, maybe, I don't know . . .

GERALDINE: I think you do know, but you're a custard. Of the cowardy, cowardy variety.

SIMON: I know, I'm sorry. Why don't we just say 'that was the autumn that was'. Let's see what winter brings.

GERALDINE: Yeah. Either that or 'Get out of my house you treacherous, gigantic, elongated bastard'. Er, but no. Probably the autumn wintery metaphor is much nicer. Much nicer for you.

SIMON: I'm sorry.

GERALDINE: Yeah. (*He goes to pick up his ice-cream tub but Geraldine takes it from him.*) No, I think not.

## Scene Eight: The Parish Hall

DAVID: Right, a couple of announcements. One, we're likely to experience some interruptions today because . . .

*A massively loud drilling noise from outside drowns David's voice.*

And two . . .

*More drilling.*

FRANK: No, sorry, why did you say we're going to experience some interruptions? I couldn't quite hear because of the drilling outside.

DAVID: Yes, that's the reason.

FRANK: What?

DAVID: That's the reason we're likely to experience some interruptions, because . . .

*And more drilling . . .*

FRANK: I still didn't get it.

DAVID: And two, I don't know if the vicar will be joining us tonight. I haven't seen a lot of her recently.

JIM: No, no, no, your brother has.

DAVID: That is just my point. If she comes can I ask everyone to be discreet. At the last meeting she asked us to be polite and civilized. I think she was right. (*Geraldine arrives.*) Ah, Vicar, you're a little late.

GERALDINE: (*in the foulest mood of her life*) Tough titties.

DAVID: (*very perplexed*) Item one, apologies for absence.

FRANK: Yes, I have a note from the last meeting to say that Jim can't be with us today.

JIM: Why can't I be with you? What have I done?

DAVID: No, you said you couldn't be with us.

JIM: I did? Where am I meant to be?

GERALDINE: I'll tell you where you're meant to be, Jim. You're meant to be where you said you'd be. But no, of course, you're a man, aren't you? So you say one thing but you mean another. You raise our hopes then you dash them. You promise us joy and then you break our hearts.

*Her voice breaks on this last statement.*

JIM: You don't want me at the meeting then?

GERALDINE: I'll tell you what I want, Jim. I want to find one man on earth who isn't the spawn of Satan.

DAVID: Oh, good heavens, really.

GERALDINE: And you can shut it, too, egghead. You're all the same aren't you? You're just a bunch of . . .

*The drilling drowns her out.*

. . . who should be lined up and force-fed Winalot up your nose till you die. Which is actually what I'd like to do to your, oh so charming, brother, who seems to keep his brains in his . . .

*More drilling.*

. . . which, frankly, is the size of a button mushroom. Here's a neat one, why don't you all just . . .

*And more drilling. She gets up to leave.*

. . . and the Crankies!

*She slams the door behind her.*

DAVID: It doesn't take a genius to work out what brought that on.

HUGO: You're right there, Father. It was Jim. Honestly Jim, sort yourself out.

JIM: Yes. I'm sorry about that.

## Scene Nine: Geraldine's Kitchen

*Geraldine is on the floor slumped against the cupboards eating ice-cream in her pyjamas. Alice has gone round to see how she is.*

GERALDINE:  I think I've eaten a little bit too much ice-cream.

ALICE:  How much? (*She checks the freezer – where there were once a thousand big cartons, one tiny tub remains.*) Oh right! I just thought I'd remind you that it's Sunday and it's time for the service and everyone's waiting in the church for you.

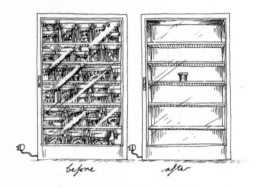

*before            after*

GERALDINE:  No, I'm not going there today. I'm not doing that.

ALICE:  Right. Interesting. Okay.

*She leaves. Geraldine rubs her hands together, opens a cupboard and a ton of chocolate falls out into a big pile on the floor.*

GERALDINE:  Right. I'd better get started on these then.

## Scene Ten: The Parish Hall

*All are gathered for an emergency meeting, including Alice. Geraldine is not present.*

OWEN: Now, my fellow villagers, I think you all know why I've called you here today. It's about our vicar. She's already missed one set of Sunday services and it's important she doesn't miss another.

ALICE: Could I just say, um, that I thought Mr Pickle gave a lovely sermon as lay preacher.

HUGO: Yes, bravo. How he kept going for two and a half hours was amazing.

OWEN: As I say it's absolutely vital that she doesn't miss another Sunday. I need hardly remind you that we actually lost a couple of the older members of our congregation during last week's sermon.

JIM: Don't worry, Frank, they were going to die anyway. And the fellow who yelled, 'If this moron doesn't stop soon, I'm going to kill myself', and then two minutes later shot himself in the head – well, he'd been gloomy for quite some time.

OWEN: Right, has anyone got any suggestions?

ALICE: I do have one suggestion.

OWEN: Mrs Horton.

ALICE: Who? Oh yes. Um, you know the series *Walking With Dinosaurs*?

DAVID: Yes.

ALICE: Well, they re-created the dinosaurs digitally, just by using the computer, and I thought maybe we could do the same with Uncle Simon.

DAVID: Re-create him digitally?

ALICE: That's right. And then send the digital Simon round to the vicarage. So that he and the vicar could kiss and things, you know, and live happily ever after.

*After sharing this masterplan she sits back down.*

DAVID: So your plan is that we get a holographic two-dimensional human to marry the vicar?

ALICE: Exactly.

DAVID: Does anyone spot the defect in this plan?

JIM: No, no, no. It sounds pretty good to me.

FRANK: All those in favour of recruiting a digital Simon for the vicar ASAP.

*All, except David, raise their hands in agreement.*

ALICE: And if that fails, I do have a plan B.

DAVID: Oh my God.

## Scene Eleven: Geraldine's Living Room

*Still in her pyjamas, Geraldine is lying on the sofa with bars of chocolate lined up on the coffee table beside her. She picks up a large bar and crams the chocolate into her mouth.*

GERALDINE: Oh yes.

*The doorbell rings.*

Go away.

*It's Alice, shouting through the letterbox.*

ALICE: I've got something to show you.

GERALDINE: Well, if it isn't your Uncle Simon's testicles on a skewer I don't want to know.

ALICE: It's some pictures. I'm going to put them through the letterbox.

GERALDINE: (*heaving herself up*) Oh God.

*Chocolate falls everywhere. The floor is strewn with chocolate and wrappers. Geraldine picks the photos up and looks at them.*

Oh Alice, they're beautiful.

*They are scans of Alice's baby. She lets her in.*

ALICE: Thank you.

GERALDINE: Oh, sweet . . .

ALICE: If you look carefully . . .

GERALDINE: Mmm . . .

ALICE: . . . that's a little tiny leg.

GERALDINE: Oh yes.

ALICE: And that's the other leg.

GERALDINE: Mmm and what's that there?

ALICE: Um. That's another leg. (*Suddenly distraught.*) Oh no, it's got three legs.

GERALDINE: No, no. I think that's probably an arm, isn't it?

ALICE: Oh phew. Some of these pictures are *amazing*. You can see the baby really clearly in this one. Look, it's the spitting image of Hugo.

GERALDINE: No, that is Hugo, Alice. It's one of your holiday snaps isn't it, that you showed me earlier?

ALICE: Oh yes. Still, apart from that one, they must have cheered you up a bit.

GERALDINE: I can't deny it, they have.

ALICE: Great. So any chance of you coming back to normal today?

GERALDINE: Ah, well, I don't know about that yet, Alice. I've been thinking about it long and hard. I just can't imagine myself standing up in that pulpit preaching about right and wrong after what's happened. Anyway, will you give this letter to your father-in-law and the rest of the Parish Council for me?

ALICE: Yeah. What is it?

GERALDINE: Just give it to them, eh?

ALICE: Okay.

GERALDINE: Lovely pics.

ALICE: Thank you. Telly bye bye. See you.

## Scene Twelve: The Parish Hall

*The men are all present.*

DAVID: Well, gentlemen, I'm afraid our crisis deepens. I have today received a letter from our vicar tendering her resignation.

ALL: Oh no. What? Shame . . .

DAVID: Well, quite, we all know our instinctive reaction but we must also face up to the fact that we have had no services now for two weeks. This is a serious situation. I have taken a photocopy of her letter. Please read it and then we'll all make up our minds.

*Hugo hands out the letter.*

FRANK: Thank you, Hugo.

OWEN: Are you sure this is the right letter?

DAVID: Of course I'm sure.

FRANK: (*reading it out*) 'Dear Miss Messenger, forgive this unusual request but my ten-year-old son, David, would like a signed photograph of you . . .'

*David snatches back the letter from everyone.*

OWEN: 'With or without top, you decide.' He's a little scamp.

HUGO: Sorry, Dad, bloody photocopier.

DAVID: Calm down, calm down. This is a very grave business. I have read the letter and it makes pretty convincing reading. Please have a look and then let me know what you think we should do. We have a very important decision to make.

*In silence they all read the letter. The atmosphere is very grave.*

Well, I think it's obvious what we have to do.

## Scene Thirteen: Geraldine's Living Room

*The next morning. Just Alice and Geraldine.*

GERALDINE: So, did they accept my resignation?

ALICE: I don't know. They just asked me to come and collect you.

GERALDINE: Right. Face the music in person, eh?

ALICE: Yeah.

GERALDINE: Fair enough. Let me just lay out a line of chocolate. In case it goes badly, I want something nice to return home to.

*She throws the chocolate bars on the floor leading to the front door. They walk outside together.*

## Scene Fourteen: The Village Green

ALICE: They wanted to see you face to face so there wouldn't be any misunderstanding.

GERALDINE: I see. (*She stops in her tracks.*) Right. Right. I get the message.

*Jim, Frank, Owen, David and Hugo are all stood on the village green underneath a banner which reads:*

*Geraldine approaches them, smiling.*

Thank you very much. I suppose I had better withdraw my resignation. (*They all cheer and clap.*) However I do feel that I need a real holiday. So that I can return bright and refreshed.

OWEN: Fair enough.

GERALDINE: So if you don't mind I'm going to ask Frank to do another month of sermons and I'll be back in November.

OWEN: No!

HUGO: No!

JIM: No, no. No, no, no, no, no. No!

GERALDINE: Just kidding, see you Sunday.

*She winks and laughs. The old Geraldine is back.*

## Epilogue: The Vestry

*Geraldine and Alice are having a cup of Darjeeling together.*

**GERALDINE:** Apparently they've come up with a new low-fat communion wafer.

**ALICE:** That's good news.

**GERALDINE:** Yeah. They've called it 'I Can't Believe It's Not Jesus'.

*And she laughs, laughs, laughs.*

**ALICE:** That's catchy. Like 'I Can't Believe It's Not Butter'?

**GERALDINE:** Exactly, yes.

**ALICE:** We should get some. Do you want me to order them?

**GERALDINE:** No, because it's a joke, isn't it?

**ALICE:** What is?

**GERALDINE:** The wafers. The low-fat wafers don't exist, they're a joke.

**ALICE:** Are you sure?

**GERALDINE:** Yes.

**ALICE:** I don't know ... because, you see, a joke is meant to be a play on words. Or a witticism or a comic juxtaposition of disparate ideas to provoke a spontaneous explosion of laughter. So what you told me can't have been a joke. Because I didn't laugh. At all.

**GERALDINE:** Oh sod off, Alice.

# Dibley Man Sets Mobile Library Land Speed Record

Gareth Jennings became Britain's fastest librarian last week, when his book-laden vehicle broke the 35 mph barrier at the Santa Pod dragster track in Bedfordshire. Ecstatic Gareth said "I suppose I'm just a velocity junkie. Driving one of these things is a real kick for me. People should realize that mobile libraries aren't just a great local resource for books, audio cassettes and jigsaws; they're also extreme machines which can burn some serious rubber. Thirty-five miles an hour! It's incredible. I'm really buzzing right now." Dibleians may remember Gareth from the 1999 village fete, where he jumped the library over an entire set of the novels of Terry Pratchett.

The twenty-eight-year-old father of two says his fascination for library hot-rodding began five years ago. "We'd just got a new Encyclopedia Britannica, and I put it on the back shelves, several feet behind the rear axle. With all that extra weight at the back, it was really easy to pull wheelies. I've never looked back since then. Some people say the library's suffered, that I'm not spending the budget on the right things. But what would you rather have; a library with a load of hardback Catherine Cooksons, or a library with five-foot monster truck tyres? Exactly!"

Local councillors are currently resisting Gareth's attempts to organize the county's first-ever Mobile Library Demolition Derby in Mr Owen Newitt's back field. Mr Newitt, himself a councillor, defends Gareth's scheme – "It is a well known fact that Beatrix Potter loved the smell of burning rubber, and Jane Austen was never happier than with her hand on a throbbing gearstick. Anyone who truly loves literature should back this event."

Got sent this by a pal in California
G.

# Funerals for Dumbos

Funerals can be complicated and – let's face it – sometimes even kinda depressing. This book seeks to explain them in terms even a real new priest on the block can understand. Soon you'll find that really funerals aren't that daunting, and before you know it, you'll be burying with confidence. You might even start having fun!

## Step One – Deciding Who To Bury

It is the undertaker's job to help you by identifying the candidate for internment. Otherwise obey the golden rule which has helped us priests for centuries – *if they're crying, they're still alive.*

## Step Two – Knowing What To Say

The best thing is to try and say something nice. As a novice, you're much better off saying 'Maria was a wonderful lady loved by friends and family' than 'What I remember most about Maria was her funny squint and her tendency to shag anything that moved, and some things that didn't'. There are exceptions – see Chapter 8: 'Burying Presidents' – but on the whole keep it light.

**Remember to get someone to dig a hole to put the coffin in. Otherwise, the coffin will just lie there when you're done, and the next day someone might open the coffin and play with the corpse. You know what kids are like!**

**You may come across all sorts of strange words and phrases when you're conducting the service. Don't worry! This book will help you decipher them.**

◆ **Soul** The bit that's left of you when you die. Like a ghost but not as scary

◆ **Dear Departed** The dead guy

◆ **Jesus** A very nice guy who will now be best buddies with the dead guy

# Winter

## Scene One: The Parish Hall

GERALDINE: Sorry I'm late, everyone, I was glued to the footy. You know with digital telly you can choose your own camera angles? I've just watched the entire Spurs match from right in front of David Ginola's shorts.

JIM: I was glued to the telly today as well.

GERALDINE: Are you a footy fan then, Jim?

JIM: No, no, no, I mean I was *actually* glued to the telly. I was trying to build an Airfix model of the starship *Enterprise* and I had a bit of spillage.

HUGO: How did you get unstuck?

JIM: Well, I didn't, I . . .

*His hand is still stuck to the television − he brings it, and the telly, out from under the table, with some difficulty.*

DAVID: Right, let's get started, shall we? First thing on the agenda is this year's Christmas Show. Now, as we know, last year was a bit of a disappointment.

GERALDINE: Your juggling for instance, Owen.

OWEN: Well, at least it was original. No one's juggled with live puppies before.

GERALDINE: Or since.

OWEN: Well, I only dropped a couple.

DAVID: Whatever, we need this year's show to be a triumph. It is, after all, the Millennium, two thousand years since Jesus's birth.

GERALDINE: Well, I think we're one step ahead of you there, doubting David. Over to you-oo-oo, Hugo.

HUGO: Whizzo!

*He gets up and stands next to a flip chart.*

Six months ago the vicar approached me, Frank and Jim.

*Frank and Jim stand up to take a bow.*

To form a Christmas Show Sub-Committee. (*He flips over to show their pictures.*) To come up with big ideas. And we've been meeting once a fortnight and we're pretty excited because just this week we had a bit of a breakthrough.

*He flips to 'The Big Breakthrough' on the chart.*

GERALDINE: Aha and what's that?

HUGO: We've agreed the date of the first full meeting.

GERALDINE: Right. And when's that going to be then?

*He flips over . . .*

HUGO: February the 10th.

GERALDINE: What, next year?

HUGO: Yeah.

GERALDINE: Two thousand?

HUGO: Yes, yes.

GERALDINE: After Christmas?

HUGO: *(realizing his miscalculation)* Yes.

GERALDINE: Well, this is very depressing, Hugo, we want this to be the best Christmas ever.

DAVID: And we don't have a show.

HUGO: Sorry.

OWEN: I could juggle with kittens – they don't mind being dropped.

GERALDINE: How do you know?

OWEN: Experience.

DAVID: Moving swiftly on.

GERALDINE: All we need is for just one of us to come up with one fantastic idea for the best Christmas Show ever.

DAVID: By tomorrow.

HUGO: Right.

GERALDINE: Um, yeah.

OWEN: I've got it, I've got it. I've darn well got it. Look, listen – Christmas is all about the baby Jesus, isn't it?

GERALDINE: Yes. And I'll warn you to be very careful Owen before you suggest juggling babies.

OWEN: On second thoughts, perhaps I haven't got it.

# THE VICAR OF DIBLEY

## Scene Two: Geraldine's Living Room

*Geraldine is on the phone to the Bishop.*

GERALDINE: Yes, of course, Bishop. Our show will be something very, very special. Very, very, very special indeed. Well, we haven't quite decided yet, but I'm sure the perfect idea is round the corner.

*Alice pops her head round the corner.*

ALICE: Nice to see me, to see me nice!

GERALDINE: Spoke too soon on that one. All right, I'll speak to you in January then. Yeah. Oh, love to Julio by the way – and Juan, of course. Has his nasty piercing infection cleared up now? Good! (*She puts the phone down.*) So how's it going, oh Lady of the Lump?

ALICE: Weird. I can feel it moving around. You've never had anything moving around inside you have you?

GERALDINE: Not a *baby*, no.

ALICE: Well, it's amazing, it's almost as if it's alive.

GERALDINE: But it is alive, Alice.

ALICE: Oh yeah. Oh brillo!

GERALDINE: Do you mind if I just get on? Got a bit of a Christmas crisis unfortunately.

*Alice sits down at Geraldine's desk, right where Geraldine wanted to sit.*

ALICE: I'll just sit here then, get out of your way. Get my breath back.

GERALDINE: Right, I'll just get my stuff then. Right.

*Alice turns on the radio and very loud dance music blares out.*

Oh, can you turn that down a bit? It's a funny thought isn't it? When they're seventy, little babies, like that one you've got cooking in your tum right now, will go all gooey over music like that. The same way that we got sentimental about Abba, they'll get all teary eyed over 'Smack My Bitch Up'.

ALICE: Yeah. Abba were always a bit experimental for me. I like my music a little more middle of the road.

GERALDINE: Oh, what would that be?

ALICE: The Wombles, really.

GERALDINE: Right, right.

ALICE: Yeah, they were a great band weren't they?

GERALDINE: Yeah.

ALICE: (singing) 'Remember you're a Womble.'

GERALDINE: Yeah. V. v. funky weren't they?

ALICE: Yeah. Funny thing – you never hear of them any more do you? It's funny that because Take That split up and Robbie Williams and Gary Barlow kept on making records, but, I mean, what happened to the Wombles? I mean you never see Uncle Bulgaria popping up on *Later With Jools Holland*.

GERALDINE: That's because Uncle Bulgaria was a man in a suit.

ALICE: No, Uncle Bulgaria never wore a suit.

GERALDINE: No, I mean there was always a man inside Uncle Bulgaria.

ALICE: I don't care what he got up to in private. Loads of rock stars are gay, Geraldine. Doesn't mean he wasn't a great musician.

GERALDINE: No, he wasn't a musician at all was he? It was just a costume wasn't it? I mean Uncle Bulgaria's in a box somewhere.

ALICE: (worried) Uncle Bulgaria's dead?

GERALDINE: Can we just finish this conversation before I stab you to death? I have got to devise a brilliant Christmas Show, something that the people of Dibley will remember for the next thousand years.

ALICE: Oh, that's easy.

GERALDINE: And not Dibley's Wombling Merry Christmas.

ALICE: Oh, right. Difficult.

GERALDINE: Yes.

ALICE: Well, I suppose the Nativity's the obvious choice.

GERALDINE: Well, of course it is, but we need to give it a twist don't we?

ALICE: Well, I suppose, I suppose you could do it like on an actual farm.

GERALDINE:  A farm? You silly girl.

ALICE:  No, so the audience can follow the story round the farmyard on a magical moonlit night, you know, visit the shepherds in a real field. Have Mary and Joseph in a real stable with real cows and sheep. You know, this sort of thing.

*Pause. Geraldine is stunned.*

GERALDINE:  Alice?

ALICE:  Yes.

GERALDINE:  How does it feel to have had your first very good idea indeed?

*Geraldine shakes Alice's hand.*

ALICE:  Hey, it feels great.

GERALDINE:  Does it? Good.

ALICE:  And here comes some more! Maybe the wise men can't see Jesus when they come into the stable and we all have to go, 'He's behind you!'

*There is no stopping her.*

GERALDINE:  Oh dear, the taxi's arrived.

*She is now on a roll.*

ALICE:  And then Jesus can escape from Herod right up a sort of giant beanstalk.

GERALDINE:  Oh, it's not a taxi. It's a spaceship come to collect you for experiments.

*She pushes Alice towards the front door.*

## Scene Three: The Parish Hall

*Geraldine, sitting behind a desk on the stage, is auditioning villagers for the Christmas Show.*

GERALDINE:  Enter, next hopeful thespian!

FRANK:  Hello, Vicar.

GERALDINE:  Oh, hello, Frank.

FRANK: I'd like to audition for one of the wise men.

GERALDINE: Oh right, lovely. Right, well, here's the script.

FRANK: Yes.

GERALDINE: I'll read in the other wise men for you, shall I?

FRANK: Right, yes.

GERALDINE: Right. Ready? Here we go. 'Lo, behold, a wondrous star in the east.'

*Frank speaks in a very strange, robotic, nasally voice out of one side of his mouth.*

FRANK: 'Oh let us follow it, my noble companions.'

GERALDINE: Right. 'Perchance we will encounter the Son of God.'

FRANK: 'Then we will worship him.'

GERALDINE: Interesting interpretation, Frank. Can't say I quite understand the voice.

FRANK: Well, I was just thinking, I'm playing a wise man. Now, who's wise? And I thought, of course, Steven Hawking. Therefore, the voice. 'Take this myrrh, it's very nice.'

GERALDINE: Well, I can see you've really thought about this, Frank. More's the pity. Can I call you about it? It's very good though.

FRANK: (*still in his Stephen Hawking voice*) Thank you.

GERALDINE: Who's next?

FRANK: It's Owen.

GERALDINE: Excellent. Can you send him in?

FRANK: Yes.

*Owen enters the room. He is dressed as Elvis Presley in a spectacular sparkly blue and white all-in-one outfit. He assumes an Elvis pose as Geraldine looks up.*

GERALDINE: Right, Owen, and, um, you've come to audition for?

OWEN: The King.

GERALDINE: Of course. There were three kings and you are obviously one of them.

OWEN: That's right.

GERALDINE:  And will you be giving us an Elvis impression on the night?

OWEN:  Well, it would be mad to dress up as him and then not lay down some serious rock and rolling. (*He produces a toilet brush and starts to sing into it.*) 'Are you lonesome tonight? Do you miss me tonight?'

GERALDINE:  Can I get back to you on it? Just store that performance and come back to you.

OWEN:  Certainly.

GERALDINE:  All right.

OWEN:  Would it help if I slept with you?

GERALDINE:  I beg your pardon?

OWEN:  Well, I've heard you can get on in acting by sleeping with the director on a couch and I for one would be only too happy to oblige.

GERALDINE:  Erm . . . no. Who's next?

OWEN:  It's Jim, he's come as one of the kings as well.

GERALDINE:  Oh right, well I hope it isn't Martin Luther King.

*She laughs. But Owen heads out again seriously and says something to Jim.*

OWEN: He says he'll come back later.

*Hugo and Alice are next. Hugo with a teatowel on his head and Alice wrapped in a blue towel.*

GERALDINE: So how can I help you two?

ALICE: We'd like to play Mary and Joseph, with me as Mary.

GERALDINE: Oh God! Oh good! Though actually, Alice, I actually was banking on you for the pivotal role of woman who sleeps through the entire thing in another room at the inn.

ALICE: Oh, that would be nice, too, but I want to play Mary.

GERALDINE: It's just that, oh dear, what a shame, you don't actually fit the vital requirements I'm afraid. For instance, Joseph was a carpenter and I'm afraid Hugo just isn't, is he?

*Hugo pops into the hallway and brings in a handmade wooden stool and bookcase.*

HUGO: Just finished them in evening class.

GERALDINE: Right, good, but the crucial thing, I fear, is that they weren't English, so I'm afraid Mary only spoke Hebrew.

*Alice suddenly speaks in completely fluent Hebrew.*

Yep, just like that.

HUGO: Please.

ALICE: Please.

GERALDINE: Look, I'll think about it.

ALICE: (crying into Hugo's chest) I wanted to play Mary.

GERALDINE: Right. I've thought about it and I think it's an excellent perfect idea.

ALICE: Hooray. Ooh! (She kisses Geraldine.)

HUGO: See you on the set, Reverend Spielberg.

GERALDINE: Yes. Er, Hugo, you don't think your father would be willing to act do you?

HUGO: Absolutely, he was rather hoping you'd ask him to play God.

GERALDINE: Actually, no, I have another part in mind.

## Scene Four: The Parish Hall

*All are gathered for the first rehearsal. Jim has turned up in a women's tennis outfit. Geraldine is wearing her director's outfit — woolly shawl and glasses resting on her nose.*

GERALDINE: Mmm. Nice try, Jim, but I really don't think one of the kings would have been Billie Jean. Now then, everyone. Welcome to your first rehearsal. Let's just whip around the circle shall we, to just check which parts we're playing. For instance, *(She assumes a very organized director's voice.)* I am Geraldine. Hi, I'm your director, I am also playing the announcing angel and the narrator.

ALICE: I'm Alice and I'm playing Mary.

HUGO: I'm Hugo and I'm Joseph.

DAVID: I'm David, I'm . . . Herod.

JIM: I am Jim and I, no, no, no, don't know.

GERALDINE: Good, moving on.

OWEN: I'm Owen, I'm third shepherd, first king and it's my farm we're performing in for a very reasonable rent.

GERALDINE: Owen!

OWEN: For free.

GERALDINE: Yes, thank you. Now since this is an experimental play, I'd like to use some of the rehearsal methods from Brook's early productions.

FRANK: Brooke Shields?

GERALDINE: No. Peter Brook. He was a director at the Royal Shakespeare Company.

JIM: I wouldn't mind being directed by Brooke Shields. 'This way to the bedroom, Jim.'

GERALDINE: Do shut up, Jim.

JIM: 'Andre Agassi, get out of that bed you lazy sod, I've got Jim Trott here.'

DAVID: Can we get on, Vicar? I've got a meeting in April.

JIM: I'm sorry, I get carried away. It's been a very long life with very little sexual experimentation.

GERALDINE: In Brook's classic productions there was a lot of improvisation to enable the actors to really explore the background of their characters. So let's do a little bit of that, shall we? Hugo, Alice, here we go. Let's clear the floor. Come on, make a big open space. That's it. Don't worry, Alice, it's just pretending.

ALICE: Oh right.

GERALDINE: Right, here we go. Now Alice you're playing Mary, you're young.

ALICE: Yes.

GERALDINE: You're unmarried, you're a virgin and yet you find out you're pregnant.

OWEN: That happened to my cousin Sally.

GERALDINE: No it didn't, Owen.

OWEN: She gave birth three times but she never ever had sex with a man.

JIM:  Except me.

FRANK:  And me.

OWEN:  And me if I'm honest.

GERALDINE:  Now then, Alice. So, unmarried, and yet pregnant, and that very day who comes home but Joseph, your fiancé, a humble carpenter. Right, so, okay and centre and go!

*Alice mimes stirring something in the kitchen, like a child. Very wooden acting all round.*

HUGO:  Knock, knock.

ALICE:  Who is it?

HUGO:  It's me, Joseph, your boyfriend, a humble carpenter.

ALICE:  Oh, come on in Joe. Cup of tea?

HUGO:  Yes please.

ALICE:  Busy day?

HUGO:  Yes, yes, I've been carpentering all day.

ALICE:  Oh good.

HUGO:  And yourself? Interesting day?

ALICE:  Er, well yes, actually. Um, I spent the morning shopping, got you a lovely supper.

HUGO:  Splendid, what is it?

ALICE:  Loaves and fishes. Family recipe.

HUGO:  Great. And this afternoon?

ALICE:  I came home and the Angel of the Lord was waiting and made me with child, who shall be Lord of all mankind.

HUGO:  Oh right.

ALICE:  Humous?

HUGO:  Please.

*This is too weird for Geraldine. She jumps up.*

GERALDINE:  No, sorry, sorry, sorry. Can I just butt in there, Hugo. I think you'd react a bit more than that, wouldn't you? It's quite big news you're hearing.

HUGO: Right, okay, yes, sorry. Get your drift. Good point.

GERALDINE: Absolutely, so – centre and go.

ALICE: A bit of a turn up for the books, Joe, I'm pregnant. And God the maker of all mankind is the father.

HUGO: Oh! (*His voice wavers.*) Actually have you got any taramasalata I'm . . .

GERALDINE: No, no, no. You're obviously completely useless at this. Sit down immediately. I'll be Joseph. Right here we go, I'll show you how to do it. (*with attitude*) Hello, Mary.

ALICE: Hello, Joseph.

GERALDINE: Any news?

ALICE: Yeah, I'm pregnant.

GERALDINE: Hang on a minute there, madam, you're telling me you're pregnant?

ALICE: Yes.

GERALDINE: (*shouting now*) Well who's the father, you little scrubber? Come on, who is it?

ALICE: (*now getting upset*) God Almighty, creator of all things.

GERALDINE: Oh sure, I've heard that story before. Come on, who is it?

*She points a finger in Alice's face.*

ALICE: (*in a tiny voice*) I don't know. I went to the loo and when I got to the loo the Angel of the Lord was sitting on the loo and he said to me, 'You don't actually need the loo, you're pregnant.'

*Geraldine steps forward to give the tearful Alice a hug.*

GERALDINE: Oh, Mary, forgive me.

*But Alice backs off.*

ALICE: Get away from me, you bastard. How could you doubt me? I never want to see you again. I'm going to Bethlehem on my own.

*Alice runs out to the door, then puts her hands on her hips and relaxes.*

GERALDINE: And out of character. Well done, Alice.

## Scene Five: David Horton's Sitting Room

*After the rehearsal, Geraldine goes round to have a drink with David.*

DAVID: Whisky?

GERALDINE: Oh, yes please, lots. I'm absolutely whacked. It's exhausting all this directing. No wonder Stanley Kubrick died.

DAVID: Right. Right. Now obviously, Vicar, I'm very happy to play Herod. But I did just wonder if we weren't missing a trick with him, a chance to make him more rounded. Perhaps bring out his nicer side.

GERALDINE: The nicer side of Herod?

DAVID: Yes.

GERALDINE: Oh, I see, you mean a little bit like the playful side of Hitler?

DAVID: Exactly. I mean, there's Herod, a cultured, sophisticated man, into music, into ancient art, and then he massacres just *one* batch of babies and suddenly that's all people can remember.

GERALDINE: It's just not fair, is it?

DAVID: So, I have written a short scenelet. Nothing definitive, but perhaps putting his side of things a little more, well, you know.

*David hands her a piece of paper.*

GERALDINE: Right. (*She reads.*) 'Herod strokes his adoring dog Cuddles then turns to two soldiers. Herod: "Soldiers, take a battalion of men to Judaea and kiss all the babies there." Soldier One: "Did he say kiss all the babies?" Soldier Two (who is slightly hard of hearing): "No, I thought he said kill all the babies." Soldier One: "Oh right, well let's go and massacre them then."'

DAVID: It's an interpretation.

GERALDINE: No, it's not. Naughty.

## Scene Six: The Parish Hall

*A rehearsal is under way with Frank, Owen and Jim. Geraldine is directing them.*

GERALDINE: Come on now. Focus, focus. Come on now. You're in the fields, you're tending your sheep just before the Angel of the Lord appears. I need a little bit of chatter, make something up.

FRANK: Right. Right. Hello, Shepherds. Did anyone see *Ground Force* last night?

JIM: No, no, no, no, yes – that Charlie Dimmock! She can propagate my seedlings any time.

GERALDINE: No, no, no, no.

OWEN: When she leans over it's like two pumpkins rolling around in a grow bag.

*They are enjoying this bit of improvisation. Geraldine stands on a box next to them.*

GERALDINE: And, lo, an Angel of the Lord appeared before them.

OWEN: Shall I prompt for this bit, as you're playing the angel?

GERALDINE: Okay, but I am a vicar, Owen. I do actually know it.

OWEN: Good. Just in case.

GERALDINE: Okay. Be not afraid. For I am an Angel of the Lord and I bring you glad tidings of great joy.

OWEN: For tonight in the city of David . . .

GERALDINE: No, no, no, no. That's a pause isn't it? That's a dramatic pause there, do you see?

OWEN: Well, it didn't look like a pause. It looked like you'd forgotten it.

GERALDINE: (ignoring him) For I am an Angel of the Lord and I bring you glad tidings of great joy . . .

OWEN: For tonight in the city . . .

GERALDINE: No, that's the pause. That's the pause.

OWEN: I thought you were pausing, but then you paused a bit longer than you did in the first pause so I thought you'd stopped pausing and you'd forgotten it.

GERALDINE: Right, okay, all right look. I'm just going to go back to the beginning, all right, and you three just don't say anything, all right?

FRANK: We won't say anything.

OWEN: No, nothing at all.

JIM: What, not even our lines?

GERALDINE: Yes, your lines. Yes, your lines.

OWEN: We've got to have a prompt.

GERALDINE: Right, fine, okay. Well then, Frank can prompt me, can't he?

OWEN: Yes.

GERALDINE: Right, thank you.

FRANK: Right.

JIM: She's not very angelic is she?

GERALDINE: And lo an Angel of the Lord appeared before them . . .

FRANK: (interrupting) Be not afraid.

GERALDINE: No. BE AFRAID. BE VERY AFRAID.

## Scene Seven: Geraldine's Living Room

*A chocolate yule log is on the table in front of Geraldine.*

GERALDINE: Oh yes. Oh yes.

*She takes a knife and cuts a small slice, then picks up the remaining large portion and is about to tuck into it when Alice comes in.*

ALICE: Sorry to disturb you, Vicar.

GERALDINE: Oh, no that's fine. That's absolutely fine.

ALICE: Yum!

GERALDINE: Yeah.

ALICE: The thing is I'm a bit worried about this giving birth business.

GERALDINE: Oh?

ALICE: It's just that I watched a video of a birth last night and it looked really quite horrible.

GERALDINE: Mmm?

ALICE: I don't want my baby bursting through my stomach like that.

GERALDINE: Was the video called *Alien* by any chance?

ALICE: That's right.

GERALDINE: Right, right.

ALICE: Also, I've heard that mothers-to-be should avoid unnecessary strain, so I was thinking maybe I shouldn't be acting in the play after all, because it is pretty stressful.

GERALDINE: Alice, I'm sorry but you've only got one line, haven't you? 'But I am great with child.' Just the six words.

ALICE: Yeah, I know, but I'm really worried I'm going to forget them and the worry might cause me all sorts of damage internally.

GERALDINE: (*ever so slightly threatening*) Yeah, see your point, but on the other hand if you leave me high and dry with this play now, this fist will cause you all sorts of damage *externally* in the face department, do you see? Obviously the choice is yours.

ALICE: I think it will be okay, don't you?

GERALDINE: Yeah, I think so, I really do. Really do.

*Alice reaches for the small slice of cake and Geraldine taps her hand away.*

Ah, ah, ah, ah no, sorry. Can you just sod off now please? Thanks. It's just that I want to watch Sean Bean on the telly; I'd like to be alone with him.

ALICE: Isn't he lovely?

*She points at the TV so Geraldine won't see her nick the slice of cake. Then she makes a dash for it.*

GERALDINE: Oi, you!

❦

## Scene Eight: The Parish Hall

*At the end of another rehearsal.*

GERALDINE: Right, well, thank you, everyone, for an excellent day's rehearsal, after a slightly shaky start. Right, the poster. What do you think?

*She holds up the poster. It says 'The Greatest Story Ever Told'.*

OWEN: Well, I don't know about that.

GERALDINE: What?

OWEN: Well, I just don't think it is the greatest story ever told. I mean there's that great story about the people whose house was burgled and they thought the robbers hadn't taken anything. And then they developed their photographs months later and they found pictures of the robbers with toothbrushes up their bottoms.

GERALDINE: So what, you think I should write 'The Second Greatest Story Ever Told'?

HUGO: And there was a fantastic story about the woman whose

husband got out of the car and she heard this banging on the roof and the police said, 'Get out of the car and don't look round.' But she did look round and it was a lunatic actually banging her husband's severed head on the roof of the car.

GERALDINE: Well, perhaps I should just write 'One of the Top Ten Greatest Stories Ever Told'.

OWEN: You're forgetting all those great Jackie Collins stories: *The Bitch, The Stud*.

FRANK: And Beatrix Potter of course. She wrote lovely stories.

HUGO: Yes and *Newsroom South East* has some excellent local stories.

GERALDINE: Sorry, can we just stop right there. Can I please just remind you all a little bit about the story we're actually telling here. Two thousand years ago a baby is born in a stable. The poorest of the poor. And yet during his lifetime he says things that are so astonishing that millions of people are still living their lives by them today. He said 'love thy neighbour'. He told us to turn the other cheek, whatever people might do to us.

OWEN: Does that include that Simon bonking you like a beach ball?

GERALDINE: Yes, it does, Owen. Sadly it does. But most astonishingly, I believe that this tiny little baby boy actually *was* the Son of God, and when he was younger than I am today he was brutally crucified for simply telling people to love each other. And the men who killed him thought 'that's it'. That's the end of it. He's dead, he's gone. And yet here we are two thousand years later, in a village in the middle of England doing a play about his birth. (*pause*) Now I think that's a pretty great story.

ALICE: Yeah.

FRANK: Yes, yes.

OWEN: Yes all right, it's a good poster, leave it as it is.

GERALDINE: Thank you. Although I do admit the one about the toothbrushes is pretty gripping. Perhaps we'll do that next year.

HUGO: Bags Frank plays the toothbrush.

FRANK: Yes please.

## Scene Nine: Outside the Church

*Alice puts up a 'Tonight' sticker on the poster advertising the play. And then gets a big twinge of pain in her stomach.*

## Scene Ten: Owen's Barn

*The cast are all dressed and ready to start. The villagers are arriving at the farm.*

GERALDINE: Right, it's time to get going. Break a leg, everybody. And don't forget if you feel like improvising, just go for it.

HUGO: Right.

GERALDINE: Right.

ALICE: (*whimpering, having stomach pains*) Oh, oh. I think it's started.

GERALDINE: Exactly like that! Very good at it, well done Alice. All right everyone, give 'em hell. Actually, no, the absolute opposite of that please, give them a quite heavenly evening please. And Jim, I'm sorry, I think this beard is just far too long.

*It extends to the floor.*

JIM: No, no, no, no, yes you could be right.

## Scene Eleven: Owen's Farmyard

*Five minutes later Geraldine addresses the crowd of villagers.*

GERALDINE: Right, hello, everybody, hi. Welcome to the Farmyard Nativity. I hope you all enjoy watching it just as much as we've enjoyed rehearsing it. As you know we haven't charged anybody anything to come in, so at the end there'll be two little angels here waiting at the gate and all donations will be welcome. Thank you.

*The two angels hold up their buckets. One has written on it 'Give us lots of cash'. The other '. . . or else'.*

So, here we go.

*Owen shouts out from behind the crowd.*

OWEN: I'd just like to say I'll be slaughtering Daisy here tomorrow, so do order your Christmas beef after the show.

GERALDINE: Right, thank you very much, Owen.
'And it came to pass that there went out a decree from Caesar Augustus, that all the world should be taxed and Joseph went to Bethlehem with Mary his espoused wife, who was great with child and riding upon a donkey'.

*Hugo comes through the crowd, pulling Alice behind him . . . on a lawn mower.*

'But the donkey did run away during rehearsals this afternoon, so in the end she actually turned up on a small motorized lawn mower. And so Mary and Joseph came unto an inn in Bethlehem and knocked upon the door.'

*Hugo knocks on the stable door and Jim, the inn-keeper, appears.*

HUGO:  Innkeeper, have you a room where we may rest?

JIM:  No, no, no, no, no, no room in the inn. We're fully booked because of the Millennium.

GERALDINE:  *(whispering a prompt to Alice)* And I am great with child.

JIM:  *(taking her up on the prompt)* Also, I am great with child, so it's particularly awkward.

GERALDINE:  *(pointing at Alice)* You.

ALICE:  Oh sorry. 'But also I am great with child.' Oh, I forgot it.

GERALDINE:  *(whispering a prompt to Jim this time)* In that case I have a stable you can use.

JIM:  In that case the vicar has a stable you can use.

GERALDINE:  'And so Mary and Joseph went into the stable the inn-keeper so kindly offered, there to make preparations for the birth of the holy child.'

*Alice and Hugo start to walk towards the stable when Alice stops, in pain.*

ALICE: I can feel it coming.

*Geraldine thinks she's really got into her part.*

GERALDINE: Oh, that's good.

ALICE: No, I really can.

*Geraldine gives thumbs up.*

JIM: She was good, wasn't she?

GERALDINE: Very convincing, yes.

JIM: I was quite good, wasn't I?

GERALDINE: No.

*On the other side of the farmyard, two minutes later.*

GERALDINE: 'And at that time in Jerusalem, Herod had heard of the impending birth of a so-called King of the Jews and he was sore troubled, for Herod was a cruel and jealous king.'

*She steps aside. David is seated on a throne with soldiers on either side of him.*

DAVID: Soldiers, go forth unto Bethlehem and kill all the infants in that region, for I shall have no other King but me.

GERALDINE: 'And so . . .'

DAVID: But kill them gently. For I am not as cruel and jealous as some would have me be.

GERALDINE: 'And so . . .'

DAVID: In fact I really love children. Indeed, I see some in my court and would give them many gifts of sweets and chocolates.

*He gets up to give sweets out to the children watching.*

For you.

CHILD: Thank you, Herod.

DAVID: And for you.

CHILD: Thank you, Herod.

DAVID: And for you.

CHILD: I love you, Herod.

*Five minutes later, in a field, Geraldine stands next to Jim, Frank and Owen, dressed as angels.*

GERALDINE: 'And meanwhile, in the fields, some shepherds were tending their flock.'

*The men are completely still. Geraldine prompts them on.*

Improvise.

OWEN: See that ewe over there? She's pretty.

JIM: No, no, no, I wouldn't mind giving her one.

GERALDINE: *(stepping in quickly)* 'And lo, an Angel of the Lord appeared before them and they were sore afraid.'

*The men shield their eyes away from Geraldine, the Angel of the Lord. She flicks a switch on her back and huge wings unfold behind her.*

'Be not afraid, for I am an Angel of the Lord and I bring you tidings of great joy.'

*A silver foil halo pops up above her head. Frank takes the opportunity to prompt her.*

FRANK: For tonight in the city of . . .

GERALDINE: *(at the top of her voice)* I KNOW, YOU PILLOCK! Sorry, sorry . . . 'great joy'.

## Scene Twelve: Owen's Big Barn

*There is a little set of the stable and the manger. Alice is on all fours, panting and moaning in pain.*

HUGO: Wow, you're good. I mean this, this is a Judy Dench-type quality performance.

*Geraldine stands nearby.*

GERALDINE: 'And so it was that the three wise men, who looked remarkably like the shepherds but who were, in fact, completely different people, approached the stable, riding camels – or at least doing very good camel-riding impressions. And as they came unto the manger they saw Mary who was extremely great with child – and looking rather hot.'

*Alice, by this time, is in a birthing position, sitting with her knees bent. Hugo beside her, trying to cool her down.*

'And in the company of only some cattle and her husband Joseph.'

*Hugo takes a peek up Alice's skirt – he sees that she's about to give birth.*

HUGO: Oh, my God.

*And promptly faints.*

ALICE: (*panting*) Oh, oh, oh.

*Owen kneels down in front of her to present his gift to the baby Jesus – he also sees that she is about to have her baby.*

OWEN: Jesus, she's having the baby.

FRANK: No, the line is 'She's having a baby, Jesus.'

OWEN: No really, she is actually having a baby, have a look.

*Frank and Jim rush over.*

FRANK: Oh. Vicar . . .

GERALDINE: (*to the audience*) Would you excuse me just one second, thank you.

*Irritated, she goes on to the set to find out what's going on.*

What are you doing? We've got them in the palms of our hands. (*She catches sight of Alice's baby about to emerge.*) Oh my God! Oh my

God! We must have some towels. Owen, run up to the house and get some towels.

OWEN: I haven't got any.

GERALDINE: What, no towels?

OWEN: Why would I have towels?

GERALDINE: To dry yourself after a bath.

OWEN: I don't have a bath.

*She turns to the audience.*

GERALDINE: Would anyone here have some towels?

JIM: I suppose you could use these. My entire costume is made of towels.

*He begins to undress.*

GERALDINE: Good, good, good. (*But she stops him from removing the flannel which is strategically placed in front of his privates.*) No, no, no, no. (*To the audience.*) Would you excuse us just one moment. Actually, is there a doctor in the house?

VET: I'm a vet.

GERALDINE: You'll do. Could you come and help?

DAVID: (*emerging through the crowd*) Over my dead body. I'm not having a grandchild of mine brought into the world by James Herriot. Come on, it's common sense surely. (*He sees up Alice's skirt.*) Oh dear, oh dear.

JIM: Are you sure it's a good idea having Herod take care of Jesus?

FRANK: He's not Herod now, he's Mr Horton.

JIM: Oh yes.

DAVID: Come on little one, push, push. Oh Geraldine, come on, give us a hand.

GERALDINE: Right, Alice. Breathe.

ALICE: Oh, it hurts.

GERALDINE: Does it? Well, next time you get a contraction you just hang on to my hand really tight, okay, grip it. Tight as you like.

ALICE: It's coming.

Frank Pickle

Hugo Horton

David Horton M.B.E., M.A. (Oxon), F.R.C.S.

Owen Newitt

Jim Trott

The Prospective Couple

The Unhinged Couple

The Unhappy Couple

The Happy Couple

The Dibley Five

The Moment of Triumph

Three Generations of Hortons, and a Twit

The British Olympic Netball Team

GERALDINE: Okay.

ALICE: Here it comes.

GERALDINE: Okay.

ALICE: Here it comes.

GERALDINE: Okay. (*Alice squeezes Geraldine's hand very tightly.*) Oww, oooh, you bitch.

*The contraction subsides.*

ALICE: Thank you. Oh my God, here comes another one.

*She grabs Geraldine's hand. Geraldine grabs David's hand to pass on the pain.*

GERALDINE: Right. All together.

FRANK: Isn't there something we can do to help? I mean, after all, we are the three wise men.

JIM: No, no, no, no we are the kings.

FRANK: Oh right.

JIM: And most kings are brain-dead inbred cretins.

GERALDINE: Now then, deep breathing, deeper, deeper, that's it. Good girl. (*Hugo comes round.*) Here's Hugo.

ALICE: Oh my God!

HUGO: Oh my God.

GERALDINE: There we are. Just, just one more push now. Oh my God, I can see the head. God, I hope that is a head.

WOMAN IN THE AUDIENCE: It's very realistic isn't it?

GERALDINE: It's coming! It's coming!

*Alice gives one more tremendous push and the baby is born. The audience clap enthusiastically.*

*Five minutes later, everything has calmed down and all the cast are in a very Christmassy tableau.*

GERALDINE: 'And there in a stable, two thousand years ago, God himself took part in the miracle of birth and Mary held in her arms a very special – and very realistic – child.'

ALICE: Brillo pads!

HUGO: Most excellent.

GERALDINE: One, two, one, two, three . . . four.

ALL: (*singing loudly*) Silent night, holy night . . .

*The baby starts crying.*

GERALDINE: Ssshh.

*They continue, singing quietly.*

ALL: All is calm, all is bright,
Round yon virgin mother and child.
Holy infant so tender and mild.
Sleep in heavenly peace
Sleep in heavenly peace.

GERALDINE: (*whispers*) Merry Christmas to you all.

## Scene Thirteen: Geraldine's Living Room

*The next day. Geraldine and the whole Horton family.*

GERALDINE: Well, she really is the most beautiful baby.

ALICE: Thank you. Could I just check something with you though, Vicar?

GERALDINE: Mmm.

ALICE: Have I actually given birth to the Son of God? Because, I'd find it a bit of a responsibility.

GERALDINE: No, Alice, you haven't, no.

ALICE: Oh phew.

GERALDINE: I mean, apart from anything, she's a girl, isn't she?

ALICE: Oh yes, so she is. Good clue.

GERALDINE: Have you thought of any names at all?

HUGO: Yeah, go on, Alice.

ALICE: Well, we've thought about it long and hard and, um, we'd like to name her after you.

GERALDINE: Oh guys – I don't know what to say.

ALICE: So I'm calling her 'Vicar'.

GERALDINE: Or, 'Geraldine'.

ALICE: Geraldine! Oh – even better.

HUGO: Splendido.

GERALDINE: Yes, 'Geraldine'.

DAVID: Good choice. Excellent choice.

## Epilogue: The Vestry

*It's late. Geraldine and Alice are having a cup of tea by candlelight.*

**GERALDINE:** Right, little Christmas gagette for you.

**ALICE:** Great.

**GERALDINE:** Santa Claus goes to the doctor with a problem.

**ALICE:** Oh dear.

**GERALDINE:** Yeah. He says, 'Doctor, I think I've got a mince pie stuck up my bottom.'

**ALICE:** I wonder how that got there?

**GERALDINE:** Don't go there, okay. So the doctor says, 'Okay Mr Claus bend over please.' And he looks and he says, 'Yes, indeed, you do have a mince pie stuck up your bottom. But you're in luck because I've got some cream for that.' (*She explodes with laughter.*) See, 'cream' for the mince pie . . .

**ALICE:** You mean, he's going to take it out and eat it?

**GERALDINE:** No.

**ALICE:** That is not hygenic.

**GERALDINE:** No, he's not going to is he? Because it's a joke.

**ALICE:** But, doctors these days – what are they going to be doing next? Taking out your appendix and having it with, I don't know, bacon and egg . . .

**GERALDINE:** Look, you're just leaving Planet Earth now. Whooh!

**ALICE:** Removing your tonsils and sprinkling them with sugar . . .

**GERALDINE:** (*singing to drown out Alice*) 'Jesus Christ our Saviour was born on Christmas Day, to save us all from Satan's power' . . . that's you.

*She gets up and leaves.*

**ALICE:** I can't believe that. I'm not eating it, no way. Not if it's been up Santa's arse. I'm sticking to brandy snaps.

Keith and Margaret welcome you to

# The Chandos Arms

### Mill Lane, Dibley, Oxon

Tired of 'trendy' pubs? We can assure you that nothing trendy has ever happened here at the Chandos, or ever will! We boast a traditional English pub ambience, where a woman coming in on her own will be tutted at disapprovingly. It's a pub steeped in history. Elizabeth I stayed the night here in 1584. Saracen from *Gladiators* popped in to ask if he could use the toilet in 1995.

Come and enjoy:
- the CD jukebox which only plays 'Wonderful Tonight' by Eric Clapton •
- the three real ale bores with glasses who smirk when you ask for a lager •
  - the real fake coal fire •

Savour the splendid flavour of the dishes in our restaurant section:

**Long, thin parcels of succulent pork sausage meat served with a delicious purée of mashed South American root vegetable – £11.50**

**Hand-fried prime beef pattie nestling inside a hand-baked individual roll, accompanied by delicious slivers of Julienne potatoes hand-fried in essence of sunflower – £16.50**

Or enjoy a snack from the bar menu:
**Sausage and Mash £3.99     Burger and Chips £3.50**

So come and join us in Dibley for an evening you'll find it hard to remember! Dogs are welcome, as long as they don't mind being mounted by Caesar, our over-sexed Jack Russell. The same goes for most people's legs.

# All the Great Things for Teenagers to do in Dibley:

# Spring

## Scene One: The Parish Hall

DAVID: Right, Vicar, I believe you have a suggestion?

GERALDINE: Yes. With the arrival of baby Geraldine, I'd like to start a crèche in the vestry. All little children under the age of six welcome every weekday morning.

JIM: And people who have a mental age of under six?

GERALDINE: Also welcome.

*Frank and Jim are pleased at this — they 'high-five'.*

DAVID: Very well, you'll have to go through the normal channels, check with the Council that whoever runs it is qualified at childcare.

GERALDINE: Of course. I think I can have it up and running inside a month, so get reproducing everyone, we'll need a crowd.

JIM: Is illegitimacy no barrier?

GERALDINE: Absolutely not.

JIM: Put me down for a dozen then, baby.

DAVID: Moving on. I believe Hugo has an announcement.

HUGO: Yes, siree. We've fixed the christening for the twenty-second and I'm delighted to say that Mr Newitt and the vicar have consented to be godparents. Mr Pickle and Mr Trott, we wanted you two to be godparents as well but . . .

OWEN: You probably won't live much longer.

HUGO: That's right. So we thought you might like to be god-grandparents instead.

FRANK: Oh, thank you.

OWEN: Am I right in thinking that I should get a present for this christening?

GERALDINE: Yeah, absolutely right, Owen.

OWEN: Ah, well I'd like a new suit then, Hugo. Can't get the pig's blood out of this one.

GERALDINE: No, no, no. You get a present for the baby, Owen.

FRANK: A godparent generally gives a spoon.

OWEN: Oh. Bugger.

DAVID: As the vicar is a godparent I thought I'd ask my old friend the Bishop of Mulberry to officiate at the service.

GERALDINE: Good idea.

DAVID: Now, I know the vicar won't like the idea.

GERALDINE: No, I do.

DAVID: I beg your pardon?

GERALDINE: I think it's a good idea.

DAVID: You mean you agree? That is the first time you've ever agreed with me.

GERALDINE: Is it?

JIM: No, no, what about the proposal that we twin Dibley with the red light district of Hamburg?

GERALDINE: That was your proposal wasn't it, Jim? And if my memory serves me correctly it was triple towning wasn't it? It was Dibley, the Reeperbahn in Hamburg and the Bangkok Pussy Club, and I did not agree with it.

JIM: Oh shame.

OWEN: Bitter disappointment.

GERALDINE: But on this christening thing, David, absolutely we do agree. Hey, maybe it's the start of a beautiful friendship.

*He smiles at this.*

DAVID: Moving on.

OWEN: I think you're in there, *chairmeister*.

JIM: Take her to the Bangkok Pussy Club.

DAVID: Moving on.

## Scene Two: Geraldine's Living Room

*Alice is visiting with the baby.*

GERALDINE: Of course, babies are meant to look like their grandfathers, aren't they? Do you think she looks like Mr Horton?

ALICE: No, not really. He's much taller, isn't he?

GERALDINE: Yeah. So how are you doing with the breast-feeding then, Alice?

ALICE: It was a bit tricky at first but then the health visitor explained that I didn't actually have to eat grass like the cows do, you know, and I'd produce milk anyway.

GERALDINE: Amazing!

ALICE: I know, so now it's great, you know, I can feed her any time any place. Just whip the old booby out and get squirting.

GERALDINE: Always best to put it away again when you're finished I think.

ALICE: I know! I keep forgetting!

GERALDINE: It was a bit of a shock when you came up for Communion on Sunday.

ALICE: I'm sorry. And you know she's very clever. She's actually started saying her first words.

GERALDINE: At three months?

ALICE: Absolutely. Yesterday she said 'goo'.

GERALDINE: What, you don't think she might just be making baby noises, Alice?

ALICE: No, no, no. We looked it up, it's a proper word – G U E. It's a sort of violin played in the Shetland Islands.

GERALDINE: I think it might be a bit obscure for a three-month-old.

ALICE: And this morning she said 'grrr', which after hours of research we found to be *guerre*, the French word for 'war'.

GERALDINE: Incredible. No – literally *incredible*.

ALICE: I know, I know.

*The doorbell rings. It's David.*

GERALDINE: Oh, David, got your favourite person here.

DAVID: Jeffrey Archer?

GERALDINE: Your granddaughter.

ALICE: Oh hello, daddy – diddy – doo doo's. Big wet kiss and lick.

*Alice reaches up and gives David a big kiss on the cheek, followed by a big lick.*

DAVID: Hello, Alice. (*Then to baby Geraldine.*) Ah, there you are. You poor thing.

ALICE: She said a whole word when I picked her up this morning. Guess what she said?

DAVID: 'Help?'

ALICE: No.

*David ignores her and speaks to Geraldine instead.*

DAVID: I've come round to discuss the christening, Vicar. Any final decisions on the baby's names?

GERALDINE: Oh, Alice?

ALICE: Yes. We finally decided on Geraldine, Wendy, Nana, Peter Pan, Tinkerbell, Tiger Lily, Captain Hook, Crocodile Horton.

*Alice is so pleased with this list.*

GERALDINE: That's great. Or what about Geraldine, Pooh, Piglet, Kanga, Eeyore, Tigger Horton?

ALICE: Don't be so childish, Geraldine.

DAVID: Either she changes them or I'll have her sectioned.

ALICE: (*to the baby*) Have you done a smelly, Geraldine?

GERALDINE: No, I have not, thank you. I think I'd know.

ALICE: I think you have, you naughty little whipper.

GERALDINE: No, I have not . . . *(She realizes that Alice is talking to the baby.)* Oh right, sorry.

*Alice takes the baby out to change her.*

ALICE: See you in a minute.

DAVID: I won't have those names, Vicar. I know you'll disagree.

GERALDINE: No, I agree.

DAVID: You do?

GERALDINE: Yes. I know what it's like to have a silly first name.

DAVID: Well, Geraldine's not that silly.

GERALDINE: No, not Geraldine, my real first name.

DAVID: Which is?

GERALDINE: Well, promise you won't laugh?

DAVID: Of course I won't laugh.

GERALDINE: Boadicea.

DAVID: Boadicea?!

*David starts laughing.*

GERALDINE: Yeah, well, thanks, thanks.

DAVID: That is very amusing. Oh, by the way I'm having drinks tomorrow night so that you can meet the Bishop before the service.

GERALDINE: Oh great.

DAVID: And he can meet the Queen of the Ancient Britons.

GERALDINE: Oh har de har, har, har, ha, ha.

DAVID: It's nice having a baby in the village again, isn't it?

GERALDINE: It is, it's lovely.

DAVID: See you tomorrow, your Highness.

GERALDINE: Shut up.

*David leaves and Alice comes back through.*

ALICE: Right. Baby's botty as clean as a baby's botty!

GERALDINE: *(to the baby)* Hi, you little gorgeous thing. You're making me feel quite broody, you milky minxes.

ALICE: Well, better find yourself a husband first though, eh?

GERALDINE: Aha ha ha ha. Yes.

ALICE: Bye, bye, Auntie Gerry! See you later.

GERALDINE: Yeah. (*Then to herself.*) Auntie Gerry. It's always Auntie Gerry.

## Scene Three: David's Hallway/Sitting Room

*Hugo opens the door to Geraldine.*

GERALDINE: Ah, and how's Daddy Hugo this evening?

*Hugo holds up a notice saying 'Schhh'.*

GERALDINE: (*whispering*) Oh, sorry.

*He turns it over: 'The Baby's Asleep'. He points towards the door to the sitting room, on which is another notice: 'Total Silence'. They go through. Already there, are Frank, Jim, Owen and Alice. They are standing in silence.*

*Frank holds up a sign to Jim: 'Did you see Eastenders last night?'*

*Jim holds up his reply: 'No no no no no'. And then flicks it over: 'Yes'.*

*Owen holds up 'This is bloody ridiculous'. Hugo holds up a reply: 'Don't swear in front of the baby'. Owen retaliates with: 'I'll swear if I f . . . ing want to', his hand placed strategically over the offending word. With that, David comes in, followed by the Bishop.*

DAVID: Through here, Bishop. (*Hugo holds up his 'Schhhh' sign.*) Idiot boy. (*But he then whispers.*) Everybody, I would like you to meet the Bishop of Mulberry. The Bishop is a very distinguished old friend of mine.

BISHOP: (*quietly*) Good evening.

ALL: (*equally quiet*) Good evening.

*Unfortunately, however, the Bishop has no volume control at all when he speaks.*

BISHOP: I see the little one is asleep, so it's best we all keep very QUIET, so as not to wake her. I must say I was delighted that David asked me to officiate at the service. A christening is something I'm not VERY OFTEN asked to perform.

*The baby starts to cry at all this noise.*

Oh, the little one's woken up.

GERALDINE: Yes, I wonder how that happened?

BISHOP: Oh, hello, little one. You're not very happy are you? And I know why. Because you've just woken up and there are all these STRANGE people here. (*Alice is worried at this strange shouty behaviour.*) Oh, you must be Alice.

ALICE: Your Majesty.

*She takes his hand and curtsies.*

FRANK: I'm Frank Pickle. I'm god-grandparent.

BISHOP: Oh, how very unusual.

FRANK: Not as unusual as the photograph of Boyzone that I keep in my wallet.

DAVID: Come and meet the vicar, Bishop.

GERALDINE: Hello. David tells me you were at school together.

BISHOP: Yes, that's right, we were old chums at school. Tell me, I don't actually remember, did we sleep together?

DAVID: Erm no, we didn't.

BISHOP: Oh, my sons are there at the moment. Not the same though, the bullying's terrible.

GERALDINE: Oh dear.

BISHOP: Whereas the bullying in our day was excellent. Yeah, well, who was that horrible little creep whose head we had to shave with a blunt razor?

DAVID: That was me.

BISHOP: Was it? Oh sorry.

DAVID: No, no, it's all part of growing up. Helped to make me what I am today.

GERALDINE: What, bald?

BISHOP: You must be one of those lady vicars.

GERALDINE: Yes, I am, holy in more ways than one. (*She cackles with laughter.*) Would you excuse me?

BISHOP: I am surprised at your judgement, tolerating her here.

DAVID: Actually, she's the best vicar we've ever had. She's a truly remarkable woman.

BISHOP: Oh, I didn't realize you were giving her one, you old dog.

DAVID: I am not giving her one.

BISHOP: Oh, so you're just in love with her, eh?

DAVID: What? What?

BISHOP: Oh, come on, David. I know that look on your face. Every time Matron Three came into the dorm in her tight little pinny. Well, let's meet some of your other charming neighbours, shall we? (*He turns to the others.*) HELLO!

## Scene Four: Geraldine's Living Room

*Geraldine is sat on her desk talking to Hugo and Alice who are on the sofa.*

GERALDINE: So, can anyone tell me why you're having her baptized on Sunday?

ALICE: You're busy on Saturday.

GERALDINE: Okay, let's do it a different way shall we? You imagine that I'm Chris Tarrant, okay? Are you having your daughter baptized because a) she'll get some nice new spoons, b) she'll get a nice wash in a font, c) it'll make a change from watching *The Antiques Roadshow* and d) – that's d) – she'll be welcomed into the family of Christ?

ALICE: I'll phone a friend.

GERALDINE: No, no, no, no, no, no.

ALICE: Fifty fifty?

GERALDINE: No, it's d), Alice. It's d), it's d), it's d).

HUGO: Not strictly though, because it will also make a change from watching *The Antiques Roadshow*.

ALICE: Yes.

GERALDINE: So we're baptizing her in order to bring her into a Christian loving family. Now remember that God is a father, very much like your own father.

ALICE: So he's drunk from dusk till dawn?

GERALDINE: No, well, probably a bit more like Hugo's father then?

HUGO: Shouting a lot, telling me I'm a cretin?

GERALDINE: No, no, no.

HUGO: Caning me when I wet the bed?

GERALDINE: No, I'm thinking more of the loving, gentle father who treasured you and cuddled you when you were little.

HUGO: I had another father? I don't remember him at all.

GERALDINE: No, no, no. Okay. Let's just forget the whole father thing.

HUGO: I don't want to forget him, you've only just told me about him. I'm going to track him down through hell and high water.

GERALDINE: No! Sit down, sit down, sweetheart. Listen, all you need to know is that we're having this service so that God can love your little Geraldine exactly the same way you do.

ALICE: (*hugging Hugo*) You see!

*Hugo's alarm goes off on his watch.*

HUGO: Oh, is that the time? Excuse me, Vicar, I'm fixing up a bouncy castle for the pensioners tea party. They love a good bounce, the over-eighties.

ALICE: Oh, Hugo. (*The door slams behind him.*) Oh dear.

GERALDINE: What?

ALICE: Oh, I've just got to catch the post to send off for my *Blue Peter* badge. Can you take care of little Geraldine for a minute?

GERALDINE: Yes, of course, it would be a pleasure and a doddle.

ALICE: Oh great. (*She kisses the baby.*) Bye, bye, Mummy's baby. Oh you wouldn't just change her little nappy would you?

GERALDINE: Yeah, course I will.

ALICE: Great. Look, here's a nappy and these are the wipes. You sure you're okay?

GERALDINE: Yes, I'm a world expert nappy changer.

ALICE: Good. Back in one minute.

*Alice leaves. Geraldine lifts the baby out of its basket.*

GERALDINE: Oh, hello little sweetums, come on then, darling. Hello. Welcome to Auntie Geraldine's house. There you are. Let me introduce you to a couple of blokes I know. That's Jesus over there, he's very nice. And there, more importantly, is Sean Bean, he's very sexy. So come on in and have a look at my kitchen.

*She carries her through to the kitchen. When she's in there we have to guess at the horrors that are happening.*

You can see my new worktop, it doubles up as a special baby changing area. There we go, let's get that nappy off then. Phew! God! What have you been eating? It's like Willy Wonka's chocolate factory down here. Oh God, the wet wipes.

*She decides to pop through to the living room to get the wipes, leaving baby Geraldine on the kitchen worktop.*

Sorry, little one, I'll be with you in a second.

*There is a loud bump — the baby has fallen on to the floor. Geraldine rushes back through to her.*

Oh! Oh my God. Are you all right? There we go. Good girl, stop crying, there we go. That wasn't too bad a fall was it? Only three feet, and the old nappy sort of acted as a cushion, didn't it? Shame you fell face first. Let's call it face painting, shall we? Who's a lovely little brown bear then? You just lie there and I'll go and find the wipes.

*The doorbell rings. Geraldine answers it with hands covered in poo. A tidily dressed lady at the door reaches out and shakes her hand.*

GERALDINE: Hello. Now don't lick that okay, that's just come out of a baby. Having a bit of a crisis here, come in. Come in, go straight into the kitchen please and wash that off immediately please. I'll be with you . . .

*Geraldine goes to fetch the wipes and the lady walks through into the kitchen. Baby Geraldine screams, clearly having been trod on.*

Oh God, I'm sorry I meant to tell you the baby's on the floor. Hang on, hang on, be right with you. Oh dear, you've got poo on your shoe. Take that off please, immediately, immediately. Give it to me. There we go, one soaking wet suede shoe. Right, why don't you just pop back in here. (*She shows the woman through to the living room.*) That's it, wait there, there, on the couch, thank you. I'll just get her cleaned up. Come on, madam, let's have a final inspection of your minky area. No, no, no, no! (*to her visitor*) I'm going to be a little longer than I expected – the leaky little thing's just weed in my face.

*The doorbell goes. Alice is back. She gives Geraldine a big kiss.*

ALICE:  Oh, funny wet face.

GERALDINE:  (*now almost insane*) You said one minute, you irresponsible cow – you've been gone an hour and a half.

ALICE:  I haven't. How's little Gerry been?

GERALDINE:  She's . . .

ALICE:  On the floor of the kitchen covered in wee.

GERALDINE:  No problem with that. (*To the woman on the couch.*) Some people are so fussy aren't they?

ALICE:  Fudgy, tudgy, naughty, Auntie Geraldine.

*Geraldine at last gets to sit down and deal with her visitor.*

GERALDINE:  So we didn't get a chance to get acquainted. How can I help you?

WOMAN:  I'm here from the local council just checking up on your suitability to start a crèche in the chapel.

GERALDINE:  (*mortified*) Right.

WOMAN: I was just coming to see how you deal with little children.

GERALDINE: Good, excellent. So, how do you think I did?

WOMAN: Well, apart from greeting me with your hands covered in faeces and then leaving the baby on the kitchen floor for anyone to step on, and then abandoning it casually to answer the front door . . .

GERALDINE: Yep.

WOMAN: (*totally sincere*) I thought you were pretty damn good!

GERALDINE: Did you? Did you? Oh, great, thanks! So, out of casual interest, how long have you been doing this job?

WOMAN: I just started today, actually.

GERALDINE: I thought as much.

WOMAN: I used to be in libraries. 'Sssh!' This is my big break.

GERALDINE: Right. Well, do you know what? I think you're going to be superb at this job. Oh yes, lucky local kiddies, eh, having you in charge. So, what say I wash the urine off my face and we all have a nice cup of tea?

WOMAN: Oh great.

*Alice comes through with baby Geraldine all cleaned up.*

GERALDINE: A new friend for you, Alice.

## Scene Five: Geraldine's Living Room

*It's night-time and Geraldine is watching the TV; shouting at it.*

GERALDINE: Go on, hit him. No, hit him! Go on, a right hook, hit him!

*The doorbell rings.*

Come in, the door's open. Oh good, he's down, good.

*It's David in a nice hat.*

Oh hello, David. Hey, nice hat.

DAVID: Oh thank you.

GERALDINE: I'm just watching *The Jerry Springer Show*. It's 'My Mum Won't Let Me Sleep with Grandma'. I was on the side of the son but it turns out grandma's been dead for two months so I'm wavering. (*She turns the TV off.*) So, Alice has decided to change the baby's names.

DAVID: Good.

GERALDINE: She's decided to name her after her grandmother and her favourite TV chef.

DAVID: Who's that?

GERALDINE: That's the bad news. So what can I do you for?

DAVID: Oh, nothing much. I just thought I'd come round for a chat, that's all. Is that all right?

GERALDINE: Of course. What's on your mind?

DAVID: Oh, I don't know. What with the baby, I've been thinking about things recently. Circle of life stuff. You know, when you first arrived I thought you were completely and utterly wrong for this village. A disaster.

GERALDINE: Lovely.

DAVID: But you weren't wrong, you were right. Then again I thought you were wrong about Hugo marrying our Alice, but you weren't, you were right – they're happy.

GERALDINE: What can I say except: 'Correct. I'm great!'

DAVID: Yes. And sometimes I think to myself, have I been a daft stupid prejudiced old fool?

GERALDINE: No, that's Prince Philip.

DAVID: I live alone in that great big house, and I think to myself just sometimes, did I let that scrofulous brother of mine seduce the woman I should have made it my aim and my mission in life to woo?

*This sinks in.*

GERALDINE: Pardon?

DAVID: Boadicea. If I may call you that.

GERALDINE: No, you mayn't.

DAVID: Geraldine, just hypothetically of course, would I ever have had a chance with you? I know you didn't like me at first, but I do believe you're getting to like me more. You have agreed with me on no less than two occasions this week.

GERALDINE: David, it's true I have grown increasingly fond of you but, well, I think even hypothetically you'd have to agree that we'd never have made a pair.

DAVID: Right. Right. Though just parenthetically can I ask why? I mean you can't be happy just here on your own every night with Jesus and Sean Bone . . .

GERALDINE: Bean.

DAVID: Bean . . . as your only companions. I mean, why wouldn't I make better company?

GERALDINE: Well, okay, let's think about it. I'm going to be frank because I know we're just fooling about here.

DAVID: Well, right.

GERALDINE: Right. Three reasons why you wouldn't be right for me. Well, one, you're a Tory.

DAVID: Doesn't make me a bad person.

GERALDINE: No, but it does mean that you can watch William Hague on the telly and not giggle and therefore you're not the bloke for me. Secondly, you can't deny it, David, you are a bit mean.

DAVID: Mean?

GERALDINE: Yes, you see a beggar on the street, what do you give him?

DAVID: I give him a kick. Tell him to stop cluttering up the highway.

GERALDINE: Exactly, and what are you worth?

DAVID: About five million pounds.

GERALDINE: What?

DAVID: All right, what's your other reason?

GERALDINE: Sorry, five million pounds? That's a hell of a lot of chocolate, isn't it? I might reconsider. No, resist temptation. The thing is David, you're very old fashioned, you live in a suit and you're not exactly romantic. If you were to propose to somebody I expect you'd do it hypothetically or parenthetically, wouldn't you? Whereas if ever I were to marry I'd like somebody to woo me properly, you know, propose to me on one knee. Not just pop round one evening to check if a deal was possible.

DAVID: Right. Right. As usual. Alas.

*Owen comes walking in.*

OWEN: The door was open.

GERALDINE: Owen! You shouldn't just barge in. I might not have any clothes on.

OWEN: All the better.

DAVID: I should go.

GERALDINE: Yes, um, bye. *(He leaves unceremoniously.)*

OWEN: You can take them off now if you like.

GERALDINE: No. Look, Owen, this just isn't the right moment, I need a bit of time to myself.

OWEN: Ah, message received and understood.

*He leaves the room.*

GERALDINE: Thanks. Oh God.

*She sits down, only for Owen to reappear two seconds later.*

OWEN: Ready now?

GERALDINE: *(resigned)* Yes.

OWEN: Good. It's about this godfather business. Frank says not only do I have to give the baby a present, I also have to teach her things.

GERALDINE: Well, that would be lovely, yes.

OWEN: Right. So I could take her on nature rambles when she's older up to Badgers Copse, where we'd gaze at the bluebells and she'd hold my hand and say, 'God-daddy, tell me about all the different pretty flowers'.

GERALDINE: Oh, excellent.

OWEN: How about teaching her to ride a bike?

GERALDINE: Well, that too, compulsory.

OWEN: Great. And slaughtering cattle?

GERALDINE: Not.

OWEN: How about smoking out moles and stoving in their heads with the flat of a spade?

GERALDINE: Definitely not, just nice things, Owen.

OWEN: Well, that is nice. You should hear the squish of their skulls.

GERALDINE: No, no, no, without killing anything, Owen.

OWEN: It's a pity.

GERALDINE: Yes, I have really got to get on now.

OWEN: Okay.

GERALDINE: Okay.

*He turns back to her.*

OWEN: Final one.

GERALDINE: Yes.

OWEN: Blowing up toads?

GERALDINE: I'll think about it.

OWEN: Good.

*Geraldine picks up David's hat which he has left behind.*

GERALDINE: (thinking out loud) What happened here this evening?

## Scene Six: The Parish Hall

*All are present for the Council Meeting, except David.*

FRANK: You know, it's not like Mr Horton to be late for a meeting.

GERALDINE: I wonder where he is.

HUGO: Search me, he's been missing for days.

GERALDINE: Really?

HUGO: He disappeared shortly after he talked to you. In fact he looked a broken man. I haven't seen him so lost and bewildered since Mrs Thatcher left Downing Street.

GERALDINE: Good Lord.

HUGO: What did you say to him?

GERALDINE: I don't know really, it was all a bit confusing.

JIM: Well, that is life, isn't it? Full of confusion.

GERALDINE: Quite.

JIM: I found this gorgeous girl in Thailand, we snogged, well, we more than snogged. I asked her to marry me. She said yes. We got married on a pineapple-strewn beach. On the first night of the honeymoon she takes off all her clothes and it turns out she's a bloke called Dwayne. She was just after a passport. She didn't love me at all.

GERALDINE: Well, this wasn't quite as confusing as that.

OWEN: What do you mean, you more than snogged?

JIM: Well, Dwayne, he used to do this . . .

GERALDINE: Yes, that's quite enough about that, thank you. There are children present.

*David arrives. Dressed in tightish jeans, a bright pink shirt, a black leather jacket and a beret.*

DAVID: Sorry I'm late, everyone. Before we start the meeting, just a few announcements. I know this should come under 'any other business' but, hey, let's go with the flow.

JIM: Who is that?

FRANK: I think it's Mr Horton.

DAVID: Hugo, I'd like you to read this.

HUGO: 'This is to certify that David Horton is a fully paid up member of the Labour Party.'

GERALDINE: That's a very wobbly signature, David.

DAVID: Yes, I was shaking at the time. And I've bought you this.

*He hands her a cheque.*

GERALDINE: A hundred thousand pounds?

DAVID: For the cause of your choice.

GERALDINE: What? Any cause? Ken Livingstone for King of England Campaign?

DAVID: If you so wish. And finally, 'one, two, three'.

*He pulls back the stage curtain to reveal a pianist and violinist surrounded by candles – they begin to play 'The First Time Ever I Saw Your Face' in soft romantic style. David pulls Geraldine to her feet. She thinks they are going to dance, until David drops to one knee before her.*

DAVID: Geraldine Granger, will you marry me?

GERALDINE: David, don't be so silly.

DAVID: No, I'm not being silly. I've never been so serious in all my life. I think we'd be happy.

GERALDINE: (*very doubtful*) Well, I'll think about it, I really will.

OWEN: Go on, Vicar, he's a millionaire, for Christ's sake.

HUGO: And very fertile.

FRANK: And strangely attractive in the right light.

JIM: No! No, no, no, no – say 'yes'.

DAVID: The simple truth is, all this nonsense aside, I love you.

*She is completely swept away by this simple declaration of love. She takes a deep breath.*

GERALDINE: All right then!

*David is overjoyed. So, too, is Hugo who gives her a huge bear hug.*

HUGO: MUMMY!

GERALDINE: Get off me, I can't breathe. Get off.

*The violinist strikes up Mambo No. 5 and Frank and Jim twirl around with their arms in the air.*

## Scene Seven: The Church

*The organ plays and the bells ring out as Geraldine enters the church for her wedding to David. She looks gorgeous in a simple wedding dress, her hair piled on her head, decorated with sweets instead of flowers. Alice enters behind her – in a bright pink tulle bridesmaid's dress, complete with fairy wings and a Statue of Liberty headdress made out of chocolate bars. She winks at Geraldine.*

ALICE: I was just thinking, in five minutes' time, you're going to be my mother-in-law. And baby Geraldine's granny. Good luck, Granny.

*Geraldine tries not to look too horrified at this. She walks down the aisle, past all her friends from the village, and a couple of people wearing 'Ken for Mayor' badges. David and Hugo, in pink morning suits, are waiting for her. It is David's favourite Bishop, with his shouting problem.*

BISHOP: We're gathered here together in the sight of the Lord to witness the marriage of this man, THIS WOMAN. Do you, Boadicea Geraldine Granger . . .

JIM: Did he say Boadicea?

BISHOP: . . . take this man, David Francis Matthew Horton, to be your lawful wedded husband?

*She's suddenly not at all sure.*

GERALDINE: Um, um.

*Then there's a shout from the back of the church . . . it's Sean Bean!*

SEAN: No! Don't do it, Geraldine. It's me you love not him. Come on, lass.

*She can't believe it — the man of her dreams wants her.*

GERALDINE: You're right. Save me, Sean! Save me.

*They run towards each other in slow motion. Then Geraldine sits upright in bed. It was, thank God and alas, all a dream.*

No, I can't. I can't.

## Scene Eight: David's Hallway/Sitting Room

*The doorbell rings and Hugo dashes to answer it, wearing an apron and rubber gloves. David continues reading in the sitting room. It's Geraldine.*

GERALDINE:  Hugo.

HUGO:  Mum!

GERALDINE:  Oh God.

HUGO:  Thank heavens you're here. Dad's got stacks of laundry.

GERALDINE:  Can I come in?

DAVID:  Of course. Soon you'll never have to ask that question again.

GERALDINE:  It's just that, um, I've got something I want to tell you.

DAVID:  Fire away, darling.

HUGO:  Shall I tootle off?

GERALDINE:  No, you stay, Hugo, I want to talk to you as well.

HUGO:  Excellent. One big happy family. Can't wait for Christmas.

GERALDINE:  Yes, yes, all right. It's just that I had a terrible nightmare last night, David.

DAVID:  I had a nightmare, too. I dreamt that you came around to tell me that you didn't love me after all and that you couldn't marry me.

GERALDINE:  Right.

DAVID:  What was your nightmare?

GERALDINE:  *(losing her nerve)* Well, it wasn't like that. It was just full of big purple monsters all going 'Raagh', like that, and people gouging eyes out and Norman Lamont and stuff.

DAVID:  So you do still want to marry me?

GERALDINE:  *(and getting it back again)* Ah, well that's another thing. I also dreamt that I was already married to you and I wasn't completely happy.

DAVID:  Ah. Right.

*She sits next to him on the sofa — this will take some explaining.*

GERALDINE:  David, I'm sorry. I think I just got swept away the other day. I really like you, but just because we're the only two people in the village with a brain cell – well, apart from you, Hugo, you've got two, haven't you? – it doesn't necessarily mean that we're right for each other. True love is what keeps marriages together, not truly stupid neighbours with a big dollop of loneliness thrown in.

DAVID: Yes. Fine. As usual you're right. If you'll excuse me for just a second I think I'll pop into my study.

*He leaves the room with dignity and a broken heart.*

HUGO: Still, at least you've made my first mum look like a real stayer.

GERALDINE: Sorry, Hugo.

*David reappears.*

DAVID: I would, however, like it to be noted, just for the minutes as it were, that in the end I did have the brains to recognize what an extraordinary woman you are and the intelligence to realize that the man who finally does spends his life with you will, indeed, be the luckiest of all men. Even though, so obviously, it cannot be me . . . Still, see you on Sunday. I'm sure with my friend the Bishop it will be an interesting experience.

GERALDINE: Yes, indeed.

*David kisses her hand and smiles warmly at her.*

## Scene Nine: The Church

*David, Geraldine, Owen, Frank, Hugo and Alice are gathered round the font for baby Geraldine's christening. The Bishop is performing the service.*

BISHOP: Now, it's normal at this point for the officiating priest to go on and on about the purpose of baptism but I don't like to think of myself as an ORDINARY CLERGYMAN.

GERALDINE: (*whispering to David*) Fair do's.

BISHOP: So if you'd like to hand her over we can all get back to David's house for some of that GENUINELY DISGUSTING sherry.

ALICE: Oh, just one moment. I wasn't quite sure how deep you'd be popping her in, so I thought I'd take proper precautions.

*Alice takes the christening gown off the baby — underneath she is dressed in a bright pink bathing costume.*

BISHOP: Geraldine La La Granny Ainsley Harriot Horton I baptize thee in the name of the Father and of the Son and of the Holy Spirit. Amen. Let us all give thanks to Almighty God and pray in silence for the truly wondrous deed that we have done here today. (*He hands Geraldine back to Alice.*) Now, total silence please.

*They all bow their heads and shut their eyes to pray. The Bishop is saying his own secret prayer.*

. . . WHO ART IN HEAVEN? . . . tiny little fingers.

*He opens his eyes.*

Excellent. May she always have God's love. But let us pray that she may one day find something which in my long experience has been MUCH harder to find.

GERALDINE: A sane clergyman . . .

BISHOP: No, the true love of another person.

*Geraldine and David look at each other. And Jim starts to play 'Baby Love' on the organ very perkily.*

## Scene Ten: Geraldine's Living Room

*They are all gathered round for post-christening drinks. Geraldine is holding baby Geraldine.*

GERALDINE: And finally, from one Geraldine to another, I wish you health and happiness and bosoms the size of basketballs! You don't need luck because you've got that already. You've been born to two of the sweetest parents that God ever made.

*Hugo and Alice make bunny faces together.*

FRANK: I'd just like to offer a little token of my affections.

ALICE: Oh Frank, you are kind.

*He presents them with a huge tower of books, bound together with ribbon.*

FRANK: These are hand-written copies that I made of the minutes of the last thirty years of Council Meetings. I assure you it's gripping stuff.

DAVID: *(to Owen)* And what did the godfather bring his goddaughter?

OWEN: As duty demands, I got her a christening spoon.

GERALDINE: Oh well done, Owen. Ah.

*He holds up a plastic spoon.*

OWEN: I got it at the local Chinky. I engraved it and everything.

GERALDINE: 'For Gerald.'

OWEN: That's all I could fit on.

JIM: Here we go. This is just a little gift.

*He hands Hugo a small giftbox.*

HUGO: Oh Jim, you really shouldn't have.

JIM: Oh no, no, no, no I'll take it back then.

*And he does. Meanwhile, Geraldine toasts the baby, who is now in David's arms. Things are quietly reconciled.*

GERALDINE: Cheers.

## Epilogue: The Vestry

*Geraldine and Alice are making palm crosses together whilst having a cup of coffee.*

**GERALDINE:** So, Superman's feeling a bit bored, because Spiderman and Batman are on a scuba diving course.

**ALICE:** Oh, shame.

**GERALDINE:** Mmm, so he hasn't got anyone to play with. So he's flying around and suddenly he sees Wonderwoman naked, spread-eagled, on the top of a tall building.

**ALICE:** She'll catch cold.

**GERALDINE:** No, it's summer.

**ALICE:** Well, thank goodness for that.

**GERALDINE:** Yeah so, he's always fancied Wonderwoman, so he thinks, 'Now's my chance', and he swoops down and faster than a speeding bullet does the business and then flies off again. A moment later, Wonderwoman says, 'What was that?' And the Invisible Man climbs off her and says, 'I don't know, but it hurt a lot!' (*Geraldine cracks up laughing.*) I know it's rude but it's very funny.

**ALICE:** I don't get it.

**GERALDINE:** No, I didn't expect that you would.

**ALICE:** Well, you seem to be suggesting that Superman committed homosexual rape upon the Invisible Man and I just don't find that funny.

**GERALDINE:** Right.

**ALICE:** In fact, you're besmirching the reputation of two of the finest superheroes this world has ever known. I mean I've never actually met them, well, I might have met the Invisible Man, I wouldn't know. He's invisible. But I've heard that they are both really nice guys. Frankly, I think you should be ashamed of yourself. Goodbye, Vicar.

*She gets up and leaves.*

**GERALDINE:** Prude.

# Geraldine Granger's
# Very Best Baptisms

### 1  Jessica Anne Babbage

I'm not sure what they're feeding babies these days but darling little Jessie managed to projectile vomit a mixture of scrambled egg, cherry cola AND pilau rice. I was particularly impressed by the late spurt she saved for David's hush puppies.

### 2  Alexandra Emily Upton

Remembered for her bright orange romper suit and a startling ability to emit goo from seven different orifices – just one less than her father. Owing to the Dibley hosepipe ban, Alice couldn't fill the font with water and decided to improvise. Probably the first baby in history to be baptized in Sunny Delight.

### 3  Bicksie Tabitha Dell-Potting

I have nothing against children being dressed in a bunny costume. But I don't think the parents should do it as well.

# in the World...

## EVER!

### 4 Arnold Newitt

Not technically a baptism on account of Arnold being a sheep. Still, Owen was very keen to have him brought into the family of God so I obliged with a quick splash and go. I have a sneaking suspicion the font was spiked with sheep-dip as I saw Jim washing his hair in it afterwards.

### 5 Geraldine La La Granny Ainsley Harriot Horton

Probably the first baby in history to be baptized in a bright pink bikini. Probably the second baby in history to be baptized in Sunny Delight.

---

## Key to symbols

 Cute baby

 Fat baby

 Baby cried through service

 Owen cried through service

 Mother wore silly hat

 Father convinced he was Lord Lichfield

 Father convinced he was in Lichfield

 Owen dropped expensive camcorder and said 'F**k' and the whole service was, well, ruined really

 Full church

 Very full nappy

# SUMMER

## Scene One: The Parish Hall

*Hugo is the last to arrive for the Council Meeting. He is carrying the baby in her Moses basket.*

HUGO: *Buenas tardes!* I said I'd mind baby Geraldine as Alice was emotionally drained by this week's *Changing Rooms.* One of the couples didn't like their new kitchen.

*He puts the baby's basket on the table.*

OWEN: Oh, I hate it when that happens. It breaks my heart.

DAVID: Right, let's not get distracted. Item one, this being Millennium year we need to commemorate it somehow.

GERALDINE: Oh, she's dropped her toy, Hugo.

*They all crowd round the basket – all except David.*

JIM: No, no, no, no, oh, she is a pretty baby, isn't she?

OWEN: Prettier than her father. You were an ugly bastard, Hugo. You looked like Mother Theresa, only even uglier.

DAVID: Can we get back to the agenda?

FRANK: Oh, absolutely. Shall we take a vote on that?

DAVID: On what?

FRANK: Jim's proposal that baby Geraldine is a pretty baby.

DAVID: Don't be ridiculous.

FRANK: All those in favour. (*All raise their hands – all except David.*) That's passed. Except for Councillor Horton, her grandfather.

HUGO: (*a bit miffed*) You don't think she's pretty, Father?

DAVID: Of course I think she's pretty.

FRANK: Right, we'll have to take that vote again. Concentrate, Chairman.

DAVID: Oh, shut up, you arch idiot.

GERALDINE: Language, David – there's a baby present.

DAVID: (losing it) I know there's an arsing baby present! Moving on, we are now into the Millennium year and we need to commemorate the event with something lasting. Any ideas?

*He looks up. Geraldine, Owen, Hugo, Frank and Jim are now all singing to the baby; totally ignoring David.*

Any ideas?!

HUGO: Yes, I think we should build something for the youth of the village.

DAVID: Ah, now that is more like it. What did you have in mind?

HUGO: A ten-screen multiplex cinema with a bowling alley and a Burger King.

DAVID: Our budget is two thousand pounds, Hugo.

GERALDINE: Either that or a statue for the green.

HUGO: Oh, good thinking, priceless preacher.

GERALDINE: Of someone who means a lot to the village.

OWEN: Carol Vorderman.

DAVID: On what grounds?

OWEN: Well, I live in the village and she means a lot to me.

JIM: Me too. I'd multiply with her any old day.

OWEN: I'd subtract her underpants any time.

JIM: Yeah, and I would divide her . . .

GERALDINE: Boys, boys, boys, please get a grip.

OWEN: I'd love to!

DAVID: Much as I would love to build a statute of the entire cast of *Countdown*, I think someone from Dibley's past who was famous might be better.

GERALDINE: Good idea, Prime Minister. Calling all brain cells, suggestions at the next meeting please.

DAVID: Very good. Meanwhile, as we all know, we've all been experiencing very hot weather.

JIM: I have taken to sleeping in the nude.

GERALDINE: On the village green. We know, Jim, as do the police.

DAVID: Let me remind you once more that there is a hosepipe ban currently in operation . . . *Vicar*.

GERALDINE: What? What? My car was dirty and let me remind you of Luke 7 Verse 11: 'And Jesus did say unto his disciples, verily, an unclean Mini Metro is an abomination before the Lord.'

DAVID: Disgraceful behaviour.

HUGO: So why were you hosing your car yesterday, Father?

DAVID: Er, moving on.

HUGO: At two o'clock in the morning.

GERALDINE: Oh yes?

HUGO: After you'd finished filling the pool and sprinkling the croquet lawn.

*David, keen to detract attention from himself, now makes a fuss of baby Geraldine.*

DAVID: Actually she really is a pretty baby, isn't she?

## Scene Two: Geraldine's Kitchen/Sitting Room

*It's morning. Geraldine has the radio on in the kitchen.*

BROADCASTER: 'Villagers are now facing their third day without mains water. A company spokesman said drinking water would be bussed in and blamed consumers . . .'

*She goes to do the dishes but realizes there is no water, so licks the plates clean. Alice is in the living room . . . watering the plants, with a small watering can.*

ALICE: Hello, you thirsty thing. Get a splosh of that.

GERALDINE: Alice, what are you doing? I only get two pints of water a day!

ALICE: I know, I know. That's why I'm giving them this. (*She holds up a bottle of vodka.*) Mum says it's better than water, she swears by it. In fact after a few glasses she can't stop swearing.

GERALDINE: Actually I'm parched – give us a sip. (*She takes a big swig from the watering can and pulls a horrified face.*) You've mixed Baby Bio with that, haven't you? Actually, you know, it's not bad. It's got a Vimto ambience about it.

*She takes another swig.*

ALICE: This water shortage makes you realize how fragile life is, doesn't it? I mean you always assume life will go on as it has and then suddenly there's no water. It's like waking up one morning and finding there's no air.

GERALDINE: Well, not really, Alice, because if there was no air you just wouldn't wake up, would you?

ALICE: Well, right. You'd sleep right through, till they put it back on again.

GERALDINE: I know what you mean about the water though. We take these fundamental things for granted, and then suddenly one day they're just not there. Like, oh dear, like Des Lynam leaving the BBC.

*Just the thought of this brings tears to Geraldine's eyes.*

ALICE: You're still upset about that?

GERALDINE: Yeah.

ALICE: Come here, come on. That's it.

*Alice gives her a hug.*

GERALDINE: Well, you know, I'm over the initial shock and I've had to accept that he'll never present *Match of the Day* again, but come on – no Des at Wimbledon making jokes about Sue Barker's weird haircut? She's going to get away with that fringe year after year. Year after year the Wimbledon final will be presented by the Bride of Chucky. There will be water again, Alice, but as for Des, he's gone for ever.

ALICE: And Noel Edmonds has gone, too. Oh and Mr Blobby – no more gunk.

GERALDINE: Thanks for that. You've really cheered me up now. Do you want a swig?

ALICE: No, I don't drink alcohol.

GERALDINE: Well, this is vodka.

ALICE: Oh.

*She tilts her head back and Geraldine pours loads of vodka into her mouth.*

GERALDINE:  There we go.

### Scene Three: The Parish Hall

*Two weeks later. They all look absolutely awful − greasy, hot, unshaven . . .*

DAVID:  We'll try to keep this meeting short as the smell really is intolerable.

GERALDINE:  Has one of us actually died and not realized?

JIM:  I like having a beard, you keep finding bits of dinner in it. I can make a meal last the entire evening. Interesting combinations. (*He finds a bit of food, then thinks.*) Rhubarb and grilled fish.

*Owen appears, looking hideously dirty in a grubby white vest.*

OWEN:  Sorry I'm late. I made the mistake of going in my toilet this morning and it hasn't been flushed for ten days. I've only just regained consciousness.

DAVID:  You'll all be pleased to know that I have written a very strongly worded letter to the Chairman of the water company.

GERALDINE:  Oh bravo, *mein führer*. What does it say?

DAVID:  Well, hold on to your hats. 'Dear Sir Michael, Dibley has now been without water for a fortnight, which is clearly, well, pretty well, you know, less than satisfactory.'

GERALDINE:  That's it?

DAVID:  That is pretty strong stuff to a Knight of the Realm.

GERALDINE:  Well, luckily, I've written my own rather strongly worded letter to the Chairman.

DAVID:  How strongly worded?

GERALDINE:  Well, you'll see. 'Dear Sir Useless Baboon's Bottom. I think you should know that down our way, you're about as popular as Judas Iscariot at a disciple reunion.'

DAVID:  And you think we should send that instead?

GERALDINE:  Just as soon as I've checked if there's a hyphen in 'dick head', yes.

DAVID: Then I'm afraid you'll be outvoted. Who thinks that we should resort to counter productive, pointless personal abuse?

*They all raise their hands.*

JIM: Absolutely.

DAVID: Oh, very well. Be it on your own head. Moving on, any ideas for the Millennium statue?

GERALDINE: Oh goody, I've been looking forward to this. Glorious Dibley in all her glorious glory. Who's going to go first?

OWEN: (*unfolding a piece of paper*) Er, me. When you said famous people from Dibley's past, does that include murderers?

GERALDINE: Well, I'd rather it wasn't a murderer, if that's all right with you, Owen.

OWEN: Right, well, that's my family out then (*and refolds the paper*).

JIM: My great, great, great, great, great grandfather, he was a famous man.

GERALDINE: Really, Jim?

JIM: Oh yes, he sailed the seven seas in search of gold and treasure.

GERALDINE: Wow, what did he bring back?

JIM: Typhus.

FRANK: Then there's Elizabeth the First. She stayed at an inn twenty yards seven inches from where we're sitting right now.

GERALDINE: That's fantastic, Frank. You're telling me that the Virgin 'I don't think so' Queen herself actually slept in Dibley?

FRANK: Not exactly. She got food poisoning and she spent the whole night vomiting.

GERALDINE: Oh, that's a lovely theme for a statue isn't it? 'Queen Elizabeth the Tudor Chunderer'.

JIM: Carol Vorderman it is then.

GERALDINE: Yeah, either that or we dump the statue entirely and spend the cash on two hundred bottles of mineral water so we can have a bath.

FRANK: All those in favour?

*Everyone raises their arms. Geraldine nearly chokes from the smell.*

GERALDINE: Oh, armpits down boys, please.

FRANK: Motion carried.

OWEN: Try not to use the word motion, or I'll faint again.

DAVID: Moving on.

## Scene Four: Geraldine's Living Room

*Ten days later. Alice is round at Geraldine's.*

ALICE: Thank goodness for the Hallowe'en party last year. I'm down to my last clean outfit.

*She walks through from the kitchen — in her witch's outfit, complete with long green wig.*

GERALDINE: Yeah, me too, I'm through my entire wardrobe.

*Geraldine follows her, holding a cup of tea, wearing a pumpkin outfit, complete with a stalk hat.*

ALICE: Hugo says that you've all decided not to have a statue.

GERALDINE: Yeah, 'fraid so, Alice. There doesn't seem to be anyone in Dibley worth remembering.

ALICE: Not even that man who discovered Bali? He lived here.

GERALDINE: No, he discovered Bali last year on holiday, didn't he?

ALICE: Oh yes.

GERALDINE: That's not quite so interesting.

ALICE: What about my Uncle Trevor? He founded the Sunday Times.

GERALDINE: (*amazed*) Is that true?

ALICE: Yeah, I think so.

GERALDINE: Great!

ALICE: No, no wait a second, he found the Sunday Times, yeah that's it. Auntie Perky had lost it and he found it in a guest room. It's not quite so good, is it?

GERALDINE: No.

*The phone rings. Alice jumps up to answer it, as Geraldine is finding movement difficult inside her outfit.*

ALICE: Hi, vicarage, home to Gerry Granger, God's most bodacious babe. Oh right. (*She covers up the mouthpiece.*) It's the water company – they got your letter.

GERALDINE: Oh, I hope it wasn't too rude.

ALICE: They say you might be interested to know there's only one D in 'pederast'. And they're not sure 'knob-guzzler' is a real word. A man is coming to talk to us tomorrow evening.

GERALDINE: Really?

ALICE: About the long-term solution to our problem.

GERALDINE: Oh, power to the people.

*She starts to dance about. Victory is in reach.*

ALICE: (*on the phone*) The vicar's delighted. She's dancing around – you should see her. Oh, it's lovely to see a pumpkin so happy.

## Scene Five: The Parish Hall

*The man from the water company has arrived to address the Council. A landscape model of Dibley is on the table in front of them.*

DAVID: First, I'm sure we'd all like to thank Mr Badcock for coming and I'm sure Mr Newitt didn't mean to spit at you on your arrival. Also, I hope you didn't find the burning effigy of your boss too disconcerting.

MR BADCOCK: Thank you. Naturally we apologize for the water shortage. As you can see from this model, you live in an area of high population growth and so traditional water supplies are fast becoming inadequate.

JIM: No, no, no – I recognize that little house. That's where I had it off this morning.

OWEN: And that's where my gran was murdered, they hid her body under the floorboards.

DAVID: If we could just . . .

OWEN: You can still smell her when the wind's in the right direction.

MR BADCOCK: The long and the short of it is, I'm pleased to say that we've found a solution which should ensure plentiful water for the next century in the form of a new reservoir. It's probably easiest to show you what I'm talking about in a simple demonstration.

*He empties a bucket of water right over the top of the Dibley model. The water completely covers the village.*

ALICE: Oh, my God, we're all going to drown. We'll be sitting at home watching Scooby Doo and then suddenly this massive bucket of water's going to flood the village.

GERALDINE: You can't do that.

MR BADCOCK: We have planning permission and government backing. The plans have been available for you to look at for months.

GERALDINE: Where?

MR BADCOCK: In a cupboard. In our basement. In the Hong Kong office. Naturally all detailed objections will be considered provided they're registered by, ah, lunchtime today.

GERALDINE: No! Just you wait. We're going to fight you all the way on this.

MR BADCOCK: So be it, dear lady, work begins in one month and I can assure you we are very determined and will be ready for anything you throw at us.

*Owen punches him in the face and Badcock hits the floor.*

OWEN: He wasn't ready for that.

### Scene Six: The Parish Hall

*At the next Council Meeting.*

GERALDINE: So how's the petition going, everyone? We need ten thousand signatures by next week.

HUGO: Here's a start.

*He hands her his personal autograph book.*

GERALDINE: Right. 'Best wishes, Harold Macmillan'. Not exactly what I had in mind, Hugo.

HUGO: I've got Benny Hill as well.

GERALDINE: No, Hugo, I need signatures of living people.

JIM: No, no, no, I got five hundred this afternoon.

GERALDINE: That's fantastic, Jim. All opposed to the reservoir?

JIM: No, no, no, they didn't give a toss for the reservoir but I asked them to sign if they thought Claudia Schiffer should get her tits out more often.

GERALDINE: Right. I see you've managed to sign it ten times, Owen.

OWEN: It's a cause I feel very passionately about.

DAVID: Vicar, much as I applaud your efforts I fear we have to accept the compensation the water company offer us. However derisory that is.

HUGO: I thought they offered you four million pounds.

GERALDINE: What?

DAVID: Yes, well, do you think I'm happy about that?

HUGO: Well, you were dancing round the rose garden singing.

DAVID: Hugo . . .

HUGO: (singing) 'Money, money, money, Must be funny . . .'

OWEN: You treacherous git! You'd sacrifice this village for your own personal greed. Have you no respect for tradition?

GERALDINE: Well said, Owen.

OWEN: For centuries my family's been massacring deer, staging illegal cock fights and gassing foxes in this valley and we don't intend stopping now.

GERALDINE: Less well said, Owen.

DAVID: Incidentally, this is what you'd be getting for your farm, by the way.

*He shows Owen his notepad with a figure written on it.*

OWEN: (singing) 'Who wants to be a millionaire? I do.' You're right, Dave, Dibley's a dump.

GERALDINE: For goodness sakes, Owen, there are people here who don't own their own properties. They won't get any compensation at all.

OWEN: Well sod 'em. Now will you sleep with me? I can pay you big time, babe.

FRANK: I'm not leaving, Vicar. I've lived in my cottage all my life. Except for the war, of course . . .

GERALDINE: I know, Frank, you're a hero.

FRANK: . . . when I hid in the woods to avoid the call up. Just me and a young farm hand called Alistair.

JIM: No, no, no, no. Where would we move to anyway?

GERALDINE: Well, I'll tell you exactly. They want to rehouse you twenty miles away in a new development. 'Twilight Towers – Happy Housing for the Nearly Dead'. (*She shows them a brochure.*) Acre after acre of soulless boxes.

FRANK: Look, there's central heating.

JIM: Look, and an inside toilet.

GERALDINE: But surely, lads, you don't want to live . . .

JIM: Remember last Christmas? I was frozen to the loo seat for the whole of Christmas week.

FRANK: Yes, I remember that. I had to wee through your legs.

GERALDINE: Let's get this right. After mature consideration you're all telling me that you actually want to move?

JIM: Soulless box, here I come. Wahay! (*He kisses the brochure.*)

GERALDINE: I see. Well I'm sorry. This is a sad, sad moment.

*She sits down at the table to contemplate the future of Dibley. The men start to sing.*

OWEN: 'Oh, happy day.'

JIM: 'Oh, happy day.'

OWEN: 'Oh, happy day.'

FRANK AND JIM: 'Oh, happy day.'

OWEN: 'When Jesus washed.'

FRANK, JIM AND HUGO: 'When Jesus washed.'

OWEN: 'He washed my sins away.'

ALL: 'Oh, happy day!!!'

### Scene Seven: David's Sitting Room

DAVID: Champagne, Jim?

JIM: No, no, no, no, yes please. I never say no, no, no to a glass of bubbly.

DAVID: (*to Geraldine*) Oh, now now, Miss Grumpy Cassocks, it's not the end of the world, you know.

*Alice bursts in.*

ALICE: Frank says you've got some exciting news. Um, my guess is, Anthea Turner's coming back to Blue Peter.

GERALDINE: No, Alice. It's the reservoir, it's still happening.

HUGO: But we're all getting loads of money to move.

ALICE: Oh nice. So where are they building the new Dibley?

HUGO: No, no there's no new Dibley.

ALICE: Oh, but we are all moving together? Vicar?

GERALDINE: I'm afraid not, Alice, no. I'll just have to go where I'm sent. Could be the Belgian Congo, could be Staines. Fingers crossed for the Belgian Congo.

ALICE: But that doesn't sound very nice at all. Mr Horton, I'll hardly ever see you again. What's nice about that?

DAVID: Well, from my point of view . . .

ALICE: We won't be able to discuss world affairs each morning.

DAVID: No, I'll miss that.

ALICE: And analyse the stick market.

DAVID: Stock market.

ALICE: While you bounce baby Geraldine on your knee.

DAVID: No. (*He will miss that.*) Still, people have always left Dibley. It doesn't mean they lose touch.

FRANK: My brothers said if they didn't leave Dibley I'd bore them to death.

GERALDINE: You can't bore a person to death, Frank. Patrick Moore tries but . . .

OWEN: Frank bored his parents to death.

FRANK: That was never proved. I just happened to be outlining Parish Council procedure when, hand in hand, they leapt out of the open window. You know, you're the only people in the whole world that don't find me unutterably boring. You've stuck with me through thick and thin. Good times and bad times. Come rainy rain, come shiny sun.

*Meanwhile, they are all beginning to die of boredom themselves. Owen points a gun at Frank. Geraldine covers his mouth with her hand.*

GERALDINE: Quit while you're alive, Frank.

JIM: To tell the truth, I don't really want to go.

GERALDINE: I see. What about you, Owen?

OWEN: As far as I can see the only people who don't want to leave Dibley are sad, lonely losers.

JIM: Like you.

OWEN: That's right. No, so, I'd rather stay.

DAVID: Oh nonsense, I for one certainly won't miss Dibley. Some people think hell is listening to Celine Dion. For me it's having to attend all those ghastly Parish Council Meetings.

GERALDINE: Which you've *never* missed.

DAVID: Oh, rubbish. Thirty-six years ago when my wife was in labour with Hugo, did I go to the village hall for a meeting? I did not.

JIM: No, no, no, no we came with you and had the meeting in the maternity ward.

OWEN: Mrs Horton wanted to name the baby straight away, but Mr Horton said she'd have to wait until 'any other business'.

DAVID: There was a lot to get through. A community to run, a village doesn't just go . . . away you know. (*The truth dawns on him.*)

GERALDINE: I was rejected by the first four parishes I was sent to. The first one wanted a man. The second one wanted a man with a full beard and moustache, just to check it was a man. The third one insisted on a full physical examination, just in case a girl slipped through with a false beard and moustache. The fourth one wanted a rabbi, but I think that was a mix up with the documents. And the fifth one, a strange little village – the inbreeding capital of the world – accepted me with open arms and became my family.

ALICE: Oh, where was that then?

GERALDINE: Here, Alice, here.

ALICE: Oh, nice.

GERALDINE: I love this village. Don't ask me why.

ALL: Why?

GERALDINE: Because it's a real country village. Because we range from the mildly bizarre to the dangerously odd – Frank – and because we live side by side, year after year.

JIM: And we're happy together.

GERALDINE: That's right. And that's why we must fight to save Dibley.

DAVID: 'This other Eden, demi paradise, this happy breed of men, this little world, this precious stone set in the silver sea. This blessed plot, this earth, this realm, this Dibley.'

GERALDINE: (*amazed at this emotional outburst*) Well, well.

*They all clap and whistle.*

OWEN:  (to Jim) Did you understand that?

JIM:  Not a word.

HUGO:  Very moving speech, Father.

DAVID:  Thank you, I thought it was the right thing to do.

HUGO:  I'm proud of you. In fact, can I kiss you, Father?

DAVID:  I don't think that's necessary.

HUGO:  Just once. I won't tell anyone.

DAVID:  Okay, don't make a habit of it.

*Hugo kisses David on the cheek and gives him a sideways hug. David remains stiff and unemotional.*

Thank you.

## Scene Eight: Geraldine's Living Room

*A campaign banner hangs above Geraldine's front door. Inside, she's on the phone.*

GERALDINE:  So let me just get this straight, you're going to donate *every* penny from the release of your new single to our campaign? That's fantastic! It'll make a huge difference, thank you so much. Bye. (*She puts the phone down.*) Bros. (*And mimes being hung by a noose.*)

*Owen comes in.*

OWEN:  I've had another superb idea, Vicar.

GERALDINE:  Oh, don't tell me, this one involves hunting water board officials with high velocity rifles and blood hounds?

OWEN: No, with this one there's an absolute minimum of sickening violence.

GERALDINE: Well, thank God for that.

OWEN: We get Dibley classified as a site of natural environmental importance.

GERALDINE: Right, how do we do that?

OWEN: We find a species of animal that isn't found anywhere else in the world.

GERALDINE: I think finding a new animal in Dibley is about as likely as finding intellectual life on Ibiza.

OWEN: That's just where you're wrong, Vicar. Dibley could be, for instance, the only place on earth with a genuine three-legged cow.

GERALDINE: You've managed to breed a three-legged cow?

OWEN: I'm very close. I've got a four-legged cow and a sharp axe. That's where the small amount of sickening violence comes in.

GERALDINE: I see.

OWEN: Or we could discover the world's only short-nosed badger. All it would take is a long-nosed badger and a big pair of secateurs.

GERALDINE: Yeah, I think I can recognize the pattern that's emerging here.

OWEN: Or, we could quickly breed the world's only genuine sheepdog. All we need is a sheep, a dog, a romantic candle-lit dinner and an animal condom shortage.

GERALDINE: Owen, bye bye. Off you go, bye bye.

OWEN: All right, just you wait. I haven't finished with this one. Hello, Mr Horton.

*He walks out and passes David on his way in.*

DAVID: Where's he off to?

GERALDINE: Oh ignore him, he's just trying to mutilate things as usual. David, we have got to come up with a fantastic original idea that will grab the press's attention. Argh! Hang on. Yes, yes, yes! I've just thought of the most fantastic village-saving idea.

DAVID: Oh good. As long as it isn't an embarrassing publicity stunt, like chaining yourself to the church.

GERALDINE: (diffidently) No.

## Scene Nine: Outside the Church

*Geraldine has, indeed, chained herself to the church. Right across the main entrance to the church porch. David walks up to her.*

DAVID: You look like an extra in a low-budget remake of a film by Ken Russell.

GERALDINE: Well, what are you doing for the cause?

DAVID: I've written to our MP, Sir Patrick Payne.

GERALDINE: The famous alcoholic?

DAVID: Well . . .

GERALDINE: Let's face it, David, the last time he spoke in the House of Commons, all he could muster was 'Hcha, ngkcha, ha'. We need publicity and we need it now.

DAVID: (*sarcastically*) Oh yes, I can see the world's press just flocking in. Afternoon, Vicar.

*He walks away.*

GERALDINE: Just you wait. Just you wait.

*Later that day . . . Geraldine is still chained up. She is taking a service.*

May the blessing of our Lord Jesus Christ be with you now and for ever more. Amen.

CONGREGATION: Amen.

*The congregation begin to emerge from the church and have to leave by crawling through her legs.*

OWEN: Vicar, most enjoyable.

GERALDINE: Thank you, Owen. Could the lady with the big hat go to the back of the queue please. Cor, you've put on some weight. The lady with the feather hat come next. Very good. Oh great.

*Later that evening Hugo fixes up a television for Geraldine to watch during the night. He sorts out the aerial and then leaves.*

HUGO: Goodnight then, Vicar.

GERALDINE: Thanks, Hugo. No, no, no. Hugo! Hugo!

*To her horror, a programme starring Anthea Turner is just starting – and she can't switch it off.*

Help. No! No!

## Scene Ten: Outside the Church

*The next day, and Geraldine is still chained up. Alice and Jim go to see her.*

JIM: If you'd like me to take over for a bit, you only have to say the word.

GERALDINE: Oh, that's very sweet of you, Jim but no, thank you. I'm determined to see this out until the press get here, even if it takes a week.

JIM: You wouldn't like just to go to the loo?

GERALDINE: No, thanks.

ALICE: She's amazing, she must have a bladder the size of Lake Titicaca. Not like me. My mum only has to go 'tinkle, tinkle', or 'ssss', or . . . (*she whistles*) and I'm absolutely bursting.

GERALDINE: (*suddenly desperate for the loo*) Actually, sorry, Jim, do you think you could take over? Quickly.

*She gets out of the chains and puts Jim in them.*

There, comfy?

JIM: Not bad. I normally have the handcuffs a bit tighter, but they'll be all right.

GERALDINE: Sorry, what do you mean normally?

JIM: Well, I have this Chinese girl . . .

GERALDINE: All right, got the picture! Got the picture!

## Scene Eleven: Geraldine's Living Room

*Geraldine runs back over to the vicarage to go to the loo, and whilst she's there she washes her hair and freshens up, not realizing that a BBC news van has pulled up outside to do a news feature on the protest . . . She hears the newscaster mention Dibley on her television, just at the moment she isn't there.*

NEWSCASTER: And finally, news is reaching us of a most unusual demonstration in the village of Dibley.

GERALDINE: At last!

NEWSCASTER: We've all heard of people chaining themselves to trees and railings, but what about a church?

GERALDINE: Yes!

*Over to the news report . . .*

REPORTER: (*in Dibley*) I'm here with demonstrator Jim Trott.

GERALDINE: No!

REPORTER: Mr Trott, can you tell me why you're chained to the church?

JIM: No, no, er yes. Because the vicar's gone to the toilet.

GERALDINE: Too much detail.

JIM: You should talk to her, she's a wonderful woman. (*Geraldine smiles.*) Lovely arse.

GERALDINE: I will kill him.

*After this broadcast, all the news programmes feature Dibley and the church protest. First, Martyn Lewis on the BBC News at Six.*

MARTYN: And Dibley's MP today spoke out in the House of Commons. 'Show me the way to go home,' he said, before falling over.

*Then Jeremy Paxman on* Newsnight.

JEREMY: And before we go, a look at tomorrow morning's front pages. The *Star* has 'Thou shalt not kill my village' about the vicar who's chained herself to her church. The *Independent* leads on the same story, 'Vicar has big reservations over reservoir' and the *Sun* has its own angle, 'The *Sun* asks, is the vicar's arse really lovely?' As if we care. That's all from *Newsnight* for tonight. We'll be back with more tomorrow night.

## Scene Twelve: Outside the Church

*The next day and Geraldine is joined in her protest by Frank, Jim, Hugo, Alice and baby Geraldine. They are now all chained to the church. Meanwhile, more news reports from around the world are seen on television — the story has captured the attention of the world . . .*

MARTYN LEWIS: As their protest enters its third week, the vicar of Dibley today received crucial backing from the most important figure in the Church of England, Sir Cliff Richard.

*An Italian newscaster then reports on the story, with a picture of the Pope making a speech in the background.*

## Scene Thirteen: The Village Green

*Photographers, reporters and TV news crews are swarming all over the place. Protesters with placards have turned up to show their support. A small marquee has been set up, providing refreshments and toilets for the crowd.*

REPORTER: The protest here in this little village seems to have struck a chord across the world. In times of increasing urbanization, who's going to stick up for the small communities, where everybody knows your name?

MARTYN LEWIS: Meanwhile the world's press continue to flock to this tiny village and its remarkable vicar. They've been joined by representatives from environmental pressure groups and assorted others.

*Protesters are seen with their placards: 'Save Dibley', 'Friends of the Earth Support Dibley' and 'Friends of the Arse Support the Vicar of Dibley'. David walks through the crowd to the church.*

DAVID: Still here, eh?

GERALDINE: Yes. Still standing firm, despite what you think.

DAVID: I think, in the end, it's not a bad idea.

*He unzips his coat to show he's wearing a 'Save Dibley' T-shirt. Then he brandishes a pair of handcuffs.*

Chain me up, Scotty!

## Scene Fourteen: Outside the Church

*Night has fallen, the news crews have packed up and the crowd has gone. Geraldine and the others are still chained up, singing 'You'll Never Walk Alone'.*

GERALDINE: Right, your turn next, Frank. Only six hours to go before dawn so make it a good 'un.

FRANK: I've got just the thing. *(He sings.)* 'One hundred thousand green bottles hanging on the wall. One hundred thousand green bottles . . .'

*And they all join in.*

ALL: '. . . hanging on the wall and if one green bottle should accidentally fall, there'd be ninety-nine thousand nine hundred and ninety-nine green bottles hanging on the wall.'

## Scene Fifteen: Outside the Church

*The next morning, the crowd has returned and Mr Badcock makes a speech to all those gathered outside the church.*

MR BADCOCK: After careful consideration of all the facts, I am instructed to inform you that the water board has decided to proceed with Dibley Reservoir.

*The crowd cannot believe it.*

GERALDINE: What?

MR BADCOCK: Sorry, sorry, sorry. Has decided not to proceed with Dibley Reservoir.

*Everyone cheers in delight.*

We wish to point out that this decision has nothing to do with the recent protest.

GERALDINE: Sure.

MR BADCOCK: We have listened very carefully to the more detailed environmental arguments and after the discovery in a local farm of a blue-crested one-legged chicken, (*Owen catches Geraldine's eye and she smiles*) we believe the area to be of unique natural importance. And therefore we'll look for other solutions to the water crisis. Thank you very much.

*Everyone claps and Owen steps up to have his photo taken with Badcock and the blue-crested one-legged chicken he is holding.*

GERALDINE: You've got the key haven't you, Hugo?

HUGO: Yeah.

GERALDINE: Good. Where is it then?

HUGO: (*very proud of himself*) I swallowed it. For security.

*Very worrying.*

## Scene Sixteen: Geraldine's Living Room

*All are gathered for celebratory drinks.*

GERALDINE: Well, the good news is Dibley's saved!

ALL: Yeah!

GERALDINE: The bad news is that Michael Winner wants to make a film about it. With Jim being played by Charles Bronson. We did have some bad times – Ant and Dec coming to cheer us up, that was pretty rough for everybody.

ALICE: Oh, I loved that!

GERALDINE: Yes. And obviously there isn't a single animal left on Owen's farm with the correct number of legs.

OWEN: Though I have to say, it's surprising how agile a one-legged pig can be.

GERALDINE: But despite that, WE WON!

ALL: Yes!

JIM: After it was all over I was so excited I made love to a Swedish journalist.

GERALDINE: We know, Jim, we were chained to you at the time.

DAVID: This is indeed a great day for Dibley. And the right moment to announce that we have decided to have a Millennium statue after all. And chosen our subject.

GERALDINE: Really?

HUGO: We haven't discussed it with you, Vicar, but we feel there's only one person it can possibly be. In fact, everyone I asked gave me the same answer. And that answer was . . . a statue of Geraldine.

GERALDINE: (*extremely flattered*) I don't know what to say.

DAVID: We just hope you'll honour us with your presence at the unveiling.

GERALDINE: I certainly will.

JIM: Is it okay if I bring Anna-Greta along?

DAVID: I should think so.

JIM: (*with a dirty laugh*) She says she's got a little surprise for me.

## Scene Seventeen: The Village Green

*All the villagers are gathered for the unveiling of the statue. Jim has a beautiful young Swedish girl on each arm. Anna-Greta and her twin. They both kiss him on the cheek. Everyone is waiting for Geraldine.*

DAVID: I'm sure it will only be a couple of minutes.

## Scene Eighteen: Geraldine's Living Room

*Geraldine is putting her make-up on, using the mirror on the wall. Alice pops up in front of her to look at herself in the mirror. She has two huge circles of blusher on her cheeks.*

GERALDINE: You look pretty as a picture, young Alice.

ALICE: Thanks. A painter did once ask me to pose for him.

GERALDINE: Really?

ALICE: Mmm, with no clothes on!

GERALDINE: No? Did you do it?

ALICE: Yeah! It was quite exciting. He was painting our kitchen at the time.

GERALDINE: I don't mind admitting I'm feeling a little bit nervous. Well this sort of thing doesn't happen every day does it? How do I look: gorgeous or Y-front-stretchingly gorgeous.

ALICE: Y-front-stretching-till-a-little-bit-of-winky-sticks-outly-gorgeous! How about me?

GERALDINE: You look like Michelle Pfeiffer, at her most beautiful. One little thing, do you mind me saying?

ALICE: No.

GERALDINE: It's just the lipstick.

ALICE: Too much or too little?

GERALDINE: Not good as blusher. Do you mind if I . . .

ALICE: No.

GERALDINE: (*She rubs a bit of it off.*) There we are.

ALICE: Thanks.

GERALDINE: Now you look babelicious!

ALICE: We make the perfect team I reckon.

GERALDINE: Yeah.

ALICE: Because while you provide the beauty and the brains, I provide the, the, er . . .

GERALDINE: The rest.

ALICE: That's it, the rest. Exactly.

GERALDINE: So, come on, let's go, Alice Amazing.

ALICE: After you, Vicar V . . . Velociraptor.

## Scene Nineteen: The Village Green

*Geraldine and Alice join the assembled crowd on the green. Geraldine stands up front with David. She is bursting with pride to think the statue of herself is about to be seen.*

DAVID: And so it gives me the greatest pleasure, now that our heroic vicar has joined us, to unveil the Dibley Millennium statue. We'll call it simply 'Geraldine'.

*David pulls the red material away to reveal a statue of . . . baby Geraldine in her cot! Geraldine is completely taken aback by this and claps overenthusiastically after everyone else to prove that she isn't completely taken aback.*

DAVID: We didn't want to commemorate the past but look to the future. What do you think, Vicar?

GERALDINE: I think it's . . . perfect. Perfect. (*Then, to herself.*) It doesn't look anything like me.

## Epilogue: The Vestry

*The girls are having a nice strong cup of Assam tea.*

**GERALDINE:** Okay, nice quick one.

**ALICE:** Hurray!

**GERALDINE:** What's brown and sticky?

**ALICE:** I don't know. What's brown and sticky?

**GERALDINE:** A stick.

*She laughs at this simple word play.*

**ALICE:** No, sticks aren't sticky.

**GERALDINE:** Well, they are, aren't they, because they're sticks so they are stick-y.

**ALICE:** Yeah, but that's not what sticky means. Sticky means all sort of sticky, you know. I mean, *some* sticks *are* sticky because sap oozes out of them and they get sticky. So if you say, 'What is brown and sometimes sticky?' then that might work.

**GERALDINE:** Yeah, but that sort of takes the edge off it doesn't it, you see?

**ALICE:** Although to be honest, some trees aren't brown either, are they? You might as well get this right otherwise you'll never get a laugh. Either you could say, 'What is sometimes brown and sometimes sticky?', and that's a stick, or 'What is sometimes brown but also sometimes greeny grey, sometimes whitish and, sometimes, like in those big American trees, red?', you see. So, 'What's sometimes, red, sometimes greeny grey, sometimes sort of white and sometimes sticky?'

*Geraldine's had enough. She gets up and grabs a big Bible – with which she hits Alice over the head.*

**GERALDINE:** Sorry about that, Alice. Even if I do go to jail, somebody had to do it.

If you enjoyed this book, why not try –

# THE BIBLE

- ◆ The runaway bestseller
- ◆ Packed with super stories
- ◆ Over 150 plagues
- ◆ Loads of violence
- ◆ Lots of funny foreign names
- ◆ More than 400 prophets – gotta catch 'em all!

**The Bible.**

## Four Gospels, Two Testaments,

# One Great Read!

Hello. I'm the Rev. Granger, and I want to talk to you about my third favourite charity, after the WTGCF (Wet T-shirts for George Clooney Fund) and my own SFHETOBAJCMTOPNLW (Sanctuary For Half Eaten Tubs of Ben and Jerry's Chunky Monkey That Other People No Longer Want). Yes, that's right: Comic Relief.

Comic Relief was set up to support some of the poorest and most disadvantaged people in Africa and the UK, by helping them to help themselves. Between 1985 and 2000, it's raised a jaw-dropping, pick-your-jaw-up-so-it-can-drop-again £174 million. And with your help, there's more to come.

For every penny raised, and that includes royalties from this book, a penny goes directly to the projects that Comic Relief supports; none of it goes on administrative costs. That's none. Nothing. Nowt. Zero. Nada. Diddly-poo. Comic Relief does of course have administrative costs, but these are all paid for by rich people with kind smiles and gentle voices, plus a little bit of the interest that comes from Comic Relief's Piggy Saver account.

Without your stunning-ass generosity, Comic Relief couldn't be doing what it does, so THANK YOU, THANK YOU, THANK YOU for helping Comic Relief to help people help themselves!

Geraldine Granger

If you'd like to know more about Comic Relief, would like to get involved in the next Red Nose Day, or if you'd just like to bring round a cartload of money, log on to www.comicrelief.org.uk, or write to Comic Relief, 5th Floor, 89 Albert Embankment, London SE1 7TP.
Registered Charity Number 326568.

# Here's how some of the cash is making a difference...

## Two thirds of the money Comic Relief raises helps projects in Africa . . .

. . . and this is about just one of them – because if we told you about the whole lot, it would be a book as long as the book you've just read.

Send a Cow might seem a joke name – but actually it's a life-changing project in Uganda, run by a group called Stockaid. Nine out of ten people in Uganda live in rural areas and less than half of those get clean, safe water. And women have the hardest time – they're amongst the very poorest, with the most precarious lives, because they very rarely own land of their own.

What Send a Cow does is organize two crucial things that help these women get the best out of their land. First – they're given lessons in organic farming, which means they recycle and use any waste from animals or crops to help with other animals and crops. Next (and this is, obviously, why they're called Send a Cow) the woman are actually lent small amounts of money to buy cows, which are completely vital to them leading a good life. With the extra cash made from having the cows, which both plough and give milk, they pay back the loan and begin to really improve their lives in a way that wouldn't be possible without your help and the help of Stockaid.

And it's not only their lives – it's the lives of their whole families. Take just one woman we've been helping, Teopista Nakanyanzi. She's a widow who has two children living with her, and four living with and supported by relatives. With the help of the cow sent by Send a Cow, she's been able to earn enough money to send all six of her children to school – and now she's actually saving money to buy more land. Your money – and her hard work – have totally transformed her life from living on the edge, to having a real, solid, hopeful future. As Geraldine might say – bless you!

## One third of the money Comic Relief raises goes to projects all over the UK.

Again, there are far too many to mention here – but one brilliant line of work we do is helping old people with dementia. One in twenty people over sixty-five suffer from this terrible disease, in which the powers of the brain progressively decline – and that figure rises to one in five with people over eighty. It makes life terribly difficult – because they can't communicate properly, and lose a lot of their memory, older people with dementia also lose the power to express themselves and to let people know what they do and do not want in the most crucial areas of their lives – like where they live, what they want to eat and even who should have control of their money.

Alzheimer Scotland is working, with your money, to make sure that people with dementia retain power over their own lives. They work with people in both the early and later stages of the disease, to make sure that they can live in an environment that is calm, and comfortable and, most importantly, familiar. They're taking the fear out of their lives – and giving them back confidence and control.

And like the very best projects, Alzheimer Scotland is spreading the knowledge their work creates – sharing everything they learn with projects working throughout the UK. The Vicar of Dibley has always got some of its laughs from older people – by buying this book, you have made sure that real older people, in real places, genuinely have better lives.

The publishers are grateful for permission to reprint the following copyright material:

'Love Is All Around' (Presley) © 1967 by kind permission of Universal Music Publishing Ltd.

'Let It Be Me' words and music by Gilbert Becaud/Pierre Delanoe/Curtis Mann.
Copyright © BMG Music Publishing Ltd. All rights reserved. By kind permission.

'Raining In My Heart' (Bryant/Bryant) Published by: Acuff-Rose Music Limited © 1959.

'My Favorite Things' Words by Oscar Hammerstein II and Music by Richard Rodgers © 1959, Williamson Music
International, USA. Reproduced by permission of EMI Music Publishing Ltd, London WC2H OQY.

The publishers and Comic Relief would like to say a BIG THANK YOU to the following
people without whom The Vicar of Dibley book would not be in your hands today:

Richard Curtis, Paul Mayhew-Archer and Kit Hesketh-Harvey for their scripts.

The gorgeous cast: John Bluthal, Emma Chambers, James Fleet, Dawn French,
Roger Lloyd Pack, Trevor Peacock, Liz Smith and Gary Waldhorn.

Also all the guest stars – in parts large and small – from nasty Clive Mantle to crazy Simon McBurney.
It would have been so much less good without Sean Bean, Orla Brady, Darcey Bussell, Peter Capaldi,
Mel Giedroyc, Richard Griffiths, Pat Kane, Nick Le Prevost, Martyn Lewis, Carol Macready,
Geraldine McNulty, Jeremy Paxman, Roger Sloman, Nina Wadia, Philip Whitchurch,
Terry Wogan and all the other wonderful actors and animals.

The Vicar of Dibley is a Tiger Aspect Production for the BBC,
and huge thanks to everyone who worked on it, including:

Executive Producer Peter Jones
Producers Jon Plowman, Sue Vertue and Margot Gavan-Duffy
Directors Dewi Humphries, Gareth Carrivick and John Howard Davies
Production Manager Rachel Salter
Musical Maestro Howard Goodall
and everyone else who brought it from scrappy page to stylish small screen.

And special thanks to:
Kevin Cecil, Andy Riley and Paul Powell for all the extra funny stuff in the book . . .

Matilda Harrison, Andy Riley and Margie Jordan for their wonderful illustrations . . . and Lindsey Jordan,
Harrie Evans, Carole McDonald and Tracey Woodward for basically making the book exist at all.

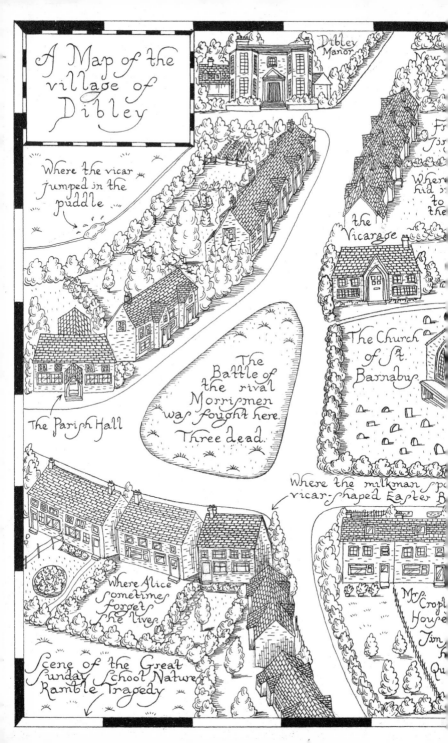